Travellers' Tales of Wonder

In memory of my mother
Ruth Laurence
16 July 1954 – 21 September 2001

And for my grandparents
Christopher and Margaret Laurence

Travellers' Tales of Wonder

Chatwin, Naipaul, Sebald

Simon Cooke

EDINBURGH
University Press

© Simon Cooke, 2013

Edinburgh University Press Ltd
22 George Square, Edinburgh EH8 9LF

www.euppublishing.com

Typeset in 10.5/13 pt Sabon
by Servis Filmsetting Ltd, Stockport, Cheshire, and
printed and bound in Great Britain by
CPI Group (UK) Ltd, Croydon CR0 4YY

A CIP record for this book is available from the British Library

ISBN 978 0 7486 7546 3 (hardback)
ISBN 978 0 7486 7547 0 (webready PDF)
ISBN 978 0 7486 7548 7 (epub)
ISBN 978 0 7486 7549 4 (Amazon ebook)

The right of Simon Cooke
to be identified as author of this work
has been asserted in accordance with
the Copyright, Designs and Patents Act 1988.

Contents

List of Illustrations

Acknowledgements

As I think of all the people in different places who have contributed in unique ways to this book, it makes sense to me that it was a traveller – Ryszard Kapuściński – who wrote: 'it is only thanks to long-established custom that we sign the text with a single name' (2008: 13). I am indebted to many more people than I can name here. But with this acknowledgement, and with the proviso that any errors can be signed with my own name alone, I offer the following, warmest thanks.

This book is on the result of research carried out at Justus-Liebig-University Gießen, Germany, where between 2006 and 2010 I was a member of the International PhD Programme (IPP) 'Literary and Cultural Studies', generously funded by the International Graduate Centre for the Study of Culture (GCSC), with a part-time post in the Department of English and American Studies. The book might have remained a *voyage imaginaire* were it not for my doctoral supervisor, Ansgar Nünning: his generosity and vision, both in his personal guidance and in his dedication to creating such an inspiring international context in which to work, have been pivotal to my research, and much else. Thanks, too, to my second supervisor, Catherine Bernard (Paris Diderot), whose insights and encouragement – especially at the delicate moment when I realised I was writing about wonder – were crucial. Thanks to Wolfgang Hallet, co-facilitator of the IPP, and my colloquium year-group, for their invaluable feedback and camaraderie. I benefited greatly from Eleonora Ravizza's insights as my dedicated respondent, and from conversations (as well as formal or informal German lessons) with Ursula Arning, Hanna Bingel, Steffi Bock and Meike Hölscher. Special thanks are due to two great friends who read and responded, with tireless generosity and sensitivity, to work in progress: Michael Basseler patiently and insightfully talked through the whole project on an almost daily basis, and his careful reading of an early draft of Part I in particular was vital; René Dietrich, with whom I was fortunate to share the doctoral journey, read and responded to the whole manuscript, often on an after-midnightly basis, and reassured me, at the end, that I was there. Where I would have been without Rose Lawson, who gave me a home when I arrived, and made me at home throughout, I am not sure; but it would not been on time, nor with the right documents, nor in such good spirits. Without these people in my life I could not have brought the work to completion, and among the other dear friends who inspired and nourished me, I would especially like to thank Farzad Boobani, Ute Dietrich, Mirjam Horn, Marija Sruk, and Jutta Weingarten.

The research was formatively influenced by teaching, especially a module on travel writing, 'The Nomadic Alternative', in 2006 and 2007: my thanks to all the students who took part in the courses. I benefited from more insights and suggestions from co-participants at conferences than I could credit here, but a conversation begun at the Hermes Summer School with one of the organisers, Timothy Mathews, in Aarhus in 2008 continues, and continues to enliven and enrich my sense of literature. Readers and editors of articles I wrote alongside the research also greatly contributed to my thinking for the book. In this regard I would like to thank Astrid Erll, Herbert Grabes, Angela Locatelli, Birgit Neumann, Ann Rigney, Bernard Schweizer, Robert A. Segal, Jonathan Skinner, Carl Thompson, Frederik Tygestrup. My thanks too to Peter Hulme, who gave invaluable feedback on an early version of the Chatwin chapter.

In 2009, I was granted the extraordinary privilege of consulting the Bruce Chatwin archive at the Bodleian Library ahead of the embargo, thanks to the generosity of Elizabeth Chatwin. Like all admirers of Chatwin's work, I already owed her a great deal. The opportunity to study 'The Nomadic Alternative', the Moleskine notebooks and the drafts, was something like the personal equivalent of Chatwin's being present at Saskatchewan for discovery of evidence of the first manmade fire – I am deeply grateful for the opportunity. My thanks to the staff at Special Collections, particularly Colin Harris, who made my request possible, and offered much advice on using the archive. The Sebald chapter, too, draws on archival research – in the Sebald *Nachlaß* at the Deutsches Literaturarchiv Marbach. I am grateful to the staff, and was fortunate to have been introduced to this fascinating archive by one of the people to whom we owe the scrupulous care with which it has been organised: Sebald's friend, colleague, reader and now translator, Jo Catling. My personal thanks, too, to Ute Sebald, for permitting me to cite drafts of *Die Ringe des Saturn*.

The bulk of the revisions were carried out as a research fellow at Wolfson College, Oxford. My thanks to the college president, Hermione

Lee, and also to Elleke Boehmer, Julie Curtis and Jon Stallworthy, for making it possible to work in such a vibrant and nurturing environment. My thanks, too, to them and to other colleagues and friends at the college – including Samuel Yi Chen, Daniel Grey and Jarad Zimbler – for their encouragement, generous conversation and good counsel. I was very lucky to meet with Clare Broome Saunders and Tom F. Wright, with whom I co-convened the research seminar Travel Cultures: I thank them for their friendship as well as for reinvigorating my sense of the subject. And I learned much from those who participated in the seminars as well as the Travel and Truth conference we co-organised in September 2011, where conversations about the research with Ottmar Ette and with Tim Youngs were particularly instructive for the present work. The opportunity to administrate the Oxford Centre for Life-Writing at Wolfson on a short-term basis – for which role Rachel Hewitt gave me generous guidance as her cover – came with the added benefit that it encouraged me to think through the relations between travel and life-writing as I revised the manuscript.

Some thanks stretch a little further back: to my unofficial undergraduate mentor at Hull University, Jane Thomas, who continued to guide my plans and ideas for postgraduate and doctoral work long after my first degree; and to John Hoyles, whose teaching on the remarkable modules on 'Literature and Totalitarianism' I was often conscious of in my research here. Special thanks are due to Alison Light: the book grew out of my MA dissertation on W. G. Sebald at UCL (2002–3), where I had the great good fortune of being supervised by her. She, and her work, have been an inspiration and guide ever since. The generosity, depth and independence of her thinking were vital to the pre-history of the book, as they have been – along with her encouragement and friendship, and that of her husband, John O'Halloran – as I revised the research and sought a publisher. In this regard, I have been extremely fortunate in Edinburgh University Press. My thanks to Jackie Jones, who has been an exceptionally insightful and responsive commissioning editor, and to the anonymous reviewers for their encouraging responses to the proposal, and their searching and thoughtful recommendations for revision. Thanks, too, to the rest of the editorial team involved – Jenny Daly, James Dale and Rebecca MacKenzie – for their encouragement, efficiency and patience guiding me through the preparation of my first monograph, and to my copy-editor, Nicola Wood, who not only picked up on many more editorial and bibliographical slips than I would care to admit, but also suggested many invaluable improvements in terms of cogency of argument, clarity and expression, with sensitivity and good humour. These final stages of revision were given a great boost, too, in coinciding with my taking up a research fellowship at Edinburgh University: my thanks to Penny Fielding, Jeremy Robbins and Jonathan Wild for making this possible, and to them and the English Department for their warm welcome on my arrival.

Finally, my deep thanks to all of my family, and those friends not already mentioned. Of other friends who have informed, sustained and encouraged my writing I would like at least to mention: Ruth Baker, Theo Bishop, Anne Frühauf, Vicky Hampton, Myles Howell, Julia Huber, Simon Neligan, Gemma Sudlow, Sebastian Verweij. The importance of my grandparents, Christopher and Margaret Laurence, will be clear from the dedication – the first thing written in the manuscript and the only thing that never changed. Their inexhaustible interest in everything and everyone may well be the source of the present argument. Much in their lives, and mine, has been made possible and happier by Dilys Jones. I have the wisest, most encouraging and loving sister in the world in Laura Edwards, whose insights always made me think in different ways. Thanks to my father, Michael Cooke, for conversations about books and place. And thanks to my parents-in-law, Richard and Ginny Taylor, for their encouragement and generosity – and for welcoming me into their family. Which brings me to the last word, which goes, with my deepest gratitude and love, to my wife, Cathy Taylor. She and her love have been my motivation, a constant support (even from a few hundred miles away), and my happiest distraction and delight. And as I submit this book about wonder experienced by travellers, I discover this great new wonder and happiness that comes with sharing the excitement of waiting to welcome a new arrival in one's home.

I gratefully acknowledge the following permissions:
Giorgio de Chirico, *The Enigma of Arrival and the Afternoon*. Copyright © DACS 2012.
Excerpts from the manuscript draft of *Die Ringe des Saturn* by W. G. Sebald. Copyright © 2013, The Estate of W. G. Sebald, used by permission of The Wylie Agency (UK) Limited.
Images from *Die Ringe des Saturn / The Rings of Saturn*. Copyright ©, The Estate of W. G. Sebald, used by permission of The Wylie Agency (UK) Limited.
Excerpts from the manuscript draft of *Die Ringe des Saturn* and other documents consulted in the Sebald *Nachlaß* used by permission of the Deutsches Literaturarchiv Marbach, Germany.

Were this world an endless plain, and by sailing eastward we could for ever reach new distances, and discover sights more sweet and strange than any Cyclades or Islands of King Solomon, then there were promise in the voyage. But in pursuit of those far mysteries we dream of, or in tortured chase of that demon phantom that, some time or other, swims before all human hearts; while chasing such over this round globe, they either lead us on in barren mazes or midway leave us whelmed.

Herman Melville, *Moby Dick* (2002: 196)

As you are not unaware, I am much travelled. This fact allows me to corroborate the assertion that a voyage is always more or less illusory, that there is nothing new under the sun, that everything is one and the same etcetera, but also, paradoxically enough, to assert that there is no foundation for despairing of finding surprises and something new: in truth, the world is inexhaustible.

H. Garro, *Tout lou Mond* (1918), anthologised in Borges and Casares,
Extraordinary Tales (1971: 95)

and then we both say that it is a small world. We say this, as people usually do, with a sense of wonder and refreshment.

Alice Munro, *The View from Castle Rock* (2006: 331)

Introduction:
The Wonder that Came Later

[W]e have said or spoken nothing of the Greater Sea nor of the Provinces which are around it, though we have well explored it all [...] I omit to speak of it, since it seems to me to be wearisome to speak that which may be unnecessary and useless, nor that which others know always, since they are so many who explore it and sail it every day, as is well known, such as Venetians and Genoese and Persians and many other people who make that journey so often that everyone knows what is there, and therefore I am silent and say nothing to you of that.

Marco Polo, *The Description of the World* (1938: 489–90)

To speak of travellers' tales of wonder in late twentieth-century literature may well strike some as oxymoronic, anachronistic, quaint: more tall tale than area of inquiry. Already at the end of the thirteenth century, the 'wise and learned citizen of Venese' (Polo 1938: 73) was beginning to tire of accounts of the Provinces. What promise for wonder voyaging, then, when the idiom of the 'global village' (McLuhan 1988: 28–31) itself rings overly familiar? Travellers' tales of wonder belong, according to most accounts, in bygone ages: to Messer Polo; to the medieval Wonder Book; to Columbus and Ralegh and the first astonishing, and then brutally violent, Renaissance encounters between Europe and what would enter Western history – in being all but destroyed – as the 'New World' of the Americas. But the contemporary world is not held to be 'new' but 'belated'; and we are the *Nachgeborenen* (Brecht 1973), 'born afterwards' in an era habitually described in terms of its posterity. Where once there were wonder voyages in a world unknown to itself, there are now 'tourists with typewriters' (Holland and Huggan 2000) in a world that can peer in on itself with Google Earth. Where once there was wonder about 'new worlds' there can now be found the ravages of empire that followed, hungry for possession, in its wake. 'Over the centuries,' writes Mary Baine Campbell, 'the marvelous and the desirable have moved from text, to margin and preface, and finally out of the book itself' (Campbell 1988: 254). And what Jaś Elsner and Joan-Pau Rubiés write with the last five hundred years in mind has become increasingly emblematic: 'Modern travel writing is a literature of disappointment' (Elsner and Rubiés 1999: 5). Disappointment, disenchantment, disillusionment, belatedness, nostalgia: these are among the most recurrent terms in discussions of contemporary travel and its writings. The *Oxford English Dictionary* entry on a well-known axiom expresses the situation concisely: '*wonders will never cease*: that is indeed surprising; now freq. *ironic*'.

This book is about the wonder that came later. It explores – and questions – the narrative of disenchantment intimated above, both in terms of its tenets as a sensibility, and by gathering and appraising a body of work that indicates a parallel emergence in contemporary literature of what will be referred to here as 'travellers' tales of wonder'. In its broadest strokes, it argues that over the course of the late twentieth century an international constellation of writers has increasingly moved towards the travel narrative form, recovering and renewing a sense of wonder, often drawing on the formal and thematic features of early, pre-modern and Renaissance travellers' tales. This, it is argued, is not simply an escape from the sources of modern disenchantment, but a profound response to them. The book moves through the wider literary and cultural landscape into readings of three works that exemplify the reach and range of the form: Bruce Chatwin's *In Patagonia* (1977), V. S. Naipaul's *The Enigma of Arrival* (1987) and W. G. Sebald's *Die Ringe des Saturn: eine englische Wallfahrt* (1995), translated into English by Michael Hulse with Sebald's involvement as *The Rings of Saturn*, without the subtitle of 'An English Pilgrimage', in 1998. This triumvirate of texts is read as both expression of and counter to a sensibility of disenchantment: a challenge to the hubris of thinking the world too well known, and an invitation to encounter and approach the present, past and future, in all its complexity, with a sense of wonder. In précis: travellers' tales of wonder are not only still possible; they have become an increasingly prominent form of engagement with the very problems for which, as we shall see, they are often held to account.

The appellation 'travellers' tales of wonder' is offered as descriptive, rather than definitive – a viewfinder rather than a frame – regarding a corpus of texts united most conspicuously by their resistance to classification. The publication of Chatwin's *In Patagonia* met with widespread confusion over its wandering across generic and disciplinary boundaries – including those between fact and fiction (see Shakespeare 1999: 310–14). *The Enigma of Arrival* is subtitled *A Novel in Five Sections* but widely regarded as 'Thinly Veiled Autobiography' (Thieme 1987) and has been described by Naipaul's biographer as 'an unusable masterpiece' (French 2008: 427). Sebald's *The Rings of Saturn* is classified, in its English-language form, as a superficially paradoxical combination of Fiction/Memoir/Travel – and the endemic use of photographs and visual materials means that even the term 'writing' only partially captures the basic form of his work. Each of these books, then, might prompt us to recall Walter Benjamin's remark that 'it has been rightly said that all great works found a genre or dissolve one – that they are, in other words, special cases' (Benjamin 1999b: 197; see Wood 1999: 38 and Santner 2006: xiv). But their resemblance to one another in their very incommensurability invites consideration as a literary historical phenomenon. When John Banville credits Sebald with creating 'a new kind of writing, combining fiction, memoir, travelogue, philosophy, and much else besides' (Banville 2001: no pagination), he echoes earlier responses to Chatwin and Naipaul, and might with equal accuracy have been responding to numerous other contemporary writers from disparate cultural and linguistic backgrounds: Roberto Calasso, J. M. G. Le Clézio, Cees Nooteboom, Claudio Magris, Predrag Matvejević, Jan Morris, Tim Robinson, Iain Sinclair, to name only a few.

How to account for a class of unclassifiable texts? The generic 'homelessness' of these writings, it can be argued, is closely, even expressively, related to the experience and theme of travel. They may be read in the contemporary literary sphere in the terms set out by Ottmar Ette in *Literature on the Move*, which charts the emergence of a 'bordercrossing literature' with 'no fixed abode': 'literatures beyond clear-cut national, continental, and territorial borderlines [. . .] that cross through and over the until now valid borders of national-literary, literature-historical, genre-historical, or cultural kinds' (Ette 2003: 13). Another reason the form of the traveller's tale is worth stressing in formal as well as thematic terms is that they also draw on, or resemble, older traditions of travel and writing. John Marincola introduces another writer – Herodotus – in strikingly similar terms to those we find in the receptions noted above: he 'lived in a time [c. 484–25 BCE] when categories of knowledge had not been rigidly separated, and his work ranges over many fields and includes geography, anthropology, ethnology, zoology, even fable and folklore. His work defies easy categorization' (Marincola 2003: xiv). Sebald's '*Annäherung an Bruce Chatwin*' (Sebald 2005) – suggesting both an 'approach' to and 'convergence' with Chatwin (cf. Prager 2010: 189) – brings these issues clearly into view:

> Just as Chatwin himself remains an enigma, one never knows how to classify his books. All that is obvious is that their structure and intentions place them

in no known genre [. . .] It probably does them most justice to see their prom-
iscuity, which breaks the modernist concept, as a late flowering of those early
traveller's [*sic*] tales going back to Marco Polo where reality is constantly
entering the realm of the metaphysical and miraculous, and the way through
the world is taken from the first with an eye fixed on the writer's own end.
(Sebald 2005: 180–1)

This study pursues the implications of this richly tentative assessment.
Why is it the case that so many writers, Sebald among them, have made
a similar move in turning to the travel narrative? What is at stake in a
'late flowering' of 'travellers' tales' in the late twentieth century and how
has the form been adapted and revised? How do such writings relate
to the literary and cultural contexts of late- or post-modernity? These
are the book's widest questions. It aims to bring to the fore the often
neglected role that wonder has played in late twentieth-century travels,
focusing in on three writers who, from diverse perspectives, have challenged the idea that the traveller's tale is rendered redundant, or inherently dubious, by the pressures of late modernity – most pertinently,
the exponential rise of tourism, the association of travel writing with
empire, and a wider sense of cultural exhaustion since the Second World
War. Travellers' tales of wonder, then, are to be read as engagements
with pervasive literary and cultural preoccupations. It is thus more than
coincidental that the scholarly fields of inquiry within which the argument is most firmly situated – studies in travel writing and studies in
wonder – rose to prominence in parallel with each other, as well as with
the emergence of the literary corpus in question.

The arrival of 'travel writing' as a fit area for scholarly research, now a
burgeoning field, is a relatively recent phenomenon. In the *Cambridge
Companion to Travel Writing*, the most authoritative state-of-the-art
guide, published in 2002, Peter Hulme and Tim Youngs alert the reader
at the outset to 'the absence within the academy of a tradition of critical
attention to travel writing', with the consequence that 'this Companion,
unlike most others in the series, whose areas of study are well-defined,
has to bring its subject into focus in order to "accompany" it' (Hulme
and Youngs 2002: 1). There is now an International Society for Travel
Writing, founded in 1997 along with the Centre for Travel Writing
Studies at Nottingham Trent University, England, and the associated
international journal *Studies in Travel Writing*, followed soon after
by *Journeys: The International Journal of Travel and Travel Writing*
(2000). The academic publishers Routledge and Ashgate, among others,
have series dedicated to travel writing. And scholarly work on the genre
has developed into a highly interdisciplinary field, involving not only

literary studies but also, most prominently, cultural studies, anthropology, tourism studies, history, geography and – almost as a prerequisite of the subject itself – often crossing the boundaries between them.

The breadth of the body of texts that can conceivably be approached as travel writing – ranging from the ancients to works by Henry James to *Lonely Planet* guides – is matched by a breadth of scholarly approaches and interpretations. Any summary account of the research area can only be partial, then. But it is fair to suggest that, in the Anglophone world at least, two seminal books have exerted a profound, even formative, influence on subsequent scholarship: Edward Said's *Orientalism* and Paul Fussell's *Abroad: British Literary Traveling Between the Wars* (cf. Mills 2003). *Orientalism*, published in 1978 and often credited as one of the foundational texts for postcolonial studies, scrutinised the travel texts of nineteenth-century European authors such as Sir Richard Burton and Gérard de Nerval, alongside novels, poetry and scholarly writing, to demonstrate their role in systematically 'producing' rather than objectively representing the Orient as the projection of an exotic cultural 'other' to confirm the centrality (and tacitly justify the hegemony) of European power. In *Abroad*, Fussell sought to counter a 'generic snobbery' (Fussell 1980: 95) against travel writing with attentive readings of travel books of the 1930s, but framed his appreciation as an elegy for the 'last age of travel', arguing that the rise of tourism had 'made the experience of genuine travel impossible' (1980: 24). These twin landmarks of scholarship brought an unprecedented degree of sustained attention and insight to a body of texts which, traditionally, had been either banished to, or ignored on, the margins of literary studies as a discipline. While having different, even conflicting perspectives, they, or the intellectual currents of which they are such eloquent expressions, have primed the continuing debate according to a pretext that travel writing in the contemporary period is epistemologically obsolete in the era of the tourist, and ethically dubious in its association with empire. Between these two poles, the combined conclusion is often that travel – what Fussell calls 'genuine' or 'real' travel – is no longer possible, and that where travel writing continues as practice it is – in its perpetuation of colonial vision – ethically dubious.

As already noted, the diversity of studies in travel writing prohibits summary generalisation, and numerous studies have elucidated aesthetic features of the genre (see for example Adams 1983; Porter 1991; Rennie 1995; Korte 1996; Russell 2000; Whitfield 2011). While feminist criticism and gender studies perspectives have often exposed the interrelations of empire, the male gaze and gender, women's travel writing has also proven a site for studies in alternative modes of travel and representation (Mills 2003; Rose 1993). In the main, however, the value of studying contemporary travel writing is often seen as cultural, rather than literary, and the perspectives taken by Fussell and Said remain pretexts. One of the most extensive and rigorous book-length analyses, Patrick Holland and Graham Huggan's *Tourists with Typewriters: Reflections on Contemporary Travel Writing*, takes as its cue the view that contemporary travel writing 'calls out [. . .] for a sustained critical analysis: one that looks at travel writers as retailers of mostly white, male, middle-class, heterosexual myths and prejudices, and at their readers as eager consumers of exotic – culturally "othered" – goods' (Holland and Huggan 1998: viii). The resulting thesis is that 'travel writing frequently provides an effective alibi for the perpetuation or reinstallment of ethnocentrically superior attitudes to "other" cultures, peoples, and places' (1998: viii). Similarly, Debbie Lisle approaches contemporary travel writing as a genre occupying a 'precarious position', and asks how is the genre 'coping with the embarrassment of its colonial past while also recognising there are no undiscovered places left to explore?' (Lisle 2006: 3). When casting a glance ahead, studies of earlier periods often take a similar view. In a study of Romantic travel, for example, Nigel Leask writes that the

> whimsicality of much modern travel writing – and the genre is now firmly situated on the parlour table rather than in the library – suggests nostalgia not just for an imperial age of travel 'before' tourism but also for an epoch of 'integrated' travel narrative when literary representation of the foreign was at the cutting edge of emergent discourses both of self and of scientific knowledge. (Leask 2002: 10)

This study shares these concerns. But though it does not contest the specific readings of many of the texts examined in such studies – nor the urgency of such critical scrutiny – it looks to a body of texts that suggest that travel writing has also been a site of engagement, rather than symptomatic complicity, with these same concerns, renewing a sense of wonder as part of that engagement. And it questions the assumptions underlying the statement that there are 'no undiscovered places left to explore' (Lisle 2006: 3) and the idea that travel writing automatically draws on a colonial heritage (2006: 3). Indeed, these currents of thought will form part of the object of study in what follows, as part of a sensibility of disenchantment with contemporary travel.

To invoke 'wonder' is of course to introduce an extraordinarily polyvalent word. The *OED* entry referred to earlier takes its place within more than eight columns (492–5) of diverse definitions, with a history as old as that of extant English literature: the earliest cited occurrence is traced to *Beowulf*, and its Anglo-Saxon form, 'wundor', dated as 840. The Germanic *Wunder* to which the English word may be traced is of uncertain origin, perhaps derived from 'intricacy' or 'complexity' (Daston and Park 1998: 16). The French equivalent, *merveille*, linked to the English 'marvel', carries over the Latin associations of *admiratio*, *mirabilia*, *miracula* and *ammirunda* – linked to *miror* and thus to the idea of reflection, with roots in the Indo-European word for 'smile' (1998: 16). Limited to the English word alone, 'wonder' has operated as a noun, a verb, an adjective, or an adverb respectively. As a verb, the word's most colloquial meanings are near contradictory: to wonder means 'to feel or be affected with wonder; to be struck with surprise or astonishment, to marvel'; but to wonder also means to 'feel some doubt or curiosity'. One stops us in our tracks; another propels inquiry. And this multiplicity extends to wonder as noun. While its first meaning is 'something that causes astonishment' – a 'marvellous object; a marvel; a prodigy' – the connotations of 'a wonder' have not always been exclusively positive. Particularly given that this study concerns writings that deal with histories which, to say the least, cannot be described as 'wonderful' in the most colloquial sense, it is worth noting that among the word's meanings are the following:

> † 5. a. Evil or shameful action; evil; *pl.* evil or horrible deeds. *Obs.*
> † b. Destruction, disaster. *Obs.*
> † c. Great distress or grief. *Obs.*

This study will have cause to question the qualifications '*Obs.*' (obsolete), particularly in the reading of Sebald's *Die Ringe des Saturn*, where it becomes clear that there may be more than alliterative and assonant relations between wonder and wound, trauma and *thauma* (the Greek root of wonder (*OED*)). What is immediately clear is that the unusual versatility of wonder means that too strict a definition is unlikely to be both conceptually consistent and historically inclusive at the same time. Even at the time of the Renaissance when the discourse of wonder was at its peak, Peter Platt observes, 'no unified vision of the marvelous existed: it was a concept full of inconsistency and variety' (Platt 1999: 16). And equally, as Lorraine Daston and Katharine Park write, the history of wonder 'is tightly bound up with the history of other cognitive passions such as terror and curiosity' (Daston and Park 1998: 15). This breadth sounds a cautionary note against too summary a definition – or dismissal – of wonder. And it is precisely this breadth and elusiveness that makes 'wonder' so important here: the unifying feature to be found in all the word's many meanings – which will provide a thread in what follows here – concerns the unknown, or the unknowable. Whether a marvellous object or an inner sensation, whether dumbfounding or propulsive, whether provocative of admiration or of scepticism, delight or profound grief, wonder always skirts the boundaries of understanding, cajoles knowledge into a state of uncertainty, harasses us out of the security, however melancholy, of knowingness.

The study of wonder, as already noted, rises in parallel, and often as part of, research in travel writing. As R. J. W. Evans and Alexander Marr observe in *Curiosity and Wonder from the Renaissance to the Enlightenment*, '[t]he last three decades have seen a veritable cornucopia of studies devoted to various aspects of curiosity and wonder, predominantly, though not exclusively, focused on the sixteenth, seventeenth, and eighteenth centuries' (Evans and Marr 2006: 3–4). Tzvetan Todorov's *The Conquest of America* (1984), Mary Baine Campbell's *The Witness and the Other World: Exotic European Travel Writing, 400–1600* (1988), Stephen Greenblatt's *Marvelous Possessions: The Wonder of the New World* (1991) and Lorraine Daston and Katharine Park's *Wonders and the Order of Nature: 1150–1750* (1998) are all singled out as seminal contributions, and inform much of what follows here. However, while acknowledging the work of Nigel Leask (2002) on curiosity and wonder in the Romantic period (Evans and Marr 2006: 4), the question of what has happened to wonder since the early nineteenth century has been less thoroughly accounted for: 'Indeed, one of the most pressing challenges facing historians of curiosity and wonder is to track the trajectories of these themes through the end of the eighteenth century into the nineteenth and twentieth centuries' (Evans and Marr 2006: 17).

That the focus of these studies is on much earlier periods makes them, strangely enough, especially relevant. For one, the fact that studies of early modern and Renaissance texts draw into focus generic and thematic issues pertinent to the late twentieth-century texts considered here in itself indicates the way that writers such as Chatwin, Naipaul and Sebald draw on and respond to older traditions, more than is often held. Such studies are also relevant as a sign of contemporary intellectual interest in wonder as something that lies in the past. Studies in travel and in wonder are, after all, components of the history, as well as the historiography, of their subjects. And it is surely not arbitrary that the story of the discovery and conquest of the 'New World' of America, the 'cornucopia' of studies of wonder, the formation of 'travel writing' as a key topic in literary and cultural studies, all rose to such prominence from the late 1970s onwards, at a time in which the possibility and viability all of these things were being brought into question in the present.

The path of wonder has recently experienced something of a paradigm shift in the humanities: a process of 're-enchantment' in response to the definitive claim by the sociologist Max Weber, that modernity has involved a process of *Entzauberung*: 'The fate of our times,' Weber argued, 'is characterized by rationalization and intellectualization and, above all, by the "disenchantment of the world"' (1946: 155). The essays in the multi-author collection *The Re-Enchantment of the World: Secular Magic in a Rational Age* accept the Nietzschean assertion of the death of God, and counter Weberian disenchantment with discussion of 'the variety of secular and conscious strategies for re-enchantment, held together by their common aim of filling a God-shaped void' (Landy and Saler 2009: 2). What follows in this study is in keeping with the overall vision of the book, and nourished by several of the essays it contains. But it is notable that it has nothing to say about travel – an omission that would be unimaginable in the discourse on wonder and its neighbouring concepts in earlier periods. And in focusing on travel in the contemporary period – with its anxieties of obsolescence, of imperial inheritance, and of exhaustion in the wake of war – there emerge other, if related, issues than rationalisation and intellectualisation to contend with. The disenchantment of the world has a traumatic aspect. And these are issues with which wonder, and travellers' tales, must contend.

Scholarly interpretations of each of the authors whose work is studied in depth here are equally rich in themselves. Chatwin is the only writer in whom we find anything like an asymmetry between the impact of his work and its scholarly reception. There are many scholarly articles and two biographies rich in critical insight (one an impressionistic 'portrait' by his former editor, Susannah Clapp (1997), the other Nicholas Shakespeare's indispensable authorised biography (1999)). But as yet there is no 'critical companion', and book-length critical studies are few (Nicholas Murray (1993) and Patrick Meanor (1997) provide the most sustained responses thus far). And for all that Chatwin insisted *In Patagonia* to be 'a modern WONDER VOYAGE' (Chatwin 2010: 275) the role that wonder might play in his work has largely been looked on askance. The archive of scholarship on Naipaul is extensive, in keeping with his profile as one of the most celebrated writers in contemporary literature (culminating in the award of the Nobel Prize in 2001), and also one of its most controversial. The crucial role of wonder in his work, however, has been obscured by a tendency, among both critics and admirers, to regard him as the 'supreme writer of disenchantment' (Hass qtd in Winokur 1997: 118) – something to be challenged in this study. The lionisation of W. G. Sebald over the course of the 1990s is among the most extraordinary stories of literary celebrity of the period, fairly described as the 'Sebald Phenomenon' (Denham and McCulloh 2006). It is in the reception of Sebald's work that wonder has figured most prominently – not least in the language of the 'mesmeric' and 'spell-binding' which, as we shall see, permeates the reviews. The artist Jeremy Millar, in a short but densely suggestive essay, makes the most direct link between Sebald's *The Rings of Saturn*, as 'a book of wonder', with medieval compendia of marvels (Millar 2007: 113). Brad Prager has illuminated many of the correspondences between Sebald and Chatwin (Prager 2010). And Peter Hulme points towards the contours of the corpus explored here in suggesting that Naipaul's later fiction may belong to a 'still emergent genre: allusive and literary meditations, with elements of autobiography and travel writing' (Hulme 2002b: 89), while the 'intricate path' of Sebald's *The Rings of Saturn* illustrates the ways in which 'the genre of travel writing is subverted and renewed' (Hulme 2002b: 99. Nevertheless, the issue of how Sebald's wonder relates to late modernity warrants further consideration. So too do the formal and thematic resonances between the work of three writers who, as yet, have not been studied together as part of a broad literary historical phenomenon.

There are, then, deep pools of thought on which to draw for a study of contemporary travellers' tales of wonder. The point of departure from which this book aims to contribute is the observation that travel and wonder seem to part company in studies of contemporary literature and culture; and that, perhaps consequently, the role of wonder in contemporary travellers' tales has received comparatively scant – or knowingly sceptical – attention. One way of summarising the present argument is to claim that these apparently disparate areas are part of the same story.

How to tell that story? The first step may well be to stand back. The title of Part I – 'Horizon of expectations': Travels in Literary History' – is drawn from what has become a critical idiom in explorations of literary genre: Hans Robert Jauss's *Erwartungshorizont* (1972). Part I aims to explore the broad dimensions of the 'horizon of expectations' through which contemporary travellers' tales of wonder come into view – or are obscured from it. Chapter 1 assesses travel writing as a genre, and makes the case for according it a vital place in literary history. Chapter 2 then focuses in on 'travel and its discontents in late modernity', aiming to identify and contend with those dimensions of a late twentieth-century cultural climate that predispose an idea that travellers' tales of wonder are either epistemologically obsolete or ethically dubious: the sense that authentic travel has given way to tourism; the idea that travellers' tales are an inheritance and expression of empire; and the wider sense of post-Second World War cultural exhaustion. Chapter 3 then attempts to demonstrate the prominence of travels in contemporary international literature, seeking to understand how, and why, writers have adopted and adapted the travel narrative form. In no small part – thus the argument here – it has been a response to precisely those problems considered to be inherent in the form itself.

Having explored the wider contexts, Part II proceeds with close readings of Chatwin's *In Patagonia*, Naipaul's *Enigma of Arrival* and Sebald's *Die Ringe des Saturn*. The argument develops, on one level, cumulatively: each case study is presented with the aim of progressively contributing to a sense that travellers' tales of wonder are not only possible in the contemporary world, but have become increasingly prominent. But there is also a historical and thematic pattern to the specific sequence chosen. In terms of the main textual focus, the readings follow a chronological history, tracking the path of wonder in the last three decades of the twentieth century. And although each book responds to the issues discussed as a whole (among other concerns), the respective emphases echo the sequence of the issues discussed in Part I, Chapter 2: Chatwin's *In Patagonia* most obviously recovers a sense of wonder in contrast to the terms of a rhetoric of exhaustion; Naipaul's *The Enigma of Arrival* brings into question the idea that travellers' tales of wonder are inherently colonial in perspective; the sense of wonder in Sebald's *Die Ringe des Saturn* most clearly engages with the sense of disenchantment in the wake of the Second World War. In each case, it is wonder itself that is explored as the means of addressing the very sources of disenchantment.

This book, then, explores why and how writers have adopted and adapted the form of the travellers' tale of wonder – and, relatedly, why it might be that this has been overlooked, underestimated, or doubted in the critical reception. Its principal aims are literary historical. But what it moves towards is an idea with a broader ethical dimension. Beside the now sometimes hubristically held view that wonder in travel is rendered 'unnecessary and useless' by the 'many other people who make that journey so often' (to allude once more to the epigraph from Polo), and undermined by the violence of history past and present, may be placed an alternative view: that if we can encounter the world and think it too well known, and if we can contemplate the complexities of our histories, including those most tragic, without a sense of wonder, then we are, like Naipaul's traveller before his awakening in *The Enigma of Arrival*, hiding ourselves from our experience, and hiding our experience from ourselves (cf. Naipaul 2002: 117). And therefore travellers' tales of wonder continue to speak of what 'everyone knows [. . .] is there', and do not remain silent or 'say nothing to you of that' (Polo 1976: 90).

Part I
'Horizon of expectations': Travels in Literary History

Chapter 1

A Question of Form:
Genre and the Journey

Voyages and travels are among the oldest and most culturally wide-spread forms in literary history. Among the earliest extant texts is a traveller's tale of an island of marvels, 'The Shipwrecked Sailor' (Tappan 1914: 41–6), written in Egypt's Twelfth Dynasty (that is, around 2200 BCE). The journey is the common denominator for accounts as varied as *The Histories* of the ancient Greek Herodotus, Egeria's pilgrimage to the Holy Land in the fourth century CE, the writings of household-name scientists such as Charles Darwin with *Voyage of the Beagle* and works by canonical literary authors such as Henry James, with *Italian Hours*. And from *The Epic of Gilgamesh*, the Sumerian quest narrative dated at around 2000 BCE, to the ancient epics, to the world's religious texts, to the emergence of the Western novel, the journey is a perennial motif. Homer's *Odyssey*, Exile and Exodus, the Norse sagas, the early Germanic *Widsith*, the Anglo-Saxon poem *Beowulf*, Thomas More's *Utopia*, Cervantes' *Don Quixote*, Defoe's *Robinson Crusoe* – all are cases in point. Travel, real or imagined, prompts tales, oral or written. In 'Der Erzähler' ('The Storyteller'), Walter Benjamin cites a German proverb: '"If one goes on a journey, one has something to tell"' (Benjamin 1977: 386; my translation). And conversely, tales, oral or written, imply a journey, literal or figurative. That German saying could well be supplemented: 'If one has something to tell, one has travelled.' Readers, too, may be 'transported'. And we are often, slightly to adapt Peter Brooks' formulation, 'reading for the journey' (Brooks 1984) – something notably evident, of course, in Jauss' *Erwartungshorizont* (1982).

The initial question, then, may well be Tzvetan Todorov's at the outset of 'The Journey and its Narratives': 'What is *not* a journey?' (1995: 60). So elastic and pervasive is travel that designating the parameters of a specific travel genre is fraught with classificatory quandaries. To cite or near-cite what is almost a literary critical topos, 'travel writing is notoriously difficult to define' (cf. Hulme and Youngs 2002: 1; Roberson 2001: xi–xxvi). The terminology itself is far from given. 'Travelogue' is used anachronistically of pre-twentieth-century texts: it was coined in 1903 by Burton Holmes to describe his travel lectures supplemented by hand-tinted photographs, and originally meant 'an illustrated lecture' (*OED*). 'Travel writing' seems to have become critically idiomatic only since the 1980s. It doesn't enter at all into the taxonomy of terms for 'Travel books as literary phenomena' in Paul Fussell's pioneering *Abroad* (Fussell 1980: 202–15). Fussell notes 'travelogues', 'travel logs' and 'literary travel', settling on 'travel books' as the term for discussion (1980: 203). And among other terms, we might refer to 'voyages and travels' – the terms used in Richard Hakluyt's collection of *Principal Navigations* (1598–1600) – or, indeed, 'travellers' tales'.

This proliferation of terms is a mark of the contested parameters, even the conceptual cohesiveness, of a specific form itself more than a question of sub-categorical distinctions. It alerts us to the fact that under the aegis of 'TRAVEL' – to use yet another term: that favoured by English-language publishers and booksellers – we are drawing together texts from diverse periods, cultures and fields into a genre that Jonathan Raban, in a much-quoted characterisation, has described as 'a notoriously raffish open house in which different forms are likely to end up in the same bed' (Raban 1987b: 253). What, then, as we look back and across literary (and not only strictly literary) history, are the criteria for inclusion in or exclusion from this 'raffish house'?

'A traveller's account of a journey taken' might seem to suffice. But even the most level-headed attempts at clarification tend to pose questions as well as answer them. Fussell's definition is as follows: 'A subspecies of memoir in which the autobiographical narrative arises from the speaker's encounter with distant or unfamiliar data, and in which the narrative – unlike that in a novel or romance – claims literal validity by constant reference to actuality' (Fussell 1980: 203). But must a travel book stress the autobiographical? Must it arise from distant or unfamiliar data? And, most contentiously, how are we to know that the 'claim to literal validity' is in fact making reference to actuality? Jan Borm has valuably drawn attention to the incongruity between the Anglophone concept of 'travel writing' and the French and German terminologies, in which a distinction is made between the 'travel report' and the 'literature of travel': that is, the *récit de voyage* and the *Reisebericht* on the one hand, and *littérature de voyage* and *Reiseliteratur* on the other (Borm 2007a: 19). Borm proposes 'a similar distinction between the *travel book* or *travelogue* as a predominantly (and presupposedly) non-fictional genre, and *travel writing* and *travel literature* (the literature of travel, if one prefers) as an overall heading for texts whose main theme is travel' (2007a: 19). Yet many use the term 'travel writing' precisely to distinguish writing based on actual travel. The *Cambridge Companion*, for example, has a chronology in which 'travel writing' – texts recounting 'actual travels undertaken' – is listed in one column, while another lists historical events and 'other travel-related texts, mostly fictional and theoretical' (Hulme and Youngs 2002: 279).

If the parameters of a genre of travel cannot be determined unanimously, though, there are nevertheless a number of questions that recur, both in the texts and in their reception, which can bring our field of inquiry into focus. Firstly, we encounter the issue of what constitutes a journey: must it be physical and if so, how much distance must be covered to qualify the text as travel writing? Does Orhan Pamuk's portrait of his home city in *Istanbul* constitute travel writing? Can Xavier de Maistre really claim to have made a *Voyage autour de ma chambre*? Secondly, there are the issues of whether the traveller must be the first-person narrator – the teller of the tale – and the vexed question of the identity or non-identity of author, narrator and traveller. Is Homer's *Odyssey* to be included? Or a multi-authored guide book? Thirdly, we encounter questions of the borderlines or bordercrossings between the fields of the arts and sciences, professionalism and amateurism, fact and fiction, literature 'high' and 'low' and so on. At this level, the most perennial and contentious question is of the 'generic pact' – to borrow Philippe Lejeune's term in reference to *Le Pacte autobiographique* (1975) – between writer and reader: the question of whether the tale is a true one – or of whether it has to be true, or has to try to be or claim to be true, or has to be read as such, in order to qualify as a 'travel book', however subjective and mediated the account may be.

This last area of contention has the most bearing on the place of travellers' tales of wonder in contemporary literature – or rather, it is here that we encounter the question of whether travellers' tales can be considered a genuinely literary form at all. It is now some time since Paul Fussell sought to counter the 'generic snobbery' that he saw behind the neglect of a form that 'seemed not to be a fiction' (Fussell 1980: 95); and numerous writers and scholars have similarly drawn attention to innovations in travel writing as a form. Yet Steve Clark could still describe travel writing, without expectation of controversy, as a 'kind of love that dare not speak its name' (Clark 1999: 3) and take it as given that the form 'has always been mixed and middlebrow' and 'unabashedly commercial': 'its force is collective and incremental rather than singular and aesthetic' (1999: 1). This horizon of low expectations rests, crucially, on an idea that travel writing is 'too dependent on an empirical rendition of contingent events, what happened to happen, for entry into the literary canon' (1999: 2). Both aspects of this critical position, however, are open to question. That travel writing – even travel writing that strives for documentary authority – is 'dependent' on 'contingent events' is questionable; so too is the implied requirement that narrative, to be of literary value, must be overtly, formally fictional.

The auto-optic claim of the witness is certainly a foregrounded component of many travel writings. As Elsner and Rubiés remark, the 'rhetorical attempt to claim authority as a direct observer' can be seen as the 'fundamental literary mechanism of legitimation in the genre' (Elsner and Rubiés 1999: 3). This mechanism has perhaps its most exemplary expression in the prologue to Marco Polo's *Description of the World*, in which 'all people who are pleased and wish to know the different generations of men and the diversities of the different regions and lands of the world' are given the injunction to

> take then this book and have it read, & here you will find all the greatest marvels and the great diversities of the Great and Less Armenie and of Persia, Median, Turquie, and of the Tartars [. . .] Master Marc Pol of the Melion, wise and learned citizen of Venese, relates because he saw them with his own eyes [. . .] And each one who shall read this book must believe it fully, because all are most truthful things. (Polo 1976: 73)

It is a paradigm example of the rhetorical claim to the authority of the eye witness. Yet it is one of the ironies of Polo's opening gambit that it promises a credible account of that which is incredible – 'the greatest marvels' – and that he 'caused the accounts [. . .] to be written by Messer S. Rusticians of Pisa' – a famous *romancier* of the day. In a sense, the long history of disdain for tall tales surrounding this area of ambiguity is the first question mark over a view that travel writing lacks the creativity of fiction. The satirical literary response can be traced to at least the first century CE, in Lucian's *A True Story* – a fantastical voyage to the edges of the universe which begins with Lucian chastising the 'charlatanry' of many travellers' tales, and making the counter-claim that 'not having had any adventures of significance, I took to lying' but 'I shall at least be truthful in saying that I am a liar' (Lucian 2007: 4). It is a model of the vein of travel satire that has its most influential expressions in Thomas More's *Utopia* (1516) and Jonathan Swift's *Gulliver's Travels* (1726). In the seventeenth and eighteenth centuries particularly, with the rise of New Science and Enlightenment thought, there is a decisive attempt to assert the authority of the witness, by decoupling travel from the marvellous with a demand for exactitude and objectivity in language as a basis for anthropological and natural historical knowledge. In *The Trial of Travel* (1630), for example, Baptiste Goodall called upon writers to dispense with 'the least of lying wonders told / [. . .] of foothigh pygmies, dog-eared men / Blue black and yellow' (1630; qtd Daston and Parks 1998: 31). And the disputes continue in the present. While Bill Buford in the influential 1984 issue of *Granta* on travel writings could celebrate 'a narrative eloquence that situates them, with wonderful ambiguity, somewhere between fiction and fact', Ian Jack's introduction to the more recent issue of the magazine, published in 2006, expresses his surprise at his predecessor's assessment: 'the thought of their "wonderful ambiguity" had never occurred to me: I imagined that what had been described was what had happened, in more or less the order it happened' (Jack 2006: 14). While Jack acknowledges the 'omission and distortion that narrative always imposes' he maintains that 'if travel writing is to be more than a persuasive literary entertainment' and have 'some genuinely illuminating and perhaps, even, these times being what they are, some moral purpose – then the information it contains needs to be trustworthy. How else do you justify the carbon emissions spent in its research?' (2006: 14).

The demand for veracity exists side by side with the equally powerful idea present in the claim that travel writing is too 'dependent on an empirical rendition of contingent events [. . .] for entry into the literary canon' (Clark 1999: 2). This seems to have its roots in the Romantic period. Rising alongside the empirical demands of the New Science is the era of the Grand Tour, in which the stress is placed on the personality of the traveller (Sterne's *A Sentimental Journey* (1768) is the archetypal example). Yet it is also as we enter the Romantic period that travellers' tales are questioned from a different perspective. The distinction is neatly encapsulated in Thomas de Quincey's division of the 'literature of knowledge' from the 'literature of power' – the latter being literature of aesthetic value, the former primarily of value for information. From the category of the 'literature of power', de Quincey wrote, 'even books of much higher pretensions must be excluded – as, for instance, books of voyages and travels, and generally all books in which the matter to be communicated is paramount to the manner or form of its communication' (qtd Leask 2002: 10). Given this enduring demand for 'trustworthy' reportage, and given that fulfilling this demand is often seen as rendering an account less than literary, it is worth spelling out the ways in which travel writings – what Polo called 'the description of the world' – can be understood, to borrow the title of Nelson Goodman's 1978 philosophical work, as 'ways of worldmaking', illustrative of the 'overwhelming case against perception without conception, the pure given, absolute immediacy, the innocent eye, substance as substratum'

(Goodman 1992: 6). In order to afford the travellers' tale a place in literature, it is necessary both to challenge the historically contingent prioritisation of fiction as a form as well as a dimension of narrative, and to demonstrate that even texts that are distinguished by their non-fictional referentiality nevertheless involve the writer in creative, rather than transcriptive, procedures.

In one of a series of series of important interventions in the debate, Manfred Pfister has argued that much travel writing and its commentaries can be seen as the 'last refuge of a romantic aesthetic of immediacy, as yet uninfected by the postmodern consciousness of the entanglement of every experience in textually mediated schemes of perception and dispositions of experience, the dialogic participation of every text in other texts' (Pfister 1993: 111; my translation). And as Ansgar Nünning has elucidated, travel writings as much as overtly fictional forms can be understood as performing Paul Ricoeur's three-stage circle of mimesis: the encounter in the journey involves 'prefiguration' by the 'context of cultures which already have certain established versions and conceptions of travelling and identity'; the representation of the journey involves 'configuration' 'through specific aesthetic, narrative and descriptive methods and refiguration'; and, in turn, the circulation of the text involves the 'refiguration' of the extra-literary reality, 'shaping and reflecting collective identity and communal ideas about travel' (Nünning 2008: 14; see Ricoeur 1984). As already noted, even the radical experience of the encounter between Europeans and the 'New World' of the Americas was filtered through the prefigurations of cultural memory: Columbus' encounters on his travels had been prefigured by his readings of Mandeville's fictions. As Neil Rennie has written of travellers to the South Seas, what was encountered 'was not a new land so much as a new location for old, nostalgic fictions about places lost in the distant past, now found in the distant present, found and confirmed, it seemed, in the form of exotic facts' (Rennie 1998: 1).

Acknowledging the role of prefiguration, configuration and refiguration in travel writings need not be seen as a critical unmasking of the potential bad faith of auto-optic claims, nor as a flat amalgamation of all writings into an equalised stratum of equally relativised, equally viable or unviable fictions. As Peter Hulme has remarked, such an enterprise can have dubious implications, in that what might be called the 'postmodern moment' of ambiguity between fact and fiction is brought into question by, most controversially, the 'powerful assaults on fact made by David Irving and other holocaust deniers' (Hulme 2002a: 237). But it does illustrate that even the most apparently referential 'rendition' of experience is productive of, as well as responsive to, 'what happened to happen' (Clark 1999: 3) at the formal level. Acknowledging the productive dimension of the account of any traveller – as will be explored in the final section of this chapter – requires that we assess the creative and expressive challenges, as well as the conditions, of any traveller who tells the tale of a journey.

Most fundamentally, what these controversies illustrate is that what we regard as 'literary' is historically and geographically variable, and that our generic horizon of expectations should not foreclose our sensitivity to literary expression in specific works. In his introduction to Rebecca West's *Black Lamb and Grey Falcon* (1942), Geoff Dyer develops a similar series of concerns:

> The book is manifestly a work of literature but since literature in English (at least as far as prose is concerned) is synonymous with the novel – with an agreed-upon *form* of writing rather than a certain *quality* of writing – it is tacitly removed from the company to which it belongs [. . .] Palpably inferior works – novels – sit far more securely on the literary syllabus than an awkward tome whose identifying quality is a refusal to fit. In danger of dislodging other volumes from the top canonical shelf – or, more radically, of bringing the whole shelf crashing down – *Black Lamb and Grey Falcon* topples from its rightful place and is tacitly stocked in a lower, less prominent but safer place. (Dyer 2006: 5; emphasis in original)

Dyer's more radical idea is, perhaps, the most tenable, in that it invites us to make general judgements based upon specific encounters, rather than vice versa (that is, maintaining a critical orthodoxy about genre despite exemplary evidence to the contrary). It involves approaching literary history with an awareness of the way a culturally and historically evolved horizon of expectations, that values an idea of 'agreed-upon forms' of writing as inherently literary, can lead to neglect of writings 'whose identifying quality is a refusal to fit'.

The questions of form raised by the journey as genre reveal, not only the resistance of travel writing to definition, or the role of form in shaping travellers' accounts, but the preformative power of a literary critical horizon of expectations that dictates a specific, and local, idea of what 'literature' is. As Gillian Beer writes in one of her many voyages across literary and cultural history, '[t]he utmost resourcefulness and probity of language are needed, both by scientists and poets, to outwit the tendency of description to stabilize a foreknown world and to curtail discovery' (Beer 1987: 56). The same is true for the reader. And one consequence of acknowledging texts that open up a field of uncertainty in our models of thought – concerning truth and fiction, and the generic schemata that shape not only how literature is read, but what is read as literary – is that they illustrate the incompleteness of our knowledge, ask us to reassess our horizon of expectations. That the contours and generic patterns of travel writing are among those things known, and unknown, in different ways at different times and in different places, is worth carrying over as we approach the specifically contemporary issues attendant on travel and travel writing in late modernity – in which a sense of narrowing horizons under the weight of too much knowledge is key.

Chapter 2

'An End to Journeying': Travel and its Discontents in Late Modernity

'An End to Journeying': thus the often-cited, era-defining title – part injunction, part lament – of the first part of Claude Lévi-Strauss' *Tristes tropiques*, his seminal anthropological memoir (and, indeed, travel account) of his years in South America. First published in 1955, it was translated from French into English by John Russell in 1961 with the substantially inaccurate, and thus all the more telling, title of *A World on the Wane*. The combative, exasperated, self-chastising opening sentences – 'I hate travelling and explorers. Yet here I am proposing to tell the story of my expeditions' (Lévi-Strauss 1976: 15) – launches an invective of superb disdain against the 'vogue' for a kind of travel book in which 'platitudes and commonplaces seem to have been miraculously transmuted into revelations by the sole fact that their author, instead of doing his plagiarizing at home, has supposedly sanctified it by covering some twenty thousand miles' (1976: 16). The distancing critique is in part the anxiety that 'the truths' anthropologists seek 'only become valid when they have been separated from this dross' (1976: 15). But it gradually gives way to the singularly eloquent yet broadly representative *tristesse* of travel and its discontents in late modernity. 'Journeys,' Lévi-Strauss writes, 'those magic caskets full of dreamlike promises,'

> will never again yield up their treasures untarnished. A proliferating and overexcited civilization has broken the silence of the seas once and for all. The perfumes of the tropics and the pristine freshness of human beings have been corrupted by a busyness with dubious implications, which mortifies our desires and dooms us to acquire only contaminated memories. (1976: 43)

It is an emblematic instance of the 'never again' that echoes through modern and contemporary travel writing and its commentaries. *Tristes tropiques* serves as a touchstone text of the sensibility of disenchantment in that it expresses and explores some of the defining preoccupations of the horizon of expectations regarding travels in contemporary literature and culture. There is a sense of belatedness and the diminishing possibilities for authentic travel, prompting the nostalgic wish to have lived 'in the days of *real* journeys, when it was still possible to see the full splendour of a spectacle that had not yet been blighted, polluted and spoilt' (1976: 50). There is the sterner consciousness of the implication of those 'real journeys' in the very 'blighting' of the world, most especially in the form of empire: 'what else can the so-called escapism of travelling do,' Lévi-Strauss asks, 'than confront us with the more unfortunate aspects of our history? Our great Western civilization, which has created the marvels we now enjoy, has only succeeded in producing them at the cost of corresponding ills' (1976: 43). And, implicit in those 'corresponding ills', and related to Lévi-Strauss' preoccupation with the 'vestiges of a vanished reality' (1976: 51), there is the wider sense of cultural exhaustion in the wake of the Second World War.

We will consider the literary historical and theoretical implications of each of these interrelated – indeed, inextricable – issues in turn. They are among the challenges which any traveller's tale of wonder in contemporary literature cannot but address, or fail to address, and they constitute some of the most powerful currents in the literary and critical climate in which contemporary travel writing has been discussed and critiqued. That the exposition of a sensibility of disenchantment is drawn here from what is itself a traveller's tale, however, already intimates that the argument moves towards the idea that the most nuanced engagement with these areas of critique may well be in the form of writing often held to account. But before considering the ways in which contemporary travel narratives address the issues, we may inquire into the theoretical and historical assumptions present in these lines of thought in themselves.

'Geography triumphant': the law of diminishing departures

Lévi-Strauss, in his invocation to the 'days of *real* journeys' and the idea that such journeys can 'never again' be experienced (Lévi-Strauss 1976: 43), voices one of the key preoccupations concerning travel in the contemporary period. 'Never again will we feel the world wide open to us,' Evelyn Waugh had written a decade earlier in the demonstratively titled *When the Going Was Good* (1946), predicting (falsely, as we now know) that 'I do not expect to see many travel books in the near future' (Waugh 2011: xii). It has surely been of significance to literary historiography that Paul Fussell's *Abroad* (1980) – the book that most decisively announced the travel book as a form worthy of sustained critical appreciation – ushers in the corpus as an 'elegy' for the 'last age of genuine travel', assuming that 'genuine travel is no longer possible and tourism is all we have left' (Fussell 1980: 190). Thus is a body of writings introduced, only to pronounce the collection most likely, if alas, complete. As one of Fussell's central themes (and chapter titles) has it, there remains 'Nowhere Left to Go' (1980: 36–43). And even critics who lament the cultural centrism of this perspective nevertheless often adopt its underlying assumptions. Debbie Lisle takes as one of her points of departure the question: 'how is contemporary travel writing coping with the fact that there are no undiscovered places left to discover?' (Lisle 2006: 3). Patrick Holland and Graham Huggan find that 'nostalgic parody' (Holland and Huggan 1998: 197) is among the few, and most pronounced, means remaining whereby travel writing has allayed an anxiety about a sense of its own obsolescence. There exists, then, what Michael Cronin has described as a 'rhetoric of exhaustion' (Cronin 2000: 2; cf. Watson 1993), which remains widespread as a horizon of expectations when approaching travels in contemporary literature.

While there can be no question that the exponential rise of tourism and the impact of globalisation have profoundly affected the forms and functions of the traveller's tale, the idea that the world has been gradually depleted of new horizons expresses a highly encultured interpretation of travel and travel writing, of both the present and the past, which, hypothetically and historically, is open to question.

What reading of the past does the 'rhetoric of exhaustion' imply? The idea that travel is 'at an end' (Fussell 1980: 217) is manifestly teleological: 'Before tourism,' Fussell writes, 'there was travel, and before travel there was exploration. Each is roughly assignable to its own age in modern history: exploration belongs to the Renaissance, travel to the bourgeois age, tourism to our proletarian moment' (1980: 38). The 'phases' of this cultural history were given an earlier expression, in terms particularly pertinent to the present study, by Joseph Conrad, in an article originally published under the title 'The Romance of Travel' (1926). The first phase, up till the Renaissance, was the age of marvels and wonders: 'Geography Fabulous'. This, Conrad wrote, was 'a phase of circumstantially extravagant speculation which had nothing to do with the pursuit of truth', in which literature was replete with 'pictures of strange pageants, strange trees, strange beasts, drawn with amazing precision in the midst of theoretically conceived-continents' (1926: 3). This was succeeded by 'Geography Militant': the age of exploration. Captain Cook was Conrad's paradigm example of 'adventurous and devoted men' who went in search of 'exciting spaces of white paper' with the aim of 'conquering a bit of truth here and there, and sometimes swallowed up by the mysteries their hearts were so persistently set on unveiling' (1926: 3). As the 'white spaces' were coloured in, 'Geography Militant' was succeeded, Conrad argues with dismay, by 'Geography Triumphant' and a time in which the modern traveller was 'condemned to make his discoveries on beaten tracks' (1926: 25). Referring back to his own Congo journey in 1890, and thus to one of the key modern journey narratives, *Heart of Darkness* (1899/1901), Conrad saw self-serving heroics as the only compensation left, compromised by 'the distasteful knowledge of the vilest scramble for loot that ever disfigured the history of human conscience and geographical exploration' (1926: 25).

Where Conrad's account, like Lévi-Strauss', stresses the ethical disfigurements at the heart of empire, his idea of Geography Triumphant has often been taken up with a less nuanced view, and transformed into a generalised idea about the experience of travel. This has been particularly pronounced with increasing cultural-historical anxiety over the era of Thomas, rather than Captain, Cook, in which the World Tourism Organization can now claim tourism to be one of the biggest industries in the world.[1] The teleology that leads from exploration to discovery to travel to overfamiliar tourism suggested by Fussell is mapped out, for example, by Daniel J. Boorstin, in the piece in which he makes the categorical claim that where travel once broadened horizons, now 'travel narrows' (Boorstin 1985: 78). The past is characterised as follows:

> In the fifteenth century the discovery of the Americas, the voyages around Africa and the Indies opened eyes, enlarged thought, and helped create the Renaissance. The travels of the seventeenth century around Europe, to America, and to the Orient helped awaken men to ways of life different to their own and led to the Enlightenment. The discovery of new worlds has always renewed men's minds. Travel has been the universal catalyst. (1985: 78–9)

By contrast, Boorstin writes, in the 'era of the tourist', '[w]e get money-back guarantees that we will see what we expect to see' (1985: 117). Thus what Conrad called 'the romance of travel' gives way to disenchantment in an increasingly predictable, homogenised world, in observance of a law of diminishing departures in which there is an inverse proportion between the number of those travelling and the transformative potential of the experience. The seemingly paradoxical idea of travel becoming less possible as it becomes more ubiquitous is founded on an idea that what was valuable – what was 'real' and 'genuine' – about former travels concerns an element of discovery, or the exceptional status of the traveller. This narrative of depletion has numerous theoretical problems.

At the most fundamental level, any argument that asserts such generalised claims about travel cannot account for the inherent elasticity of its object. The 'travel narrows' argument is, simply put, too narrow. Philosophically, it presumes that 'travel' is something that can be isolated and assessed as a constant among variables. But the activity of 'travel', and thus any account of travel, is inconceivable, or at least indescribable, in a pure, elemental state, as it always takes place in specific circumstances. Historically, it privileges a certain view of the past. As Ian Ousby has argued in one of the prime critiques of the Boorstinian–Fussellian view, 'what is being proposed is not a historical definition but a vision of a Golden Age, a phantasm, compounded of modern self-dislike, intellectual snobbery and sentimentality about the past' (Ousby 1990: 6–7). To superimpose an idea that experience of the new is the all-defining motivation and reward for travel is to forget that the world can only ever be 'new' in the relational sense – new to the traveller and the culture reported back to – and to forget the breadth of motivations that have been part of travel's cultural history. It is also to forget that there never was a time in which the world was encountered entirely free from the influence of expectation and prefiguration. Indeed, what was the 'discovery of the New World' as it was rendered by Columbus, Drake and Ralegh, if not, itself, a 'vision of a Golden Age'? And a vision, at that, which led to what was, according to Tzvetan Todorov, the most extensive genocide in human history (Todorov 1999: 5)?

This points to another area in which late modern nostalgia misapprehends the past it implores: the continuity of nostalgia as a feature of travel writings. The term was coined in 1688 by a Swiss doctor, Johannes Hofer, as a medical term to describe the 'homesickness' experienced by diasporic emigrants and exiles of the French Revolution (Hofer 1934). And it is itself an amalgamation of the Homeric *nóstos* (homecoming) and *álgos* (pain or ache) (Boym 2001: viii–xiv). And the anxiety that the world is being depleted of its potential for travel, too, has a longer history than is implied in the contemporary lament. As James Buzard has shown, it is central to eighteenth-century writings: 'If there is one dominant and recurring image in the annals of the modern tour, it is surely that of the beaten track, which succinctly designates the space of the "touristic" as a region in which all experience is predictable and repetitive, all cultures and objects mere "touristy" self-parodies' (Buzard 1998: 4). The idiom of the 'beaten track' itself is drawn, Buzard notes, from a letter of 23 February 1767 from Laurence to Lydia Sterne, in which he describes his ideas for what would become *A Sentimental Journey*: 'I have laid a plan for something new, quite out of the beaten track' (qtd Buzard 1998: 4). And when that book came to pass, we may add, Sterne already felt he lived in 'an age so full of light, that there is scarce a country or corner of Europe whose beams are not crossed and interchanged with others' (Sterne 2005: 14). Indeed, the sense of elegiac nostalgia for an age of genuine travel is very much part of Fussell's last age of travel, the 1930s, too. Much of the pathos of the texts that Fussell recalls as having been written when the going was still good often seems to derive from precisely that same sense of a lost world. Here is D. H. Lawrence, one of Fussell's case studies, in *Sea and Sardinia* (1921), looking up and back at the same time, and suggesting some of the complexities of memory and imagination at work in the traveller's encounter with the present:

> Morning came sunny with pieces of cloud: and the Sicilian coast towering pale blue in the distance. How wonderful it must have been to Ulysses to venture into this Mediterranean and open his eyes on all the loveliness of the tall coasts. How marvellous to steal with his ship into these harbours. There is something eternally morning-glamorous about these lands as they rise from the sea. And it is always the Odyssey which comes back to one as one looks at them. All the lovely morning-wonder of this world, in Homer's day! (Lawrence 2007: 318)

Lawrence here illustrates that nostalgia was as much part of the age of 'real travel' as it has been of its elegy. But it also intimates the ambivalences of that longing. Does Lawrence's apostrophic exclamation register the 'the world-weariness of the late-comer' (Porter 1991: 217)? Or does it register a tremor of ambiguity? The 'lovely morning-wonder of this world' is phrased in such a way that we cannot be entirely sure what the exclamation expresses. Is it a nostalgic desire to voyage 'in Homer's day', as suggested by the conditional perfect imaginings of what it must have been like to be Ulysses? Or does it express the jubilation of there being something '*eternally* morning-glamorous about these lands' (emphasis added), as if the narrator himself is experiencing the 'lovely morning-wonder of this world, in Homer's day', in the present? Even if we must see this as an invocation of the past, is there not still something more like wonder than weariness? Either way, it is clear that a sense of what has been lost has long been as much a feature of travel writings as the sense of what has been found.

A rhetoric of exhaustion distorts our view of travels in the present as well as the past. Even if we maintain an epistemology of discovery, the idea of there being nowhere left to go displays a peculiar insensitivity to the many places that have not figured highly in the 'description of the world' even in this vein: Venice remains an attraction for travel writers today as much as ever; *A Year in Pontefract*, however, has yet to be written. The repost is based on an approach involving indexing the world catalogue and noting those places that have not figured highly in travel accounts as potential sources of epistemologically worthwhile travellers' tales. The flippancy of the repost points to the flippancy of the ideology itself. It also points to the deeper problems in this line of thought: an assumption of the completeness, comprehensiveness and permanence of an understanding of the world.

The clearest and most contentious problem with considering the world exhausted of grounds for travel narratives is that it takes no account of the perspective of the traveller. To claim that the world and the potential to encounter it has been gradually eradicated, and that in the 1930s a handful of 'young and clever and literate' Englishmen 'in the final age of travel' (Fussell 1980: vii) exhausted the potential descriptions of the world would be volatile – or, perhaps, more so – if it were not so quaintly self-contained. It is insular in terms of gender and class, taking no account, say, of Rebecca West, and paving the way for the denigration of the 'Ryanair class' of traveller. But it is most ironically insular in terms of language and international culture – that is, in terms of travel. For Fussell, Boorstin and those who argue in a similar vein, date the 'end of travel' at the dawn of the postcolonial era; an era defined, surely, by global movement. Yet, despite the travels and readings of travel books, it does not seem to occur to Fussell – or other critics who assume a depletion of new horizons – that it might be worth wondering about the literary cultures they travel among deal with travel themselves. A personal anecdote Fussell uses to illustrate what he means by 'genuine travel' is quite telling: 'it was as a traveler, not a tourist,' he explains, 'that I once watched my wallet and passport slither down a Turkish toilet at Bodrum, and it was the arm of a traveler that reached deep, deep into that cloaca to retrieve them' (Fussell 1980: 40). It is not only that, for such highlights of 'genuine travel', surely, any number of toilets the world over await. The more serious concern is that, if discomfort is the mark of the 'real traveller', are there not millions of people who have had to, and continue to, endure considerably more discomfort than this (to say the least)?

This concern leads into the postcolonial issues to be discussed shortly. But it also invites us to consider another element of this nostalgia that has its most exemplary expression in the final pages of Fussell's book. The post-war world, Fussell remarks, is not a place

> in which either travel or the travel book could flourish. The going was good for only twenty years, and after the war all that remained was jet tourism among the ruins, resulting in phenomena like the appalling pollution of the Mediterranean and the Aegean. (Fussell 1980: 226)

Fussell cites George Orwell's closing lines in *Homage to Catalonia*. Returning from the Spanish Civil War, Orwell finds England absurd in its obliviousness: with its cricket matches, bowler hats, red buses and blue policemen, England is 'sleeping the deep, deep sleep of England, from which I sometimes fear that we shall never wake till we are jerked out of it by the roar of bombs' (2000: 187; qtd Fussell 1980: 227). To this, Fussell responds: 'The British did awake, but to a different world, one in which the idea of literary traveling must seem quaint and a book about it a kind of elegy' (1980: 227). Here is the deeper theme of Fussell's book; a theme implicit in literary travelling 'between the wars'. For surely the sense of elegy derives not from the memory or fantasy of a time of 'genuine travel' before the advent of 'jet tourism', but from the disenchantment of living 'among the ruins'? Between the experience of discovering that one is a tourist and the experience of war, the latter poses a greater threat to freedom; between the loss of an aristocracy of travellers and the loss whose monument is the 'ruins', the latter makes the greater demand on elegy. It is not tourists who make the thought of innocence seem 'quaint'. Disdain for tourists, nostalgia for a time in which one could go unshaven, rely on poor French and fish one's passport from the toilet without the assistance of a tour guide . . . Is this almost an instance of what might in psychoanalytic terms be identified as transference?

This is the sense of elegy, I think, that is most important in Fussell's book – which remains, after all, perhaps the most sustained and eloquent appreciation of the travel book form yet published. This dimension of the elegy, in contrast to the argument, imparts a sense that the world will never be 'fully discovered' if only because the 'world' is not only geographical but temporal; the very word has as one of its meanings: 'a unit of human time' (*OED*). A traveller can only write of their experience of a specific time as well as a specific place. Rebecca West would have to resubtitle *Black Lamb and Grey Falcon: A Journey through Yugoslavia* if she were to write it today. Naipaul could not have written of journeys through a country called Pakistan before 1947. And urgency may derive not only from the sense of a place being seen for the first time, but of being seen, potentially, for the last. Thus the poignancy of Raja Shehadeh's *Palestinian Walks: Notes on a Vanishing Landscape* (2007), for example, hovering as it does between warning and elegy. The transience of the world, as much as its multiplicity, makes demands on literature for expression.

The problem for contemporary travellers' tales is not the loss of the possibility of primacy in encountering the world, but the persistence of the ideology of primacy itself – a discourse which sees the traveller's tale as deriving its wonder from the discovery of 'new' territories. Whenever we set out with the assumption that the travel narrative occupies a precarious position in a world too well known for the form to have epistemological value, we have already adopted this rhetoric of discovery and conquest. But if one problem in the idea of the rhetoric of exhaustion is that it fails to take account of the variety of perspectives in the postcolonial, globalised world, this also has implications for the ethics of the travellers' tale itself.

Travel writing and power: the legacies of power

Implicit in the sense of there being 'nowhere left to go' (Fussell 1980; Graves 2003) is an idea of the centrality, validity and comprehensiveness of the accounts to which this anxiety defers. In one sense, the awareness that only a limited and culturally specific version of the worlds narrated is provided by travel writing produced by writers from a specific cultural and historical perspective – namely, writers who travelled from Europe to the 'rest of the world' and back again – may be seen as a defence of the possibility of travel writing in the contemporary world. The exponential increase in mobility and exchange across the globe in terms of people and media brings home the inexhaustibility of 'worlds', asserting the open field of encounter in what Jan Borm calls 'polyidentity' (Borm 2007: 16). Yet it is also an awareness of the links between travel writing and power, most especially in the form of empire, that has contributed to the most incisive critique of the genre – and, indeed, has constituted the most pressing and often-stated reason for attending to it. Brian Musgrove goes so far as to say, reasonably, that '[i]t is virtually impossible to consider travel writing outside the frame of postcolonialism' (Musgrove 1999: 32).

As noted in the Introduction, this current draws most clearly on Edward Said's *Orientalism* (1978). Said's analysis of a 'textual attitude' involved in the European 'production' of the colonial other draws theoretically on Michel Foucault's analysis of discourses of power (1989; 2008), and has a more direct precedent in Frantz Fanon's *The Wretched of the Earth*: 'the colonist', Fanon wrote, 'is right when he says he "knows" [the colonized]. It is the colonist who *fabricated* and *continues to fabricate* the colonized subject' (2004: 2). But Said's analysis is nevertheless a foundational text for postcolonial studies, and 'Orientalism' has become a watchword for European hegemonic practices. British and French pilgrims from Volney on, Said argues, 'planned and projected for, imagined, ruminated about places that were principally *in their minds* [. . .] Theirs was the Orient of memories, and an almost virtuosic style of being, an Orient whose highest literary forms would be found in Nerval and Flaubert' (1978: 169–70). This pervasive discourse, Said argued, 'reduced the personalities of even its most redoubtable individualists like Burton to the role of imperial scribe' (1978: 197). Thus Orientalism 'was fully formalized into a repeatedly produced copy of itself' (1978: 197), replete with 'summational statements' about the object they produced, but purported to perceive (1978: 255).

Said's work, and that of scholars following in his footsteps, has played a crucial role in exposing the ways travel writing has served the cause of empire. But Said's approach to specific texts has, in a manoeuvre not without irony, sometimes been adopted to make a range of 'summational statements' (Said 1978: 225) about the form of travel writing in general. To write a travel account is often seen, from the outset, as a mark of the inheritance of, and nostalgia for, a questionable legacy. As Robyn Davidson writes in her Introduction to *The Picador Book of Journeys* (2001):

> It's as if the genre has not caught up with the post-colonial reality from which it springs. One would think it should collapse under the weight of its paradoxes, but quite the opposite is happening. There is a passion for travel books harking back to a previous sensibility when home and abroad, occident and orient, centre and periphery were unproblematically defined. Perhaps they are popular for the very reason that they are so deceptive. They create the illusion that there is still an uncontaminated Elsewhere to discover, a place that no longer exists, located, indeed, somewhere between 'fiction and fact'. (Davidson 2001: 2)

Davidson's alertness to the attractions of the travel book in the late twentieth century Anglophone market, for writers as for readers, requires careful note – as does her own travel book, *Tracks* (1980), an account of her journey through the Australian outback which might well be considered an exception to this colonial nostalgia, as well as prime example of innovation in the genre. The critique Davidson expresses in modulated ways can reach a higher pitch, exemplified in Charles Sugnet's sharp-eyed diatribe against travel writing of the 1980s (Sugnet 1991). The travel books promoted by *Granta* magazine, Sugnet argued, 'restore the lost dream of empire'; 'a curious fusion of the 1880s and the 1980s is what keeps all those *Granta* travel writers up in the air, afloat over various parts of the globe, their luggage filled with portable shards of colonialist discourse' (1991: 85). In one of the most recent and robust engagements with the genre, Debbie Lisle, though taking the case to an extreme, thus expresses a powerfully present line of thought. Taking as a point of departure the claim that '[h]istorically, travel writing participated in the international realm by disseminating the goals of Empire: stories of "faraway lands" were crucial in establishing the unequal, unjust and exploitative relations of colonial rule' (Lisle 2006: 2), Lisle asks the double-question that has lain behind much of the most penetrating analysis of contemporary travel writing:

> How is contemporary travel writing coping with the embarrassment of its colonial past while also recognising there are no undiscovered places left to explore? Given this precarious position, can travelogues tell us anything relevant, let alone provocative, about contemporary global life?' (2007: 3)

Lisle's answer is, essentially, that travel writing has not coped, and that it can tell us about contemporary global life only in symptomatic terms: 'as a whole, the genre encourages a particularly conservative political outlook that extends to its vision of global politics' (2007: i). It has failed to cope with the 'embarrassment' of colonial history, and has dealt with the feeling that there are 'no undiscovered places left to explore' by either overtly and nostalgically recalling and perpetuating the days and values of empire (presumably despite the embarrassment) with 'colonial vision' (2007: i), or by obscuring it through an attempt at 'cosmopolitan vision', which, Lisle finds,

> is not as emancipated as it claims to be; rather, it is underscored by the remnants of Orientalism, colonialism and Empire. In effect, travel writers currently articulating cosmopolitan visions of the world do not avoid the 'embarrassing' attitudes of their colonial predecessors – they actually produce new forms of power that mimic the 'previous sensibility' of Empire. (2007: 5)

While attending to the way in which travellers' tales have supported and motivated conquest has undoubtedly yielded important results (see especially Pratt 1992), the wholesale association of travel writing and empire does run the risk of oversimplifying both. Travellers' tales undoubtedly played a major role in the rapacious expansion of empire; but so too did tales of home and family, novels as well as travelogues, poetry as well as prose: the whole architecture of 'fictions of empire' (Nünning and Nünning 1996) in a wide range of literary and cultural and societal forms and media. This, indeed, is a central point of Said's own approach. Conversely, just as empire cannot be limited in its literary expression to 'travel writing', nor can the corpus of travel writing be limited to the colonial project. One need only visit the Travel section of most bookshops to observe, as we have seen, that the form is one of the oldest and most culturally ubiquitous. Ibn Battuta, Olaudah Equiano and Matsuo Bashō, for example, are hardly obscure and inaccessible to the Anglophone reader. Such texts call into question too exclusive an association of travel writing with European colonialism, and precisely this breadth may be one of its attractions for writers seeking forms less encultured within European discourses – a point we will return to in Chapter 3. Indeed, the peculiarity of the critique that holds travel writing to be both a source and resource of European colonialism is that it tends to express the very parochialism it purports to oppose – in its non-acknowledgement of the writings of other cultures.

It is striking that the two judgements most frequently made of travel writing are firstly that it is generically indeterminate; and secondly, that it is ideologically over-determined. There is little consensus about what travel writing is, but strong convictions about what it does: what Fredric Jameson called the 'ideology of the form' (Jameson 1983: 141) – the idea that 'form is immanently and intrinsically an ideology in its own right' (Jameson 1983: 141) – has been especially prevalent in analyses of travel writing. In his assessment of Orwell's *The Road to Wigan Pier*, for example, Philip Dodd observes that 'forms not only permit, they also *condition* meaning' (Dodd 1982: 136), going on to claim that 'to have shown the working class active in its own making, Orwell would need to have chosen some literary form other than the travel book' (1982: 136). But should there not be space within the recognition of the generic sedimentation of meaning for a co-existent recognition of the ways writers adapt and use form? Though the relations between form and ideology demand careful scrutiny, they also demand appreciation – they are part of a writer's work. And, historically, the association of travel writing and European empire is somewhat lopsided, given the cultural and historical ubiquity of travel narratives. If there is a genre that rose to prominence concomitantly with the rapid expansion of the European colonial project, it was the novel. Concomitance is not the same thing as complicity; but if we wish to make an assertion of the association of a form with a specific cultural and historical ideology, it is more tenuous still to do so with a kind of writing that is neither historically co-eval nor geographically co-emergent.

It may be more tenable to contend that the prejudices found in travel writing produced during the age of empire and its aftermath or refor-mulations reside in culture and in writing itself. Travel writing brings into view perhaps one of the deepest problems of the ethics of language, and written language especially: the dynamics of power involved in representation, brought into sharp relief in the context of intercultural encounters. In *The Conquest of America*, Tzvetan Todorov notes the remarkably neat coincidence that 1492 is both the year of Columbus' 'discovery' of America, and the year that sees the publication of the first grammar of a European language: the Spanish grammar of Antonio de

Nebrija, who writes in his Introduction (by way of commendation): 'Language has always been the companion of Empire' (qtd in Todorov 1999: 123). As this implies, this dimension of language is not limited, or limitable, to the travellers' tale as a form.

The issue surfaces in Lévi-Strauss' *Tristes tropiques*, in an episode which has proven a point of controversy over the writing of the 'other'. The chapter is called 'A Writing Lesson' (Lévi-Strauss 1976: 385–99). Lévi-Strauss is staying with the Brazilian Nambikwara tribe, who (so he records) had no written language. He is making notes. The tribespeople become interested. Lévi-Strauss hands out pencils and paper. The chief is most ambitious; and the scene culminates with an exchange in which the chief 'made a show of reading' the wavy lines he had made on his paper to demonstrate to the tribe (so Lévi-Strauss interprets the situation) that he understands the secret language (1976: 388–9). Writing – thus the analysis – is borrowed for a 'sociological rather than intellectual purpose' (1976: 390), and Lévi-Strauss extrapolates a disturbing hypothesis on the function of writing:

> The only phenomenon with which writing has always been concomitant is the creation of cities and empires, that is, the integration of large numbers of individuals into a political system, and their grading into castes and classes. Such, at any rate, is the typical pattern of development to be observed from Egypt to China, at the time when writing first emerged: it seems to have favoured the exploitation of human beings rather than their enlightenment. This exploitation, which made it possible to assemble thousands of workers and force them to carry out exhausting tasks, is a [. . .] likely explanation for the birth of architecture [. . .] My hypothesis, if correct, would oblige us to recognize that the primary function of written communication is to facilitate slavery. The use of writing for disinterested purposes, and as a source of intellectual and aesthetic pleasure, is a secondary result, and more often than not it may even be turned into a means of strengthening, justifying or concealing the other. (1976: 392–3)

The historical accuracy of this hypothesis is beyond the scope of this study to assess, but the concern it expresses for the 'colonial' nature of writing enters into the open centre of questions of writing and power. Jacques Derrida has argued that 'the essential confrontation that opens communication between peoples and cultures, even when that culture is not practised under the banner of colonial or military oppression' always involves 'a violence of the letter' – 'of difference, of classification, and of the system of appellations' (Derrida 1976: 107). Yet to speak of 'peoples and cultures' at all is already to make use of 'difference, classification, and of the system of appellations' being brought into question. The 'violence of the letter' is not limitable to what, in a move making use of just this practice, we call intercultural encounters. Similarly, the impasse often reached in even appreciative studies of travel writing is that, as one becomes more aware of the stereotypes and prejudices generated, circulated and legitimised by travel writing, one comes to the conclusion that it would have been better had these never been written at all (see Porter 1991: 304). But to assert as much is essentially tantamount to saying that when an 'I' encounters a 'You' and responds narratively, the result can only be detrimental. Partly as a result of this perhaps, criticism of travel writing has been more concerned with the traveller's accounts as cultural autobiography than as a window onto other cultures. Thus Susan Bassnett pinpoints one of the central tasks, even responsibilities, of criticism as the need to 'expose subtexts beneath the apparently innocent details of the journeys in other lands that enable us to see more clearly the ways in which travellers construct the cultures they experience' (Bassnett 1993: 93).

Given that we are increasingly in what Mary-Louise Pratt calls the 'contact zone' (Pratt 1992) between cultures – and given that this itself is only a version of the demarcation of individual and environment that can be identified in innumerable forms of self and other – it is near impossible to think of a language that does not potentially involve a violence of the letter at some level. Self-reflexivity as a component of intercultural encounters is thus clearly imperative. Yet if we take to its logical conclusion an approach which involves examining travel accounts exclusively for what we can expose about the traveller's prejudices, we can never encounter anything but the domestic, in that accounts of that which is perceived as foreign can only ever be made from the perspective – the subjective and culturally specific perspective, conditioned in incalculably many ways – of the traveller. Cultural self-reflexivity, if it is to retain its value in an ethics of the encounter, must be a component of, rather than substitute for, engagement with the other. Engagement with the other is what gives cultural reflexivity its value, even its substance. This means tackling the question of how, despite the endless regress of conditions and pre-conditions, the other can be encountered, and how that encounter can be spoken or written of. Mary Baine Campbell describes this as 'the subversive side of travel literature, at the roots of the legend of that secular exoticism which in *Mandeville's Travels* will turn at last to *charitas*' (Campbell 1988: 57). That an interest in the exotic – etymologically, 'from abroad' (*OED*) – can lead to a desire for conquest, or reify a sense of otherness, requires vigilant attention. But, equally, there can be no *charitas* without *curiositas*: without wonder, no concern.

Contemporary travellers' tales are indeed implicated in the history of empire, and the critical horizon of expectations that fosters alertness to the ways in which travel writing of the past and present feeds from and back into this history is an essential element of their interpretation. But the view is limited by a too-simple equation of the individual text with a generic ideology of form, and by implicitly sequestering the issues of writing and power within that form. In order to approach travellers' tales themselves as a means of engagement with the other (whether delineated culturally, linguistically, or in any other way) we must be able to look upon them in terms of their expressive and creative encounters with these issues. If we approach them with the preformed theoretical aim of exploring such texts as manifestations of discourses of power, we foreclose our sensitivity to their adaptations of form and efforts to undermine the colonial potential of language. Ironically, to approach travellers' tales as automatic and specific manifestations of a predetermined ideology both utilises a constituent aspect of the colonial mind-set in its generality, and, as importantly, hinders the suggestion made by Said early on in *Orientalism*: that the 'most important task of all would be to undertake studies in contemporary alternatives to Orientalism, to ask how one can study other cultures from a libertarian, or a nonrepressive and nonmanipulative, perspective' (Said 1978: 24).

The 'disenchantment of the world': cultural exhaustion and postmodernity

The third dimension of travel and its discontents in late modernity to be discussed here has been less pronounced, though ever present, in critical commentary on what is often referred to as 'postcolonial', 'postmodern', 'postwar' travel writing: that is, the sense of belatedness and posterity that permeates Western culture more widely in the twentieth century, and the late twentieth century especially. Contemporary travellers' tales of wonder emerge – or are interpreted as ironically parodic – in part against a literary-cultural climate in which forms of disenchantment are, while of course not in any sense undisputed or unanimous, nevertheless powerfully present. The discontents we have considered above – a sense of anxiety about the exhaustion of what remains to be discovered or made; a loss of faith in the ethical viability of writing and its complicity with dubious political enterprises – these are far from the private province of the contemporary traveller's tale. On the contrary: the central preoccupations of contemporary travel are among the salient concerns in postmodernity per se.

The continuity of the terms of the critique of travel writing as a specific genre with wider cultural-historical preoccupations is surprisingly rarely remarked, though so ubiquitous as to be easily evoked by a handful of names and titles: George Steiner's *In Bluebeard's Castle* and its lament for the 'The Great Ennui' of 'post-culture' (Steiner 1971: 1–26); Frank Kermode's *The Sense of an Ending* (1966); John Barth's often-quoted, often misrepresented 'Literature of Exhaustion' (Barth 1984); Baudrillard's theorisation of simulacra and the desert of the real (Baudrillard 1983). Indeed, the idioms of disenchantment regarding travellers' tales – nowhere left to go, beaten tracks, an end to journeying – could be applied, figuratively, to a dimension of the postmodern cultural condition in general. Barbara Hernstein Smith captures something of the mood in suggesting that the world has been 'heir to too many revolutions':

> We know too much and are sceptical of all we know, feel and say. All traditions are equally viable because all are equally suspect. Where conviction is seen as self-delusion and all words as lies, the only resolution may be in the affirmation of irresolution, and conclusiveness may be soon seen as not only less honest but less *stable* than inconclusiveness. (Hernstein Smith 1968: 240–1)

The third dimension to be discussed, then, like the last, offers both a form of defence and an additional challenge for travellers' tales of wonder. On the one hand, it draws attention to the way that travellers' tales are equally, perhaps especially, but by no means exceptionally implicated in sources of disenchantment. Yet it also introduces other areas of concern. What place do travellers' tales of wonder have in the advanced stages of an industrialised age which Max Weber famously argued to 'be characterized by rationalization and intellectualization and, above all, by the "disenchantment of the world"' (Weber 1946: 155)? And how to speak of travellers' tales of wonder, or of wonder at all, after world wars, genocide, the atomic bomb; at a point in the cultural history of travel in which deportations to concentration camps must be counted among the last century's definitive journeys?

Max Weber's categorical pronouncement of the 'disenchantment of the world' primarily focused on the role of the scientific and industrial in society. By the early twentieth century, he argued, modernised societies 'no longer have recourse to magical means in order to master or implore the spirits, as did the savage, for whom such mysterious powers existed. Technical means and calculations perform the service' (1946: 42). Industrial and scientific advances, he claimed, meant that there remained 'no mysterious incalculable forces that come into play, but rather that one can, in principle, master all things by calculation'

(1946: 42). His phrase draws on the current of thought powerfully expressed in Nietzsche's pronouncement of the death of God, in *Also sprach Zarathrustra* (1966–7), which raises the spiritual issue of how to overcome the gap left by a retreating divinity in a secular universe. But Weber's categorical pronouncement of the 'disenchantment of the world' may be seen as the outcome of a cultural history of the retreat of wonder from the intellectual sphere which proceeds most clearly from the 'New Science' of the late seventeenth century and the Enlightenment in particular, to the point of becoming a 'disreputable passion' among modern intellectuals (Daston and Park 1998: 14–15).

René Descartes and Sir Francis Bacon issued perhaps the most influential voices of dissent against wonder – or, rather, in questioning its excesses, marked the turning of the tide. Descartes distinguishes 'wonder' (*admiration*) from 'astonishment' (*étonnement*), 'which makes the whole body remain immobile like a statue, such that one cannot perceive any more of the object beyond the first face presented, and therefore cannot acquire any more particular knowledge'; thus is 'astonishment' to be scorned as 'an excess of wonder' (qtd in trans. in Daston and Park 1998: 317). Bacon, one of the principal instigators of the Royal Society, founded in 1660 for the furtherance of science, issued a challenge to those who 'ever breaketh off in wondering and not in knowing' in his *Advancement of Learning* (1857–74), seeing wonder as 'broken knowledge': though it is, as such, the 'seed of knowledge', sustained wonder is chastised as 'nothing but contemplation broken off, or losing itself' (Bacon 1857–74: (vol. 3) 266). Among other discourses, the Society had tales of wonder in its sights when warning against propagating clouds of unknowing and falsehood in its (still current) motto: *Nullius in verbia* ('nothing on another's word'). And it was in a continuation of an effort to purge the language of marvels and wonders that Thomas Sprat, in his *History of the Royal Society*, placed figurative and metaphorical language 'amongst those general mischiefs [. . .] which have been so long spoken against', regarding them as 'mists and uncertainties on our knowledge', favouring what he envisaged – apparently untroubled by the metaphorical nature of his description – as 'a close, naked, natural way of speaking' (Sprat 1722: 113). As Lorraine Daston and Katharine Park write in their extremely rich study, *Wonders and the Order of Nature: 1150–1750*: 'Central to the new, secular meaning of enlightenment as a state of mind and a way of life was the rejection of the marvelous' (Daston and Park 1998: 331). Their longer history of the decline of wonder as an intellectually respectable mode of thought nuances the Weberian idea of secularisation and rationalisation as the source of modern and contemporary disenchantment:

How marvels fell from grace in European high culture has less to do with some triumph of rationality – whether celebrated as enlightenment or decried as disenchantment – than with a profound mutation in the self-definition of intellectuals. For them wonder and wonders became simply vulgar, the very antithesis of what it meant to be an *homme de lumières*, or for that matter a member of any elite. This marked the end of the long history of wonder and wonders as cherished elements of European elite culture [. . .]. (1998: 19)

In the Epilogue, they look ahead to the contemporary period and see in tabloids and *The Guinness Book of Records* a resemblance to early modern broadsides of the period Conrad had called Geography Fabulous – a link that Mary Baine Campbell also makes in her equally rich study, *The Witness and the Other World: Exotic European Travel Writing 400–1600* (Campbell 1988: 83). Both see the role of wonder in the contemporary period as debased (while bringing this debasement into question in their own work). 'Among the learned,' Daston and Park write, 'wonders and wonder are often objects of mild condescension [. . .] Indeed, wonder and wonders define the professional intellectual by contrast: seriousness of purpose, thorough training, habits of caution and exactitude are all opposed to a wonder-seeking sensibility' (Daston and Park 1998: 367). They continue:

If the screaming headlines of the latest tabloid recall the heavy black letter of an early modern broadside, their readerships nonetheless diverge. One cannot imagine a diarist of the social and literary stature of Samuel Pepys – Leonard Woolf, say, or Edmund Wilson – faithfully recording monsters he read about or saw. To be a member of a modern elite is to regard wonders and wonder with studied indifference; enlightenment is still in part defined as the anti-marvelous. But deep inside, beneath tasteful and respectable exteriors, we still crave wonders. (1998: 367–8)

It is this horizon of expectations as much as anything in the texts themselves that predisposes us to read wonder in contemporary travel literature as either naïve nostalgia or knowing parody. We read with what Daston and Park describe as the physiognomy of the 'incredulous, ironic, and faintly patronizing smile of the savant or man of letters confronted with [. . .] a breach of *vraisemblance*' (1998: 350) – a stance we will encounter in relation to Bruce Chatwin's *In Patagonia* in particular. Where wonder is discussed with reference to the specifically late twentieth-century literary and cultural sphere, it tends to be found with regard to the worlds of fantasy and science fiction (for example Knight 1967; Barron 2004), and children's books (Pendry 2004): in fantastical, speculated worlds and in journeys into the unexperienced, imagined reaches of space. It is notable that even a study of contemporary travel writing with the title *The Wonder of Travel* (Pordzik 2005) seems to hold a sceptical distance to the 'wonder' in its title. Wonder, when discussed directly, is located in its present-day manifestations in overtly fantastical narratives: not Chatwin, the focus of two chapters, but Canadian writers who are said to reject 'the set idea of literature as always dealing with factual persons and real geographic space' and instead enter 'the region of the marvellous and the fantastic' (2005: 12). The 'wonder of travel' is located in the *'voyage imaginaire'* (2005: 12) rather than in accounts (however imaginatively rendered) of actual journeys made.

The physiognomy of the incredulous, ironic savant has of course been a contested one: the Romantic rejection of Enlightenment philosophy itself had already challenged the foundations of the Weberian idea of calculability; science as much as the arts cannot be reduced to a too-simple narrative of disenchantment (Richard Holmes, for example, has described the early nineteenth century as the 'age of wonder' (Holmes 2008), with the scientist John Herschel as a guiding presence). And against Weber's statement of calculability must be placed that of his contemporary Franz Kafka, in his definitive rejection of such a philosophy in his 'Letter to His Father': 'Nothing alive can be calculated' (Kafka 2002: 116). But the 'disenchantment of the world' has lodged itself trenchantly enough that a recent challenge in scholarly terms noted in the Introduction, *The Re-Enchantment of the World: Secular Magic in a Rational Age* (Landy and Saler 2009), has been described on the jacket sleeve as a 'paradigm shift' in the humanities. Its persuasive discussions of the wide range of modern, secular enchantments – from sport to gardening to elements of psychoanalysis – provide diverse evidence of the forms of enchantment that persist in modern and contemporary thought and culture. As noted in the Introduction, however, travel does not feature in the terms of this 'paradigm shift', while travel and wonder are almost inseparable in the accounts of earlier periods discussed above.

Equally worth stressing for our purposes is that rationalisation and secularisation are not the only source of disenchantment in contemporary intellectual history (nor unanimously shared). Indeed, there is another side to the relations between modern disenchantment and calculation, rationalism, industrialisation (as intimated above by the reference to Kafka). If, as numerous intellectuals in diverse disciplines have argued (see for example Bauman 2000; LaCapra 1994), political totalitarianism, and the most iconic modern atrocity, the Holocaust, have been as much an expression of industrial modernity as an aberration of it, then the disenchantment of the world does proceed from a perspective shaped by rationalisation; rationalisation itself is one of the dimensions of culture with which we have been disenchanted: our disenchantment as much as our enchantments may place us at odds with the laws of rationality. And the recovery and renewal of wonder in the contemporary world must contend with more than the explanatory drive of the natural sciences. The disenchantment of the world results in part from the knowledge of what we have been capable of doing to one another; the extremity and violence of our histories.

This is one of the traumatic dimensions of the disenchantment of the world. And it is this traumatic history that most profoundly challenges – but also, it may be argued, demands – an aesthetics and ethics of wonder. Earlier, I suggested that the elegy in Paul Fussell's lament that 'after the war all that remained was jet tourism among the ruins' (Fussell 1980: 226) derived more from the ruins than the tourists. And we might now note the perturbing paradox in the concurrency of the anxiety of there being 'nothing left to see', as it were, with the deep sense of coming after experiences and events which take the possibility of witness to breaking point – the radical caesura represented by the Holocaust as a limit case of knowing and feeling. Primo Levi wrote with great eloquence in *The Drowned and the Saved* of the way that even those who suffered the atrocities of the concentration camps were not the 'true witnesses':

> we, the survivors, are not the true witnesses [. . .] We survivors are not only an exiguous but also an anomalous minority: we are those who by their pre-varications or abilities or good luck did not touch bottom. Those who did so, those who saw the Gorgon, have not returned to tell about it or have returned mute. (1988: 83–4)

Such concerns clearly pose an indirect challenge to the rhetorical claim of the authority of the witness in the traveller's tale; and such events and experiences render thought of enchantments and wonder poten-tially highly dubious, as much as they render lyric poetry barbaric (to allude to Adorno's famous dictat). But while there is a clear conflict here between wonder as *admiratio* and the traumatic in history, there is simultaneously a striking echo between the language of wonder and the vocabulary with which the indescribable has been registered. The exotic and the traumatic share in this feature: they stretch language, reveal its insufficiency, its localism, its attachment to things and experi-ences and its limits in facing that which has no precedent in those things and experiences that have found issue in language. There is an uneasy affinity, too, between what Bacon called the 'broken knowledge' (Bacon 1857–74: (vol. 3) 266) of wonder and the break in knowing and feeling iconically embodied by the Holocaust.

Such histories compel us to acknowledge the limits of knowledge – the limits of calculation to explain our world and the dangers of calculability as a faith. Wonder, in its broadest history that includes within it admiration, amazement, great distress or grief, destruction, disaster, horror, doubt – is by no means sufficient as a response; but it may be necessary. Its invitation to consider how such various emotions may live among one another is a beginning of a response to what Shoshana Felman and Dori Laub write in their seminal study of issues of witness, *Testimony: Crises of Witnessing in Literature, Psychoanalysis, and History*, of 'the ways in which our cultural frames and our pre-existing categories which delimit our perception of reality have failed, essentially, both to contain and to account for, the scale of what has happened in contemporary history' (Felman and Laub 1992: xv). How close this is to the language with which Daston and Parks figure the nature of wonder: 'To register wonder was to register a breached boundary, a classification subverted. The making and breaking of categories – sacred and profane; natural and artificial; animal, vegetable and mineral; sublunar and celestial – is the Ur-act of cognition, underpinning all pursuit of regularities and discovery of causes' (Daston and Park 1998: 14). At the very least, both trauma and wonder challenge the idea that we have exhausted what can be said of the journeys that have been made and are still being made in the world. Perhaps the opening chapter of Lévi-Strauss' 1955 *Tristes tropiques*, 'An End to Journeying', should be read alongside the first chapter of another book that gained worldwide attention around the same time, in 1958: Primo Levi's *If This is a Man*. It is called 'The Journey':

> With the absurd precision to which we later had to accustom ourselves, the Germans held the roll-call. At the end the officer asked 'Wieviel Stück?' The corporal saluted smartly and replied that there were six hundred and fifty 'pieces' and that all was in order. They then loaded us on to the buses and took us to the station of Carpi. Here the train was waiting for us, with our escort for the journey. Here we received the first blows: and it was so new and senseless that we felt no pain, neither in body nor in spirit. Only a profound amazement: how can one hit a man without anger? (Levi 2004: 22)

Among so much else, such a passage of writing indicates that we should not speak too easily of the world-weary exhaustion of the traveller, nor of the ideological oppression inherent in the form of an account of a journey taken. It may illustrate too, that there is an ethical ground for sustaining a 'profound amazement' in our response to the most troubling elements of our histories. If the discontents of contemporary travel are to be addressed, the form of the traveller's tale itself may be a site in which such engagement is possible and necessary. Though Lévi-Strauss' *Tristes tropiques* announces itself as an ending, then, it might also serve, with all the artificiality such a statement involves, as marking a beginning of sorts – pointing the way towards the issues and themes that will make up some of the key concerns of travels in contemporary literature.

Note

1. Available at <http://www.untwo.org/aboutwto/why/en/why.php?op=1> (last accessed 16 July 2012).

Chapter 3

Forms of Recovery and Renewal: Travels in Contemporary Literature

It might at first appear an irony: the peak in anxieties about the end of travel coincides, almost exactly, with what has been described as the 'renaissance of the travel book' (see for example, Graves 2003). But this convergence in the late 1970s and 1980s is more likely an expression of a broad literary and cultural engagement with questions of travel in a world increasingly on the move, increasingly interconnected. The publication of Bruce Chatwin's *In Patagonia* in 1977, alongside that of Patrick Leigh Fermor's *A Time of Gifts*, is often given as the literary historical moment in which travel writing was most conspicuously asserted and formally renewed (Hulme and Youngs 2002; Graves 2003; Borm 2007). The work of writers like Paul Theroux, Colin Thubron, Jonathan Raban, Robyn Davidson and Peter Matthiessen further demonstrated the vitality of the form. This reinvigoration of the travel book in Anglophone terms was prominently heralded in a 1984 edition of the influential literary magazine of new writing, *Granta*, which was dedicated to 'Travel Writing', and advertised as follows:

> Travel writing is undergoing a revival: not since the 1920s and '30s has it been so popular or important. What accounts for its sudden appeal? A need for escape? Nostalgia for an experience that means not tourism but adventure? Or does travel writing – being part reportage, part fiction, and part meditation – express concerns that we rarely see addressed in other forms of writing? (Buford 1984: ix)

Answers to these questions have, as we have seen, often stressed the element of nostalgia – the way the travel book creates a fiction, so to speak, of its own continuing relevance. Thus Holland and Huggan, in summarising the reasons travel writing has continued to thrive against the odds, suggest that it has done so 'by invoking a number of late-capitalist cultural possibilities [. . .] commodification, specialization, and nostalgic parody' (Holland and Huggan 1998: 197). Though these are unquestionably prominent aspects of the contemporary travel book and particularly the popular British travel book, there may also be a more edifying range of options available for explaining how and why writers have adopted and adapted the form – not least a resistance to commodification and specialisation, and engagement with history. But to do so, we must look beyond the remits of the British and North American travel book to wider shifts in contemporary literature, delineated more by formal and thematic concerns than by cultural origin, destination, language, or commercial success. Alongside Chatwin, Naipaul and Sebald, may be placed J. M. G. Le Clézio, Claudio Magris, Predrag Matvejević, Jan Morris, Cees Nooteboom, Tim Robinson, Iain Sinclair, among others. How and why have writers, from a diverse range of cultural and linguistic backgrounds, adopted and adapted the form?

It is significant that the profession of 'travel writer' as such arose following the Second World War. 'For the post-war generation,' Peter Hulme suggests in an interpretation in accordance with Buford's analysis above, 'travel writing could become the basis of a writing career, perhaps because those who had just fought a war felt the need for the kind of direct engagement with social and political issues that journalism and travel writing seemed to offer' (Hulme 2002b: 89). The concretisation of 'travel writer' as a profession thus takes its place within a current in twentieth-century literature that moves towards forms of literature not overtly novelistic; or perhaps, rather, that incorporate the techniques of fiction into narratives in which the traditions of the classical novel – plot and character – are not dominant: autobiography, the literature of fact, and witness literature, as well as travel narratives. The centenary publication of the Nobel Academy, edited by the then permanent secretary, Horace Engdahl, is a prime example of the recognition of the place that 'witness literature' has come to occupy in contemporary literature, as the 'most profound change in literature since the breakthrough of modernism' (2002: 6). There is a kind of witness literature that tragically redefines the idea of travel as freedom but compels us to acknowledge the necessity of the account, exemplified above with reference to Primo Levi's *If This Is a Man*. The other side of this is an awareness of the urgency of engagement across cultural and political borders. Ryszard Kapuściński, a writer comparable to Naipaul in the breadth of his inquiries, suggests the first reason why the form of the travel narrative may have become prominent in his last, posthumously published essay, *The Other*:

> Does modern literature help to break down [. . .] prejudices, our ignorance or our plain indifference? [. . .] I don't think it does much. I looked through

the French literary awards for the past year, and did not find a single book
with something to say about the widely understood modern world. There
were love triangles, father-daughter conflict, a young couple's failed life
together – things that are certainly important and interesting. But I was
struck by the disdainful attitude towards the whole new trend in literature,
just as fascinating, whose representatives are trying to show us the modern
cultures, ideas and behaviour of people who live in different geographical
latitudes and who believe in different gods from us, but who actually constitute part of the great human family to which we all belong. I am thinking for example of *The Innocent Anthropologist* by Nigel Barley, of Colin
Thubron's superbly written book *Behind the Wall* or Bruce Chatwin's excel-
lent *Songlines*. These books do not win prizes, they are not even noticed,
because – in some people's opinions – they are not so-called real literature.
(Kapuściński 2008: 59)

Kapuściński may exaggerate: these books have won prizes, after all
(Thubron's *Behind the Wall* won the Hawthornden Prize as well as
the Thomas Cook Travel Book Award, and the other writers mentioned, including Kapuściński himself, have won numerous awards).
Neverthless, he is right that such books are still sometimes considered
not to be 'so-called real literature' in Euro-American letters. And
while we should not devalue literature that does not engage directly
or indirectly with the concerns of travel expressed here, and while we
might certainly look to a wide range of literary forms, including novels
about love triangles, for insight into modern cultures, ideas and beliefs
– including those of different geographical latitudes – Kapuściński's
further concern that 'so-called real literature isolates itself from the
problems and conflicts experienced by billions of our *Fremde*' (2008:
59) deserves consideration. He recalls the Iranian Revolution; he recalls
that it failed to have any impact on literature (though he overlooks
Naipaul's *Among the Believers* (1981)). He protests that

> the fact that literature can completely ignore a world drama being played
> out before our very eyes, leaving it entirely up to the television cameras and
> sound operators to tell the story of major incidents, is to me a symptom of
> a deep crisis on the front line between literature and history, a symptom of
> literature's helplessness in the face of modern world events. (2008: 60)

The prominence of travel writing may have to do with responding to
a similar concern about what Kapuściński calls the 'front line between
literature and history' (2008: 59). What might be termed literary travel
reportage has been a component of writings of the late twentieth century
that belie the idea of a world too well known. It is often related to a
sense that the novel as a form emerges from the specific cultural circumstances of bourgeois European culture. We will encounter the strongest

and earliest argument in these terms in the reading of Naipaul. But here we might look to a writer like Philip Gourevitch for its broad relevance. Gourevitch describes *We Wish to Inform You that Tomorrow We Will Be Killed with Our Children: Stories from Rwanda* as being inspired by 'what fascinates me most in existence: the peculiar necessity of imagining what is, in fact, real' (2000: 7). This imagining of what is real involves bringing imaginative processes to bear in approaching what we call 'reality'. But part of the moral force of Gourevitch's account, as is implicit in the tension between the horrific subject matter and the measured, matter-of-fact delivery in the title of the book, lies in the fact that such things enter into the cycles of the media without registering with the same force as other 'events'. It concerns, then, the way that the world remains 'unknown' to itself, but also the way that the world is only known through selective circulations shaped, in part, by economic, political and commercial interest.

The broadest and most often remarked tendency in travel writing of the late twentieth century is its increasing subjectivisation and pronounced self-reflexivity. Travel narratives, in their basic formal thematisation of displacement, always carry within themselves a negotiation – sometimes foregrounded, sometimes resisted, but always present in the process of production as well as reception – of relativism. The very proposition that there are other places where things are done differently and on the basis of different values – whether fictionally produced, or experienced through however many layers of mediation – suggests the contingency of perspective in cultural terms. The awareness of the subjectivity of the traveller's viewpoint is thus not a postmodern precedent as such: the Vicomte de Chateaubriand wrote in the nineteenth century that '[e]very man carries within him a world which is composed of all that he has seen and loved, and to which he constantly returns, even when he is travelling through, and thinks he is living in, some different world' (as qtd in trans. in Lévi-Strauss 1976: 52). Nevertheless, if this was once a concession, it is increasingly stressed as an assertion, and forms of self-reflexivity have been a crucial component of contemporary travels. 'As the earth's wildernesses get paved over,' Peter Hulme suggests, 'travel writing increasingly emphasises the inner journey, often merging imperceptibly into memoir' (Hulme 2002b: 94). And as the level of the journey and that of the traveller diversifies, so too the diversity of inner journeys, and their interaction with the encounter, assume a growing importance.

Self-reflexivity comes in many guises. One, to be sure, is the ironic self-parody of which Paul Theroux is perhaps the most distinguished practitioner. His breakthrough travel book, *The Old Patagonian*

Express (1979), exemplifies what can be read as the motto of a particular travel sensibility, close to that which we encountered in Fussell and Boorstin:

> The literature of travel has become measly, the standard opening that farcical nose-against-the-porthole view from the plane's tilted fuselage. The joke-opening, that straining for effect, is now so familiar it is nearly impossible to parody. How does it go? (Theroux 2008a: 12)

In a sense, this represents a continuation of the discourse of discovery. The self-reflexivity of asserting that the genre one is practising is 'the lowest form of literary self-indulgence: dishonest complaining, creative mendacity, pointless heroics, and chronic posturing' (2008b: 1) – as Theroux writes in a more recent travelogue (2008b) – is closely related in its claims to knowledge to the rhetorical presuppositions of Polo's claim to the authority of the eye witness. It claims the authority of being aware of what others might suspect; it is the knowledge of the second-guess. As Holland and Huggan have astutely and relatedly observed of the ironisation of the figure of the English gentleman in much British travel writing of the late twentieth century, 'self-irony [. . .] affords a useful strategy of self-protection – as if the writer, in revealing his/her faults, might be relieved of social responsibilities' (Holland and Huggan 1998: 7). The pleasure we derive from such complaints – and their registration of frustrated, perhaps unrecognised longings – can easily be underestimated. But that self-reflexivity with one eyebrow raised can serve to perpetuate continuing practice at the same time as bringing it into question is clear.

However, there are forms of self-reflexivity that move in other directions. The 'prologues' of two very different travel texts can be taken as exemplary of the extent of the epistemic reversal: from an idea of empirical objectivity (as embodied in the claim to the authority of the eye witness) to one of epistemological reflexivity. Kapuściński's own *The Shadow of the Sun* (2001b) prefaces his account of his experiences in Africa with the assertion of the unimaginable size and variety of the continent: 'Only with the greatest simplification, for the sake of convenience, can we say "Africa". In reality, except as a geographical appellation, Africa does not exist" (2001b: no pagination). We find a similar foreword in a very different travel account of which it has justifiably been said that it 'marks an end of travel literature as we have known it in the West' (Porter 1991: 302): Roland Barthes' *Empire of Signs* (1970). The epistemology of representation and conveyance of the faraway is, in Barthes' account, both discarded and deconstructed. *Empire of Signs* is Barthes' account of a journey to Japan, but 'in no way claiming to represent or analyze reality itself' (Barthes 1983: 3). Rather, its 'object' is the 'system which I shall call: Japan' (1983: 3). Published in the original French in 1970, it seems directly to counter what Edward Said would discuss in *Orientalism* later in the decade: rather than 'lovingly gazing toward an Oriental essence', Barthes writes towards the 'history of our own obscurity' (1983: 4).

The reference to Roland Barthes signals the confluence of reflexive travel with the concerns of contemporary theory, in which 'travel' is one of the mastertropes. Indeed, while travel writing's position in literary esteem has been somewhat unstable, the metaphor of 'travel' has come to occupy an increasingly definitive position in intellectual history. Susan Sontag once suggested that '[t]o travel becomes the very condition of modern consciousness, of a modern view of the world' (Sontag 1984), and from Deleuze and Guattari's conception of nomadology (Deleuze and Guattari 1980), to Mieke Bal's idea of 'travelling concepts' (Bal 2002), to Wolfgang Welsch's philosophy of 'transversal reason' (Welsch 2002), the theoretical work of intellectuals is replete with metaphors of travel, exile, homelessness, otherness, as a style of thought. Friedrich Nietzsche provides a precursor of this intellectual position in his aphorism, 'The Wanderer', in *Human, All-Too-Human*:

> He who has attained the freedom of reason cannot, for a long time, regard himself otherwise than as a wanderer on the face of the earth – and not even as a traveller towards a final goal, for there is no such thing. But he certainly wants to observe and keep his eyes open to whatever actually happens in the world; therefore he cannot attach his heart too firmly to anything individual; he must have in himself something wandering that takes pleasure in change and transitoriness. (1964: 405)

If travel writing as a genre has been critiqued for holding onto an empirical idea, then, much theory of the late twentieth century has been engaged with a kind of 'travel writing' in which the locatedness, or dislocatedness, of thought is at issue. There is James Clifford's observation that to theorise is to become a traveller (the Greek *theorin* means a 'practice of travel and observation, a man sent by the polis to another city to witness a religious ceremony' (Clifford 1989: 177)). Postcolonial theory, so John Phillips suggests, 'may itself be read as a form of travelogue articulating the historical and geographical displacement undergone by the populations of the colonial periphery' (Phillips 1999: 63). And if deconstruction has been one of the intellectual currents that most decisively break with the empirical tradition, Jacques Derrida has been regarded as a 'travel writer' whose work can be seen as a kind of 'counter-Odyssey' (see Malabou and Derrida 2004). As he writes:

The time for reflection is also the chance for turning back on the very conditions of reflection, in all the senses of that word, as if with the help of a new
optical device one could finally see sight, could not only view the natural
landscape, the city, the bridge, and the abyss, but could 'view' viewing.
(Malabou and Derrida 2004: 154)

The cultural history of theory is as significant here as the theory of cultural history. It is surely no coincidence that this style of thought rose
to such prominence in an era affected more universally than ever before
by global travel and exchange, or that a sense of a surfeit of conflicting
representations coincides with a study of how those representations are
made. But it also draws attention to the question of how such theoretical
awareness can be brought to bear in accounts of actual travels themselves. Recent anthropological theory in particular has been particularly
engaged in this issue. As George E. Marcus and Michael M. J. Fischer
write in *Anthropology as Cultural Critique*:

> in experimental works that focus on the representation of experience and
> describe encounters between fieldworker and specific others [. . .] the motiva-
> tion to develop more effective ways of describing and analysing cross-cultural
> experience makes the use of explicit fictional narrative devices tempting,
> and with this temptation, the status of ethnography as scientific or factual
> description, analogous to journalistic reporting, comes into question. (1999:
> 75)

Self-reflexivity, the foregrounded consciousness of the partiality and
perspectivity of the account, has its complement in a foregrounding of
cultural memory. At its most fundamental poetelogical level, the narrative of a journey evokes an extraordinarily rich and varied cultural
history. The resonance of the travel narrative derives in part from the
way that it necessarily combines the old and the new, invoking a deep,
archetypal structure on the general level, involving departure from the
familiar on the specific level. The template appears to be inherent; the
specifics are manifestly not. It is at once part of an idea of newness and
discovery and at the same time always linked in to a sense of a connection to something fundamental, a mythic structure the pervasiveness of
which in literary history we encountered in the first part of this chapter.
Manfred Pfister has observed

> a general tendency in modernist and postmodernist travel writing to stage
> self-consciously what previous travel writers have tended to play down: the
> fact that travelling is always a travelling in traces, is always the pursuit of
> traces to be followed and read, and that the reading of these traces is more of
> an adventure than the travelling itself. (Pfister 2006: 5)

We have seen the Venetian Marco Polo's assertion that the value of his account derived from the authority of his having seen what his audience had not. Reflecting on contemporary travel generally, as well as on a journey to Venice itself, the Dutch traveller and writer Cees Nooteboom describes how the traveller's experience today is, in diametrical contrast to that of Polo's, that

> what your eyes see is what the no longer existent eyes of millions of others have seen [. . .] while you are looking they go on talking, you are constantly accompanied by both the living and the dead, you are involved in an age-old conversation. (Nooteboom 2007: 8)

This sense of the 'age-old conversation' in which the travelling writer takes part has, contrary to the ideology whereby the function of travel writing is undermined by an ostensible surfeit of accounts, become one of its principal concerns. Borrowing from Richard Holmes' *Footsteps: Adventures of a Romantic Biographer* (1985) there is what is sometimes considered a kind of sub-genre within travel writing: the 'footsteps' genre (Hulme 2002a and 2002b; Pfister 2006), which involves both the re-covering of paths already taken, and the recovery and renewal of the early traveller's tale. Iain Sinclair's *Edge of the Orison: In the Footsteps of John Clare's 'Journey out of Essex'* is a fine example of how tracing the paths of a predecessor can involve recovery and renewal of the past and a transformation of the present (we will encounter this, to some degree, in all of the readings that follow). It is a process of intertextual revision that can have a more politically acute function in the contestation of previous travel accounts. Raja Shehadeh's *Palestinian Walks: Notes on a Vanishing Landscape*, for example, reviews the prospectus of the Palestinian Exploration Fund, founded in 1865, and places itself as a corrective to

> a process that continues to this day of travellers and colonizers who see the land through the prism of the biblical past, overlooking the present realities. Eager to occupy the land of their imagination they impose their vision and manipulate it to tally with that mythical image they hold in their head, paying scant notice to its Palestinian inhabitants. (Shehadeh 2007: 47)

Perhaps the central insights to be drawn from these varied voyages in terms of cultural memory and cultural forgetting are that a sense of the subjectivity of the account nevertheless leads to a sense of the danger of 'paying scant notice to the [. . .] inhabitants' of the shared environment; and that the accounts of the past are not a separate entity to the 'world' they describe, but part of it. The accounts of the past are an element of the composition of the present, part of what is to be found in the world rather than the mark of the exhaustion of its potential to be innovatively or ethically described. It is a revision of that ideology of newness that permeates much of travel and its discontents, and that is given eloquent, aphoristic expression by Tim Robinson in his profound and poetical *The Stones of Aran*: 'If it is true that Time began, it is clear that nothing else has begun since, that every apparent origin is a stage in an elder process' (Robinson 1986: 5).

Travels tend to concern encounters more than relationships. There are travel books in which the traveller is accompanied: Boswell's *The Journal of a Tour to the Hebrides with Samuel Johnson* (1785), for example, D. H. Lawrence's *Sea and Sardinia*, or Rebecca West's *Black Lamb and Grey Falcon*. But even such shared voyages tend to be punctuated by encounters with strangers. This, perhaps, is one of the experiences of the contemporary world that the travel narrative, as a form, accommodates and speaks to. The development of modernity has made encounters increasingly important. We lead more interconnected lives. The literature of travel, even when it concerns rural journeys, thus bears a certain thematic and poetological resemblance to the literature of the metropolis, with its emphasis on encounters and anonymity – I am thinking of Edgar Allen Poe's 'Man of the Crowd' (1840) and the detective stories of the nineteenth century, as well as modernist fictions such as Joyce's *Ulysses* (1922) or Woolf's *Mrs Dalloway* (1925). Both contend with rapid meetings, flows and exchanges. In both, encounters radiate through the text – and this points towards one of the paradigmatic ethical problems of the contemporary period implicit in the etymology of the word 'contemporary' itself. That etymological meaning is there in the title-piece essay of Susan Sontag's last book *At the Same Time*, which explores this issue:

> To be a traveler – and novelists are often travelers – is to be constantly reminded of the simultaneity of what is going on in the world, your world and the very different world you have visited and from which you have returned 'home'. It is a beginning of a response to this painful awareness to say: it's a question of sympathy [. . .] of the limits of the imagination. (Sontag 2007: 228)

Sontag refers to Voltaire's 'Poem on the Lisbon Disaster' (1756), which neatly encapsulates the sense of ethical paradox arising from this awareness of 'elsewheres' (Sontag 2007: 228): 'Earth Lisbon swallows; the light sons of France / Protract the feast, or lead the sprightly dance' (Voltaire 2000: 100). It is a version of what has been called the 'meanwhile problem' (Buzard 1998), and has been linked, historically, to the way in which the diaspora in the wake of the French Revolution led to a 'dramatic reorganization of modern time and space, so that contemporaries felt themselves *contemporaries*, as occupants of a common time zone' (Fritzsche 2004: 9–10). Stephen Kern links the inception of World Standard Time and the rapid development of telecommunications, which 'worked to create the vast extended present of simultaneity' (Kern 1983: 318).

This, it may be argued, is the other side of what Mary-Louise Pratt has identified as one of the principal functions of travel writing in developing, over the course of the eighteenth and nineteenth centuries into the present, an emergent 'planetary consciousness [. . .] marked by an orientation toward interior exploration and the construction of global scale meaning through the descriptive apparatuses of natural history' (Pratt 1992: 15). As Pratt conclusively illustrates, much of the travel writing of the imperial period involved a 'global resemanticizing' in which 'the (lettered, male, European) eye that held the system could familiarize ("naturalize") new sites/sights immediately upon contact, by incorporating them into the language of the system' (1992: 31). We will see in the readings that follow that this sense of 'planetary consciousness' has another aspect, in its openness, its opening of the cultural imagination to its implication in wider history. The requirement that we inhabit our worlds, however delineated, with a sense of elsewheres, will be one of the central facets of each of the books considered in what follows.

While much has been written about the ideological conditioning of travel writing, one of the attractions of the form may be precisely the freedom it allows the writer – not only in terms of the journey, but in terms of form. Charles Darwin made the astute observation of Alexander von Humboldt's *Personal Narrative of a Journey to the Equinoctial Regions of the New Continent* (1995) – which had been criticised by some contemporaries as overly digressive and unfocused – that it was precisely because the travel narrative offered a 'convenient vehicle for miscellaneous discussions' that Humboldt had adopted the form (qtd Nicolson 1995: xxvii). W. H. Auden, in one of his two collaborative admixtures of poetry and narrative in a travel account, *Letters from Iceland* (with Louis MacNeice), touches on a similar theme:

> I want a form that's large enough to swim in,
>   And talk on any subject that I choose,
> From natural scenery to men and women,
>   Myself, the arts, the European news [. . .] (1985: 19)

In addition to the writers whose work will be studied in depth in the next chapter, writers like Nooteboom (particularly *Roads to Santiago: Detours and Riddles in the Lands and History of Spain* (1998), Predrag

Matvejević (with *The Mediterranean: A Cultural Landscape* (1999)) and Claudio Magris (with *Danube* (2001) especially) have used the form in precisely this way, as a 'convenient vehicle for miscellaneous discussions' and a 'form that's large enough to swim in'. Reading *Danube*, an account of a journey down that river from West to East, it is not always possible to say if the teller of the tale is recalling a journey made, or tracing his finger along the map and allowing the course of the river to dictate the stories and cultural historical episodes he may relate. The important aspect of the journey here is that it allows the writer to travel across memory and experience and forms of knowledge – in whatever genre or discipline they might be considered to fall – with a structure in place that ensures the narrative maintains a certain momentum, even if this momentum is frustrated. The form allows the writer to cross boundaries between different kinds of writing; its form allows for the recovery and renewal of the already experienced and already thought in redistribution along the narrative journey as much as the discovery of new experience – and the navigation between the two forms much of the dynamic tension. To paraphrase Italo Calvino's fine compliment to Roberto Calasso's *The Ruin of Kasch*, they are books with two subjects: the first is the place they travel to, the second is everything else.[1]

It is perhaps in this last feature of travellers' tales in contemporary literature that they are at once most contemporary and most in touch with older traditions – most linked, formally, to the wonder voyages of the past. For the assembly and juxtaposition and blurring of many and varied phenomena, and their integration into a summary whole, is not only analogous with the concerns of postmodernity – and the preponderance of 'Blurred Genres' (Geertz 1983). It is also strangely reminiscent of the travellers' tales of the pre-modern world, particularly the medieval *mirabilia* genre, or Wonder Book, of which *The Marvels of the East* is an old English example, in which the reader encounters word and image, galleries of wonders and grotesques, and the compilation of ostensibly factual and fictional narratives alongside different kinds of narrative.[2] Mary Baine Campbell, as we have seen, makes the agile link that the wonder book's 'closest modern analogues [. . .] are the *National Inquirer* and *The Guinness Book of Records*', which continue the tradition of the gallery of wonders and grotesques (Campbell 1988: 83). Yet there is also a parallel between the way such books gather together galleries of the culturally incommensurate with the substance of the writings that will be considered in depth in the following chapter, and those noted above. The otherwise heteroclite can be gathered together, connected not by plot or character – not by consequentiality – but by flights of association and memory around the thread of the journey.

Each of the reformulations of the travel narrative we have considered illustrate that the world has by no means been exhausted of its capacity to inspire wonder. And as we move into our readings of travellers' tales of wonder in contemporary literature, we may make the more general point that just as travel poses problems – the difficulties involved in representation, the implication of apparently disparate places and times, the tensions between different kinds of narrative – so its narrative provides, or requires, a form in which these issues can be addressed.

Notes

1. Calvino's original remark, which appeared in an Italian review of Roberto Calasso's *The Ruin of Kasch* (1994), is quoted in James Atlas' interview with Calasso, who 'likes to cite' Calvino's remark that '*The Ruin of Kasch* has two subjects: The first is Talleyrand; the second is everything else' (Atlas 1994). Worth noting, too: Calasso, a publisher as well as a writer, counted Bruce Chatwin among his clients (Shakespeare 1999: 306).
2. *The Marvels of the East* is stored in three versions: the Cotton Vitellius A.xv, Nowell Codex, housed at the British Library in London, in which it is bound with *Beowulf*; and in the Cotton Tiberius B.v., in Latin and Old English, stored at the Bodleian 614 manuscripts at Oxford University's Bodleian Library. See Mary Baine Campbell's *The Witness and the Other World* (1988: 57–9).

Part II
Readings in Contemporary Travellers' Tales of Wonder

Chapter 4

Bruce Chatwin and the 'modern WONDER VOYAGE': *In Patagonia* (1977)

> One arrives in the world and is disappointed. Then one goes to Rome and is disappointed. Paris, Brussels, London. Again one is disappointed. Berlin is not the city one wants to live in. One does not steal horses on the Puszta. Everywhere, the mountains are less high than one had thought. The plains less wide. The waters less deep. And in Holland, one finds the sails of the windmills too small. So one seeks out the harbours. So one deserts Europe. So one crosses the sea. But again one is disappointed. One wanders out to India and is disappointed. In China, everything is as it was at home, only a little bigger. To Patagonia one travels no more.
>
> Jürg Amann, *Patagonien: Prosa* (1985: 7; my translation)

When Bruce Chatwin published an account of a journey to a part of the world which had come to symbolise, in the Western cultural imagination, the distance to which 'one travels no more', it appeared as both novelty and relic, at once literary newfoundland and lost world regained. As its premise was the mythically resonant, marvellously unlikely quest for a replacement for a scrap of Giant Sloth skin which the traveller had gazed upon in wonder as a child in his grandmother's cabinet of curiosities, believing it to be a 'piece of brontosaurus', and which had been discarded after her death (Chatwin 1977: 1). Many found this redolent of Victorian adventure, of 'the kind of book that used to be common a century ago when our planet was still being explored' but that was 'a vanishing genre now' (Barkham 1978: no pagination).[1] Some, such as the poet Alastair Reid, looked further back, and suggested that *In Patagonia* had taken travel 'back to its magic roots' (Reid 1978: 190). To this day, the book is introduced on the jacket sleeve as 'an exhilarating look at a place that retains the exotic mystery of a far-off, unseen land' (Chatwin 1977). Yet the sense of what the book retained or returned to was equalled by a sense of what it resisted in terms of genre. The ninety-seven short chapters, zig-zagging across an eclectic range of stories, episodes and forms of writing, as well as across the hazily defined region of Argentina and Chile known as Patagonia, seemed to be a travel book, but a travel book which dissolved the boundaries of the genre so thoroughly as to create a form as exotic as the 'Patagonia' of myth which it recalled.

Chatwin responded to the (almost unanimously appreciative) critical confusion this engendered with a series of letters. He informed his agent, Deborah Rogers, ahead of US publication, that *In Patagonia* – pronounced already by no less than Graham Greene to have been 'one of [his] favourite travel books' – should be removed from the travel category (Shakespeare 2003: xiv; xix). Chatwin's explanation that '[a]ll the stories were chosen with the purpose of illustrating some particular aspect of wandering and/or exile' (Chatwin 2010: 277) clarified the thematic focus. But his classificatory proposal seems unlikely to have provided much guidance for publisher, bookseller, or librarian. As he wrote to a friend, Cary Welch, designating the book with the term that supplies the title of this reading:

> the FORM of the book seems to have puzzled them (as I expect it did the publisher). There's a lot of talk of 'unclassifiable prose', a 'mosaic', a 'tapestry', a 'jigsaw', a 'collage' etc. but no one has seen that it is a modern WONDER VOYAGE: the Piece of Brontosaurus is the essential ingredient of the quest. (Chatwin 2010: 275)

Despite the capitalised amplification, Chatwin's assertion that *In Patagonia* should be read as a 'modern wonder voyage' has not registered with like volume in assessments of the book. *In Patagonia* has certainly been recognised and illuminatingly discussed, Chatwin's protestations notwithstanding, as 'the book that redefined travel writing' (Clapp 1989: 37). The winner of the Hawthornden Prize upon publication, it has been a 'Vintage Classic' of 'Travel' at Random House since 1998 and at 'Penguin Classics' since 2003. It is proposed in Peter Hulme's judicious discussion of the postwar period in the *Cambridge Companion to Travel Writing* (Hulme and Youngs 2002: 87–101) as one of three books – the others being Peter Matthiessen's *The Snow Leopard* (1978) and Robyn Davidson's *Tracks* (1980) – which, through their experimental formal techniques, 'announced a decisive shift in modern travel writing' (2002: 87). Yet, while Chatwin's role in that shift has generated a wide array of critical responses, whatever might be at stake in his characterisation of *In Patagonia* as a 'modern wonder voyage', though frequently noted in passing, has not yet been explored in depth.

Perhaps – so at least is the wager of this reading – this is because it is as a modern wonder voyage that the book is most counter-cultural. For it is as a modern wonder voyage that Chatwin's book stands most decisively at the opposite end of the spectrum to the 'widespread rhetoric of exhaustion' (Cronin 2000: 2–3) with which it is contemporary. But as the inclusion of that quieter, uncapitalised but decisive word 'modern' implies, there is a creative tension in the ambiguity between continuity and change, recovery and renewal. *In Patagonia* registers and engages with, rather than escapes, those cultural pressures that lie behind belatedness and disenchantment – including, most problematically, the ethical charge against travellers' tales of wonder as an ally of empire. Yet wonder becomes a means of approaching these very issues. *In Patagonia* issues an oblique but dazzling indictment of the complacency of thinking that the world has been exhausted of its capacity to inspire wonder. One of the principal and distinguishing features of Chatwin's originality is his rejection of arriving in the world 'disappointed' – his tireless 'search for the miraculous' (Chatwin 1996: 282) and the sense of wonder, by turns elegiac and celebratory, that propels and infuses all his travels and writings. It is as a modern wonder voyage that *In Patagonia* lives most fully in the story of Chatwin's writing, in the history of travel and in literary history. It is the exemplary requirement that we question what it means to inhabit a world in which it makes sense – has become, indeed, a hubris – to say that 'to Patagonia one travels no more'.

'The last place on earth': the persistence of distance

Wellington Island, Beagle Channel, Tierra del Fuego ('Land of Fire'), Desolation Island, Hermit Island, Last Hope Sound ... The map that prefaces *In Patagonia* reads like a superlative poem of the prehistory and preoccupations of belated travel: less a chart of a place than of the vanities of European empire, the conquests of science, obscure longings run aground in disenchantment and – silently among those European names – of the obliteration of other peoples and cultures in their wake. One reason *In Patagonia* is so exemplary a modern wonder voyage is the special resonance Chatwin creates between the cultural history of Patagonia and the climate of disenchantment and exhaustion so prevalent at the time of his voyage. As Chatwin wrote, later, in *Patagonia Revisited* (Chatwin and Theroux 1985):

> Since its discovery by Magellan in 1520, Patagonia was known as a country of black fogs and whirlwinds at the end of the habited world. The word 'Patagonia', like Mandalay or Timbuctoo, lodged itself in the Western imagination as a metaphor of the Ultimate, the point beyond which one could not go. Indeed, in the opening chapter of *Moby Dick*, Melville uses 'Patagonian' as an adjective for the outlandish, the monstrous, and the fatally attractive. (Chatwin and Theroux 1992: 44)

Chatwin's own addition to this cultural mythology marshals a vast Patagonian archive illustrating the point: the voyages of Renaissance explorers like Pigafetta and Magellan (1977: 94–7); Shakespeare's *The Tempest* (1977: 95–7); the writings of Edgar Allan Poe and Samuel Taylor Coleridge (1977: 126–32); and – perhaps the most famous name associated with Patagonia before Chatwin – Charles Darwin's *Voyage of the Beagle* (esp. 1977: 13–15 and 126–32). All respond to the enduring gravitational pull of what Lucas Bridges described, in another of *In Patagonia*'s intertexts, as the *Uttermost Part of the Earth* (Bridges 1948). Patagonia stands, on the one hand, for what globalising modernity is supposed to have made impossible – an outlandish world, far away. On the other, it presents modernity's exaggerated image: a symbol of futility, endings and posterity. Chatwin thus transforms his destination into the *locus classicus* for exploring anxieties about what Claude Lévi-Strauss had called, in the opening chapter of *Tristes tropiques* (1973), 'An End to Journeying'. One way into the question of how *In Patgonia* operates as a modern wonder voyage, then, is to gauge some of the different ways in which Patagonia can – or cannot – be regarded as the 'The Last Place on Earth' (Chatwin 1977: 3).

To speak of Patagonia as 'the last place on earth' in terms of geographical distance, as a country 'at the far end of the world' (1977: 1), is immediately to invite J. M. G. le Clézio's perfectly economical critique: 'distant from what?' (2008: 154). But, as is implicit in an understanding of Patagonia as 'metaphor', Chatwin was writing with a keen and foregrounded awareness of the European bias in the divergence and interaction of place and imagination. As Chatwin put it in another context:

> There are two Timbuctoos. One is the administrative centre of the Sixth Region of the Republic of Mali, once French Sudan [. . .] And then there is the Timbuctoo of the mind – a mythical city in a Never-Never Land, an antipodean mirage, a symbol for the back of beyond or a flat joke. (1997: 27)

That the pursuit of the 'metaphor' was at the tragic cost of the actual people and cultures who furnished the dream of distance is one of *In Patagonia*'s abiding themes, if not its most central. We will move towards Chatwin's homage to the Yaghan people and their language. But we move towards it, as Chatwin does, through a climate of fantasies and anxieties about the 'fatally attractive' idea of the 'last place on earth' – in its temporal, as well as its spatial, sense. 'At least part of the book,' Chatwin had written in his proposal, 'will discuss the End of the World from the end of the world' (I.1 'O Patagonia': 8).[2]

The first manuscript Chatwin delivered to his publisher – *At the End: A Journey to Patagonia* (Clapp 1997: 27; Shakespeare 1999: 307)

– illustrates the significance of this dimension to Chatwin's conception of the book. Indeed, the narrative point of departure invokes two lost worlds: that of the personal past of childhood in the narrator's recollection of visiting his grandmother's house, and that of the prehistorical world represented by 'the piece of brontosaurus'. There is also the world potentially lost: in the memory of apocalyptic Cold War fears as a child in the 1940s and '50s. This is what is named, in fact, as the source of the traveller's awakening to the map of the world:

> for the Cold War woke in me a passion for geography. In the late 1940s the Cannibal of the Kremlin shadowed our lives; you could mistake his moustaches for teeth. We listened to lectures about the war he was planning. We watched the civil defence lecturer ring the cities of Europe to show the zones of total and partial destruction. We saw the bones bump one against the other leaving no space in between. The instructor wore khaki shorts. His knees were white and wobbly, and we saw that it was hopeless. The war was coming and there was nothing we could do. (Chatwin 1977: 3)

Hoping 'to survive the blast', the Cold War child takes part in an 'Emigration Committee', which settles on Patagonia 'as the safest place on earth', 'somewhere to live when the rest of the world blew up' (1977: 3). Patagonia, then, is imagined as the 'last place' left in the event of total war: it is the last place temporally, because, geographically, it is the furthest place from European power. As Manfred Pfister has suggested, Chatwin's book 'teems with too much and too variegated life to strike an apocalyptic note' (Pfister 1993: 255) – as is implicit in the mischievous comedy of the image of the wobbly-kneed defence, and borne out by Chatwin's own remarks: 'I had my apocalyptic phase early; doom-mongers of today leave me rather cool' (I.1 'O Patagonia': 8). But this hinterland of war should not be underestimated in Chatwin's writing, nor in the significance of Patagonia as destination. Chatwin's 'early childhood', as he wrote in the first draft of *In Patagonia*, 'was war and the feeling of war. We were homeless and we were always travelling up and down England' (I.6 'First draft': 1). This is an autobiographical element he would return to, later, and integrate into *The Songlines* (2005: 5–10). The fact that the tone is not apocalyptic is thus more than incidental: it is a decisive feature of the narrative.

This problematises another prominent element of the reception of Chatwin's book: that it conveys a sense of Patagonia being the last place left, as it were, for what Paul Fussell, as we have seen, was to call 'genuine travel' (Fussell 1980: 40). As already noted, Penguin recognises a selling point in advertising the book as 'an exhilarating look at a place that retains the exotic mystery of a far-off, unseen land'; and

Paul Theroux, reviewing *In Patagonia* not long before the publication of his own South American travel book, *The Old Patagonian Express*, is among the most notable commentators to have adopted the language of 'real travel' in his response. For Theroux, Chatwin had 'fulfilled the desire of all real travellers, of having found a place that is far and seldom visited, like the Land Where The Jumblies Live' (Theroux 1977: no pagination; cf. Morgan 1978). Here is Alastair Reid, neatly illustrating, without quite succumbing to, this worldview in one of the fullest recognitions of *In Patagonia* as wonder voyage, 'The Giant Sloth Skin and Other Wonders' (Reid 1978):

> Since tourists took over from travellers, the times have not been kind to those few, rare writers who have always seen the world well for us – who filter unknown landscapes through the screen of their curiosity, who travel at a human pace, and who keep notes that allow us to take armchair journeys with them. Now even the waste places of the world are discovered regularly for us by documentary crews, and the records of articulate, lone travellers have given way to anonymous guidebooks, which list what to see and where to eat, drink, sleep, and be gratified in varying degrees of comfort. The unknown looks sometimes like a beaten track. (Reid 1978: 186)

This direct example of the currency of the tourist versus traveller paradigm and the idiom of the 'beaten track' is offered as the horizon on which Chatwin's work appeared so unexpectedly. Thus, *In Patagonia*, Reid concludes,

> jogs us with the realization that what we have come to regard as travel is no more than a geographical transference, where hardly anything changes, where map and guidebook obliterate the landscape, where journeys are taken for the purpose of summing up, of reaching a conclusion – the very opposite of a wonder voyage. (1978: 186)

Yet part of the originality of Chatwin's wonder voyage is precisely its freedom from the desire to get 'off' the 'beaten track'. *In Patagonia* in no way validates itself as a report on an insufficiently discovered place, or a newly rediscovered lost world. Indeed, its most recurrent discovery is that Patagonia and the Europe the traveller imagined he could escape there as a child, are intricately and irrevocably interconnected. How to maintain Theroux's idea that Patagonia is a place that is 'far and seldom visited', given that, as Manfred Pfister has noted without much exaggeration, Chatwin's Patagonia contains hardly any Patagonian Patagonians (Pfister 1996: 256)? Chatwin's Patagonia is inhabited by travellers from everywhere but Patagonia (this is the tragedy). If *In Patagonia* has a sense of 'exoticism', it derives not from the geographical or cultural unfamiliarity of Patagonia so much as from the surfeit of ways in which it has been imagined, and the longevity of this mythology. It evokes, but also exposes, this fantasy, and is thus diametrically opposed to what Robyn Davidson identifies as one of the chief tropes of contemporary travel writing: the fantasy of 'an uncontaminated Elsewhere' (Davidson 2001: 2).

A critique of the colonial dimensions of a history of pan-Atlantic 'contaminations' may sound like belated disenchantment. But it is part of Chatwin's revision of the colonial discourse of discovery and conquest. *Pace* the view that an absence of blank spots on the map of the world renders travellers' tales obsolete and disenchants the present, the sense of coming after other travellers is a source rather than a scourge of wonder. The title *In Patagonia* itself announces its place in a long lineage of travel books in which the '*In . . .*' formulation is used (see Cocker 1992: 253–5). The mode of travelling foregrounds, rather than disavows, its followings in the traces of others in a version of what, following Richard Holmes' *Footsteps: Adventures of a Romantic Biographer* (1985), is sometimes called the 'footsteps' genre (see Hulme 2002a and 2002b; and Pfister 2006). As Chatwin later wrote of himself (and Paul Theroux): 'If we are travellers at all, we are literary travellers. A literary reference or connection is likely to excite us as much as a rare animal or plant' (Chatwin and Theroux 1992: 7–8). And his book is more an exploration of Patagonias imagined by generations of travellers and writers, from Shakespeare to Darwin to Poe, than an empirical report. More explicitly, when the motivations for the journey are stated, they are most often related, specifically, to the desire to go where someone else has been before, precisely because they had been before. Specific directions are often taken in order to track predecessors. The route via Mount Spión follows the tracks of the author of *The Uttermost Part of the Earth*, Lucas Bridges: 'I had always wanted to walk the track' (Chatwin 1977: 139). Indeed, the most fundamental organising principle of the voyage to Patagonia is conducted as a following in the footsteps of an ancestor: the storyteller's first cousin twice removed, Charley Milward the Sailor.

Milward's story, and his provision of the piece of brontosaurus that was to become the object of his descendant's quest, is of self-evident importance in motivating the journey. Chatwin's working papers show that Milward's unpublished memoirs were also instrumental in the composition of the book itself, in terms of its form. Chatwin's first draft in particular bears striking similarities to Milward's. Like Chatwin, Milward begins with a childhood memory – 'a small thing in itself destined to have a great effect on my life' (I.4 'Milward's Memoirs': 1)

– and an episode that resonates powerfully with Chatwin's own story. On a visit to a Somerset seaside village, the young Milward is frightened by the sea (not to mention the sight of his two aunts 'clothed from head to foot in long blue serge bathing gowns [. . .] with their heads done up in sponge bags' (I.4: 2)). He makes a run for it, but is 'quickly caught, and these two big girls took me each by a hand and dragged me down the beach, I holding back all the time and gasping out from time to time, "What is on the other side? "What is on the other side?" Must I go?':

> Carry quieted me after a time by telling me 'That when I was a man, I should go and see for myself'. This idea never quite left me, and I often said afterwards 'That when I was a man I was going to see what was on the other side'. (I.4: 2–3)

The importance of Milward's memoirs to Chatwin's account concerns the sense of the journey being a following in the footsteps of the ancestor; not a seeking out of 'new' tracks so much as the recovery of those made in the past. Such footstepping by no means originates with Chatwin: the ancient practice of pilgrimage by definition involves tracing the paths of others, and it can be said that it is 'an axiom of recent travel writing that writers offer tribute to their predecessors' (Holland and Huggan 2000: 7). But there is more at work here than a case of 'paying statutory respects to previous writers' (ibid.: 7). Nor is it the case that Chatwin realises, reluctantly, that his 'own endeavours have come too late' (ibid.: 7). On the contrary, as we have seen, the predecessors are the source of the wonder voyage, and we detect nothing in Chatwin's work – much of which is composed of the words of others – that might, in Harold Bloom's sense, be considered an Oedipal 'anxiety of influence' (Bloom: 1997). Chatwin is never moved symbolically or rhetorically to kill off his predecessors, contemporaries, or successors. Far more, the presence or absence of others is invoked and pursued. *In Patagonia* diverges from the assumption of the virgin territory as the traveller's motivation: Chatwin's Patagonia becomes the destination of a wonder voyage not because it is the 'last place' unseen, but, on the contrary, because of the innumerable living encounters it evokes.

There is another, vital element to Chatwin's account, which concerns the way travellers' tales have as one of their primary, even primal, features the idea that they speak of survival: Ancient Mariners live on to tell the death-defying tale. In his notes to *The Book of Wonder Voyages*, Joseph Jacobs writes that in most wonder voyages 'there are traces of the influence of the last voyage of man' as journeys into 'the other world as the bourne from which our travelers do return: in fact, we have the free play of the Folk mind on man's last home. The travelers cross the bar and come out into the Unknown; their peculiarity is that they return and cross it' (Jacobs and Batten 2008: 216). It is in this dimension that Chatwin's *In Patagonia* is both most exemplary and exceptional of its form. As Peter Hulme has drawn attention to, Chatwin's journey travels south – to Ushuaia, the 'southernmost town in the world' – and the journey south, as in Dante's *Divine Comedy*, is symbolic of the journey towards death (Hulme 2002a: 227). But the traveller's arrival at Ushuaia, under the page-heading 'A Town at the End of the World' (Chatwin 1977: 121–2), is emplotted within a cluster of stories in which the different meanings of the 'last place on earth' confront and problematise one another, and which culminates in a chapter under the page-heading 'The Uttermost Part of the Earth' (1977: 142–3). Arrival at the southernmost point at the 'End of the World' represents the traveller's own symbolical encounter with death: the teller of the tale recalls an 'apparently childless town' (1977: 121), which he left 'as from an unwanted tomb' (1977: 132). But threaded through this crux of the tale of the traveller who survived is Chatwin's most direct elegy to those who did not.

As the traveller reaches the 'last place on earth', the narrative weaves a complex knot of stories. The town 'began' in 1869 with the landing of Anglican missionaries among the Yaghan Indians, followed by the Argentine Navy: the 'Indians died of measles and pneumonia' (1977: 121). The town becomes the location for an account of the anarchist Simón Radowitzky in an exemplification of Chatwin's *idée fixe* of the conflict between nomadism and settlement, to be considered in the following section: 'the same old quarrel: of Abel, the wanderer, with Cain, the hoarder of property' (1977: 122). There is then the story of 'Jemmy Button', the Wulaian boy kidnapped by Captain Robert Fitzroy of the HMS *Beagle*, who played so important a role in Charles Darwin's voyage, and 'who lived into the 1870s to see a proper mission established at Ushuaia and see the first of his people die of epidemics' (1977: 131–2). The traveller seeks out the 'last of the Yaghans' on nearby Navarino Island (1977: 132) and proceeds to recover what he can of the Yaghan language from Thomas Bridge's *Yaghan Dictionary* (1977: 134–9). It is from this that Chatwin draws something like a philosophy of language:

> the concepts of 'good' or 'beautiful', so essential to Western thought, are meaningless unless they are rooted to things. The first speakers of language took the raw material of their surroundings and pressed it into metaphor to suggest abstract ideas. The Yaghan tongue – and by inference all language – proceeds as a system of navigation. Named things are fixed points, aligned and compared, which allow the speaker to plot the next move. (1977: 136)

What is celebrated at the point at which the metaphor of the Ultimate is embodied most emblematically, then, is a language understood as rooted in things, resistant to a language of transferable, abstract metaphors. It is not coincidental that the chapter is followed by the most extended engagement with the flora and fauna of the land itself: Chapter 36 is one of the only ones in which the journey on foot is described in detail.

The senses in which Patagonia can be understood as the 'last place on earth' – as the 'metaphor of the Ultimate' in the Western cultural imaginary; as the furthest place to which humankind walked; as last place at the outer rim of the Cold War zones of destruction; as a 'last place left' for 'real travel'; as the symbolic last mortal home of the traveller himself – as these come into most precise focus at the superlatively southernmost point at the uttermost end of the earth, they are subordinated to the story of those for whom this was, in concrete terms, the last place on earth. Central to the wonder voyage of *In Patagonia*, then, is that it works to undermine the principles of exoticism and distance which it so emblematically evokes. Implicit in this is an equally poignant rejection of the anxieties of their exhaustion.

'The Nomadic Alternative' and other prehistories

Just as Patagonia, as 'the last place on earth', resonates with and brings into question a cultural sense of belatedness and posterity, so Chatwin's own literary publications are the product of a personally 'late' start. A start, at least, that the writer perceived as late: he was thirty-seven years old when *In Patagonia* was published, and was to warn other writers not to delay: 'I've left it far too late' (qtd Shakespeare 1999: 285). This dimension of Chatwin's literary career creates a tension with one of the prominent elements of the writer's 'image'. Chatwin has been described and is readily recalled – for example, by Sybille Bedford (Bedford 1978: 46), a writer whose own work Chatwin greatly admired (see his introduction to Bedford's *A Visit to Don Otavio*) – as a 'true traveller', one of Baudelaire's '*vrais voyageurs*' who

> are those alone who leave only
> To leave; hearts light, like balloons,
> From their fate they never swerve,
> And without knowing why, say, always: let us go!
> (Baudelaire, 'Le Voyage' (2006): 241; trans. adapted)

It is the Baudelairean traveller who 'leaves only to leave' who is evoked, for example, in the most famous story about Chatwin, which finds its way into the Vintage Classics profile that prefaces his books in that series: 'Between 1972 and 1975 he worked for the *Sunday Times*, before announcing his next departure in a telegram: "Gone to Patagonia for six months." This trip inspired the first of Chatwin's books.' Thus the Chatwin legend. And there is certainly something of Chatwin the 'congenitally absent' and 'inveterately mobile' wanderer (Buford 1984: 6) in what he himself described as 'Baudelaire's own incomparable "Le Voyage"' (Chatwin and Theroux 1992: 46). But if Chatwin did indeed have the '*coeur léger, semblable au ballon*' of Baudelaire's 'true traveller', it was heavily ballasted – with preparation and prognostication, as well as formidable scholarly and professional 'baggage'. His writing draws on, redeploys and sometimes defines itself against, the harvest of a long and varied apprenticeship – or rather, aborted apprenticeships in other 'fields'.

The story is well known, if 'known' is the right adjective to apply to a biography in which legend plays so prominent a part. Versions have been told with verve and insight by Chatwin's editor at Cape, Susannah Clapp (1997) and his biographer Nicholas Shakespeare (1999), both indispensable as critical interpretations of Chatwin's work as well as biographical renderings of his life. Only a cursory account, drawn from these sources, need be provided here. At eighteen, direct from public school to Sotheby's auction house (rather than to university), where he began as a porter, quickly rose through the ranks and finished up one of the firm's youngest directors, in the Impressionist department. Then, training at Edinburgh as an archaeologist (abandoning his studies midway). Then, working as a journalist for the *Sunday Times Magazine*. And in the midst of all this, labouring on the ambitiously expansive anthropological-cum-historical treatise and '*ur*-text' of Chatwin's œuvre, which he called, provisionally, 'The Nomadic Alternative'.

The story in sum is illustrative of Chatwin's extraordinary scope of interests, and of a resistance to specialisation reminiscent of the figure of the 'Renaissance Go-Between' (Höfele and Koppenfels 2005) so prominent when the discourse of wonder was at its height. But 'The Nomadic Alternative' was the project in which Chatwin had invested most fully. The power of *In Patagonia* as a wonder voyage derives in part from its being written after great exertion and exhaustion, and disappointment: the suspension of the project by the commissioning publisher, Tom Maschler at Jonathan Cape, in 1970, four years before the journey to Patagonia (see Shakespeare 1999: 257). *In Patagonia* is the book that Chatwin submitted, seven years later, under the commission for 'The Nomadic Alternative'. This book, perhaps the most famous never published in twentieth-century English literature, is both everywhere present, and everywhere resisted, throughout Chatwin's literary work.

For all that 'The Nomadic Alternative' remains unpublished, the argument is nevertheless well known through the articles Chatwin published on the work in progress (see Chatwin [1997: 12), and through its fullest literary exposition and formal expression in *The Songlines*. His theory was, in summary, that the entire history of the human species, and indeed of natural history itself, can be understood as a primal conflict between the forces of civilisation or settlement on the one hand, and nomadism or wandering on the other, as exemplified most archetypally in the myth of Cain (the settler) and Abel (the wanderer). 'There are two conditions for men,' Chatwin writes early on in 'The Nomadic Alternative', 'to wander and to settle – to dig in or to move – two conditions with two incompatible ideologies. The wanderer exults in his freedom, the settler compensates for his chains' (Chatwin G.1 'Nomadic Alternative': 18). Chatwin found this duality expressed in conflicts between societies, between individuals within societies, and within individuals themselves. The conflict was never more strikingly dramatised than in Chatwin, the desert-wandering art collector, himself.

The argument, and his style of argument, has followers, sceptical admirers and hostile critics. The sceptical admirers are probably the most insightful: to be a follower requires a consistent didactic argument that could be adopted as a mantra – something 'The Nomadic Alternative', let alone the literary works in which its argument can be identified, does not provide. Thus followers tend not to notice the paradoxes and difficulties that Chatwin himself was aware of and discusses, while the more hostile critics tend to occupy precisely the position of civilisation and specialisation that Chatwin brought into question. We find a striking example of this in the Introduction to the exhibition catalogue *'Animal Style' Art from East to West* (1970), to which Chatwin contributed an article which is also a condensation of 'The Nomadic Alternative' in progress. In seeking answers to 'one of the world's most difficult historic problems', Gordon Bailey Washburn writes in his Foreword, 'it is not to be wondered if our trio of scholars were inclined to differences of opinions':

> Mr Chatwin, an anthropologist at heart, is inclined to find shamanism the most likely inspiration for the Animal Style in its various ramifications – seeing in it the natural explanation for the style's apparent encirclement of the globe [. . .] Mrs Bunker and Dr Farkas are less interested in an unprovable hypothesis and more concerned with the exacting research that traces the movements of ancient peoples and their styles of ornament across the vast face of Asia and the smaller one of Europe. They belong to that very small band of specialists, an international group of scholars, whose largely invisible research may in the end restore to us some of the many lost pages of ancient history. (Washburn 1970: 7)

It is because of his interest in 'an unprovable hypothesis' then – more akin to wondering than to verifiable knowing – that Mr Chatwin attracts this arch scepticism. He and the specialists share in the aim 'to restore to us some of the many lost pages of ancient history'; but the approaches, for all Chatwin's exacting research, are counterpoints. At the top of one of Chatwin's many pages of notes on nomads, among the author's reflections on Chillait theories of apocalypse, Bowlby's *Attachment and Loss* (1969), the relationship between the primate's ability to climb and the development of its 'teeth, skull, vertebrae, and viscera', and, perhaps most appositely for our discussion, the nervousness of the baboon 'at the edges of its periphery', Chatwin writes:

> A —— I am not a specialist of any kind. I am unspecialised. I must therefore state my aims and biographical detail —— and self-flattering to think that the generalist —— may be able to articulate something to a general pattern of ideas (G.1 'Research': no pagination)

The long straight lines in the quotation above represent longer, curving lines that connect the components of the sentence as it finds space amid other notes. The 'A' – which recurs in the margins of the notes – appears to stand, not for 'aims' or 'approach' but 'autobiography'. Here it is again, a few pages on:

> 'They are using my path.' Myself at 4, Derbyshire. (Reason for jealousy of traveller's – A) I quite definitely prefer to adhere to a fixed range revisiting rapidly a number of points. Random walks in Paris rarely deviate from a set pattern of the Guars Bvd St Germain. —— Security of commuter trains. (G.1 'Research': no pagination)

This recurring 'A' is worth noting when considering the two problems raised most frequently with Chatwin's thesis. The first, eminently sensible reservation that Chatwin meant too much by the term 'nomad' was first made by Desmond Morris, author of *The Naked Ape* (1967), when Maschler asked him to comment on the thesis (Shakespeare 1999: 218). Chatwin responded to Morris' criticism, as is known, with at least apparent delight (1999: 218). This might not have been so much out of magnanimity in the face of criticism, as because the criticism is persuasive but, in a sense, beside the point. It is certainly an important reservation regarding Chatwin's account of nomadic culture. But while the defence of nomads was certainly his aim, his conception of the conflict was mythic in proportion, rather than strictly anthropological: it was less a thesis than a worldview. The second problem often raised is that Chatwin projects his own condition as the human condition – this is the usual explanation for the first flaw, as concisely expressed by John Ure: 'Because he was a rolling stone himself, he wanted to believe this was a superior way of life' (Ure 2003: 63). Though there is surely much in this, it must be acknowledged that this was hardly something Chatwin was unaware of or sought to conceal: he presented his thesis from the first as deeply influenced by 'A'.

While Chatwin's thesis has often, even among admirers, been indulged as a Chatwinian flight of fancy rather than entertained as an idea, its dilemmas have become noticeably more prominent in more recent historical inquiries. Felipe Fernández-Armesto, for example, writes that the 'world's earliest known full-scale battle was fought at Jebel Sahaba, near the modern Egyptian – Sudanese border, about 11,000 years ago, in a context when agriculture was in its infancy' (2006: 10). This 'slaughter of unmitigated ferocity' leads Fernández-Armesto to speculate that

> the earliest warfare was between settled communities contending to control of resources. At least, wars seem to have taken on a new intensity or to have been waged in a more systematic way once people settled down to tend stands of crops. (Fernández-Armesto 2006: 10)

Similarly, Stephen Greenblatt writes that '[f]or the urban Greeks nomadism was the indelible mark of the Scythians' distance from civility, the sign and substance of an alien existence, the quintessence of otherness' (Greenblatt 1991: 124) and asks a highly Chatwinian question: 'But if nomads are always elsewhere – people, as Columbus said of the Indians, "living in highlands and mountains, having no settled dwellings, and apart from us" – how can the historian know anything about them?' (1991: 124).

This last point is the deeper issue that Chatwin was working through in 'The Nomadic Alternative' – the question that poses the deeper question in literary terms. The paradoxes that repeatedly stall the book, or register as a tension in its tone, are questions of form. Clapp reports that Chatwin told her: 'In the Cairo museum I saw all these masks of the pharaohs, row on row. I asked myself: Where are the masks of Moses? I started liking people who had no garbage to leave. I wanted to find the other side of the coin.' (Clapp 1997: 127) His fascination was for the '"lives that were invisible to the archaeologist's spade" [...] nomads who travelled through history "leaving no burnt layer"' (1997: 127). It was a history, then, of that which has no written history; of that which was perceived as specifically anti-literary. Its opening line was: 'The best travellers are illiterate' (G.1 'Nomadic Alternative': 1). How to write what, in being written, ascribes itself to the very thing it aims to critique? How to adopt the tradition of the city in the name of the outcast?

'[W]hen literature first comments on the antithesis,' Chatwin suggests, 'it sings the triumph of the settler, because the settler is closer to the source of literature.' He continues:

> In any case, *writing* develops hand in hand with specialisation, standardisation, and bureaucracy, and with them a stratified social and economic hierarchy, and the repression of one group by a ruling minority. The first written tablets record how much the slaves are bringing in. Literate Civilization freed some for the higher exercises of the mind, for the development of logical thought, mathematics, practical medicine based on scientific observation rather than faith healing and so on. But in Mesopotamia the two highest gods were Anu (Order) and Enlil (Compulsion). Breasted writes of the 'dauntless courage of the architect of the Great Pyramid'. However, the 2.5 million blocks were *lashed* into place. We inherit the load. (Chatwin 1997: 78–9)

This critique of writing is not the modernist issue of the attempt to express the inexpressible – the difficulty, as Eliot's Prufrock puts it, of it being 'impossible to say just what I mean' (Eliot 1961: 15). Here the problem – one we will encounter again in Sebald, and which is redolent of Claude Lévi-Strauss' speculations in *Tristes tropiques* concerning the links between writing and power (Lévi-Strauss 1973: 392–3) – is the sense of there being an ethical dilemma at the heart of writing in itself. The problem is a matter of form as much as content. Thus, we find that other writers have made very similar points in terms of argument, but without the same pressures of proof drawing the same kind of critique. Among Chatwin's papers (G.1 'Research'), for example, is a piece by Jorge Luis Borges, 'The Gaucho and the City: Stories of Horsemen' (1982):

> Distant in time and space, the stories I have assembled are really one. The protagonist is eternal [. . .] There is a pleasure in detecting beneath the masks of time the eternal species of horseman and city. This pleasure, in the case of these stories, may leave the Argentine with a melancholy aftertaste, since [. . .] we identify with the horseman, who in the end is the loser [. . .] (Borges 1982: 7)

Borges' remark that '[f]rom the farmer comes the word "culture" and from the cities the word "civilization", but the horseman is a storm that fades away' (1982: 9), too, sounds very close to the ideas Chatwin had been working though.

Unlike Borges' poetically oriented vision, however, or the historical hypotheses noted above, Chatwin's book was not only aiming to propose a theory or express a spirit of affiliation. It was written with the aim of polemical intervention in the conflict, with the commitment to bringing about a change in the conditions of life and the lot of humanity. All this against a profound but as yet unfulfilled commitment to story over rhetoric as a mode of understanding, detail over argument, anomaly over normalising thesis. In what appears to be a suggestion for a sleeve-note, we find the following: 'The question is, "Do you belong to MAN or the MACHINE?" With each day more and more reply, "We belong to MAN, and there's nothing wrong with him"' (G.1 'Nomadic Alternative': no pagination). Such sentences illustrate the strain of the voice, the tension of the conviction with the troubling thought of its unlikeliness. Thoughts of a Penguin Special to rally Man into action against the Machine interfere with the voice. The 'argument' – Chatwin's *idée fixe* of a 'nomadic' ideal – never really changed. But the nature of his involvement in the argument did, and profoundly. The paradoxes of a fixed obsession with movement and transience, of writing that which slips through history, present an immobilising cul-de-sac rhetorically, but they provide a mobilising creative tension. And we can see the variety of adaptations – Chatwin's never settling into any genre – as a formal expression of this nomadic ideal. His literary work expresses, rather than resolves, the tensions: the 'problem' becomes one of its mainsprings.

In *In Patagonia*, Chatwin becomes a character in the narrative, rather than the faux-objective author of a treatise. Whether consciously or not, he follows the advice given to Charlie Milward in a letter of 4 March 1924, responding to his memoirs:

> Your work is a serious work, therefore use studied language, cultured, without slang. State yourself definitively. In writing 'It is my opinion' or 'I am of the opinion' the expression qualifies for argument. You are not expounding a theory and inviting discussion. You see; you know, so you state it. (Chatwin I.4 'Letter to Milward': 1)

We do not find any instances of 'my opinion' in Chatwin's finished prose, and *In Patagonia* avoids the presentation of direct argument. Though Chatwin's conviction on the 'nomadic alternative' remains strong, he scrupulously avoids allowing it to gain direct rhetorical expression in his book. The nearest we come to an explicit presentation of the thesis is with a resident ornithologist in Puerto Deseado, with whom the narrator 'talked late into the night, arguing whether or not we, too, have journeys mapped out in our central nervous systems; it seemed the only way to account for our insane restlessness' (Chatwin 1977: 86). Chatwin's polemic has been softened to the point that we cannot be entirely sure whether this 'seemed the only way' to the narrator, or the interlocutor. The absence of the rhetorical drive, the restraint of the narrative from overt judgement – something which has sometimes been chastised, or inquired into, as an elusive non-engagement with political issues (see, for example, Sugnet 1991 and Youngs 1997 respectively) – can be understood, then, as one of its most intrinsic responses to the association of writing and power – an attempt both to express the ideas and escape from the manifest ideology of the form of 'The Nomadic Alternative'.

In Patagonia is also a personal embodiment of one of the theoretical assertions made within the treatise. The 'wonder voyage' itself is explored as a stage in individual development – one which, so Chatwin argues, civilisation has suppressed. Chatwin outlines the model as follows:

> A young man, bursting with vigour and often credited with superhuman audacity in childhood, leaves home on a long journey. After a sequence of adventures in remote and fabulous lands, he faces the Jaws of Death. A fire-breathing monster menaces with fangs and claws [. . .] and jealously hoarding a treasure, threatens the inhabitants of the land with total destruction unless they cringe before it and appease its bloodthirstiness with sacrificial victims. The hero fights and kills the monster, rewards himself with the treasure and a bride, returns home to the jubilant acclamations of his proud parents and people, and they all live happily ever after. (Chatwin G.1 'Nomadic Alternative': 36–7)

This, Chatwin argues, is an 'archetypal sequence [. . .] rooted in the psychology of every individual' (G.1 'Nomadic Alternative': 37), expressed in the stories of national histories, of Columbus, of the Israelites, of Jason and Odysseus, of Ché Guevara (who will figure notably in the second chapter of *In Patagonia*):

> A human life is a journey of initiations in which the hero faces the monster, 'dies' a little, only to be reborn and enjoy the rewards of life. Thereafter he may disappear. The Wonder Voyage is thus indissociable from the biological fact of life, and it matters little if the Road of Trials leads to the Otherworld in the brain, the Otherworld of Outer Space, a remote archipelago or a Land of Punt with its dancing pygmies and frankincense trees. It is meaningless to decide if the hero lives out the myth or the myth lives itself out in the hero. (G.1 'Nomadic Alternative': 37–8)

This model of the wonder voyage is both recovered and renewed in *In Patagonia* – its archetype is adopted, but the specifics of the quest are, as we will see in the following section, made equal to the pressures of modernity. What is indisputable is, firstly, that Chatwin's wonder voyage is founded upon long meditation on power: on territorialism and oppression, and the implication of writing in this history. Secondly, while Chatwin's move away from the theory to the practice of wonder voyaging involves placing a first-person traveller at the centre of a form usually inhabited by a fictional character or third person, this is less a case of individualistic self-aggrandisement than it is, at a deeper level and rather more remarkably, an effort at a kind of radical human- ism, a conformity with what Chatwin perceived as a deeper cycle of human life that had been suppressed by contemporary culture. Chatwin approached *In Patagonia*, as a wonder voyage, with an understanding that such a venture was to live out a human myth, or allow the myth to live itself out in the traveller.

It may be appropriate, then, that the first thing we learn about Chatwin when we open his books is most likely apocryphal. Chatwin did claim to have sent a telegram announcing his departure for Patagonia, but the duration does not tally with the publisher's account: 'GONE TO PATAGONIA FOR FOUR [rather than six] MONTHS' (Chatwin 2010: 234). And whether this telegram was even sent is doubtful. If there was a 'telegram', it was most likely a letter received by one of Chatwin's mentors, his former editor at the *Sunday Times*, Francis Wyndham. Whether this telegram is more accurate or not, it provides a glimpse of the hinterland and evolution of the book, as a journey and an idea with the weight of prehistory behind it, a prehistory that predates even 'The Nomadic Alternative':

> I have done what I threatened. I suddenly got fed up with N.Y. and ran away to South America. I have been staying with a cousin in Lima for the past week and I am going tonight to Buenos Aires. I intend to spend Christmas in the middle of Patagonia / I am doing a story there for myself, something I have always wanted to write up. (Chatwin 2010: 234)

The impulsive, offhand persona on which the author biography draws is there in the man who 'suddenly got fed up [. . .] and ran away'. But so too is the retentiveness of the long-harboured, 'threatened' plan. Chatwin was, like many postwar writers, 'travelling to write' (Hulme 2002b: 87–101). And more: he was 'travelling to write *up*': it might be more fitting to say, not that the 'trip inspired the book', then, but, vice versa, that the book inspired the journey. It is that phrase, 'I always wanted', that is the deeper secret of Chatwin's voyages, intimating the prehistory that lends the departures such pathos. Desire, in Chatwin's writing, has as its most habitual tense the past or present perfect (Chatwin 1983; 1977: 65–6; 2005: 271): 'I always wanted' is his most characteristic formulation of longing, his most habitual grounds for saying, with Baudelaire, '*Allons!*' Chatwin's travels, all of them pub- lished after his thirty-seventh year, are not so much whimsical departures as tardy voyages of requitement – stories of the fulfilment, or at least the expression, of undying desires. The apparently impetuous desertions point obliquely towards the endurance of the imaginative life preceding the journey, as well as the alert sense of mortality that prompts their realisation. And it is to these deeper longings, to those prehistories that live in us, that lie dormant in us, that his work so powerfully speaks.

'A piece of brontosaurus': the resurrection of the quest

Of all the voyages in this study, *In Patagonia* presents the most exemplary 'wonder' in the sense of a 'marvellous object; a marvel; a prodigy' (*OED*): the 'Piece of Brontosaurus' which was really a piece of *Mylodon Listai*, or giant sloth, and that Chatwin had insisted was the 'essential ingredient of the quest' (Chatwin 2010: 275). Yet, as Peter Hulme has put it, 'the narrative structure of *In Patagonia* is so attenuated, the interpretative focus tends to fall on how seriously to read that quest' (Hulme 2002a: 226). In the main, scholars have seen the bizarre quest as parodic. The point is made most convincingly by Manfred Pfister, who figures the quest for the scrap of brontosaurus skin as a parody of Jason's quest for the Golden Fleece in the *Argonautica*. As Pfister puts it, there is a 'marked down-grading from the mythical heights of the Golden Fleece to a brontosaurus skin' – a down-grading 'continued, when it turns out, that the skin can't be that of a brontosaurus [. . .] but is that of a mylodon' (Pfister 1997: 256). Thus is the 'topos of questing [. . .] ironically deflated and emptied' (Pfister: 256). While for Pfister 'the hollowing out of the quest structure' is part of a 'postmodernizing thrust against all totalizing claims' (Pfister: 256), others have been more sceptical of the enterprise. Patrick Holland and Graham Huggan, for example, see the skin as an 'object lesson' not in parody but in the salience of 'hoaxes' in contemporary travel writing: 'the Mylodon skin is of doubtful authenticity; it seems much more than likely that it is an utter fake' (Holland and Huggan 1998: 13). Whether admired as postmodern irony or doubted as false, however, the assumption of the inauthenticity of the quest – aside from notable exceptions, such as that of W. G. Sebald (2005) – remains.

There is surely something in the reading of *In Patagonia* as a parody. Chatwin himself hedges his bet a little in suggesting the book is 'supposed to fall into the category or be a spoof of <u>Wonder Voyage</u>' (Chatwin 2010: 277; underlining in original), and the narrator himself describes the quest as a 'ridiculous journey' (Chatwin 1977: 194). But Chatwin's quest for a piece of brontosaurus is more than a straight spoof, hoax or conceit; it is not a Hitchcockian 'maguffin'. It is, after all, the story of a traveller who '*accomplished* the object of this ridiculous journey' (Chatwin 1977: 194; emphasis added). The quest for the piece of brontosaurus that was really a piece of mylodon is, it can be argued, as pivotal to Chatwin's aesthetic and ethic as Keats' Grecian Urn was to his – as open to interpretation, and as carefully wrought. What should we make of it?

The deftness with which Chatwin draws us into the story may be discovered by anyone who attempts to paraphrase it. For the subtlety with which fact and fiction, memory and imagination, are interwoven is one of poise and tone, rather than logic, rendering it impossible to 'straighten out' the story without changing the nexus of relations. Tempting then, to quote the three-page chapter in its entirety, free from commentary; but the opening may suffice to show the composure and gathered quiet with which Chatwin finds what T. S. Eliot, in 'Burnt Norton', called 'the still point of the turning world', where 'past and future are gathered' (Eliot 1961: 16–19):

> In my grandmother's dining room was a glass-fronted cabinet and in the cabinet a piece of skin. It was a small piece only, but thick and leathery, with strands of coarse, reddish hair. It was stuck to a card with a rusty pin. On the card was some writing in faded black ink, but I was too young then to read.
> 'What's that?'
> 'A piece of brontosaurus.'
> My mother knew the names of two prehistoric animals, the brontosaurus and the mammoth. She knew it was not a mammoth. Mammoths came from Siberia.
> The brontosaurus, I learned, was an animal that had drowned in the Flood, being too big for Noah to ship aboard the Ark. I pictured a shaggy lumbering creature with claws and fangs and a malicious green light in its eyes. Sometimes the brontosaurus would crash through the bedroom wall and wake me from my sleep.
> This particular brontosaurus had lived in Patagonia [...] (Chatwin 1977: 1)

Intimate, decided but undemanding, the voice has an almost parenthetical, confidential quality. It requires no agreement; it only invites a listener. The Russian doll of the first sentence sets out rather like a children's story, drawing us in; syntactically and epistemologically letting us in on a secret. Indeed, enchantments, wonders, miracles, things that teeter between astonishing reality and incredible fabrication, portals to other worlds – all are common to both fairy tale and the traveller's tale. Both are written, or spoken, from a position of privileged experience and knowledge. It turns out, of course, that the 'piece of brontosaurus' was in fact a scrap of skin from the extinct *Mylodon Listai*, or Giant

Sloth. The grandmother's cousin, Charley Milward the Sailor, had found the 'skin and bones preserved by the cold, dryness and salt, in a cave on Last Hope Sound in Chilean Patagonia'. Such is the version 'less romantic' but with the 'merit of being true' (1977: 3). But the 'beast of the imagination' survives the new version of the truth. Just as it is the 'brontosaurus' that comes crashing through the wall at night in the boy's dreams (1977: 1), so it is a piece of brontosaurus of which Chatwin writes: 'Never in my life have I wanted anything as I wanted that piece of skin' (1977: 2). And when the Mylodon Cave at Last Hope Sound is finally reached: 'I tried to picture the cave with sloths in it, but I could not erase the fanged monster I associate with a blacked-out bedroom in wartime England' (1977: 194). The childhood fantasy survives the inconvenience of fact. *Pace* the Weberian idea that disenchantment results from scientific rationalisation, the spell of wonder remains, regardless of the explanation.

What kind of object is it that the child is drawn towards? What is the 'object' of the quest? It is not an aesthetic object in any standard sense: it was not made; it is not 'beautiful'; it is more of a grotesque (it might provoke disgust at the same time as curiosity). The piece of brontosaurus is – to borrow a phrase from Chatwin's biographer – an 'all-suggestive fragment' (Shakespeare 1999: 4); it requires that the creature in its wholeness be imagined from the fragment. And it is a relic of a former time, indicative of a 'fascination with provenance and the origin of things' (1999: 4). It is dislocated in form, space and time. The object is older than written history – it is prehistorical – and the prehistorical is echoed in the personal, in that it is a memory of a pre-literary time in the narrator's life: 'I was too young then to read' (Chatwin 1977: 1). The object is organic, but it is dead, and more than that, it is a fossil: a record of extinct life. In the narrator's personal mythology, it is a remnant of 'an animal that had drowned in the Flood, being too big for Noah to ship aboard the Ark' (1977: 1). Thus, natural history and myth, fact and fiction, are folded into each other to produce an imaginary creature: the skin is experienced and desired as something it is not: as a piece of brontosaurus rather than a piece of mylodon. The justification provided for its being a brontosaurus is a carefully weighted send-up of logical reasoning, in which certain facts add up to fabulation: it cannot be a mammoth, and therefore must be a brontosaurus, because it is not from Siberia (1977: 1). In both its fictional and factual form, however, it is a reminder that the world was once a very different place, and that entire species and ecosystems have risen and fallen. The child does not need to know of evolutionary theory to experience the skin as evidence of what the natural historian George Gaylord Simpson noted to be the inheritance of Darwin: an idea that 'in the mists of time loom antique monsters' (Simpson 1982: 60). The object is also inextricably bound up with another story of a more recent past: it is the talismanic vehicle of the story of a distant ancestor, the narrator's first cousin twice removed: Charley Milward the Sailor, finder and sender of the object.

This much (at least) is available to the child who 'was too young then to read' (Chatwin 1977: 1). The pre-literary source of the desire for the piece of brontosaurus is worth bearing in mind when we begin to consider the more historical and psychological significances that may be attributed to a search for what is, in fact, a piece of *Mylodon Listai*. But the animal has deep historical significance, too. In one of the few scholarly engagements with the specificity of the object, Peter Hulme has shown that at the height of imperialist science in the Victorian era, the giant sloth

> was *the* emblem of Patagonia, congruent with its surviving indigenous population in that both offered keys to the prehistoric past, but also symbolic of that population's lumbering slowness: behind the times, at the back of history, the last in the human race. That population's subsequent genocide owed much to the scientific picture of Patagonia which had that sloth as its central image. (Hulme 2002a: 226; emphasis in original)

We might take this association as evidence that Chatwin's work resuscitates Victorian imperialism. But the quest itself is clearly more related to a desire to recover and pay tribute to that which was lost, and to a sense of the magnitude of all else that is forgotten, than to the symbolic economy of those who brought about the loss. In W. G. Sebald's meditation on Chatwin's work, 'The Mystery of the Red-Brown Skin' (Sebald 2005: 179–87), he links the piece of brontosaurus with Honoré de Balzac's *The Wild Ass's Skin* (1977), in particular the paragraphs concerning the geological treatises of Georges Cuvier. What Balzac writes of Cuvier might also be said of Chatwin: he 'calls aeons back into being without pronouncing the abracadabra of magic; he digs out a fragment of gypsum, descries a footprint in it, and cries out: "Behold!" And suddenly marble turns into animals, dead things live anew and lost worlds are unfolded before us!' (Balzac 1977: 41). This points towards a vital difference between Chatwin's 'hunt for a strange animal in a remote land' and the paradigm of such hunts, which Chatwin had described in 'The Nomadic Alternative' as one in which the 'hero fights and kills the monster, rewards himself with the treasure and a bride, returns home to the jubilant acclamations of his proud parents and people and they all live happily ever after' (Chatwin G.1 'The Nomadic Alternative': 36–7). Chatwin's quest is for a fossil, a remnant of a beast that not only died long ago, but that belongs to an extinct species. The monster poses no threat; and Chatwin's quest is not to kill. As George Gaylord Simpson writes in his natural-historical memoir *Attending Marvels*: 'The fossil hunter does not kill; he resurrects' (Simpson 1982: 82). It is in this sense, too, that Chatwin's search for a replacement piece of brontosaurus may be understood as performing the 'resurrection' of the quest.

Part of what is resurrected by the quest for the object as replacement is also the personal, more libidinal memory. The object recalls any number of Freudian psychoanalytical models, but most pertinently, as Sebald, again, suggests, 'there is no mistaking the fetishistic character of the sloth relic. Entirely without value in itself, it inflamed and satisfied the lover's illicit fantasy' (Sebald 2005: 184). That Chatwin's 'fleece' has a fetishistic quality was something he himself, in his first draft, had considered including within the book:

> I cannot say if my impulse to cling to a piece of antediluvian fluff was an atavistic ~~memory~~ nostalgia ~~to cling to~~ for the pelt of a hairy ancestor. And it is unclear if my mother was present when I first saw the piece of brontosaurus. But throughout my childhood I ~~longed~~ yearned for it with a persistent longing. (Chatwin I.6 'First draft': 6)

A little further in, drawing on considerable research, Chatwin notes that the 'Viennese doctor' would likely 'point to an atavistic impulse, in an insecure child' (I.6 'First draft': 6). It is significant in this regard that the fossil is a piece of skin: in Chatwin's opening, the organ of touch is something the child can see but cannot touch behind the glass of the cabinet: looking is a substitute for touching. The 'Viennese' element of the skin – does the small hairy patch of skin have an almost genital connotation? – is suggested more strongly when, upon reaching the object of his quest, the Mylodon Cave in Last Hope Sound, the narrator considers spending the night in the cave (itself susceptible to innuendo), but hears the singing of a troop of nuns and is removed by none other than a mother superior (Chatwin 1977: 194). The scene – almost so available to sexual innuendo that it seems a red herring – is echoed in *The Songlines*, when Chatwin's narrator recalls that his 'most treasured possession' as a child was a 'conch shell called Mona': 'I would ram my face against her sheeny pink vulva' and pray that 'a beautiful blond young lady would suddenly spew forth' (2005: 7). Again, what is remarkable is the recovery or endurance of desire and memory.

Here is the passage in which the quest is ostensibly consummated. It is an example, too, of the way humour in Chatwin's writing so often arises as the absurd drily observed, as lunacy looked on through reversed binoculars:

I tried to picture the cave with sloths in it, but I could not erase the fanged monster I associate with a blacked-out bedroom in wartime England. The floor was covered with turds, sloth turds, outsize black leathery turds, full of ill-digested grass, that looked as if they had been shat last week.

I groped in the holes left by Albert Konrad's dynamiting, looking for another piece of skin. I found nothing.

'Well,' I thought, 'if there's no skin, at least there's a load of shit.'

And then, poking out of a section, I saw some strands of the coarse reddish hair I knew so well. I eased them out, slid them into an envelope and sat down, immensely pleased. I had accomplished the object of this ridiculous journey. And then I heard voices, women's voices, voices singing: 'María . . . María . . . María . . .'

Now I too had gone mad. (Chatwin 1977: 194)

The syntax very finely works up the comic sense of a vertiginous, intoxicating spiral into madness, finely poised against the impeccable, sober control of its presentation: the triplicate incantations of the 'turds, sloth turds, outsize black leathery turds' is echoed by the 'voices, women's voices, voices singing' and the 'María . . . María . . . María . . .'. And there is comic bathos in the ultimate moment of consummation, when the traveller, having 'accomplished the object of this ridiculous journey', sits down, 'immensely pleased'.

Did the real Bruce Chatwin really find a real piece of mylodon skin? Or is it, as Holland and Huggan suspect, an 'utter fake' (Holland and Huggan 1998: 13)? We have only a handful of mutually contradictory stories on which to decide whether Chatwin himself actually consummated the quest (one of Chatwin's hosts on his return suggested that Chatwin found only a 'ball of fossilised mylodon dung which he plonked on the tea-table' (Shakespeare 1999: 303)). 'This spurious quest ended,' Chatwin reminisced later, 'one stormy afternoon in 1976, when I sat at the back of the cave, after finding a few strands of mylodon hair and a lump of mylodon dung, which looked a bit like last week's horse (so much that my cleaning lady took exception to it and, the other day, chucked it out)' (Chatwin and Theroux 1992: 16). The question is: is this the right question? The stance of incredulity towards Chatwin's quest sounds remarkably like that identified by Daston and Park in arguing that '[i]f the Enlightenment had a physiognomy, it was the incredulous, ironic, and faintly patronizing smile of the savant or man of letters confronted with [. . .] a breach of *vraisemblance*' (Daston and Park 1998: 350). Yet it is through teasing the line between fact and fiction that *In Patagonia* comes into view as a wonder voyage, the 'root of the whole idea' of which, as Jacobs writes, is 'scepticism with regard to travelers' tales and sailors' yarns' (Jacobs and Batten 2008: 215). *In Patagonia* lives through its miraculous – and subversive – unlikeliness, which prompted Jean-François Fogel's finely appreciative remark: 'No one goes on such a journey' (qtd Shakespeare 1999: 318).

What is most important about the 'piece of brontosaurus' as an object for a quest is its workings as a portal into an imaginary world – or rather, into the memory of imagining the world as it was but can never be seen again. When Robert Taylor wrote in the *Boston Globe* that the book 'celebrates the recovery of something inspiring memory, as if Proust could in fact taste his madeleine', Chatwin responded: '*ENFIN* somebody's got the point' (qtd Shakespeare 1999: 353). And as with Proust's madeleine – the piece of brontosaurus' closest literary ancestor – it is what the object releases that counts. Unlike Proust's madeleine, the desire for a replacement piece of brontosaurus is not an accidental, involuntary memory: the point about involuntary memory being precisely that it is a question of chance and thus beyond questing (Proust 1997: 17). Chatwin's quest is for an object which is identified with the memory of an experienced past in which an unexperienced past was imagined. It suggests a need, cultural and historical as well as psychological, to attend to those pasts which lie dormant in us, and which – for all the questing – remain, and can only remain, enigmatic. Chatwin may have been thinking of the last chapter of W. H. Hudson's *Idle Days in Patagonia*, and a paragraph that sounds uncannily akin to Proust's *mémoire involuntaire*:

> when, after a long interval a forgotten odor, once familiar and associated intimately with the past, is again encountered, the sudden, unexpected recovery of a lost sensation affects us in some such way as the accidental discovery of a store of gold, hidden away by ourselves in some past period of our life and forgotten; or as it would affect us to be met face to face by some dear friend, long absent and supposed to be dead. The suddenly recovered sensation is more to us for a moment than a mere sensation; it is like a recovery of the irrecoverable past. (Hudson 2006: 244)

Chatwin's piece of brontosaurus is ridiculous, comical, pointless and useless. It has none of the purpose of Jason's quest to secure his inheritance as King of Iolkos. It has none of the violence or glory of the quest to find and kill a monster. But if it parodies these ideologies of power and conquest, then it is the ideology of the Fleece, not that of the Piece of Brontosaurus, that is brought into question. Given that travel writing generally is so often associated with power and conquest, and given that Chatwin himself has so often been critiqued for nostalgia for imperialism, it is worth stressing how fundamentally the quest at the heart of *In Patagonia* celebrates the personal and idiosyncratic (the ridiculous), rather than serving any 'political' purpose; rather than questing for victory and power, it seeks to recover what has been lost or defeated. It is in thus reformulating the quest as a voyage of recovery and renewal in search of a fragment of an extinct creature bound up with an imaginary one that *In Patagonia* invites us to a sense of wonder; and it is as such that it is so emblematic a modern wonder voyage.

A literary *Wunderkammer*: travel, text and the collection

The foregoing reading of the quest and its quarry has necessarily involved sidestepping the feature of the book that most immediately strikes most commentators, and which itself goes some way to explaining the tendency to see the quest as a mere conceit. That is, the multitudinous variety that characterises the book and its reticence in terms of its means of transport from one chapter to the next: *In Patagonia* is a story about looking for one thing and finding a thousand-and-one other things. The myriad wonders do not detract from the quality of quest – a genuine obsession can weather any number of distractions, and the detours, in any case, often supplement and at most defer, rather than obstruct, the traveller's quest. But it does recast and relativise it. Just as the piece of brontosaurus was located in a cabinet of curiosities, so, in searching for a replacement, Chatwin places the quest within a literary *Wunderkammer*. These 'wonder chambers' or *Kunstkammern* (art chambers) are large cabinets in which collectors would store a wide range of curious objects gathered from around the world, and which experienced their heyday from the sixteenth to the eighteenth century. They can be seen as a precursor of the modern museum (Pomian 1990; Shelton 1994; Martels 1994: xiii), and they embody a number of facets of Chatwin's own thought and style, and *In Patagonia* in particular. Two areas are of immediate concern here. The first is the way the book itself resembles a *Wunderkammer*, the narrative cabinet in which Chatwin deposits (or distributes) the spoils of a collector's passion, bringing together a diverse and heterogeneous range of objects, stories and forms of writing. The second is the way that, in part through this multifaceted quality, the book itself is like a moveable object, and attempts to contain it seem like the literary historical equivalent of the idiosyncratic collector's arrangements.

The art critic Robert Hughes is among those to have observed that Chatwin's admiration for the cabinet of curiosities was 'a very important component of [his] imagination' (qtd Shakespeare 1999: 35). The function and ideology of such cabinets and their collections straddles the boundary between exoticist familiarisation and subversive defamiliarisation. As Anthony Alan Shelton argues, such cabinets 'expressed a visual image of the inclusiveness of the European view of the world and its facile ability to incorporate and domesticate potentially transgressive worlds and customs' (Shelton 1994: 203). This prompts the conclusion that the 'truly marvellous and extraordinary accomplishment of medieval thought was that it made marvellousness itself a category of the mundane' (1994: 203). Conversely, Steven Mullaney describes such cabinets as containing 'things on holiday, randomly juxtaposed and displaced from any proper context [. . .] Taken together, they compose a heteroclite order without hierarchy or degree, an order in which kings mingle with clowns' (qtd Shakespeare 1999: 35). We find the same tension in views of travel writing, in which, as Holland and Huggan have argued, the 'world of wonders is in one sense a world already known – one made available to readers "back home" through the comforting reiteration of familiar exotic myths' (Holland and Huggan 2000: 5). Conversely, Mark Cocker argues that the travel book is the form in which 'we discover all over again the newness of the world' (Cocker 1992: 260). The tension exists, too, in *In Patagonia*, which pulls in two directions: both drawing on the Renaissance sense of wonder in bringing things together, and in a more modern sense of seeing things fall apart in a kind of travellers' tale equivalent of the 'heap of broken images' of T. S. Eliot's *The Waste Land* (Eliot 1961: 51). The tension, which is analogous to that between settling and wandering, is lucidly described by Manfred Pfister:

> The process and the product of collecting involve both moving about and settling – wandering in search of the desired objects, and a safe place to store them. Or, to draw the meta-poetic conclusions from this: writing has to remain light and mobile, in the state of flux of an on-going open process and at the same time it cannot but stabilize into some *Gestalt* or enclosed structures. (Pfister 1996: 261)

The tension is, of course, irresolvable, either by Chatwin or by any maker of forms. Whichever tendency we stress, there is always the potential in any collection of objects, stories, or ideas, that they implicate other constellations of relations, just as an assortment, however apparently incongruous, can accrue its own logic. What is clear in the case of *In Patagonia* is that Chatwin had found in the travel narrative a form far better suited to his breadth of interest and lack of specialism than the rhetorical mode of 'The Nomadic Alternative'. As a literary form, the travel narrative shares with the cabinet of curiosities the capacity to accommodate the apparently incommensurate. The journey model provides – to borrow Darwin's insight into Humboldt's motive in adopting the travel narrative form once more – a 'convenient vehicle for miscellaneous discussions' (qtd Nicolson 1995: xxvii). That is, a literary equivalent of the cabinet, an architecture which can accommodate a dizzyingly diverse, and potentially limitless, range of data. As we have seen, 'The Nomadic Alternative' had troubled Chatwin in part because his breadth of interests chafed against the requirement for a coherent rhetorical argument. And it seems clear that, in principle at least, Chatwin's attraction to the *Wunderkammer* was more closely aligned with its potential for defamiliarisation than domestification. Louis Aragon, writing in *Paris Peasant* (1994), might have written the following as a manifesto for Chatwin's own enterprise:

> Reality is the apparent absence of contradiction.
> The marvellous is the eruption of contradiction within the real.
>   Love is a state of confusion between the real and the marvellous. In this state, the contradictions of being seem *really* essential to being.
>   Wherever the marvellous is dispossessed, the abstract moves in.
> (Aragon 1994: 204–5; emphasis in original)

Chatwin, like Aragon, is instinctively opposed to those 'who divide the mind up into faculties' (1994: 205), and his method was one which, as Susannah Clapp writes, shows that he was 'keen to be hospitable to as many stories as possible in his first publication' (Clapp 1997: 32). The journey through 'Patagonia' serves as exhibition space as much as exhibit, providing a narrative momentum that allows for any number of digressions into other stories, past or present.

   The links between chapter and chapter, place and place – or absence thereof – is one of the features that most clearly distinguishes Chatwin's book from travel books of the time. The most obvious counterpart is Paul Theroux's *The Old Patagonian Express* (1979). Theroux's early, enthusiastic review of *In Patagonia* had expressed his wish to have heard more about the journey itself (Theroux 1977). It was a point he was to return to:

> My friend Bruce Chatwin had told me that he took the trip for *In Patagonia* after he'd read *The Great Railway Bazaar*. I had always wondered how he had travelled to Patagonia – he left that out of his narrative. He had written about being there, but I wanted to write about getting there. This thought was always in my mind, and it made me meticulous about my own trip. I knew that as soon as I got to Patagonia I would just look around and then go home. Mine was to be the ultimate book about getting there. (Theroux 2008: vii–viii)

The distinction between 'being there' and 'getting there', Theroux finds, also extends to the journeying within Patagonia itself:

I used to look for links between the chapters, and between the conversations or pieces of geography. Why hadn't he put them in?

'Why do you think it matters?' he said to me.

'Because it is interesting,' I said. 'And because I think when you are writing a travel book you have to come clean.'

This made him laugh, and then he said something that I have always taken to be a pronouncement that was very near to being his motto. He said – he screeched – 'I don't believe in coming clean.' (qtd in Clapp 1997: 40)

One can, in fact, plot Chatwin's journey by pursuing the links between the chapters with relative ease (several writers, after all, have reproduced the journey as the basis for their own books (Sepúlveda 1989; Pilkington 1991; Hutton 1998). But there can be little doubt that *In Patagonia* does indeed contravene the expectations of a reader in the Theroux mould. Though Chatwin's response suggests the lack of clear links was incidental, his lack of interest in describing this dimension of the journey is crucial to the narrative form. As with the *Wunderkammer*, Chatwin's narrative assembles and juxtaposes, rather than explains and emplots, its units – be they places, stories, or objects. Throughout, the actual travelling is almost always described, if at all, with a single sentence, with very little ornament: 'I took the train to La Plata to see the best natural history museum in the world' (Chatwin 1977: 3); 'In the evening Bill drove me to Bahía Blanca' (1977: 5); 'I took the nightbus to Chubut Valley' (1977: 10). With a very few exceptions, these are almost as comprehensive as the book gets in terms of its 'description of travel'. Even walking – the god of which is the only one the narrator professes to follow (1977: 16) – is not described in much depth outside of the single chapter mentioned earlier (1977: 66).

We thus encounter *In Patagonia* as a series of stills; movement is evoked according to the same principle as the rapid succession of images that make up the cinematic illusion. They are essentially short stories – Cartier-Bresson-style snapshots (cf. Shakespeare 2003: xxi) – each of which is a telling fragment of the life journey of the individual concerned, and which cannot be considered as 'discrete': they lead into and out of other stories. We are presented with a kind of *milieu* of strangers, their community formed by a travelling observer only, rather than through acquaintance. We are introduced to so many people, so many stories; then we move on. Any desire for narrative continuity, or for familiarisation, is frustrated. In reading Chatwin, then, we must extend our sympathies in rapidly changing directions, and always with a sense that each intricate miniature is part of a larger, potentially infinite, collection. It creates a sense of the interconnection, the implicatedness, of apparently disparate people, places and times. And this carries over into the autobiographical narrative, too: we are given an individual composed only of these sequential encounters. Our narrator does not 'develop'. Amid the dazzlement there is the startlingly calm evenness of the narrator's perceptions and voice.

The most audacious leap is that between the first and the second chapters. There is no mediation between the reminiscence about the traveller's childhood – which implies, rather than directly states, the reasons why a voyage to Patagonia has long preoccupied the teller of the tale – and the account of the adult traveller being in Buenos Aires. The narrative journey from the grandmother's house in England and the Cold War childhood, to Buenos Aires in the 1970s, could have had any number of itineraries en route. We are in a reminiscence about child-hood in England after the Second World War, aware that Patagonia had been 'held in reserve' (1977: 3), and then – more as if by magic than by boat or plane – we are transported instantaneously not only across the Atlantic and most of South America but across an unspecified number of years, to Buenos Aires, where it was 'lovely summery weather' (1977: 4). As in the enchantments of fairy tale, the narrative makes use of the prerogative recorded in the Sicilian storytelling formula noted in Italo Calvino's *Six Memos for the Next Millennium*: '"*lu cuntu nun mette tempu*" (time takes no time in a story)' (Calvino 1996: 35).

As Nicholas Murray notes, one of Chatwin's characteristic devices was his reliance on the 'corroborative anecdote or observation' (Murray 1993: 47). What Malina Stefanovska writes of Saint-Simon in her elu-cidation of the tension in the anecdote between the exemplary and the singular, we might also say of Chatwin:

> A passion for accumulating eccentric, anomalous, and strange examples, or just for capturing a striking detail, drives many of his anecdotes. When inter-preted as evidence, his anecdotes point to a meaning [. . .] But, as curiosities, they gain in autonomy and acquire the status of a collectable. They no longer point to a precise (ideological) category, but to the entire collection, a collec-tion that exemplifies only the endless diversity of humankind and the real. (Stefanovska 2009: 26)

The anecdote, Stefanovska continues – and again the relevance to Chatwin is clear – thus 'has something unsettling about it', remaining 'heterogeneous to the traditional purpose of history': their appeal can be attributed to 'their exemplary singularity, which points to meaning while negating it' (2009: 26–7). Anecdotes are portable; they can be redeployed, re-emplotted. There is, for example, the story of the tramp. In 'The Nomadic Alternative', Chatwin writes of a tramp whom he bought lunch, and who after talking 'incoherently' said, 'suddenly, without prompting': 'I'm like the Arctic Tern, Guv'nor. That's a bird, a beautiful white bird, what flies to the North Pole to the South Pole and back again. *It's like the tides was pulling gradually to highway*' (Chatwin G.1 'Nomadic Alternative': 22; emphasised sentence added to typescript in blue ink). The tale is a four-times-told one: in addition to this version, we find it in Chatwin's notes (G.1 'Research'); in the *Vogue* article that was (against Chatwin's wishes) entitled 'It's a Nomad Nomad Nomad World' (1997: 100–8); and in *The Songlines* (2005: 273–6).

The structural interconnection of the chapters, however, does follow scrupulous compositional concerns. And it tends to be compositional and thematic concerns, as much as the traveller's itinerary, that provide the locomotion from one chapter to the next. Manfred Pfister suggests that 'Chatwin employs two basic structural devices here: concatenation and embedding': where concatenation 'juxtaposes stories', embedding 'creates a hierarchy of them, a mise en abîme of subordinate stories reflecting upon the superordinate story of stories [. . .] Again, vistas of an infinity of stories are opened up, this time in the form of an infinite regress of recursive embedding, of stories within stories within stories *usque ad infinitum*' (Pfister 1996: 257). Within these overarching structural devices, it is worth noting that both between neighbouring chapters and across the larger canvas of the book, thematic echoes and motifs create patterns of association and interaction that sometimes nuance the more overt meaning of the episodes. Chapters 2 and 3, for example, are not only linked as points on an itinerary, but thematically: by *machismo*. In Chapter 2, Ernesto Guevara is described by a 'lady novelist' as 'very *macho* [. . .] like most Argentine boys' (Chatwin 1977: 5). Immediately afterwards, in Chapter 3, we encounter 'two everyday victims of *machismo*, a thin woman with a black eye and a sickly teenage girl clinging to her dress', opposite whom sits a boy with knife-blade patterns on his shirt (1977: 5). The references to a 'lady novelist', and the quip – 'trust a Frenchman [. . .] to see through all the cant about gaucho' (1977: 4) – read rather differently in isolation than when set off, immediately, against an encounter read as an instance of chauvinism and national stereotyping. As so often, the specific passage or object is illuminated from various angles, and, like an object in a cabinet of curiosities, takes on a different set of potential meanings in its different places.

This is as much as to say that Chatwin was a writer intensely concerned with, as well as often dogged by, questions of form. Any inventory of the forms taken by the six books Chatwin published in his lifetime tells a story of formal restlessness of a piece with his geographical travels. His output tends to be split up into different categories in English-language bookshops, with *In Patagonia*, *The Songlines* and *What Am I Doing*

Here in the Travel section, and *The Viceroy of Ouidah*, *On the Black Hill* and *Utz* in the Fiction section – although the publishers classify only *In Patagonia* and *What Am I Doing Here* as Travel, and the rest as Fiction. According to Francis Wyndham, Chatwin's editor at *The Sunday Times*, Chatwin had been delighted when Rebecca West commented on *In Patagonia* that the 'photographs were so good there was no need for a single word of the text' and reported that Chatwin had indeed intended to exhibit his photographs (Chatwin 1993: 10). An undated proposal among Chatwin's miscellaneous writings envisages a book – which in theme and method anticipates aspects of Sebald's work – to be called *On the Silk Road*, which would 'take the form of a travel diary with diversions' to be used 'as a vehicle for my photographs' [. . .] alongside 'some taken from Persian and Indian miniatures such as the Babur-Nama; also with 19th–20th Century photographs' (B 'On the Silk Road': no pagination).

That *In Patagonia* itself resists classification, and tends to seem like a curiosity in whatever category we place it, is an intrinsic feature of Chatwin's work in the individual books and in sum: a formal expression of Chatwin's restlessness and his resistance to the coercive potential of categorical delimitations, and his openness to alternative points of view. Yet if there is cause to see *In Patagonia*, in one aspect, as the literary equivalent of a cabinet of curiosities, as well as a curiosity in itself, then to assess how this operates in its ethical as well as its aesthetical point of view, we might look to Chatwin's own remarks concerning the only other writer whose work he defines as a '"Wonder Voyage"' ('quite simply a book of marvels'): Sybille Bedford, with *A Visit to Don Otavio: A Traveller's Tale from Mexico* (Bedford 1990: 12). Bedford, Chatwin writes – and we can say the same of his own book of marvels – 'never moralises or scores a political point. What she does convey – here and in all her novels – is that everything is problematic; and that the human condition consists of millions and millions of people being tossed up and down the earth, trying vainly to connect but somehow being prevented from doing so' (Bedford 1990: 12).

A '*livre simultané*': a contemporary voice

Chatwin draws the first item in his literary *Wunderkammer* – his epigraph – from Blaise Cendrars' poem *Prose du Transsibérien et de la petite Jehanne de France*:

> *Il n'y a plus la Patagonie, la Patagonie,*
> *qui convienne à mon immense tristesse* [. . .]

One source of the 'immense sadness' to which only Patagonia remains equal, in Chatwin's book as in Cendrars', is linked to the consciousness of the simultaneity of heres and elsewheres, nows and thens, for which Cendrars found an objective correlative in the form of what he described as *'le Premier Livre Simultane'* (Cendrars 2001: i). *Prose du Transsibérien* was a 'simultaneous book', firstly, in that it was first published in a collaborative venture with the painter Sonia Delaunay, in which Cendrars' entire poem was reproduced vertically on a two-metre high 'book' alongside Delaunay's illustrations in such a way as to allow that the whole, and the two media, could be experienced simultaneously. The simultaneity of form, however, expressed a parallel preoccupation with an experience of simultaneity derived from, or made more pronounced by, the experience of travel:

> The rails' tracks constitute a new geometry
> SYRACUSE
> ARCHIMEDES
>   & the soldiers who cut his throat
>   & the galleys
>   & the vessels
> & the extraordinary machines that he invented
>   & all the carnage
>   Ancient history
>   Modern history
>   Whirlwinds
>   Shipwrecks
> Even the loss of the Titanic which I read about in the paper
> So many associations that I can't find a way to include in my verse
> For I'm still a truly lousy poet
> For the world overwhelms me
> For I've omitted to get insurance against accidents on railways
> For I've no idea how to see it through to the end
> And am afraid. (2001: no pagination)

The idea of there being 'so many associations that I can't find a way to include in my verse' chimes with Chatwin's project. As we have seen, the ninety-seven chapters amass an astounding range of phenomena. One of the ways in which its literary form takes shape – one of the elements which makes it a specifically modern wonder voyage – is in its thematic and formal response to what James Buzard calls the 'meanwhile problem' (1998). This is the issue, discussed in Part I, Chapter 3, of what Peter Fritzsche has described as the 'dramatic reorganization of modern time and space' following the diaspora of the French Revolution, and which has accelerated and diversified ever since, by which 'contemporaries felt themselves *contemporaries*, as occupants of a common time zone'

(Fritzsche 2004: 9–10; emphasis in original). A second issue concerns the relationship of the narrative voice to its own specific contemporary moment in history, political as well as literary, and that most frequently levelled critique: the charge of nostalgia and closedness to the political realities of Patagonia. The question, then, is of the ways in which Chatwin's wonder voyage may or may not – in the different senses of this word – be 'dated' in late modernity.

Chatwin, as strikingly as Cendrars, creates in *In Patagonia* a kind of '*livre simultane*' – a kind of writing alert to the potential to make connections across any spatial distance via narrative. Consider the following passage:

> At the precise moment that Darwin and Fitzroy were settling down to their narratives, a copy of Captain Weddell's book turned up in Richmond, Virginia, and lay on the desk of the Editor of the Southern Literary Messenger, Edgar Allan Poe, who was writing a different kind of narrative. Poe, like Coleridge, whom he idolized, was another night-wandering man, obsessed by the Far South and by voyages of annihilation and rebirth – an enthusiasm he would pass on to Baudelaire. He had recently become acquainted with the theory of J.C. Symmes, an ex-cavalry officer from St. Louis, who claimed in 1818 that both Poles were hollow and temperate. (Chatwin 1977: 130)

Crucial here in the passage is the opening phrase: 'At the precise moment . . .'. In addition to the role of direct influence (Coleridge on Poe, Poe on Baudelaire) and similarity, there is the category of simultaneity. Many of Chatwin's subclausal points, many of his new chapters, could logically be preceded by the word 'incidentally', or 'coincidentally'. It requires that the narrator be conscious of two places at once, not necessarily inhabiting either. It allows leaps across time, too: 'About the time of Hudson's visit, the Río Negro was the northern frontier of an unusual kingdom which still maintains a court in exile in Paris' (1977: 15); and from here, one hundred years forward in time, to a November afternoon in Paris when Chatwin met a descendant of the self-appointed first and last king of Patagonia and Araucanie, long before Chatwin himself set off on the Patagonian journey we are ostensibly reading about. By the time we finish this story, it is six pages later, and we return without mediating emplotment to 'I left Río Negro and went on south to Port Madryn' (1977: 21). A 'November afternoon' in an unspecified year in Paris was part of the experience of Río Negro. Río Negro was part of that afternoon. There is a kind of spatial and temporal simultaneity at work, or potentially at work, at all times.

Nicholas Shakespeare has made the observation that although Chatwin 'hated computers almost as much as he did the combustion engine [. . .]

he was in a sense a precursor of the Internet age: a connective super-highway without boundaries, with instant access to different cultures' (Shakespeare 1999: 542). The same can be said of Chatwin's narrative form itself. We often think of narrative mimesis as indexical: that is, we see language and narrative as indexically representing or imitating the action it directly describes. But perhaps mimesis can also operate analogously, or performatively: not in terms of the form's indexical representation of its immediate contents, but in the analogous relationship between its modes of connecting the units of language and the modes of connection in contemporary cultural contexts. The narrative form of the passages cited above, and more generally of the overall interconnectedness that is formally thematised throughout, might be thought of as 'mimetic' in its narrative configuration of a textual world analogous to an increasingly interconnected world in historical and cultural terms. Chatwin's narrative form may be understood in the terms offered by Jerome Bruner in 'The Narrative Construction of Reality' (1991), in claiming that all narrative forms are not only 'representations of social ontology, they are also invitations to a particular style of epistemology' which reflect not only 'the content of imagination but its modus operandi [. . .] providing a guide for using mind' (Bruner 1991: 15) in the context of specific histori-cal circumstances. Chatwin may well have drawn the idea for this nar-rative technique from the logic of the *Wunderkammer* we have already considered. But the world resembles this art more ubiquitously now, and the way in which things are connected here bears a certain resemblance to the way in which internet search engines can yield collections in order of 'the most relevant first' according to (sometimes) coincidental, even apparently bizarre, overlaps. It is a kind of thinking characterised by openness and by relations not governed by explanatory or rhetorical affiliations; and it always implies the possibility of additional intercon-nections and affinities. Even in its most densely intertextual, deeply erudite qualities, knowledge is thus always exposed in Chatwin's writing to its open side: to the wonder that is a kind of unknowing. As a modern wonder voyage, Chatwin's sense of simultaneity thus represents a revi-sion of one of the features that has often been found to be the source and expression of cultural centrism in texts from the 'the scriptural past or the unnarratable, unvisitable present' of the medieval *Wonders of the East* (Campbell 1988: 121) through to twentieth-century anthropology: the denial or suppression of the idea of coevalness, of a shared world, that Johannes Fabian finds at the heart of ethnographic othering in *Time and the Other: How Anthropology Makes Its Object* ([1983] 2002).

If the simultaneity above is that of consciousness hovering over geo-graphically and temporally separated moments, it has a counterpart in

Chatwin's talent for distraction by the unpredicted in the more immediate contemporary environment. This registers in the way he writes in his notebooks. As Chatwin conducted research into Milward's history in Patagonia, the single word '*Interesting!*' interrupts his work in the margins of his notes (Chatwin I.3 'Patagonia Notebook 1': 9). A few pages on, he makes notes on the incident that caught his attention, in ways that are intriguing in their method:

> Jose Mansilla   barber late seventies   slid off the barber's chair   swivelled to the left   well preserved man   thick steel grey hair   though he had come from Chiloe ---------------------------- Indian blood [illegible] Chiloe, wore a clipped moustache. Eyes of a man who had seen horror. Fastidious in habits. Rose early. Cleaned street pebbles of footpath. House washed a pale blue modern style   tin plates nailed over & [illegible]. Barber shop tidy – pack wood cabinet
> (I.3 'Patagonia Notebook 1': 14)

Chatwin edges around his object – and the story seems like an object here – picking up its characteristics in a manner akin to his object descriptions in catalogue entries when he was at Sotheby's (cf. Clapp 1997: 89). It is largely free of punctuation at this stage. The indeterminate space seems a record of alert, undirected patience, waiting for impressions to form, allowing the story's details to reveal themselves. It is as if Chatwin is avoiding prescribing a grammar on their relations; not allowing a grammar to guide his line of thought. True, there is the influence of Hemingway, both in the short 'sentences' that are not quite complete, and in the kind of details Chatwin selects (Chatwin had *In Our Time* with him on the journey (Shakespeare 2003: xxi)). And the story emerging here, the most Hemingway-esque in the book, could well have borrowed the title of another Hemingway story: it is a tragedy in 'A Clean, Well-Lighted Place' (1926). But we may remain alert to the allusiveness and still sense that the aim here is that of objectivity, of a shift of balance between the self and object of contemplation. It is reminiscent of Christopher Isherwood's 'A Berlin Diary (Autumn 1930)': 'I am a camera with its shutter open, quite passive, recording, not thinking. Recording the man shaving at the window opposite and the woman in the kimono washing her hair. Some day, all this will have to be developed, carefully printed, fixed' (Isherwood 1998: 9). What is remarkable is the endeavour of patience and the attentiveness to that which is on the periphery of the journey and its objectives.

One of the most persistent lines of critique taken against Chatwin concerns the idea of his place as part of 'a cult of the English gentleman' (Holland and Huggan 2000: esp. 36–40), as belonging to a cluster of writers 'still living in the nineteenth century' (Sugnet 1991: 5). Attendant on this, it is argued, is a nostalgia for the time of the British Empire coupled with a blindness to the present, protected by a dandyish distance which 'liberates him from moral judgement' (Holland and Huggan 2000: 38). Dressed like Hergé's Tintin on safari in the most widely distributed press photograph of the time, Chatwin certainly projected something of the image of the gentleman explorer, and it is not incomprehensible that he earned himself a cartoon in *Rolling Stone* magazine, standing in the Patagonian desert with a cup of tea in hand (Greil 1978). It is an image that attracts critique as much as curiosity. As Chris Moss writes in *A Cultural History of Patagonia* (2008):

> Chatwin's *In Patagonia* has [. . .] become canonical, unhealthily influential, the subject of academic scrutiny and literary hysteria, and an easy text for all those engaged in analyzing post-colonial discourse. But Chatwin's Patagonia also seems like a closed world, perhaps because the prose – for all its craft and carefully modulated elegance – suffers from a certain stylistic opacity. Somehow, his travelogue is beginning to seem dated and dusty, a remnant of the oddly Victorian 1970s. (Moss 2008: 278–9)

The interesting idea of the 'oddly Victorian 1970s' itself, we might think, casts doubt on the issue of whether or how *In Patagonia* can be described as 'dated': a voice pitched anachronistically from the first has an uneasy place in literary history. More importantly, one of the most subtle features of *In Patagonia* is that its site and date of writing are indeterminable. At no point is the narrator's 'current' location revealed: we do not know if *In Patagonia* is a 'letter home' or the recollection of an excursion after the traveller's return; we only know that the child grew up in wartime England, and when in the final chapter the traveller leaves Patagonia, where he is bound is not disclosed: there is no 'return'. And just as the site of writing is not revealed, nor is the controlling present of the narrative. There is enough in the narrative to reveal that the journey was made in the early 1970s (most specifically in the references to Perónism). But any knowledge of the present from which the narrator narrates can only be superimposed based on extratextual information: the date of publication, knowledge of the author biography and so on. The writing maintains a scrupulous placelessness and datelessness throughout. No historical markers disclose the time that has passed since the journey; there are no incursions from the intervening time between the journey and its narrative. In the entire book there is only one instance in which the narrator expresses what might be called an afterthought. This is its final line, approached as follows:

> In the morning, black petrels were slicing the swells and, through the mist, we saw chutes of water coming off the cliffs. The ladies' lingerie salesman from

Santiago had got out of hospital and was pacing the foredeck, chewing his lip and muttering poetry. There was a boy from the Falklands with a seal-skin hat and strange sharp teeth. ''Bout time the Argentines took us over,' he said. 'We're so bloody inbred.' And he laughed and pulled from his pocket a stone. 'Look what he gave me, a bloody stone!' As we came out into the Pacific, the businessman was still playing *La Mer*. Perhaps it was the only thing he could play. (Chatwin 1977: 199)

With this laconic speculation, Chatwin's modern wonder voyage unmoors into an unspecified present that can only ever be here and now. However much time passes the voice of *In Patagonia*, strictly speaking, remains contemporary. It invites us to wonder about the beautifully inconsequential detail of whether 'La Mer' is the only thing the businessman could play – and to wonder, too, how to wonder about such delicate details when, in the space of a single paragraph – and by extension, at any moment at all – there are such multitudes of lives and stories, known and unknown, all implicated one in the other. It does not bring us 'home'; and it provides no travel guide for navigating this cosmos of stories. It leaves us, instead, with a sense of their inexhaustibility, and the fragility and wonder of the worlds of experience they begin to imply. In closing, then, *In Patagonia*, as modern wonder voyage, leaves the world more open.

Coda: Patagonian afterlives

In Patagonia now has its own legacies, as varied and complex as its own fibre. On 15 August 1978, for example, alongside an unattributed review of *In Patagonia* illustrated with a photograph bearing the caption, 'THE RED DRAGON flies alongside the Argentine blue and white flag, their masts framing the monument erected in Trelew, Chubut, to the Welsh Patagonian pioneers', the *North American Welsh Newspaper* found an unusual opportunity for the following advertisement:

> **PATAGONIA**
> **UNUSUAL OPPORTUNITY!**
> For the first time a tour to
> the WELSH COLONY in
> PATAGONIA.
> 17 days of fun.
> [. . .]
> **BOOK EARLY!**
> (Chatwin I.8 'Reviews': no pagination)

Chatwin's book, perhaps more than most, has encouraged travellers to follow in his path for their '17 days of fun': it has been described as the Patagonian tourist's 'Bible' (Shakespeare 2003: xxiv). And Chatwin himself has become something of a cult figure (adored and debunked, as such figures inevitably and zealously are, in equal measure). Even those who have never read his work may encounter 'Bruce Chatwin' among a dynasty of names – including Vincent van Gogh, Pablo Picasso and Ernest Hemingway – whose patronage of 'Moleskine' qualifies the notebooks, according to the manufacturer, as 'legendary'. We find Chatwin's ideas, or versions of them, popping up in pop lyrics (Everything But the Girl's 1991 hit, 'One Place' (1991)) and his 'fiction' cited in works of sociology as scholarly source material (Sell 2006: 6). Bookshops, publishing houses and art galleries have been named after him or his works (a Paris publishing house named Utz; a travel bookshop in Berlin called Chatwins; and an art gallery, Songlines, in Amsterdam (Shakespeare 1999: 537). And as noted earlier, many followers have themselves been writers who have set about tracking Chatwin's footsteps as precisely as possible as the basis for their own books (Sepúlveda 1989, Pilkington 1991 and Hutton 1998).

In one sense, it could be said that Chatwin invites such followings, and thus might be held to account for their influence: indeed, the inextricability of writing in culture is stressed in the very texture of *In Patagonia*. But nothing in the book requires that a reader, or writer, follow the traveller to Last Hope Sound. It invites wonder, not verification; imagination, not emulation. Chatwin's fascination with Patagonia fomented over decades; it drew on a deeply personal and unrepeatable preoccupation; it was not an 'angle'. The literary example set in *In Patagonia* to writers is not to find an enigmatic place, but to identify the piece of brontosaurus – the enigma that is the writer's theme – and to create a form and voice equal to it. Closer to Chatwin than his footsteppers in the Patagonian library are the memoirs of the director of *Shoah*, Claude Lanzmann's *Le Lièvre de Patagonie*, in which 'the Patagonian hare' is the totem animal, sighted in Patagonia and brought startlingly to memory as its Polish cousin is seen passing under the wire fence of a concentration camp (Lanzmann 2009: 192). Closer to his literary forms and sensibility are not the writers of 'the new wave of British travel writing' (Graves 2003: 52), nor those delineated according to origins or destinations or commercial success, but those, as international as his own influences, who have found in voyaging a means of liberating literature from narrow conventions of form or focus: Roberto Calasso, Cees Nooteboom, Claudio Magris, V. S. Naipaul, W. G. Sebald, among others. Of English-born contemporaries, perhaps John Berger is most comparable in the independence and engagement of his fascination and forms. At a time of high conservatism in Britain – from the Winter of Discontent through to the end of the Thatcher years – Chatwin widened the horizons of literature. To read *In Patagonia* and imagine that another item in a finite catalogue has been spoken for, leaving the description of the world one more step closer to completion, one degree closer to total exhaustion, is deeply to misunderstand it. It is to maintain the conquistadorial desire for new territories that Chatwin's book so thoroughly undermines. And it is to inhabit, without attending to, the vast and fragile world that *In Patagonia*, as modern wonder voyage, lays before us.

Notes

1. Many of the reviews referred to in this chapter were consulted as cuttings in the Bruce Chatwin archive, held at the Bodleian Library, Oxford. The reviews are listed in the references according to author-date system, but where the review was consulted in the archive, the shelfmark is also provided. Where possible, page numbers have been provided, but in some instances these were not visible as a result of the cut.
2. Where references are to documents consulted in the Bruce Chatwin Catalogue of Papers at the Bodleian Library, Oxford, the in-text reference cites the document's number as listed in the Bodleian's Table of Contents for the papers (in the format A.1, B.2 and so on), and an abbreviated title ('Title') and page number where applicable. The documents referred to in the chapter are listed in the Bibliography with full titles and shelfmark locations under: Chatwin Archive. Oxford, Bodleian Library. Catalogue of Papers of (Charles) Bruce Chatwin, 1963–1989.

V. S. Naipaul and the 'gift of wonder':
The Enigma of Arrival (1987)

And sometimes Pangloss would say to Candide:
'All events form a chain in the best of all possible worlds. For in the end, if you had not been given a good kick up the backside and chased out of a beautiful castle for loving Miss Cunégonde, and if you hadn't been subjected to the Inquisition, and if you hadn't dealt the Baron a good blow with your sword, and if you hadn't lost all your sheep from that fine country of Eldorado, you wouldn't be here now eating citron and pistachio nuts.'
'That is well put,' replied Candide, 'but we must cultivate our garden.'
Voltaire, *Candide, or: Optimism* (2000: 78)

If Chatwin's *In Patagonia* had dazzled into literary consciousness an idea that 'Patagonia' as place and figurative possibility may still inspire, or require, wonder in the contemporary world, then V. S. Naipaul's *The Enigma of Arrival* is the late twentieth century's most exemplary and subtle monument to the idea that 'after Patagonia' there do indeed remain strange, distant and mysterious places in the world: 'unknown Wiltshire' (Naipaul 2002: 111), for example, deep in the archipelago of the British Isles. Before we even begin to explore *The Enigma of Arrival* as a text which both unflinchingly portrays and profoundly questions a sensibility of exhaustion, the author biographies that preface his books (amalgamated slightly here) might be enough to cast doubt on the idea of the completeness of the world picture that such a sensibility implicitly defers to:

V. S. Naipaul was born, of Indian ancestry, in Trinidad in 1932. He went to England on a scholarship in 1950. After four years at Oxford he began to write, and since then has followed no other profession. In 1960 he began to travel. He is the author of twenty-eight books of fiction and non-fiction and the recipient of numerous honours, including the Nobel Prize in 2001. He lives in Wiltshire, England.

It is a story of journeys – great personal upheavals with and against the tides of history – that cross the borders of geography, culture, social class

and literary form. In itself, it shows that the basic traveller's question –
where do you come from? – is, for Naipaul as for so many human beings
in a world characterised by global movement, extremely complex. The
division between 'home' and 'abroad' that infiltrates so much of the
literature and criticism of travel is almost impossible to maintain.

Placing Naipaul's work within this story is among the most volatile
controversies of contemporary literature, and to speak in terms of 'the
gift wonder' of a writer accused by his Trinidadian compatriot and
fellow Nobel laureate Derek Walcott of 'professional pessimism' (qtd
Winokur 1997: 121), and famously satirised as 'V. S. Nightfall' in his
poem 'The Spoiler's Return' (1981), is to enter into complicated and
emotive territory. Few writers are so decorated as Sir Vidia: a Nobel
laureate, he received a knighthood in Britain for services to literature
in 1990 and, among numerous other awards, was the first recipient, in
1993, of the David Cohen British Literature Prize, bestowed in honour
of a 'lifetime's achievement of a living British writer' (2002: sleeve
notes). But few writers have been so vilified – particularly regarding
the political implications inherent in a Trinidadian-born writer of
Indian descent being honoured as, and seen as identifying himself as, a
'British writer'. Naipaul's travels in particular have divided commentators between those who hail him as a prescient and uncompromising
'kerygmatic voice' (Hughes 1997: 209) – committed to truth, however
unpalatable – and those who condemn him as a 'postcolonial mandarin', as the sub-title of the most rigorous critique in this vein has it
(Nixon 1992). According to this view, Naipaul serves as an apologist
for empire, taking rhetorical advantage of his own displacement to
perpetuate Third World stereotypes in a bid to ingratiate himself to the
coloniser. But there is nevertheless something of a consensus between
admirers and critics. Appreciations and invectives alike often share in
a view of Naipaul as being, in the Berkeley-based poet (and admirer)
Robert Hass' formulation, 'the supreme writer of disenchantment' (qtd
in Winokur 1997: 118). 'Most Western writers,' Hass explains, 'grew
up in a rationalized world hungry for enchantment, whereas he grew
up in an enchanted world and was hungry for rationality' (1997: 118;
emphasis in original).

There is another side to this, however, and that is the central role of
wonder in Naipaul's work. Naipaul has proffered nothing so consistently
for the vocation of the writer as to 'awaken the sense of true wonder'
(Naipaul 2003c: 180). Again and again it is the ability to survey one's
experience and the world with wonder that Naipaul finds most decisively impressive in writers as diverse as R. K. Narayan, Thomas Mann,
Jacques Soustelle (Naipaul 1972: 12, 23, 192). And a 'lack of wonder,

the medieval attribute of a people who are still surrounded by wonders' (Naipaul 2003c: 141) is the object of Naipaul's critique in writers from Walter Ralegh to Mahatma Ghandi (Naipaul 1972: 58). The title of this chapter takes from Naipaul's critique of Ralegh's account of the New World, in *The Loss of El Dorado*: 'Believing in wonders, he had no gift of wonder' (Naipaul 2003b: 5). This 'gift of wonder' – of a piece with the 'disenchantment' of 'wonders' – is what envelops or brings into question the stages of experience and emotion, including the most painful or objectionable, that Naipaul's work records, recreates or dramatises.

It is in *The Enigma of Arrival* that this is given fullest and most nuanced literary expression. Marketed as fiction, it is widely regarded as the most autobiographical of Naipaul's books. The basic architecture of the story is that of the publisher's précis cited above: a first-person account of the journey of an emigrant from Trinidad to England, his becoming a writer, his settling in the rural county of Wiltshire. It is a reversal, but also a revision, of the traveller's tale of wonder: it approaches the former imperial centre as an exotic land, telling the story of a personal renaissance in the ruins of empire, but submits the processes of enchantment and disenchantment to profound analysis. It has been read as being, 'like many other West Indian arrivals in England, a narrative of disenchantment' (Hayward 2002: 44). And it has been read, in terms of its more immediate promptings, as part of a dying fall: the product of a period in the mid-1980s when, as Patrick French writes in his biography, Naipaul 'had a sense that his years of creation were behind him' (French 2008: 419). What has been overlooked in such characterisations of the book is that it speaks of recovery and the renewal of wonder. In its broadest narrative arc, it tells of passage from the 'dream of exhaustion' and the 'curse' of belatedness – the idea that the traveller 'had come into a world past its peak' (Naipaul 2002: 23) – to the 'new wonder' (2002: 387) that opens out in the closing pages, as in Proust's *In Search of Lost Time*, into the generation of the book itself. It is this 'new wonder' – all the more powerful for rejecting all Panglossian solace, for having passed through the griefs and disappointments of 'that fine county of El Dorado' – that is the abiding tone of the book. It is also this wonder that moves outwards, towards concern, to say with Voltaire's Candide, that 'we must cultivate our garden'.

'Unknown Wiltshire': travel the other way ('Jack's Garden')

Wiltshire, along with Hampshire and Devon, may be thought of by many who travel there – I quote from the 2009 edition of the *Rough Guide to*

England – as among the places in which '[t]he distant past is more tangible [. . .] than in any other part of England' (Andrews et al. 2009: 229). Among the notable features to which we may be guided are the many signs of earlier civilisations: Roman ruins and the Neolithic remainders in the sites of Avebury and, most famously, Stonehenge (2009: 229). *The Enigma of Arrival* certainly shares this sense of the presence of the distant past. The narrator speaks of his 'sense of antiquity' and 'feeling for the oldness of the earth' (Naipaul 2002: 19). But the book reverses and revises traditions of travel, including those implicit in this kind of guided tour. One of those revisions – in its reflexivity on form – is implicit in the book's subtitle, *A Novel in Five Sections*. The question of form raised by the designation 'novel' will receive consideration in the next section; but the five-section structure is also significant. It recalls the five-act drama of the ancients and the Elizabethans – exposition, rising action, climax, falling action, resolution – and patterns the book into a cyclical sequence which proceeds, as the narrator remarks of his own experience in the valley, 'like successive illuminations in a Book of Hours' (2002: 249). It is predominantly a dramatology of deepening understanding rather than developing plot, and though themes recur and deepen throughout, this narrative structure can thus provide a rough guide for the exemplary material on which to base the following thematic discussion.

Part One, 'Jack's Garden', may be thought of as the 'exposition': the part that sets the scene. The narrator introduces most of the central scenes, themes and characters to be developed, supplemented, or revised in the course of the narrative. The narrator tells of his arrival in a rented manor cottage in a valley in Wiltshire, where he experiences a 'second childhood of seeing and learning', a 'second life, so far away from the first' on the 'tropical island' of his birth (2002: 93), through to the end of this 'cycle' and his move to another part of the county (2002: 93). Time-frames are intricate and elusive. But – while mindful that we are not dealing with a directly literal account – we may calculate based on the autobiographical markers embedded throughout the book that the arrival is in winter in the early 1970s, the departure in the early 1980s (2002: 191). The renaissance is one of healing, of first finding solace in ruination and then of a navigation between the idea of decay and the idea of 'flux' (2002: 56). We catch glimpses of figures to be developed more fully later, including the traveller's landlord, the owner of the estate built on the spoils of empire (2002: 56). Thematically central, both to the chapter and to the book as a whole, however, is the Jack of 'Jack's Garden', whose 'garden in the midst of superseded things' (2002: 15) and the tending of it, whose way of living and dying, provides what could almost be called, in a narrative full of allusions to fairytale (not least in the name 'Jack'), the 'moral of the story'. But the arrival at Jack's story is itself one of the accomplishments of a reversal and revision of the traveller's tale of wonder. We begin, then, by considering the ways in which the tale of a traveller from a tropical island to the former imperial centre of England travels 'the other way', in 'unknown Wiltshire' (2002: 111), in terms both geographical and imaginative.

In a fine appreciation of Naipaul's work (in the Swedish Academy's press release for the announcement of Naipaul's being awarded the Nobel Prize), Horace Engdahl has written of how in *The Enigma of Arrival* Naipaul

> visits the reality of England like an anthropologist studying some hitherto unexplored native tribe deep in the jungle. With apparently short-sighted and random observations he creates an unrelenting image of the placid collapse of the old colonial ruling culture and the demise of European neighbourhoods. (Engdahl 2001: no pagination)

The south-west English landscape is a terrain as exotic and paradisical, in its way, as Robert Louis Stevenson's South Sea Islands: Stonehenge is as mysterious a relic as the Easter Island Moai; the strangeness of the region is not a matter of jungles but of the excitement of snow (Naipaul 2002: 3); and the indigenous population is susceptible to the kind of descriptive analysis one could find, with less eloquence or concern – and, of course, without irony – in many a European traveller's tale of the New World. Of some of the locals in the valley, the narrator comments:

> What terrors must there have been in town for them! How could people like these, without words to put to their emotions and passions, manage? They could, at best, only suffer dumbly. Their pains and humiliations would work themselves out in their characters alone: like evil spirits possessing a body, so that the body itself might appear innocent of what it did. (2002: 34–5)

It is in this ironising reversal that *The Enigma of Arrival* most directly brings into question both the rhetoric of exhaustion and the wholesale association of the traveller's tale with a colonialist inheritance. In its wintery opening scenes, in the anticipation of snow, it recalls a tradition of travelling the other way geographically, with echoes of Olaudah Equiano's *An Interesting Narrative* (1789), the eighteenth-century travelogue of an African former slave who becomes a gentleman in English society, and whose narrative is an early example of the transformation of the colonial 'centre' into a 'peripheral' land of exotic wonders. Equiano's arrival in England is followed immediately by his 'wonder at a fall of snow' (Equiano 2003: 62):

It was about the beginning of the spring 1757 when I arrived in England, and I was near twelve years old at the time. I was very much struck with the buildings and the pavement of the streets in Falmouth; and indeed any object I saw filled me with new surprise. One morning, when I got upon deck, I saw it covered with the snow that fell over-night: as I had never seen anything of the kind before, I thought it was salt; so I immediately ran down to the mate [. . .] He asked me if we had no such thing in my country? and I told him, No. I then asked him the use of it, and who made it; he told me a great man in the heavens, called God: but here again I was to all intents and purposes at a loss to understand him [. . .] (2003: 67)

What the sociologist Zygmunt Bauman has said of the traveller generally – that the stranger among strangers reveals 'the "mere historicality" of existence' (Bauman 1991: 59) – accrues pointedly unsettling value in this reversal of perspective, in which the indigenous mate's culture is revealed in its localism in the incomprehension of the traveller at a loss to understand the prospect of 'a great man in the heavens, called God'. This historicality is self-consciously, ironically thematised in Naipaul's narrative. The situation and its effects become its very substance:

> [A] man from another hemisphere, another background, coming to rest in middle life in the cottage of half neglected estate, an estate full of reminders of its Edwardian past, with few connections with the present. An oddity among the estates and I a further oddity in its grounds. I felt unanchored and strange. Everything I saw in those early days, as I took my surroundings in, everything I saw on my daily walk, beside the windbreak or along the wide grassy way, made that feeling more acute. I felt that my presence in that old valley was part of something like an upheaval, a change in the course of the history of the country. (Naipaul 2002: 14)

As John Thieme notes, 'private history functions as a microcosm of late colonial/post-colonial historical processes' (Thieme 1987: 1376). In placing the man from a tropical island at the centre of a traveller's tale of wonder in the former imperial centre, *The Enigma of Arrival* is thus, in one sense, as paradigmatic as Milton's making the story of the fall of Man the theme of an epic poem in *Paradise Lost*, or Wordsworth's placing his own development as a poet at the centre of an epic poem in *The Prelude*, or Joyce's casting of an advertising canvasser as the hero of a modern Odyssey in *Ulysses* – or, for that matter, Naipaul's own placement of an outcast of the Trinidadian islands as the hero of a tragi-comic, classical, nineteenth-century-style epic novel, in *A House for Mr Biswas* (Naipaul 1961). But its subtlety, and its wonder, lies in the way it brings into question the exoticism and romanticism implicit in this ironic reversal, in its revision of the basic tenets of the traveller's encounter.

The opening paragraph contains in embryo several of the processes and techniques, syntactical and thematic, that will be developed and deepened through the narrative: perception, deception, revision and the role of literary prefiguration in the traveller's experience. It establishes, too, the strange tone of meditative retrospective clarity, of illusion apprehended with a lucidity that is itself implicitly relativised:

> For the first four days it rained. I could hardly see where I was. Then it stopped raining and beyond the lawn and outbuildings in front of my cottage I saw fields with stripped trees on the boundaries of each field; and far away, depending on the light, glints of the little river, glints which sometimes appeared, oddly, to be above the level of the land. (Naipaul 2002: 3)

As a traveller's tale, *The Enigma of Arrival* begins, then, not with a claim to the authority of the eye witness, but with something like its opposite: the observation that the traveller had been 'hardly able to see' where he was. The first thing the narrator remembers seeing was an illusion – the river appeared, falsely, to be above the level of the land. A series of carefully deployed, effective because strictly unnecessary repetitions, each syntactically closer than the last, prepare the way for the assessments and reassessments that will form much of the substance of the book, in which a thing or word resurfaces throughout the text, at different places, considered in different lights – 'rained' is echoed in 'raining', 'field' in 'fields', 'glints' in its repetition – in a kind of spooling process of syntactical retention, which then creates a structural echo between the respective repetitions themselves. It contributes to a steadiness in the voice: half measured, controlled and precise; half almost dreamlike and incantatory. We are being alerted to the illusory in a tone that is itself half-mesmeric, as if we are being lulled and awoken at the same time. The narrator speaks – and it is to what he has 'said' in the narrative, rather than what he 'wrote' that the narrator always refers – like a man trying to describe, with the utmost alertness and precision, a vivid but vague dream. The book, then, can be understood as an attempt to reach the fifth day, as it were, of vision – of seeing where the traveller was, and understanding what it was that he saw, or did not see, and the processes by which this encounter occurred.

The traveller arrives in an environment very different from that of his previous knowledge and the environment is thus, in a sense, opaque: 'I saw what I saw very clearly. But I didn't know what I was looking at. I had nothing to fit it into' (2002: 5). Does understanding ever exist except as a form of connection between a perception and an idea? A *re*vision, a *re*making, is implicit in the very word *re*cognise; and understanding – articulate understanding at least – consists in making connections, in conceptualisations. Thus it is only later, 'when the land had more meaning', that the traveller was 'able to think of the flat wet fields with the ditches as "water meadows", and the low smooth hills in the background, beyond the river, as "downs"' (2002: 3). Yet the necessity of foreknowledge as a vehicle of recognition has a counterpart, in that knowledge prefigures and reconfigures experience. The first proper name in the book, in the second paragraph, belies a horizon of expectations that is second-guessed in the dashing: 'The river was called the Avon; not the one connected with Shakespeare' (2002: 3). The encounter with the river, then, is between the options of whether it is, or is not, the river associated with that most famous English writer. As the narrative progresses it develops this idea of an environment perceived as either a confirmation or disconfirmation of preformed expectations. The traveller knew from the paintings of the popular English landscape artist Rowland Hilder that 'summers were sunny and that in the winter the trees went bare and brush-like' (2002: 4) and approaches Salisbury with a painting by Constable in mind, a 'four-colour reproduction which I had thought the most beautiful I had ever seen' (2002: 5). The knowledge that 'walden' and 'shaw' mean 'wood' predispose the traveller to thinking – falsely again – that he 'saw a forest' at Waldenshaw (2002: 5). As the narrator more explicitly notes a little later:

> So much [. . .] I saw with the literary eye, or with the aid of literature. A stranger here, with the nerves of the stranger, and yet with a knowledge of the language and the history of the language and the writing, I could find a special kind of past in what I saw; with a part of my mind I could admit fantasy. (2002: 17)

Perception is 'aided', but also limited by the 'literary eye'. And even as the literary prefigurations are stripped away, the narrative creates its own allusive and formal echoes. The philosophically alert, reflexive subtlety is thus nuanced with irony in that it expresses and problematises formally what it is analysing discursively: the language in which the literary imagination is assessed conjures its own dream, too – not least in the sense that such an interpretation as has been offered here derives from a generic horizon of expectations. This is what registers the arrival as a revision of the auto-optic claim to the authority of the witness. To return briefly to the opening lines once more: the first two sentences provide a rhythmic prologue to the theme of the limitations of perception wrought by a literary horizon of expectations, as much as by any rain. It is written in one of the most familiar meters in the English language, and the most common, too, in Greek tragedy and comedy: iambic trimeter.

˘   ˘ /   ˘   /   ˘ /
For the first four days it rained.
˘ ˘   /   ˘ /   ˘   ˘ /
I could hardly see where I was. (2002: 3)

We are thus approaching the environment from a perspective in which the perceptual configurations and literary prefigurations, configurations and refigurations are explored on many levels simultaneously.

The rhythmic familiarity of those opening lines extends into a highly allusive narrative, in which the most pervasive and complex association is with the voyages of Columbus and Ralegh, and the search for El Dorado. In the first movement in 'Jack's Garden', the traveller goes on one of the walks that form much of the material of the Wiltshire sections of the narrative. He is ostensibly looking for Stonehenge. In another inversion of expectations, this first destination is never reached. The passage ends, instead, with the traveller finding gold, of sorts. Walking in the valley, the traveller happens upon a shed full of hay, and the 'hay in this shed was new, with a sweet, warm smell; and the bales unstacked into golden, clean, warm-smelling steps, which made me think of the story about spinning straw into gold and of references in books with European settings to men sleeping on straw in barns' (2002: 10). But, in a carefully deployed revision of the wonder voyages in quest of gold, this 'gold' is folded into a vision of decay. Indeed, it is precisely the lack of gold, the greyness of the dust, that is 'wonderful': the 'straw was golden, warm; the grain was golden; but the dust that fell after the grain had poured into the trays of the trucks was grey [. . .] This dust – the mound firm at the base, wonderfully soft at the top – was very fine and grey, without a speck of gold' (2002: 13).

In a similarly, resonantly allusive scene – and in one of the comparisons that stretch the Wiltshire countryside across the globe – a snow drift reminds the narrator of childhood memories of 'a Trinidad beach where shallow streams [. . .] ran from tropical woodland to the sea' (2002: 46). It created the impression of a landscape in miniature, and 'always brought to mind the beginning of the world, the world before men, before the settlement' (2002: 46). It is an echo of the same 'dream of the untouched, complete world' that Naipaul had identified in Defoe's *Robinson Crusoe*, closely allied with the 'dream of total power' (Naipaul 1972: 206). The narrator here, however, acknowledges this element of his emotional engagement, and supplements it posthumously, with the intimate directness of the parenthetical aside: '(Romance and ignorance: for though there were no longer aboriginal people on the island, they had been there for millennia)' (Naipaul 2002: 46).

It is in the 'romance and ignorance' of approaching the world through the filters of literary romance or the quest for wonders that is most significantly undermined in Naipaul's writing. It recounts the gradual replacement of a perception of the land and people as an expression of a literary idea, with a reflexive reassessment of the traveller's own perceptions. The name of the chapter, 'Jack's Garden', as noted, recalls fairytale: the children's rhymes of 'Jack and Jill' and 'Jack and the Beanstalk', as well as the Edenic connotations of the garden. The suggestion of 'Little Red Riding Hood' is there too, at Stonehenge, seen from a distance, where there was 'always someone in red, among the little figures' (2002: 19). The narrator gradually unpicks this literary fairytale, with characters worked up through a series of thumbnail sketches caught at different angles and moments – encounters rather than prolonged relationships – at an angle of vision that has the unintrusive, benevolent attentiveness, only almost involved in the action, of the camera work of the director of *Pater Panchali* (1955), Satyajit Ray, for whom Naipaul has expressed admiration (Gussow 1987). Many of these lives gradually absorb the traveller's vision, but the central figure on the periphery, as it were – here and in the book as a whole – is that of Jack, a farm worker and gardener on the estate.

The centrality of Jack is conveyed not only in the title but in the self-evidence of his introduction, which suggests that what has gone before was leading up to this only: as the traveller goes looking for Stonehenge, and must choose between two ways (one of many allusions to Proust's *In Search of Lost Time*), the narrator recalls: 'There was no problem, really. You came to a lane if you turned left; you came to another lane if you turned right. Those two lanes met at Jack's cottage [. . .]' (2002: 6). And then, a little later, still looking for Stonehenge:

> I had to ask the way [. . .]. Such a simple inquiry, though, in the emptiness; and I never forgot that on the first day I had asked someone the way. Was it Jack? I didn't take the person in; I was more concerned with the strangeness of the walk, my own strangeness, and the absurdity of my inquiry. (2002: 7–8)

Where Jack enters the traveller's journey as a peripheral feature, not noticed, he enters the narrative as a preoccupation: its primary source. The narrator revises the traveller's concern with his own strangeness, which at first obscured Jack from notice. The traveller begins with an impression that Jack – a man in his late forties, with a pointed beard, at work in the garden and allotments, his clothes emblematic of the particular season (2002: 29) – is a feature of the landscape, of a vision of England: 'part of the view'; a 'man fitting the landscape' (2002: 14); 'something from the past, a remnant, something that would be swept away' (2002: 99). And with what subtlety each feature of Jack's character and life is revealed to the reader by effect leading to cause in reflection of this process: we find out almost everything retrospectively, just as the narrator does, even in terms of sentence construction. The syntax of the following, for example, echoes the theme in reaching subject via the subordinate clause: 'Of literature and antiquity and the landscape Jack and his garden and his geese and cottage and his father in law seemed emanations' (2002: 21).

The Enigma of Arrival, here and throughout, is the narrator's recovery of the traveller's oversights, and arrival at a different view of Jack. And Jack's example, for the narrator, becomes the opposite of an 'emanation'. His example is that, in the midst of dereliction, he had 'created his own life, his own world, almost his own continent', in his work in his garden (2002: 100). The 'pleasures of work in his garden as a free man' become symbolic of the vocation of care and the primacy of life. And it is in Jack's final act that the narrator identifies the central motif of the book. Jack becomes ill; the garden becomes wild; but on Christmas Eve, a week before his death, Jack, with 'blocks of ice for lungs [. . .] had roused himself and found the energy to dress and had driven to the pub for the holiday, before his death' (2002: 50). It is a 'final journey' that 'served no cause except that of life' (2002: 50). It is this sentiment that is echoed towards the end of the chapter, in a kind of eulogy, which gathers the impressions of the chapter, and lays out the terms that will reverberate through to the final lines of the book:

> Jack himself had disregarded the tenuousness of his hold on the land, just as, not seeing what others saw, he had created a garden on the edge of a swamp and a ruined farmyard: had responded to and found glory in the seasons. All around him was ruin; and all around, in a deeper way, was change, and a reminder of the brevity of the cycles of growth and creation. But he had sensed that life and man were the true mysteries; and he had asserted the primacy of these with something like religion. The bravest and most religious thing about his life was his way of dying: the way he had asserted, at the very end, the primacy not of what was beyond life, but life itself. (2002: 100)

Here we have, in kernel, the vital ethical discovery of the book. It too, of course, is an impression, an interpretation; and the eulogy is succeeded, immediately, in the last section of the chapter, with a revision, 'something new about Jack' (2002: 101). His widow has cut her hair; she had worn it long because Jack liked her to 'wear it in a bun'; perhaps, 'in his own way, he had been a tyrant' (2002: 101)? In closing the chapter, the central story becomes an element of someone else's, becomes 'another cycle in the life of Jack's wife' (2002: 101). But the uncertainties do not undermine, but rather supplement, the lesson the narrator draws: that life is the true mystery, the true enigma, the source of wonder, and that it remains unexhausted when the lesson has been drawn. The 'exposition', then, introduces both the scene and the way of seeing that the narrator has arrived at – a reversal of the tradition of the traveller's tale that it evokes. Beyond the irony of this reversal is the revision of the basic tenets of the authority of the witness and the exoticism of romance, opening into a sense of wonder at that which remains 'unknown' – in Wiltshire, or anywhere else.

'Voyage in the Dark': forms of homelessness ('The Journey')

That *The Enigma of Arrival* – with its subtitle of *A Novel in Five Sections* – may be discussed in terms of its reversal and revision of the traveller's tale of wonder is a mark of the variety of text forms that it evokes, rather than its at-homeness in a specific genre. Indeed, much of the irony of the perspective derives from the tension between the traveller's cultural and historical background and the forms evoked by his account: the rambler on the estate, wonderer at the country, finder of 'gold', is not quite at home in the genre in which he comes into being. The difficulty of placing *The Enigma of Arrival* in generic terms was as much a feature of its reception as it was in the case of Chatwin's *In Patagonia*, and as we will see again with W. G. Sebald's work. It was 'unlike any other book, a work of intermittent brilliance, a cross between a partially fictional autobiography and an essay and a slowly revealed study of the life of the mind, but billed as a novel', writes Patrick French: and as such, it is 'an unusable masterpiece' (French 2008: 427). How does the form of *The Enigma of Arrival*, and the forms that precede it, relate to Naipaul's themes? The book, and Naipaul's other writings, may be seen as forms of homelessness, equal to the experience of dispossession and displacement – a response to the prefigurations of experience by a generic horizon of expectations, and an opening to wonder.

Part Two, 'The Journey' – dramatologically, the 'rising action' – retells those first four days of rain as a different version, before moving back, tracing the preconditions, rather than pursuing the plots, of Part One. The process unmoors the text from itself; relativises its precedents; registers the partial nature of each version of events; and becomes 'a book concerned in a large part with the process of its own creation' (Hayward 2006: 96). The journey is from Trinidad to England in 1950, and from there to becoming the writer who had been able to write the story of Jack and his garden. It passes through and retrospectively

Figure 1 Giorgio de Chirico, *The Enigma of Arrival and the Afternoon* (1912). (Source: http://arthistory.about.com/od/from_exhibitions/ig/Chirico_Ernst_Magritte_Balthus/CEMB_strozzi_10_02.htm (last accessed 17 Sept. 2012). © DACS 2012.

revises and supplements the 'voyage in the dark' – to borrow the title of a book (1934) written by one of Naipaul's literary predecessors in the journey from the Caribbean to England, Jean Rhys – through which the traveller had, at first, missed his material while looking through the filter of a literary idea. The blurring of its forms in the book is of a piece with this revision; and reflects, analogously, the narrator's own sense of strangeness in the journey itself. The blurring of forms is most pronounced in the retelling of the first four days of rain. Many paintings and books mentioned are in the pastoral vein (Constable and Hilder have been noted already) but it is a Surrealist painting that adorns the cover and shares its title: Giorgio de Chirico's *The Enigma of Arrival and the Afternoon* (Figure 1); so named, as the narrator notes, by Guillaume Apollinaire (Naipaul 2002: 105–6).

The traveller encounters this painting when he arrives, among the books left behind by the previous tenant, in 'The Little Library of Art Series', and 'felt that in an indirect, poetical way the title referred to something in my own experience' (Naipaul 2002: 105). The traveller identifies, then, with a painting named by someone else, found among the remainders of another person's books (cf. Piedra 1989: 36), in a kind of multilayered borrowing of and burrowing into forms as adopted, temporary homes. What the painting and its donated title trigger is the first of Naipaul's 'versions': a story told in the conditional tense, a story the narrator would have written, detailing the approach that would have been taken – a story by proxy, as it were. It is a technique that will become yet more prevalent in the 'unwritten stories' that make up many of the chapters in *A Way in the World: A Sequence* (Naipaul 1994). The 'unwritten' story that comes into being as it is retrieved is the parable of the very book in which it is contained, and, brief and absorbing as it is, is worth quoting in its entirety:

> My story was to be set in classical times, in the Mediterranean. My narrator would write plainly, without any attempt at period style or historical explanation of his period. He would arrive – for a reason I had yet to work out – at that classical port with the walls and gateways like cut-outs. He would walk past those two muffled figures on the quayside. He would move from that silence and desolation, that blankness, to a gateway or door. He would enter there and be swallowed by the life and noise of a crowded city (I imagined something like an Indian bazaar scene). The mission he had come on – family business, study, religious initiation – would give him encounters and adventures. He would enter interiors, of houses and temples. Gradually there would come to him a feeling that he was getting nowhere; he would lose his sense of mission; he would begin to know only that he was lost. His feeling of adventure would give way to panic. He would want to escape, to get back to the quayside and his ship. But he wouldn't know how. I imagined some religious ritual in which, led on by kindly people, he would unwittingly take part and find himself the intended victim. At the moment of crisis he would come upon a door, open it, and find himself on the quayside of arrival. He has been saved; the world is as he remembered it. Only one thing is missing now. Above the cut-out walls and buildings there is no mast, no sail. The antique ship has gone. The traveller has lived out his life. (Naipaul 2002: 106–7)

It is a story almost Kafkaesque in its sense of menace, its melding of concrete simplicity and vivid parabolic resonance (as the opening scenes of Part One are reminiscent of the landsurveyor K's arrival in the province of Kafka's *The Castle*). It is a story about existential solitude, but in the anonymity of the allegory, could be about any of us. The story is not only another version of the preceding account, but – the narrator realises – a version of a book he had been working on at the time of arrival, a book about 'freedom and loss' set in an African country, involving a 'day-long journey made in a car by two white people at a time of tribal war' (2002: 107). It corresponds with Naipaul's *In a Free State* (1971). The borders of the text begin to fray and merge with others, then. The story corresponds, too, to a recurring dream 'that had been brought on by intellectual fatigue and something like grief' (Naipaul 2002: 108), following soon after the disappointment of the rejection by the publisher of a book about 'discovery, the New World, the dispeopling' – and how acutely that almost bureaucratic word registers the callousness of the act – 'of the discovered islands' (2002: 109). This closely resembles what is probably Naipaul's most underrated work, *The Loss of El Dorado* (Naipaul 1969). In the dream, the traveller experiences an 'explosion' in his head, is thrown flat on his back in crowded places, leaving the dreamer with the sensation of 'consciously living through, or witnessing, [his] own death' (Naipaul 2002: 108). It is in response to this dream that the period of life in the valley is experienced as a 'miracle', a 'second chance, a new life' (2002: 111). And it is this dream that returns when the narrator, nearing the end of this period, succumbs to a 'serious illness', and to the idea of 'death, the nullifier of human life and endeavour' (2002: 112). In both time-frames, there is a dynamic tension between the dream of exhaustion and the recovery of the will to write – which, for the writer, is tantamount to the will to live – registered in the existence of the writing itself; to become, as the narrator puts it, 'a doer again' (2002: 112).

The presence of this 'version' within *The Enigma of Arrival* – in which the conditional tense renders the voice both more direct and more distanced, as if speaking in confidence, as an aside, with the story itself at one remove – is one of the marks of Naipaul's adaptations of form. In its fluid relations between autobiography and fiction and fictions imagined in the account of a journey, *The Enigma of Arrival* marks the fulfilment of a process of questioning and altering literary form as extensive as Naipaul's circumnavigatory travels. The two are intimately related. Questions of form and travel have been at issue from the beginning. The first book Naipaul wrote was only the third to be published: *Miguel Street* (1959) was more a collection of interlinked short stories than a novel, and – so the publisher André Deutsch insisted – stories only sell if they are those of known writers (see French 2008: 159–60). Naipaul was asked for a novel; and only two years later, after the publication of *The Mystic Masseur* (1957) and *The Suffrage of Elvira* (1958), did *Miguel Street* go to press. *The Mystic Masseur*, which was therefore, in part at least, a commission, seems almost to have thematised this experience. The protagonist, Ganesh, is told by the headmaster: 'the purpose of this school is to form, not to inform. Everything is planned' (Naipaul 1978: 20). Looking out at the ocean liners at anchor, Ganesh 'allowed the idea of travel enter his mind and just as quickly allowed it to go out again' (1978: 20). Challenging that ethic – 'form not inform' – has been pivotal to everything Naipaul has written; and allowing the thought of travel to enter and remain in his mind has been crucial to his approach to form as a means of challenging formal constraint.

It is Naipaul's travels – the travels that were made after the emigration to England – that have had the most evidently profound effect on the forms of his writing. It began with a commission from the government of Trinidad and Tobago that led to the publication of his first travel book, *The Middle Passage*, in 1962, soon after *A House for Mr Biswas* (1961), his tragi-comic epic and one of the standard works of postcolonial fiction. From this point onwards his production of travel writings has kept pace with and increasingly taken priority over his fiction. In a career spanning from 1957 to the present and comprising over thirty books, Naipaul's travel writing now accounts for over a third of his output. The 'Indian trilogy' that commenced with *An Area of Darkness* (1964), and his researches into the New World (most especially *The Loss of El Dorado*) represent his most personal explorations of the 'areas of darkness' in his own heritage as the descendant of indentured labourers. His travels in the Islamic world, beginning with *Among the Believers* (1981), represent his other most significant, and controversial, area of inquiry. His work is divided by publishers into two categories: fiction and non-fiction, and to a degree the division is a useful one. With the customary caution regarding the idea of non-fictional narrative, it can be helpful to think of *A House for Mr Biswas* as 'fiction', and Naipaul's essays and travel books as 'non-fiction' (Naipaul was reportedly 'incandescent' when, in 2006, the German publisher Classen brought out a translation of *India: A Million Mutinies Now* (1990) as a 'Roman' (Shakespeare 2007: no pagination)). But, as Bruce King has written, gradually these distinctions become more difficult to maintain: 'The more he wrote about the modern world and tried to analyse it the more significant he regarded his travel books and essays, with the result that literary genres began to blur, mix and blend' (King 2003: 5). In works such as *In a Free State* (1971), *Finding the Centre: Two Narratives* (1984), *The Enigma of Arrival* and *A Way in the World* (1994), he created 'his own, original blend of fiction, reportage and autobiography – new literary forms for our time' (2003: 5).

We thus encounter *The Enigma of Arrival* as a text without a clear generic home, or as a text which inhabits different forms simultaneously. It is the fulfilment of a blurring of forms that began most notably in *In a Free State* (significantly, this closely resembles the book that the narrator in *The Enigma of Arrival* is working on upon arrival in Wiltshire). *In a Free State* included three narratives connected thematically rather than by plot, framed by autobiographical narratives. But

Picador now publishes two versions of the Booker Prize-winning work: the original version, which includes the autobiographical framing narratives drawn from Naipaul's journals and is designated 'A Sequence'; and now a version stripped of these sections, as a 'novel' (though even the novel comprises three sections, related thematically but not in terms of plot or character). *Finding the Centre* contained two narratives, one a 'Prologue to an Autobiography' and one a travel piece. In *The Enigma of Arrival*, all these various strands are brought together. And, rather as Chatwin's *The Songlines* might be regarded as reworking 'The Nomadic Alternative' in a new form, *A Way in the World* recasts the work that went into *The Loss of El Dorado*.

What is at stake in Naipaul's equal commitment to travels, and his blurring of genres in the later works? Naipaul's doubts about the novel began soon after the publication of *An Area of Darkness* (1964). Reviewing Patrick White's *The Burnt Ones* in the *Spectator* magazine, his observation that there were now 'as many emergent literatures as there are emergent countries' led him to feeling 'uncertainty about the function of the novel, and a conviction that the novel has done all it can do and that new forms must be found' (qtd French 2008: 245). Naipaul's allergic pronouncements on the death of the novel are famed for their incendiary nature: Salman Rushdie is among those who have taken him to task for what he calls 'easy gloom' (Rushdie 2002: 58). But Naipaul's view is a detached long-shot. His argument recurs in other places, but is given in most depth in 'Reading and Writing', in arguing that literature 'is the sum of its discoveries':

> Literature, like all living art, is always on the move. It is part of its life that its dominant form should constantly change. No literary form – the Shakespearean play, the epic poem, the Restoration comedy, the essay, the work of history – can continue for very long at the same pitch of inspiration. If every creative talent is always burning itself out, every literary form is always getting to the end of what it can do [. . .] It is a vanity of the age (and commercial promotion) that the novel continues to be literature's final and highest expression. (Naipaul 2003c: 30)

Naipaul's concern over the form of the novel has been cultural as well as historical: 'The great societies that produced the great novels of the past have cracked', he writes in 'Conrad's Darkness and Mine' (2003c: 180). And as he told Ahmed Rashid, '[w]hat happens when you pour your content into this form is you ever so slightly distort the material. Different cultures have different visions, ideas of human achievement and behaviour. If you try to write like Hemingway and you are writing about India it will not match' (Rashid 1997: 167). We might note that the power of *A House for Mr Biswas* derives – like much postcolonial fiction – in part, through precisely this hybridity. Placing Mr Biswas at the centre of an epic novel almost radically classical for the period is one of the sources of its pathos – the protagonist inhabits a form that evokes the Victorian novel and thus the period in which the empire that engineered his tragedy was at its peak. And writers committed to the novel are understandably perturbed by assaults on the form; and understandably defensive of its variety. Virginia Woolf's famous definition of 'that cannibal, the novel' that 'has devoured so many forms' (Woolf 2008: 80) still applies. But Naipaul is not alone among writers feeling a similar need to move in different directions in terms of form.

Central to Naipaul's interrogations of the assumptions of formal convention has been a sense of the loss of the capacity to awaken a sense of wonder. Naipaul makes the connection most explicitly in 'Conrad's Darkness and Mine':

> The novel as a form no longer carries conviction. Experimentation, not aimed at the real difficulties, has corrupted response; and there is great confusion in the minds of readers and writers about the purpose of the novel. The novelist, like the painter, no longer recognizes his interpretive function; he seeks to go beyond it; and his audience diminishes. And so the world we inhabit, which is always new, goes by unexamined, made ordinary by the camera, unmeditated on; and there is noone to awaken the sense of true wonder. That is perhaps a fair definition of the novelist's purpose, in all ages. (Naipaul 2003c: 180)

Though Naipaul is inconsistent – the novelist now becomes a writer to be found in 'all ages' – it is not taxonomical precision he is working towards but a sense of the living nature of form as a part of the writer's craft and vocation, and its inextricability from the content of the writing. This is anything but resignation about literature, or 'easy gloom' (Rushdie 2002: 58). It is a statement of its demands and responsibility: 'All great writing has its own new form' (Theroux 2000: 334), as Naipaul said to Paul Theroux when asked whether *The Enigma of Arrival* and *A Way in the World* were novels or non-fiction. 'If you want to write serious books, you must be ready to break the forms, break the forms', he advised James Wood (Wood 2008: no pagination). His perspective does not preclude the possibility of breaking the forms of the novel, and using the novel as the means of breaking the forms. It is, more essentially, a protest against adopting a form as a given. In terms of the contestation of genres, perhaps the final word in Naipaul's argument is his remark in the Nobel lecture, 'Two Worlds' (2001): 'you will understand why for me all literary forms are equally valuable' (2003c: 195).

The issue of form plays a crucial role in the account of the journey from Trinidad to England in 1950. The traveller, driven by a literary ambition, misses the material at first because of an idea of what literary experience should involve. He does not note anything down in his journal about the farewell at the airport in Trinidad, 'the last of the big Hindu or Asiatic occasions in which I took part' (Naipaul 2002: 115–16). He works on a piece called 'Gala Night': 'It was wise; it suggested experience and the traveller [. . .] it might have been written by a man who had seen many gala nights' (2002: 131). The traveller's anxieties of unbelonging, and the uprootedness of those he encounters at Earls Court boarding house upon arrival in London, are buried: 'concentrating on my experience, eager for experience, I was shutting myself off from it, editing it out of my memory' (2002: 135). Seeking a specific, romantic idea, the traveller 'grew to feel that the grandeur belonged to the past; that I had come to England at the wrong time; that I had come too late to find the England, the heart of empire, which (like a provincial, from a far corner of the empire) I had created in my fantasy' (2002: 141). Disappointment is a product of specific expectations. It is in this dimension that Naipaul's account of the journey has been read as a 'narrative of disenchantment' (Hayward 2002: 44). But the disenchantment is a component, rather than an evacuation, of retrospective wonder. The traveller is, at the outset, like Columbus: looking for specific things, not seeing what does not fit into the 'world's finite catalogue' (Naipaul 2003b: 5). The traveller, the part of the traveller that was conscious and willed, could say with Columbus: 'where there were no wonders, there was nothing' (2003b: 5). But the essential element here is that this is a deficit of wonder:

> I was, in 1950, like the earliest Spanish travellers to the New World, medieval men with high faith: travelling to see wonders, parts of God's world, but then very quickly taking the wonders for granted, saving inquiry (and true vision) only for what they knew they would find even before they had left Spain: gold. True curiosity comes at a later stage of development. In England I was at that earlier, medieval-Spanish stage – my education and my academic struggles the equivalent of the Spanish adventurer's faith and traveller's endurance. And, like the Spaniard, having arrived after so much effort, I saw very little. And like the Spaniard who had made a long, perilous journey down the Orinoco or Amazon, I had very little to record. (Naipaul 2002: 156)

The traveller's disappointment in England, then, to borrow from Proust, derives from being 'like people who set out on a journey to see with their eyes some city of their desire, and imagine that one can taste in reality what has charmed one's fancy' (2002: 3). But the narrator looks back on himself as a traveller, rather like the narrator of Conrad's *The Shadow-Line*, as a figure dwelling in a fairytale without knowing it, failing to be astonished by the world he inhabits. In Conrad's narrative, the narrator remembers having been given the command of a ship 'in a twinkling of an eye, not in the common course of human affairs, but more as if by enchantment', and sagaciously remarks of people in fairytales: 'Nothing ever astonishes them. When a fully appointed gala coach is produced out of a pumpkin to take her to a ball Cinderella does not exclaim. She gets in quietly and drives away to her high fortune' (Conrad 2003: 33).

The sense of wonder, retrospectively, crucially concerns the dispossessed who are to become one of the traveller's themes as narrator:

> Because in 1950 in London I was at the beginning of that great movement of peoples that was to take place in the second half of the twentieth century – a movement and a cultural mixing greater than the peopling of the United States, which was essentially a movement of Europeans to the New World. This was a movement between all the continents. Within ten years Earls Court was to lose its pre-war or early-war Hangover Square associations. It was to become an Australian and South African, a white–colonial, enclave in London, presaging a greater mingling of peoples. (Naipaul 2002: 154)

It is by the dispossession of the literary expectation that these stories become the writer's 'material'. The equivalence Naipaul suggests between his own travels, his attempt to adopt a literary tradition, and the 'medieval Spanish stage' (2002: 156) is what points towards the association between his own forms of homelessness as an expression of a sense of wonder. Naipaul's disenchantments, his unmasking of illusion, and those whom he regards as having fallen for them not only move always from and towards a sense of wonder (though they do). The revolt against enchantments is itself an expression of wonder, inasmuch as it is a protest against the addition of magic tricks to the world. It is akin to Kafka's dislike of detective stories as a 'narcotic which distorts the proportions of life' in that they are 'always concerned with the solution of mysteries which are hidden behind extraordinary circumstances. But in real life [. . .] [t]he mystery isn't hidden in the background. On the contrary! It stares one in the face. It's what is obvious. So we do not see it' (Janouch 1971: 133).

As *The Enigma of Arrival* unsettles itself within the conventions of form, begging the question of the degree of its fictionality, evoking generic cultural memory with acutely ironised distance, following links and connections that cannot be explained in terms of plot, it becomes itself an analogue of Naipaul's own cultural dispossession, and that of the people and peoples whose histories he treats. Naipaul himself, asked of the relationship between these forms and contemporary history, tentatively makes this connection:

there are many writers and many kinds of writing, the world is very varied, and writing also has to be varied. Shall we say this form where the material is linked together by associations – that begin very simply and then radiate through the text – is very good for this particular material. (Hussein 1997: 159)

This, which intimates the analogous relationship between the displacement of global movement and a form that seeks links thematically, associatively, rather than through plot, seems a fitting description of *The Enigma of Arrival*. And the resonance of this ever-present formal homelessness is worth bearing in mind as we move into the most controversial dimension of Naipaul's affiliations.

In 'the garden of the oppressor': controversies of assimilation ('Ivy')

The title of this section is borrowed from that of Frank Kermode's review of what he suggests is 'really the story of an arrival in a new homeland – of an immigrant finally assimilated, an inhabitant of the colonial world who puts down roots in the ancient soil of the oppressor, and lives among his crumbling glories' (Kermode 1987: no pagination). Kermode's view of Naipaul as having assimilated to English society in 'the garden of the oppressor' sums up a prevalent strain in the reception of *The Enigma of Arrival*. Indeed, to 'those of us for whom this direction has always been clear' writes Derek Walcott in a reading which has the intensity and intimacy of elegy in its critique, 'this arrival is neither enigmatic nor ironic but predictable' (Walcott 1998: 122). In her reading of *The Enigma of Arrival* in *The World Republic of Letters*, Pascale Casanova characterises Naipaul as one of 'The Assimilated' (Casanova 2004: 205–19), in contrast to the 'Rebels', 'Translated Men' and 'Revolutionaries' (2004: 205–347) of world literature. '[H]e tried,' Casanova argues, 'actually to make himself English – to understand the landscape, the passing of the seasons, the history and the life of the people of his adopted land' (2004: 210). Similarly, Walcott asks: 'What is the cost to his Indianness of loving England (because that is what to love the English countryside means)?' (Walcott 1998: 125).

Leaving to one side the question of whether a desire to understand something is illustrative of a desire to assimilate to it, there can be no doubt that in *The Enigma of Arrival* Naipaul writes devotionally of the Wiltshire countryside and is concerned with a kind of homecoming at the heart of the former imperial 'centre'. Indeed, it is hard to imagine a situation more likely to provoke, or confirm, accusations that Naipaul aligns himself with the British Empire than his identification with the decadent landlord of an English estate built on the wealth of imperial pillage. Early in the book, the narrator recalls that he 'felt a great sympathy for my landlord' (Naipaul 2002: 56). This 'sympathy' is made more volatile not only by the book itself, but by the backstory: the most persistent critique of Naipaul's work generally has been based on the perception of his writings, and travel writings particularly, as degrading the Third World with contempt, while paying homage to the First, grounded in a perception of Naipaul's identification with European values, and those of the British Empire in particular. Edward Said, in the frequently cited article 'Intellectuals in the Post-Colonial World', alleges that Naipaul has been akin to an ethnographic informant and 'allowed himself quite consciously to be turned into a witness for the Western prosecution' as a means of making the case 'that we "non-Whites" are the cause of all our problems, not the overly maligned imperialists' (Said 1986: 53). Rob Nixon's *London Calling* (1992) – the most extensive and sophisticated scholarly study to contribute to the polemic – castigates Naipaul as a 'postcolonial mandarin' who has 'enlisted the idiom of displacement to exaggerate his distance from mainstream Anglo-American traditions' only to use this position to speak as an apologist for the prejudices and values of empire (Nixon 1992: 15).

Naipaul has always insisted that he 'can't serve a cause' (Schiff 1997: 138); and he has transformed his dilemma of dispossession into an ethical and aesthetic resistance to being claimed by any faction. A reading of his work in terms of alliances, and the double standard involved in readings of non-Western writers, is something that Naipaul has been keenly aware of, and satirised, from early on. In a response to some sundry remarks on his own work from various sources – that his 'whole purpose is to show how funny Trinidad Indians are' (unnamed publication); that he 'looks down a long Oxford nose at the land of [his] birth' (cited as the *Daily Telegraph*); and, equally, that he 'writes of his native land with warm affection' (in the *Evening Standard*) – Naipaul suggests:

> None of these comments would have been made about a comic French or American novel. They are not literary judgements at all. Imagine a critic in Trinidad writing of *Vile Bodies*: 'Mr Evelyn Waugh's whole purpose is to show how funny English people are. He looks down his nose at the land of his birth. We hope that in future he writes of his native land with warm affection.' (Naipaul 1972: 11)

The high satire – an example of the way Naipaul's fury is often chan-nelled into sharply focused, exasperated comedy – is written out of self-respect but also out of a humanistic refusal to patronise his subjects. As his work moves into travel writing, these issues become more pronounced, leading into appropriations as well as castigations. In a remark by turns insightful and highly dubious, Robert Boyers, editor of the US journal *Salmagundi*, has remarked to Scott Winokur:

> He identifies with white, Western intellectuals and he has *every right to do that*. There's no reason why a person of color *needs* to be writing out of a perspective associated with the Third World, why he should be *expected* to manifest solidarity with the group from which he issues. There is something grotesque about demanding of a world-class writer that he hew to a partyline or an ethnic perspective. He's been very frankly associated with Western values and he's used that perspective to criticize what is happening in the Third World – quite justifiably, some of us would say. (qtd Winokur 1997: 123)

This contains an acute critique but proceeds to perpetrate the flaw it condemns. True, and well put: there is something 'grotesque' – patronising and exoticising – about demanding Naipaul 'hew to a partyline or an ethnic perspective'. But in this case it must also be 'grotesque' to condemn and simultaneously conduct this 'demand', in reducing and appropriating Naipaul's writing by claiming that he 'identifies with white, Western intellectuals' – which he demonstrably and vociferously does not. The partisanship begins to show itself in the last sentence of the quote, where the writer aligns himself within a jostling community ('some of us would say'). It is precisely this slippage towards ideological 'sides' that Naipaul has loudly condemned in his public provocations, and quietly and totally exposed in the unplaceable forms of his work.

We might question the critique against Naipaul most effectively not so much in defence of his 'pessimism' as in contesting the view that he is fundamentally pessimistic. Even Naipaul's most incendiary remarks – the claim that 'History is built around achievement and creation; and nothing was created in the West Indies' (Naipaul 2001a: 20); the Churchillian tones with which he writes that Indians 'defecate on the beaches; they defecate on the hills; they defecate on the river banks; they defecate on the streets; they never look for cover' (Naipaul 1985: 70) – are always provocative. That is, to the degree that the writing is an address, an engagement in society, it volubly seeks, even demands, a response. And such passages take place within what is surely one of the most sustained engagements in contemporary literature with the ramifications of empire in living human experience, present and past. It is tempting to draw a parallel between the accusations against Naipaul of contempt, and those made against D. H. Lawrence of sexual sordidness in *Lady Chatterley's Lover*. Both involve reading for the vocabulary and the scenes, but not for the deeper resonance of the work as a whole (Hoggart 2005: 21–9). 'One can't write out of contempt,' Naipaul has said. 'If you try to do that, the book won't survive and won't irritate. Contempt can be ignored' (Muckherjee and Boyers 1997: 90). And when asked by Cathleen Medwick, in an interview in 1981, about what Irving Howe called Naipaul's 'dark vision' in his work, he responded: 'But if the vision were really dark then it would be very hard to put pen to paper. One would be so . . . distressed. There'd be no point, the experience has gone beyond writing. You've got to compose yourself in order to write, after all' (Medwick 1997: 59). In an interview with Adrian Rowe-Evans, Naipaul picks up on a similar theme:

> I may sit down in an enormous rage to write something; I might even begin in terms of caricature and animosity; but in the course of writing, something will happen. That side of me, that comes out in the writing, is the better side, and better not because it's nicer, but because it's truer; it's the side that in one's rage one might wish to forget [. . .] If one wasn't angry, wasn't upset, one wouldn't want to write. On the other hand it isn't possible to get anything down until you've made sense of it, made a whole of it. To write one has to use all the senses; all the pores must be open. (Rowe-Evans 1997: 30)

Wherever we stand on Naipaul's interpretations of society, it is difficult to entertain the idea that such energy and such intense interest does not have concern as its mainspring: 'The primary difference between my travel and theirs [Graham Greene and others] is that while they travel for the picturesque, I'm *desperately* concerned about the countries I'm in' (Michener 1997: 70; emphasis in original).

One way of seeing in Naipaul's position in *The Enigma of Arrival* something other than conservatism is to focus on his personal perspective, as suggested by Helen Tiffin: 'Postcolonial texts always offer, by their placement in relation to Britain and British literature, sites of resistance to it' (Tiffin 1988: 39). The problem with this is not so much that it 'smacks of an attempt to rescue Naipaul for radicalism' (Hayward 2002: 59) (such an attempt is not in itself illegitimate if one considers Naipaul a radical writer). The problem is that it disempowers the text of the postcolonial writer; it commits the writer to a circumstantial radicalism which, paradoxically, defuses the autonomy that very radicalism would, by definition, require. If we believe a text is radical because of the cultural origins of its author, we privilege the circumstantial over the autonomous (it is the other side of requiring a writer hew the party line). For any writer to be radical, it must be possible for that writer to have been conservative. Where Naipaul's text is 'radical' is in its concern, linked to wonder. And this is crucially at issue in the association – and dissociation – of the traveller of *The Enigma of Arrival* with his land-lord, particularly in 'Ivy' where the issues are most concentrated.

The narrator stresses the identification from early on. He ruminates on the irony of the traveller having found his 'nerves soothed' in an estate that 'had been created in part by the wealth of empire', alone in the valley shared only with the landlord. The landlord – the only figure never named, and thus rendered more imagined, less concrete – is first introduced as reclusive, 'elderly, a bachelor', and suffering from a 'malaise' which the narrator, having no direct knowledge of it, interprets as 'something like accidia, the monk's torpor or disease of the Middle Ages' (Naipaul 2002: 56):

> I felt a great sympathy for my landlord. I felt I could understand his malaise; I saw it as the other side of my own. I did not think of my landlord as a failure. Words like failure and success didn't apply. Only a grand man or a man with a grand idea of his human worth could ignore the high money value of his estate and be content to live in its semi-ruin. My meditations in the manor were not of imperial decline. Rather, I wondered at the historical chain that had brought us together – he in his house, I in his cottage, the wild garden his taste (as I was told) and also mine. (2002: 56)

We can find many more expressions of this sense of sympathy, based on the briefest of encounters (the traveller never meets the landlord and glimpses him only twice (2002: 199; 229)). It deepens at times from a disinterested sense of wonder at the historical chain that brought them together in a Wiltshire valley, into gratitude: 'I felt a kinship with him; was deeply grateful for the protection of the manor, for the style of things there. I never thought his seclusion strange. It was what I wanted for myself at that time' (2002: 208). And even: 'I felt at one with my landlord' (2002: 209). The figure of the landlord is built up 'in frag-ments' (2002: 206), through glimpses and imagination – as a product of the narrator's own needs, as it were – before being revised by stray information. The traveller glimpses him being driven by car, 'knew at once [. . .] had an immediate idea' it was the landlord (2002: 204), and imagines seeing 'a benign elderly man in a brown jacket making a shy wave' (2002: 206). This turns out to be a fabrication; as does the 'con-trary, slightly sinister picture [. . .] of a fat, round-faced man buttoned up in a suit, with dark glasses and a hat' (2002: 206). The physicality of the landlord remains shadowy to the end; though a picture is built up of his former socialite lifestyle, his homosexuality, his self-published romances and his retreat, in illness, into a reclusive lifestyle. The opposi-tions between the landlord and tenant also connect them, almost in the role of a *Doppelganger*:

I was his opposite in every way, social, artistic, sexual. And considering that his family's fortune had grown, but enormously, with the spread of the empire in the nineteenth century, it might be said that an empire lay between us. This empire at the same time linked us. This empire explained my birth in the New World, the language I used, the vocation and ambition I had; this empire in the end explained my presence there in the valley, in that cottage, in the grounds of the manor. But we were – or had started – at opposite ends of wealth, privilege, and in the hearts of different cultures. (2002: 208)

As this passage illustrates, *The Enigma of Arrival* is so much about its own production, so meditatively autoreferential and analytical regarding its own ironies, that it tends to contain the questions we might raise of it. How, approaching this through the Saidian view, for example, are we to interpret so perfect a case study as a text in which the landlord, inheritor of imperial fortunes, sends his colonial tenant Orientalist poems about Krishna and Shiva (2002: 231)? The reflexive irony is one way in which the text resists assimilation to its narrative situation, even as the traveller finds solace and space in the decay, and resists appropriation: it always hovers above, and outside, the world it creates. But the sympathy with the landlord also has a more concrete dimension that is obscured by reading the account as one of a desire for adoption, as a direct insertion into the 'garden of the oppressor' (Kermode 1987: no pagination).

Beyond the historical chain that brings them together in the valley, the traveller's identification with the landlord is based, most crucially, on a shared malaise rather than value: 'I felt I could understand [it]; I saw it as the other side of my own' (Naipaul 2002: 56). The landlord's malaise, the narrator names 'accidia'. Accidia – the 'disease' from which the traveller's landlord, and the dilapidated manor, suffers – is a special choice of word. It means sloth, laziness; it is one of the seven cardinal sins in the Christian religion. But it has its etymological root in the Greek *akedia*, which means, literally, an 'absence of caring' (*OED*). *The Enigma of Arrival* is about the recognition of and recovery from this malaise. While the narrative directly links landlord and tenant in a sympathetic – if largely fantastical – bond, the narrator's point of view is pervasively at odds. The chapter in which the landlord is scrutinised is called 'Ivy' – the plant grows around the manor grounds and, at the landlord's order, is allowed to choke the trees (2002: 309). There are many kinds of gardens in 'Ivy': there is discussion of plantations (2002: 244–5); the Royal Botanical Gardens (2002: 247); a secret garden (2002: 257–8); allotments (2002: 246); the garden department of Woolworths (2002: 308). The criterion of judgement is revealed in a remark on the figure of the gardener as one 'who caused the unremarkable seed to grow into leaves, stalks, buds, flowers, fruit, called this all up from the seed, where it has lain in kernel, the gardener as magician, herbalist, in touch with the mystery of seed and root and graft' which is 'one of the earliest mysteries the child discovers' (2002: 259). Robert Pogue Harrison's poetic essay, 'Homeless Gardens' (2009), comes closest, without reference to Naipaul, to what is at stake in the gardens in *The Enigma of Arrival*, in a discussion of the 'makeshift gardens that homeless individuals, with painstaking effort and care, created for themselves in some of the most degraded urban areas of New York City' (2009: 73–4). Harrison sees these gardens as part of a history which is made up of 'the terrifying, ongoing, and unending conflict between the forces of destruction and cultivation, both of which probably arise from the same source in us, namely care' (2009: 79). The following could have been written in appreciation of Naipaul's eulogy and elegy to Jack:

> There is so much about us that remains opaque, mysterious, and unfathomable, but nothing more so than the subterranean connection between our capacity for destruction – even self-destruction – and our capacity for devotion. This is the legacy of care, which obliges us to strive time and again to become what we already are, that is, human. (2009: 79)

This is where the reading of *The Enigma of Arrival* as, in Walcott's eloquent critique, 'mercilessly honest in its self-centredness, in its seasonal or eruptive sadnesses', in being 'true as life, in the terrible sense that nothing really concerns us' (Walcott 1998: 125), in being 'modest enough to be messianic' (1998: 130), misses the underlying tone of the work. A monolithically self-absorbed and self-aggrandising first-person narrative is precisely what *The Enigma of Arrival* is not. The central figure in the narrative, the text's exemplary gardener, is Jack, a figure 'peripheral' to the narrator's life (Naipaul 2002: 376). The discovery of the journey is that the writer's subject was 'not my sensibility, my inward development, but the worlds I contained within myself, the worlds I lived in' (2002: 161). And the first travel story we read in *The Enigma of Arrival* – which, incidentally, disproves on page one Salman Rushdie's suggestion that there is no mention of 'love' in the book (Rushdie 1987: no pagination) – is not that of V. S. but rather Shiva Naipaul, the author's brother:

> *In loving memory*
> *of my brother*
> *Shiva Naipaul*
> *25 February 1945, Port of Spain*
> *13 August 1985, London*

The Enigma of Arrival concerns healing the malaise – the traveller's dream of exhaustion, linked with the landlord's accidia – and, in turn, leads out to other lives. It begins and ends and is written through with an interpretation of the story of the life of a peripheral figure, Jack, who – as the narrator notes, perhaps not insignificantly at the centrepoint of 'Ivy' – 'made his life appear like a constant celebration' (2002: 254).

This element of celebration is there in Naipaul's narrative, too – in its expressions of wonder. Naipaul, early in his writing, criticised Columbus because he 'was looking less for America or Asia than for gold; and the banality of expectation matches a continuing banality of perception' (Naipaul 1972: 204). Columbus' quest, Naipaul argues, instrumentalised all he had encountered: the 'natives are studied' but his observation that '"they are not at all black"' is not 'an anthropological interest, not the response of wonder – disappointment rather: Columbus believed that where Negroes were, there was gold' (1972: 204). Columbus' attempts to capture a sense of wonder are thus 'even lower than the recent astronaut's "Wow" – there is nothing like this pure cry of delight in Columbus' (1972: 204). It is instructive to compare this reading of Columbus with a nicely drawn vignette in Scott Winokur's interview with Naipaul. Winokur took Naipaul to see the Muir Woods, the redwood forest in Marin County, California, 'the idea being to introduce a monument to a monument and see what came of it' (Winokur 1997: 123). What came of it, Winokur reports, was that 'Muir Woods stunned him'. And the reaction of V. S. Nightfall, the professional pessimist, the consummate Nay-sayer, was as follows:

> 'Yes! Yes!' he cried. 'Amazing! Yes! Yes!'
> He tilted his head backward to see the forest canopy, plunged his hands into his pockets and whirled around, the hem of his coat flying outward, like a skirt.
> 'Yes! Yes! Yes!'
> For several minutes he was speechless. Then he said Muir Woods must be a perfect place for meditation. After that, he was filled with questions about the height and age of the fog-shrouded trees. (Winokur 1997: 124)

The Enigma of Arrival, unlike Columbus' account, is full of variations on the astronaut's 'pure cry of delight' (Naipaul 1972: 204), instances of the stunned but affirmative 'Yes!'. All of the exclamations in the book – even those called up by pain or horror rather than, or mixed in with, pleasure – are expressions of wonder and invitations to wonder; and the voice is raised for no other reason. It may be while walking the wolds and encountering evidence of former settlements: 'Daily I saw the mounds that had been raised so many centuries before. The number of those mounds!' (Naipaul 2002: 18). It may be the recollection of his first departure: 'Romance!' (2002: 139). It may be in admiration of a former champion race horse, now neglected, near death, in a field: 'How tall he was!' (2002: 39). The exclamation marks provide a register of some of the things that are experienced with wonder, in the midst of things and in recollection. Nearly always, they concern that which is somehow not seen, or forgotten, in the past or the present. In their sheer number they bring into question the idea that the tone is of 'unbroken melancholy' (Rushdie 1987: no pagination). It is in these exclamations of wonder that we encounter in Naipaul's work the clearest evidence of what Milan Kundera, thinking of Kafka, has called 'a poetics of surprise; or beauty as perpetual astonishment' (Kundera 1996: 48). And it is in this that we find the deepest ethical dimension of the book: its recovery from disappointment and exhaustion; its concern; its wonder. One gives us especial pause for thought concerning the claim that in *The Enigma of Arrival* the 'clouds have not lifted, but deepened' (Rushdie 1987: no pagination). The narrator recalls his first flight and reflects:

> Always above the cloud, the sun! So solid the cloud, so pure. I could only look and look; truly to possess that beauty, to feel that one had come to the end of that particular experience, was impossible. To see what so few men had seen! Always there, the thing seen, the world above the clouds, even when unperceived: up there (as, down below, sometimes at sunset) one's mind could travel back – and forward – aeons. (Naipaul 2002: 114)

'Philosophy failed me now': death and dissolution ('Rooks')

Part Four, 'Rooks', is the first of the parts of the book to move on chronologically from the last, rather than approaching from another angle or drawing out other dimensions. Mr Pitton, the gardener who had replaced Jack, leaves the valley at the end of Part Three (Naipaul 2002: 310); at the beginning of Part Four, a figure who has been on the edges of the narrative – an unfulfilled English would-be writer and radio broadcaster, Alan comments on the departure (2002: 313). We move on chronologically for the first time, then, in the fourth 'act' – for the 'falling action'. And there is something ominous about this passage of time in itself, in its intimation that chronology is always also moving towards eschatology, and about that unmooring of the text from the calm of its meditative returns and reappraisals, a calm subtly registered by the narrative's slipping into chronology as a meditative, retentive protection against the exhaustion, or departures, of the passage of time. The theme – the motif that has been there throughout, but is to be brought to the surface more fully now – is death. It is announced symbolically in the title, which refers to the arrival in the manor grounds of a flock of rooks. The traveller is told by a neighbour, 'old Mr Phillips', whose later bereavement is perhaps the most poignant of them all, that '[t]hey lost their nests when the elms died' – a result of the ivy we have considered in the previous section – and are now 'prospecting. They need tall trees. They'll choose the beeches. You know what they say about rooks. They bring money to a house [. . .] Of course it's an old wise tale [. . .] If you think they're birds of death you can't stand the noise. If you think it's money, you don't mind' (2002: 324).

The awareness of death has played a formative role in Naipaul's writing. In a letter to his then fiancée, Pat Hale, while still a student at Oxford, he wrote:

> My first memory of sadness – cosmic sadness – came in 1941 or therea-bouts. We were living in a small house in the country, far away from everybody. It was late tropic evening, rapidly growing dark. I looked out of the window to the kitchen that was downstairs and began to cry. I had seen my mother and some of my sisters. I suddenly felt that we were all hopelessly lost, without any purpose. My mother saw me crying and asked why. Naturally I couldn't say. Then it was, too, that I came across some of my mother's girlhood possessions and the futility and waste of her life struck me. I was nine at the time. When I was twelve, I went to the seaside. Three people – a brother & 2 sisters – had been drowned. They could have been saved, but the fishermen had wanted to know how much they would be paid! Oh, the terror I felt then. The fishermen pulled in the seine [fishing net] and brought in the bodies and caught an extraordinary number of catfish, always anxious to get the helpless. The three bodies relaxed in the sand. The sun going down. And, from a cheap beach café, a gramophone: 'Besamé mucho' – Kiss me often, my darling, and say that you will always be mine. I don't know what people of 12 feel, but I have never forgotten that. (qtd French 2008: 104)

The complexity of the scene, the pathos of the concentrated details all problematising one another, contains in kernel many of the themes that have made up the fibre of Naipaul's writing, and this 'cosmic sadness' is very much at issue in *The Enigma of Arrival*. It is in 'Rooks' that this comes to the fore, surpassing the consolations of a philosophy of change or 'flux'. The omen of the rooks presages, in part, the narrator's own gathering sense of mortality: the chapter moves towards a deeper focus on his own succumbing to a 'real illness', a 'sensation of internal cold-ness such as I had never had before' (Naipaul 2002: 364). It is primarily a book of hours in others' lives. James Wood has described Naipaul as a 'wounded wounder' (Wood 2008: no pagination) – that he is wounded, as well as wounding, being a defence of sorts. But it is others' griefs that compose the bulk of the text here, and death is linked to the theme of dissolution, and to a ramification of perspectives. If the reflective narrative emphasis thus far has been on a revision of the traveller's impressions – the relativism of his own understanding and its chang- ingness through time as it gravitates around a single period – it now moves outwards to the manysided perspectives on the valley. As 'old Mr Phillips' tells of the death of his cousin, in 1911, with 'real tears for that death more than sixty-five years before' (2002: 325) by the river, it prompts the reflection that the 'wet river banks, the downs: everyone saw different things. Old Mr Phillips, with his memories of chalk and moss; my landlord, loving ivy; the builders of the manor garden; Alan; Jack; me' (2002: 325).

It is Alan, the 'writer' from London from whom 'no book came' (2002: 313) – who planned, but never wrote, a big book about contem- porary literature, an 'Isherwood-like book about post-war Germany', and an 'autobiographical novel' (2002: 314) – whose death is embedded in the narrative first, and whose perspective unsettles the traveller's own hold on the valley. Alan's 'incompleteness' (2002: 315) as a writer is the- matised as part of his lack of fulfilment, and – as with Jack and with the landlord – there is a kind of identification between the traveller and the character observed. The narrator interprets Alan's literary ambition as one governed by the need 'to say to the world (as I understood too well): "I too have witnessed these things and felt these emotions"' (2002: 314). (It is, incidentally, an interesting dimension to the issue of witness: that it can, for the literary sensibility particularly perhaps, be driven not only by a wish to tell the tale that has not been told – 'for I have seen it and lived to tell the tale' – but also by a wish to have experienced life, and to express that experience.) In assessing Alan's literary ambitions, the nar- rator feels he is 'considering an aspect of [myself] from some years back' (2002: 315). But there is a more contemporary issue in that Alan, too, feels a special relationship to the place: the landlord is among the jewels in his socialite sphere; he refers to 'being met "at the station", with all its old-fashioned country-house-weekend suggestions' and uses the 'name Phillips without the "mister"' (2002: 323) in playing a role, living a literary fantasy. But he is refused a tenancy in the valley, and after his death from alcohol-related illness, he is remembered 'at the place he thought of as his special retreat' as a narrowly avoided 'calamitous' addition to the community (2002: 322).

The judgement is made by the 'Phillips' that Alan had called to the station as part of his half-literary world in the valley. The world of the valley becomes more attenuated, divided, conflicted. The bereavement that resonates through the text most widely is that of 'old Mr Phillips' at the death of his son, Stan, who, along with his wife, are in the employment of the landlord on the manor estate:

> He had coped with the deaths of his father, mother, sister, wife. The death of
> his cousin in 1911 – as he had told me more than once – had prepared him
> for all their deaths. Now, to his great surprise, in his mid-seventies and near
> the end of his life, he had found in the unexpected death of his son a grief that
> had surpassed that earlier grief. He was broken. (2002: 350)

And it was as if, the narrator reflects, 'it was of this death – his son's
– that he had spoken when we had seen the first rooks squawking
and flapping about the manor beeches' (2002: 351). From a distance,
Naipaul's narrator circles around this death and its ramifications in the
complexities of the relations of the bereaved: the landlord is furious
not to have been informed (2002: 351); Mrs Phillips, the wife of Stan,
experiences the grief as if 'it repeated, like a continuation of the grief for
her first husband' (2002: 349), and moves from the valley to make a new
life relieved of what turns out to have been the 'strain of her life with
Mr Phillips' (2002: 371). None of these griefs is sentimentalised; each is
part of a wider network of relations. And it is this sense of the sorrows
of others that wrests the traveller from his own security in his second
life in the valley. The land becomes an echo of countless experiences,
some known, some not; none of which can be discounted. And the
symbol of the primacy of life itself, Jack's garden, 'had been destroyed
in stages and finally concreted over' (2002: 366). As this sense of others'
losses mounts, diversifies, so too does the traveller's hold on the land
of his imagination. Philosophical speculation is no longer equal to the
experience:

> I had lived with the idea of change, had seen it as a constant, had seen a
> world in flux, had seen human life as a series of cycles that sometimes ran
> together. But philosophy failed me now. Land is not land alone, something
> that is simply itself. Land partakes of what we breathe into it, is touched by
> our moods and memories. And this end of a cycle, in my life, and in the life
> of the manor, mixed up with the feeling of age which my illness was forcing
> on me, caused me grief. (2002: 366–7)

This grief is what loosens the traveller's hold on the land, on his adopted
home, where he had found healing. It dispossesses the traveller once
more. But the analytical expression in the passages quoted above find
their place within a narrative which registers, both in its very existence
and in its attentiveness, the recovery and renewal that this grief issues.
It is often said that writing derives from unhappiness; it was well put
by André Gide in *The Immoralist*: 'The finest works of mankind are
universally concerned with suffering. How would one tell a story about
happiness? One can only tell of the origins of happiness and its destruction' (Gide 2001: 55). But it is also true, if less often remarked, that

complete despair generates no writing either. The very existence of the writing is a record of the recovery from, or at least active questioning of, the insufficiency of the philosophical point of view it expresses. But where we hear the counterpart to the philosophy that failed the traveller is not in any of the philosophical ideas of decay, flux, change, but in the narrator's fascination, his alertness to the experiences of others – in wonder. As the traveller prepares to leave, he discovers where he was, without realising it, once again.

Of 'this new wonder' ('The Ceremony of Farewell')

We have followed the five-section structure of *The Enigma of Arrival* as a means of structuring this discussion, and now, in entering the final part, the 'resolution', we reach the issue of conclusion, or completeness, in a narrative that has consistently relativised its conclusions. The final section is presented as a kind of post-script, an explanation of the book itself. It traces its sources once more and, in a sense, places itself outside the narrative in its presentation of how he – and here, given the distancing, the distinctions between Naipaul, narrator and traveller seem to blur even more fully than before – 'had thought for years about a book like *The Enigma of Arrival*' (2002: 375). The fact that the specific number of sections is highlighted in the subtitle, as noted at the outset, suggests it is significant (and might be significant even if it were not envisaged consciously by its author). As we have noted throughout, it links the book to drama, to the ancients and Elizabethan five-act structure. But in bringing the cycle to completion in the fifth part, there are other more subtly suggestive dimensions to the narrative, as it moves towards its close, that suggest an idea of completion that opens out into a 'new wonder' in its final lines (2002: 387).

We might initially relate the number to the novel's preoccupation with perception (the five senses). As noted earlier, the narrative begins with the statement, 'For the first four days it rained. I could hardly see where I was' – and it is thus on the fifth day that an – albeit imperfect – prospect of the land comes into view. But in addition to the five-act drama, other literary allusions can illuminate the significance of the structural sequence. One significance of the number five is provided by *Sir Gawain and the Green Knight*, the book that the traveller sets out to Salisbury to find and reread early on in the course of the narrative (2002: 20). Sir Gawain is readying himself for his terrible quest to find the Green Knight and receive what he expects to be a fatal blow: Sir Gawain bows to the moral, close to that of *The Enigma of Arrival*, that

'"Kind or severe, / We must engage our fate"' (Cooper 2008: 564–5). Sir Gawain has a new shield fashioned, to bring him luck; the shield bears the symbolic five-pointed star, the pentangle:

> a design that Solomon devised, a sign
> And token of truth – quite rightly too,
> For its figure comprises five points
> And its lines overlap and link with each other
> With no ending anywhere; and men in England
> Call it, accordingly, the Knot without End. (2008: 24, ll. 625–30)

It is possible that Naipaul's five-section structure echoes this idea of the pentangle. At the very least, the 'Knot without End' bears a clear correlation with Naipaul's themes. The pentangle, as Helen Cooper explains in her notes to a recent edition of the poem, in its 'unbroken form [. . .] represents wholeness, perfection. Mathematically, it carries a relationship to the perfect proportion known now (but not in the Middle Ages) as the Golden Section' (Cooper 2008: 97, n.24). In *Sir Gawain*, the five-pointed star symbolises the knight's being 'Ever faithful, five times, five ways in each' (2008: 24): the five senses, the five fingers, the five wounds of Christ on the cross, 'the five joys / The Queen of Heaven had from her child' and the 'fifth group of five', made up of '[. . .] generosity, good fellowship, / Cleanness, and courtesy, uncurbed and unimpaired; / Lastly, compassion, surpassing all' (2008: 25). Compassion, surpassing all: this too is very close to the wonder of concern we have explored in Naipaul's work. But this five-pointed structure relates, too, to another text, more ancient still, and going further back in the traveller's personal and cultural past: *The Bhagavad Gita*, the Hindu text which Naipaul had included in the reading list he had prepared for his then fiancée, Pat Hale, as one of the books that could 'reveal the world of his childhood' (qtd French 2008: 96–7). We hear pre-echoes of *The Enigma of Arrival* in some of its passages: 'God dwells in the heart of all beings, Arunja; thy God dwells in thy heart. And his power of wonder moves all things – puppets in a play of shadows – whirling them onwards in the stream of time' (Mascaró 2003: 85). *The Baghavad Gita* also refers to 'the five elements, [. . .] the five powers of feeling and the five of action, the one mind over them, the five fields of sense perception' (2003: 62) and – the only set of five to be specified as well as invoked and the most pertinent to *The Enigma of Arrival* – the 'five sources of all action': 'The body, the lower "I am", the means of perception, the means of action, and Fate' (2003: 80).

At the most fundamental structural level, then, we may find in Naipaul's text a textual navigation or linkage between cultures, with something like the delight that his traveller feels upon discovering that the gladiolus flourishes in both tropical and temperate climes (Naipaul 2002: 30–1). Whether this interpretation holds or not, the issue of cultural meetings is very much at issue in this last section. The few pages draw on an extraordinarily wide range of world events and histories: a Republican Convention in Dallas (2002: 376); the shooting of Indira Ghandi (2002: 377); a visit to East Berlin (2002: 377). But the section gravitates around the death of a sister, Sati, and the return to Trinidad for the cremation.

'The Ceremony of Farewell' figures the preceding narrative as a response to this grief. It figures it as a response, too, to a period in the more distant and the recent past, in terms that suggest *The Enigma of Arrival* to run directly counter to a rhetoric or sensibility of exhaustion: 'in my late thirties the dream of disappointment and exhaustion had been the dream of the exploding head'; 'in my early fifties, after my illness, after I had left the manor cottage and put an end to that section of my life, I began to be awakened by thoughts of death [. . .], by a great melancholy' (2002: 375). As a literary voyage, *The Enigma of Arrival* tells of passage from exhaustion to reawakened wonder, from paralysis to doing, from that 'dream of disappointment and exhaustion' (2002: 375) to a stage at which, in the book's last lines, the writer and the man, now one, has a 'new wonder about men', 'laid aside my drafts and hesitations and began to write very fast about Jack and his garden' (2002: 387). It is a Proustian moment: the narrative line is circular – like *In Search of Lost Time*, it ends with the idea of how to write the book in our hands, closes with the prospect of its own beginning, the epiphany that leads to the writing of the book itself (cf. Proust 2000: 451). And as in Proust's narrative, we are thus invited to begin again, and read once more with this new knowledge which casts all that went before in a new light. Here, in Naipaul's cyclic narrative, it echoes the theme of the narrator's retrospective reassessment of his travels – his gathering understanding and unmasking of his former illusions and omissions. What is perhaps most powerful, most telling of Naipaul's ethic, is that the personal grief leads to an extended sense of attention to the lives and deaths of others. In the closing paragraphs of *The Enigma of Arrival* we are brought back to the events of 1498, and Columbus' 'discovery' of the New World – to the larger historical canvas which had so decisive and destructive an effect on the narrator's own family and culture, among so many others. We are brought to a personal grief: the loss of a sister. We recall the dedication to the writer's brother on the frontispiece. But the story told, when faced with this grief, is the story of a character 'peripheral to my life': of 'Jack', the exemplary tender and celebrator of life. Here is how

Naipaul draws his traveller's tale of wonder to a close, with a wonder of concern, the wonder that will double the voice that describes the earlier traveller's enchantment of illusion:

> But we remade the world for ourselves; every generation does that, as we found when we came together for the death of this sister and felt the need to honour and remember. It forced us to look on death. It forced me to face the death I had been contemplating at night, in my sleep; it fitted a real grief where melancholy had created a vacancy, as if to prepare me for the moment. It showed me life and man as the mystery, the true religion of men, the grief and the glory. And that was when, faced with a real death, and with this new wonder about men, I laid aside my drafts and hesitations and began to write very fast about Jack and his garden. (2002: 387)

It is with this 'new wonder', a wonder that celebrates life even as it grieves – that celebrates precisely because it grieves where melancholy had created a vacancy – that is the mainspring, tone and issue of *The Enigma of Arrival*.

Coda: 'Strangers to ourselves' – the cause of wonder

The Enigma of Arrival is a traveller's tale of wonder that both reverses and revises the basic tenets of the form. Moving beyond enchantment with 'wonders' that confirm or disappoint expectations through to a profound meditation on the way these wonders are formed, and a sense of wonder at all that remains hidden from view even as it is before our eyes, it manifests that the world is always new through its apprehension from different perspectives and its changingness, and always part of a vaster living history that stretches back and across the world and its versions. It is the fulfilment of a process of questioning and challenging the conventions of form as part of a response to the localism, historical and geographical, of assumptions about what literature is or should be, and which finds in its unsettled relations to genre an analogue of the experience and theme of dispossession. It studies profound exhaustion, and treats of it unflinchingly, but its voyage is one of recovery and renewal, to arrive at the new wonder that infuses the narrative from the outset, even as the traveller doubts it. It is less the watershed of a dying fall than the midway point that points the way to the opening out into the recoveries of lost histories and manysided perspectives that we find in *A Way in the World* and *India: A Million Mutinies Now*, in which the traveller's view and the narrative of the experience increasingly become composites of oral histories and untold stories.

Few writers, if any, have had their place in literary history more con-tested than V. S. Naipaul. Much of the debate has hinged on the ques-tion of whether he can be seen as an isolated, unique case; whether his insistent rejection of all political and cultural sides is genuine, or a means of more effective service to an elected, adopted heritage. A passage in *A Way in the World* (Naipaul 1994) is instructive here. The story is of one (appositely named) Leonard Side, a decorator of cakes and dresser of bodies, a Mohammedan with a picture of Christ on his wall, who may or may not have come from a Shia Muslim group in India. And yet it is in what is not known that the deeper mystery of Leonard Side lies. Naipaul writes of him in such a way that the description is both irreducibly individual in its detail, and yet, in its openness, could be said of anyone, anywhere, at any time:

> I can give you that historical bird's eye view. But I cannot really explain the mystery of Leonard Side's inheritance. Most of us know the parents and grandparents we come from. But we go back and back forever; we go back all of us to the very beginning; in our blood and bone and brain we carry the memories of thousands of beings. I might say that an ancestor of Leonard Side's came from the dancing groups of Lucknow, the lewd men who painted their faces and tried to live like women. But that would only be a fragment of his inheritance, a fragment of the truth. We cannot understand all the traits we have inherited. Sometimes we can be strangers to ourselves. (1994: 9)

'We go back and back forever; we go back all of us to the very begin-ning': it is an inexhaustibly astounding, yet incontrovertible, 'fact' – a source of wonder, and a dimension of our identities that places any sense of affiliation in terms of ethnicity or culture or history in an unimaginably vast perspective. We do not know the fullness of our own inheritance, we do not know the inheritance of others, and we do not know when and how the past exerts its power in us. It is as strangers to ourselves that Naipaul's work, in even its most controversial dimen-sions, speaks to us. *The Enigma of Arrival* invites us to encounter our worlds with that same sense of wonder. To read it as an expression of narrow identification and of disenchantment is to read it for the malaise it treats, and miss the work of healing it performs. Naipaul's work may well be claimed by those who would have him as an ally, and resisted by those who object to his views. But his 'gift of wonder' – like Jack's trip to the pub on a wintery Sunday afternoon to be with his friends for the last time – serves no cause but life itself (2002: 50, 100).

Chapter 6

W. G. Sebald's Travels through *'das unentdeckte Land'*: *Die Ringe des Saturn* (1995)

Alles würde man wundervoll empfinden, wenn man alles empfände, denn es kann ja nicht eines wundervoll sein und das andere nicht. [One would sense everything to be wonderful, if one sensed everything, for it surely cannot be that the one thing is wonderful and the other not.]

Robert Walser, as quoted in a frieze of quotations found in the interiors of Swiss trains

It seems fitting for a study in contemporary literary history to culminate in a reading of W. G. Sebald. The body of work he brought into expression from the late 1980s through to his death in a car accident in 2001, not far from his adopted home of some twenty years near Norwich, England, was itself a culmination, the harvest of a long personal apprenticeship: a German émigré, Sebald had been active as an academic in England since the 1960s, and was a professor of European literature at the University of East Anglia when his first major 'non-academic' work, the 'elemental poem' *Nach der Natur*, was published in 1988 (Michael Hamburger's translation, *After Nature*, was published in 2002). In literary and cultural terms, too, Sebald's work seems to respond, uniquely but representatively, to any number of preoccupations in late modernity. Born in 1944 in the village of Wertach im Allgäu in the German Alps, Sebald figured his own biography as indirectly but profoundly marked by the catastrophe of the Second World War: his work has frequently been read in terms of its tangential but pervasive response to traumatic history, and to the Holocaust in particular. The texture of his work, particularly in the four 'unclassifiable' prose works on which his reputation principally rests – *Vertigo, The Emigrants, The Rings of Saturn* and *Austerlitz* – has the quality of a *summa summarum* in its compendious gathering together of innumerable forms of writing, and its intrinsically intermedial integration of photographs and other visual materials (cf. McCulloh 2003; Horstkotte 2005; Patt 2007). Classified with apparently paradoxical combinations of Fiction/History/Memoir/

Travel, Sebald's books seem to absorb, blur and take to their furthest margins any number of generic traditions. As a gathering of pasts, it has also set a precedent. 'Post-Sebaldian' has been added to the vocabulary of posterities, as a term for writings that blur genres, disciplines and media in meditative autobiographical or autofictional writings.

The resulting lionisation of Sebald as evidence that 'literary greatness is still possible' (Sontag 2000: 5) in what has been called the 'Sebald Phenomenon' (Denham 2006) has been one of the most remarkable in contemporary literature. Indeed, the tenor of the reception, in its rapturous reverence occasionally perforated by resistant debunking, has been akin to that of a Messiah: hailed as a prophet and, on rare occasions, doubted as an impostor. There is a certain irony in the contrast between Sebald's celebrity stature and his own modest, humorous aversion to it, as well as his sympathetic association with the eccentric recluses who populate his pages: he often figured his enterprise in terms that recall the Carl Spitzweg caricature of 'The Poor Poet', huddled under an umbrella in a dank attic, waiting for inspiration (see Spitzweg 1976: 36–7). But what is most remarkable for our purposes is that it is in the reception of a writer recognised for his engagement with the most harrowing of histories that we find the most recurrent language of wonder and enchantment. On the one hand, Sebald may be seen as the literary realisation of Walter Benjamin's interpretation of Paul Klee's 'Angelus Novus': the 'angel of history' who has his 'face turned towards the past', perceiving a 'single catastrophe which keeps piling wreckage upon wreckage' while the storm of progress 'irresistibly propels him into the future to which his back is turned' (Benjamin 1999a: 249). On the other, the 'swirling paths' of his work 'cast a spell' (Schwartz 2007: 12); he is the 'conjuror of what is missing' (Pye 2003: 15); and among the terms that arise most frequently in the snippets of reviews on the inside cover of the English translation of his last prose work, *Austerlitz*, are 'haunting', 'mesmeric, 'sublime', 'spellbinding' and 'wonderful' (Sebald 2001: front matter).

In this effect, as well as in the fibre of his texts, Sebald's work reveals important oversights in the 'rhetoric of exhaustion' (Cronin 2000: 2–3) even as it profoundly engages with the sources of contemporary disenchantment. The fusion of the horrific and the language of wonder suggests that the ostensibly meagre remainder for contemporary travels in 'jet tourism among the ruins' (Fussell 1980: 226) – a fitting description, perhaps, of the travels of a writer who has been described as the 'Rubble Artist' (Banville 2001: no pagination) – may itself be the source of both ethical engagement and something like wonder; even if, as the eponymous fictional biographee of *Austerlitz* remarks of the impact of the vast edifice of the Palace of Justice, it is 'a kind of wonder which in itself is a form of dawning horror' (Sebald 2001: 23). Like Naipaul, Sebald explores 'an area of darkness' that is personal as much as geographical or historical, arguing in his study of the air raids on Germany, *On the Natural History of Destruction*, that 'when we turn to take a backward view, particularly of the years 1930 to 1950, we are always looking and looking away at the same time' (Sebald 2005a: ix). And Sebald's work, both in word and image, registers a sense of both the necessity and impossibility of witness; the challenges to language and ethics posed by that which both demands and defies representation, subverting at the root the lament of there being 'Nowhere Left to Go' (Fussell 1980: 36–43). Sebald's writing brings to the fore the parallel between Francis Bacon's characterisation of wonder as 'broken knowledge' (Bacon 1857–74 (vol. 3): 266) and the epistemological break represented in the Holocaust, as the 'limit case of knowledge and feeling' (Carroll 1997: xi). And in the sense of interconnection that permeates his work in both form and content – that everything is implicated in everything else – his œuvre embodies the idea expressed in Walser's aphorism, borrowed for the epigraph above: that we would experience wonder in our encounter with all things, if we sensed them fully; but that nothing encountered as wonderful is entirely discrete, sequestered off from the illimitably vast category of *'das andere'*.

Die Ringe des Saturn: eine englische Wallfahrt was published in the original German in 1995, and translated into English by Michael Hulse, with Sebald's involvement, for publication in 1998 as *The Rings of Saturn* (without the subtitle's designation, to be discussed in what follows, of *An English Pilgrimage*). While all of Sebald's work takes shape around the Sebaldian traveller's journeys, and walks especially, *Die Ringe des Saturn* is the most immediately recognisable as a travelogue – albeit, in the German publisher's phrase, a *'Reisebericht besonderer Art'* ([1995] 2011). As 'a travel report of a special kind', the account seems to evoke and subvert every tradition one can imagine. It recounts a journey through the not inaccessible county of Suffolk as if it were, as emblematically as Chatwin's Patagonia, 'the outermost limit of the earth' (Sebald 1998: 51–2). It problematises the authority of the witness, in being, among other things, self-reflexively preoccupied with déjà vu on the one hand and what the traveller did not directly witness on the other. It studies the Suffolk landscape and the traveller's place in it as part of a vast network of complexity. And it foregrounds issues of translation. *'Das unentdeckte Land'* is borrowed as a title here from an essay Sebald wrote about one of the most perennial points of reference in his densely allusive prose, Franz Kafka (2003: 78–93), and which he himself borrowed (and translated) from Shakespeare: Hamlet's famous characterisation of death as 'the undiscover'd country from whose bourne no traveller returns' (Shakespeare, *Hamlet*, III, i, 79–80). The allusion is made once again in *The Rings of Saturn* itself (Sebald 1998: 89). In reading Sebald's *Die Ringe des Saturn* as a traveller's tale of wonder profoundly engaged with the disenchantments of the modern world, we will be guided by the many different ways in which Sebald's narrative travels through, and insists we still inhabit, an 'undiscovered country' (cf. Zisselsberger 2010).

The marvels of the East: Suffolk's *Mirabilia*

'In August, 1992, when the dog days were drawing to an end, I set off to walk the county of Suffolk, in the hope of dispelling the emptiness that takes hold of me whenever I have completed a long stint of work' (Sebald 1998: 3). Thus the opening sentence of *The Rings of Saturn* announces itself, inconspicuously enough, as a travelogue – albeit one that from the first links matter-of-fact dates with astrological influences and unmoors its referentiality with obscure emotional longings. It very soon becomes clear that the book is indeed, as the German publisher's phrase has it, a '*Reisebericht besonderer Art*': within the course of the first chapter, the narrative has parted company with the journey that it begins to narrate. It leaps forward to exactly one year after the end of the walking tour, when the narrator was interned in Norwich hospital in a 'state of almost total immobility' (1998: 3); it passes through elegies to lost friends; recounts a search for the seventeenth-century doctor and writer Thomas Browne's skull; conducts an ekphrastic reinterpretation of Rembrandt's *Anatomy Lesson*; engages in a critique of Cartesian rationalism; discusses levitation; and considers Browne's cabinet of curiosities – among other things. The second chapter returns the narrative to the journey itself – almost exactly repeating the opening lines of the book (1998: 29) – but setting out on a very different narrative. The traveller does complete his walk; the journey can, in principle, be traced. But, as Robert MacFarlane found out in attempting to recreate Sebald's walks, the routes are 'littered with false turnings, decoys, and red herrings' (MacFarlane 2007: 82). And in any case, the most immediately striking feature is the dynamic openness of the relations between the journey and its narrative; the way the account wanders through different times and places, through dreams and reminiscence relating to times before and after the walk, and across innumerable forms of writing and image. There is thus a tension between the sense of a story foretold from the start (leading inexorably towards the traveller's hospitalisation) and the freedom expressed through the narrative. It is this transgressive liberalism that is most pronounced in readings of Sebald's work generally as 'a new kind of writing, combining fiction, memoir, travelogue, philosophy, and much else besides' (Banville 2001: no pagination), and in finding in *The Rings of Saturn* in particular an example of the ways in which 'the genre of travel writing is subverted and renewed' (Hulme 2002b: 99).

The term *'renewed'* is carefully chosen here. As Andrew Motion has suggested, 'what felt new in [Sebald's] work had as much to do with subtle adaptations of tradition as it did with pioneering a brand new kind of non-fiction': a 'descriptive ramble along the edge of East Anglia [. . .] interspersed with more or less freestanding reflections on characters and ideas' can be linked to 'late nineteenth- and early twentieth-century travelogues of the kind written by Edward Thomas' (Motion 2007: no pagination). Indeed, what is perhaps most counter-cultural about Sebald's writing is precisely his openness to cultural forms of the past, his digression from an ideology of novelty. The very fact that claiming Sebald for one genre or another is, surely, to miss the most fundamental feature of his forms – their resistance to generic limitations – makes it worth considering Sebald's formal borrowings from writings that pre-date the classificatory systems that his work, in its incommensurability, confounds. *Die Ringe des Saturn* is, as the subtitle in German makes more explicit, *'eine englische Wallfahrt'*: the journey involves 'an English pilgrimage' to the ancient site of Walsingham, as well as taking in en route the site of the sunken village of Dunwich, which had become 'a place of pilgrimage for melancholy poets in the Victorian age' (Sebald 1998: 159), and a visit to see a miniature, exact replica of the Holy Temple of Jerusalem, near Harleston (1998: 239–68). And there are striking points of comparison, too, between Sebald's book and the medieval *mirabilia* genre. Jeremy Millar, in a short but illuminating essay, makes the link, describing *The Rings of Saturn* as 'a book of wonder' (Millar 2007: 113). An Old English example of such compendia of marvels, miracles and monsters at the edge of the world, believed to have been written at around CE 1000, is *The Marvels of the East* – a title which seems especially apposite for Sebald's East Anglian tour.

The very title of *The Rings of Saturn* intimates a symbolic economy drawn from belief systems of a piece with such texts. Throughout his work, Sebald draws on the symbolic system of astrology, figuring his own biography in terms of the 'cold planet Saturn' which is described in *After Nature* as having 'ruled this hour's constellation' on the day of his birth (Sebald 2002a: 88). The first thing that the narrator of *The Rings of Saturn* 'wonder[s]' is whether 'there might be something in the old superstition that certain ailments of the spirit and the body are particularly likely to beset us under the sign of the Dog Star' (Sebald 1998: 3), to which he attributes, tentatively, his illness a year later. It is a view inherited from the Middle Ages and Renaissance, when it was considered an 'incontestable fact that melancholy, whether morbid or natural, stood in some special relationship to Saturn, and that the latter was to blame for the melancholic's unfortunate character or destiny' (Klibansky et al. 1964: 127). The *Schönspergerscher Kalender* of 1495 contains an entry of specific relevance to Sebald's eastern pilgrimage:

> The planet Saturn [. . .] is hostile to our nature in every way and stands over to the east, and is a planet of wicked and worthless men who are thin, dark and dry, and is the planet of men who have no beard, and white hair, and who wear unclean garments. Children who are born under Saturn are misshapen of body and dark with black hair [. . .] are unchaste and do not like to walk with women and pass the time, and also have all evil things by nature. The hour of Saturn is the hour of evil. In that hour God was betrayed and delivered to death. [. . .] (qtd Klibansky et al. 1964: 195)

Saturn, hostile to our nature in every way, standing over to the east: such an ideology frames *The Rings of Saturn*, as it does much of Sebald's work. This may be deployed in such a way as to convey the psychological make-up of the narrator: the comical quality of such wide-eyed terror, slipping into paranoiac totalisation, is often self-consciously parodied in Sebald's writing. But the symbolism is too pervasive to be seen as simply and knowingly satirical. We will return to its relationship with freedom, fate and melancholy. At this point, what is notable is that this places the book at odds with Max Weber's characterisation of modernity as being a time 'of rationalization and intellectualization and, above all, of the "disenchantment of the world"' (Weber 1946: 155). It contributes, too, to the atmosphere in which the traveller approaches East Anglia as 'the outermost limit of the earth' (Sebald 1998: 51–2) – where strange and monstrous creatures, alarming miracles and bizarre peoples, can be found.

The Rings of Saturn chimes with Mary Baine Campbell's account of *The Marvels of the East* as dealing with the 'East' as 'a concept separable from any purely geographical area. It is essentially "Elsewhere"' (Campbell 1988: 48). The narrator frequently refers to the 'extraterritorial' atmosphere (Sebald 1998: 237), balanced by the way in which the traveller himself is sometimes encountered as if he 'had arrived from another planet' (1998: 175–6). As the walk moves down the coastline from Lowestoft, there come into view (also in a photograph) 'tent-like shelters' along the beach. The narrator reflects:

> It is as if the last stragglers of some nomadic people had settled there, at the outermost limit of the earth [*Rand der Erde*], in the expectation of the miracle [*Wunder*] longed for since time immemorial, the miracle which would justify all their erstwhile privations and wanderings. (1998: 51–2; Sebald 2011: 68)

Much hangs, of course, on that 'as if', the linguistic mark of the consciousness of the gap between experience and object, of the essential 'fictionality' of the experience apprehended as such. Indeed:

> In reality [. . .] these men camping out under the heavens have not traversed faraway lands and deserts to reach this strand. Rather, they are from the immediate neighbourhood, and have long been in the habit of fishing there and gazing out to sea as it changes before their eyes. (1998: 52)

We might sense a certain comic bathos here. It registers in the extremity of the distance between the 'as if' and the 'reality' – not only not 'faraway lands', but the 'immediate neighbourhood' (not exotic, but as domestic as could be). Yet the bathos itself marks the distance between objective and subjective, and opens out into a sense that the reality is as strange as that which had first been imagined, redeploying the idea of the *Rand der Erde*:

> I do not believe that these men sit by the sea all day and all night so as not to miss the time when the whiting pass, the flounder rise or the cod come in to the shallower waters as they claim. They just want to be in a place where they have the world behind them, and before them nothing but emptiness. (1998: 52)

What remains is a sense of strange, obscure longings, which, even in being explained, remain opaque. The sense of being on the edge of the world, for all that it is brought into question through bathos, endures.

There may be, as we saw in Naipaul's *The Enigma of Arrival*, a similar subversive process of exoticising the 'centre' at work here – a defamiliarisation of East Anglia into the 'edge of the world', a recognition of the subjectivity and perspectival source of distance. The ironisation involved may be seen as a revision of the *mirabilia* form. Yet the sense of marvels and monsters, even when presented with this conscious irony, is often overtaken by a more psychologically committed investment. At one point, the traveller looks over a cliff edge and sees that

> A couple lay down there, in the bottom of the pit, as I thought: a man stretched full length over another body of which nothing was visible but the legs, spread and angled. In the startled moment when that image went through me, which lasted an eternity, it seemed as if the man's feet twitched like those of one just hanged. Now, though, he lay still, and the woman too

was still and motionless. Misshapen, like some great mollusc washed ashore, they lay there, to all appearances a single being, a many-limbed, two-headed monster that had drifted in from far out at sea, the last of a prodigious species, its life ebbing from it with each breath expired through its nostrils. (1998: 68)

There is, of course, no question in the text as to whether the traveller has encountered an actual sea monster – and the scene is delivered with carefully weighted comedy in the mounting syntax, even as it registers the unsettling nature of the experience as a kind of Freudian primal scene. Yet, as Margaret Bruzelius has noted, as the traveller moves on from the cliffs, the narrator records turning back, and reflects that he 'could no longer have said whether I had really seen the pale sea monster at the foot of Covehithe cliffs or whether I had imagined it (1998: 69) – and thus, in Bruzelius' alert observation, the 'initial sight of a couple making love on the beach has now been completely displaced by the fantastic vision of the sea monster' (Bruzelius 2007: 40). The sense of the marvellous and monstrous, even when ironically self-aware, unmoors a grip on reality. To travel *as if* is itself a doubling consciousness generating its own defamiliarisation: the traveller is in some ways wandering through a generic landscape that contributes to his disorientation. Any ironic awareness adds to, rather than subtracts from, the experience of the marvellous.

The Rings of Saturn collates marvels in compendious numbers. From the strange glow of the herring after death (still, the narrator claims, unexplained) (Sebald 1998: 58–9) to Sebald's namesake, Saint Seybolt's lighting of a fire with icicles (1998: 86), to Algernon Charles Swinburne's 'truly unusual head' and 'fiery red shock of hair' making him 'an object of amazement at Eton' (1998: 162). What is striking about Sebald's presentation of such phenomena is the way that it leads always into engagement or reflexive disengagement, either into a deepening empathetic concern with the experience of that which falls into the category of the marvellous – as in the case of all of the examples listed above – or as a mark of the traveller's own state of mind. The way Sebald's narrative patiently describes friends' working methods, in tones of sobriety shaken by baffled admiration, almost has something about it of Dr Watson's loyal but respectfully distant affection in telling the stories of his friend Sherlock Holmes: the narrator 'marvelled at the degree of dedication' Michael Parkinson 'always brought to his work' (1998: 6); he reports that 'Janine quoted thousands of pages from [Flaubert's] correspondence, never failing to astound me' (1998: 7). Conversely, the narrative allows the encounter with the miraculous to reveal as much about the traveller as the object of vision. It figures the marvellous as a foundation for recognition, but not reification, of otherness. The compendiousness itself, including the gathering of different text-types and images, also bears a certain similarity to the compilations in which books of wonder have been preserved. Though Sebald's endemic use of photographs and other visual materials can be linked with Surrealist works such as André Breton's *Nadja* (cf. Long 2007: 142; Patt 2007: 26–7), the *Marvels of the East* is among the older forms involving a compound of word and image. The debate as to the degree or kind of evidentiary function performed by Sebald's visual materials recalls the speculation among contemporary and subsequent commentators on the *mirabilia* genre over whether the images were 'intended to lend a note of authority' to the scenes described (Karkov 1998: 80).

Part of the resonance and subversiveness of *The Rings of Saturn* in postmodernity lies in the way it evokes and reformulates such pre-modern forms. Partly, it is a matter of literary historical note: we have seen that studies in books of wonder of the past, when casting a glance ahead, find that we 'cannot imagine a diarist of the social and literary stature of Samuel Pepys – Leonard Woolf, say, or Edmund Wilson – faithfully recording monsters he read about or saw' (Daston and Park 1998: 367–8). Sebald's work, certainly regarded as of high literary stature and replete with accounts of marvels, suggests otherwise (even if the record is not always made 'faithfully'). More importantly, it suggests the depth of Sebald's sense of the past. As J. J. Long has argued, we 'need to see Sebald not only as a chronicler of post-Holocaust trauma but as a historian of the *longue durée* of modernity if we are fully to understand why his work matters' (Long 2007: 174). For Long, 'the Holocaust, trauma and memory, melancholy, photography, travel and *flânerie*, intertextuality and *Heimat*' as 'individual topoi' 'can in fact be seen as epiphenomena of a much wider "meta-problem" in Sebald's work': that is, 'the problem of modernity', with modernity understood as 'the seismic social, economic, political and cultural transformations that took place in European societies from the eighteenth century onwards' (2007: 1). This puts its finger on a central concern (and the argument is richly and persuasively realised). But surely trauma, memory, melancholy, travel, intertextuality and *Heimat* all have histories stretching back rather further than the eighteenth century? Indeed, Sebald's evocation of pre-modern forms is very much part of his critique of modernity: it resists a tendency towards presentism; and it loops back to recuperate ways of thinking considered discredited by modernity. On the one hand, these aspects of the text register the persistence of a language of marvels. In marshalling the language of wonder alongside an equally unflinching sense of the horrors of history, it also suggests that Sebald's approach to the traumatic maintains a stance of wonder – of incomprehension, rather than too much knowledge. It draws on a similar idea to that which Gustav Janouch reports Kafka to have expressed: that '*das Wunder und die Gewalt, das sind nur zwei Pole des Unglaubens* [wonder/the miracle and violence are but two poles of disbelief]' (Janouch 1971: 156). These issues become especially pronounced in Sebald's engagement with questions of witness.

Aris Kindt's hand: questioning the witness

The atmosphere of marvels and monsters, extraordinary encounters and inexplicable incidents, in itself raises the question of the credibility of witness. If one of the enduring rhetorical claims of the traveller's tale has been that the scenes described were seen with the traveller's own eyes, and faithfully reported, Sebald's work seems to bring this into question at every level, while also – and herein lies the ethical question – registering the ethical necessity of bearing witness to the present and the past. Among Sebald's abiding obsessions are the questions of the reliability of witness and the ways in which horizons of expectation prefigure what the observer encounters. His work displays a preoccupation with mediated memory and events not directly witnessed, and thus with what Marianne Hirsch calls 'postmemory', in which an 'object or source is mediated not through recollection but through an imaginative investment and creation' (Hirsch 1997: 22). And this interest in bearing witness to what has not been witnessed has a counterpoint in the recurrent experience of déjà vu (of already having been here and now).

We are alerted to the centrality of this preoccupation with witness early on, in the interpretation of Rembrandt's *Anatomy Lesson of Nicolaes Tulp* (Figure 2), which depicts the autopsy of a petty criminal, Aris Kindt. Sebald's interpretation, and its presentation, crystallises his subtle reconfiguration of the issue of witness around the question of Aris Kindt's thumb. That the interpretation of this representation of an autopsy takes place just a few pages into a book ostensibly recording a walk in Suffolk, already, in a sense, dissents against the generic expectation that a travel account engage in an empirical rendition of a journey made, in its digression from the walk. And it is intensely concerned with the way in which expectations and schemata frame the witness's experience. The narrator's essential point is that the gaze of the medical students gathered around the corpse is not directed at the body in question, but at the book at his feet, the 'anatomical atlas in which the appalling

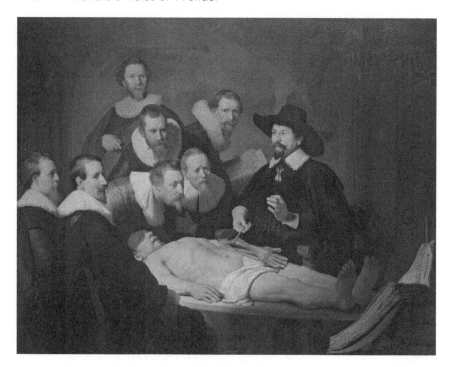

Figure 2   Rembrandt Harmenszoon van Rijn, *The Anatomy Lesson of Dr Nicolaes Tulp* (1632), The Royal Picture Gallery Mauritshuis, The Hague. (Source: http://www.artres.com)

physical facts are reduced to a diagram, a schematic plan of the human being' (Sebald 1998: 13). Rembrandt registers his opposition to this epistemological deference to the 'schematic plan', the narrator suggests, by including in the image a 'crass misrepresentation at the exact centre point of its meaning, where the incisions are made': the thumb, it is claimed, is on the wrong side of the exposed hand (1998: 16).

The narrator makes his case: 'It seems inconceivable that we are faced here with an unfortunate blunder. Rather, I believe there was a deliberate flaw in the composition' which 'signifies the violence that has been done to Aris Kindt' (1998: 17). The 'error' in the painting thus signifies that it is with the victim, 'not the Guild that gave him his commission', that Rembrandt identifies: 'His gaze alone is free of Cartesian rigidity. He alone sees that greenish annihilated body, and he alone sees the shadow in the half-open mouth and over the dead man's eyes' (1998: 17). The auto-optic account of the journey is thus deferred for a critique of empirical auto-opsis, which urges we overcome the Enlightenment philosopher Descartes' logic – his philosophical investigations are regarded as 'one of the principal chapters of the history of subjection' (1998: 13) – and attend to the creaturely, living form as itself.

By extension, this warning against allowing any anatomical atlas to shape our perception feeds into Sebald's self-reflexivity as a writer, and, indeed, goes some way to explaining his preference for the first-person, autobiographical or travel narrative form (involving fictionalisation within it) over the classical novel. Sebald once remarked that the 'traditional novel doesn't give you enough information about the narrator, and I think it's important to know the point of view from which these tales are told, the moral make-up of the teller' (McCulloh 2003: 127). His work, accordingly, has a kind of respiratory quality, fluctuating between introversion and extroversion as its dominant mode, reconfirming the perspective of the teller of the tale between excursions into the lives and experience of others. This happens within the books themselves, and within passages and even sentences. But it also happens across Sebald's œuvre. The first and third prose fictions – *Vertigo* and *The Rings of Saturn* – have as their centre of gravity the psychology of the narrator, while the second and fourth – *The Emigrants* and *Austerlitz* – orbit the experiences and recounted memories of others. The latter books are markedly more 'novelistic' than the former. As with the self-reflexivity of Sebald's presentation of monsters and marvels, the movement of his writing allows, even provokes, the reader to bring into question the way the information is being presented.

The visual materials are so inherent a part of Sebald's books that to ask what function they serve can be answered no more comprehensively than the question of what function the language serves. At times, Sebald has suggested his writing originates in the photographs: 'It was these photographs that eventually got the better of me,' he told James Atlas (Atlas 1999: 278) as an explanation for what got him started on his non-academic work, as if the writing were a kind of response to the photographs, a way of dealing with photographs and all the issues they suggest, close to Roland Barthes' reflections in *Camera Lucida* (1980). The inclusion of photographs is also the most foregrounded way in which the issue of documentary veracity is raised. Photographs are the evidentiary material of choice – and yet there is something (perhaps literally) short-sighted about claiming Sebald hopes to lend a straightforward bulwark of authenticity by the inclusion of images. Sebald's books are full of nomadic images and objects dense with unknown associations – postcards, bric-a-brac, leftovers, photographs found as well as made; fragments of forgotten histories. Very often the power of the found images especially lies in their divorce from their associations, the sense of them being cut adrift, heavy with imponderable

Figure 3   W. G. Sebald, *The Rings of Saturn* (1998, p. 41) © 2013,
The Estate of W. G. Sebald; image courtesy of Eichborn Verlag.

associations and meanings that can only be imagined. They raise the
issue of provenance as well as authenticity (or, to put it another way,
they provoke the traveller's question: 'where do you come from?'). And
though the photographs lend an air of the documentary, this claim is
as often dashed as not, offered as much in evidence, or as a subversion,
of the narrator's viewpoint as much as of any objective verification.
They not only highlight the insufficiency of language; they are often
'contra-depictions' rather than corroborations. The narrator recalls, for
example, that it was 'already after six in the evening when I reached the
outskirts of Lowestoft' and reports that 'not a living soul was about in
the long streets I went through' (Sebald 1998: 40–1), 'verifying' this with
an image that directly contradicts the claim (Fig. 3).

What are we to make of this, then, given that in the bottom right
corner a couple walk arm in arm, and across to the left, a car is pulling
out of the T-junction? The image brings the narrative and the narrator
into question. Yet it seems unlikely that this is an oversight on Sebald's
part. The deployment of images that contradict the narrator's assertions invites the reader to wonder about the narrator's world or state
of mind. But the contra-depiction also creates a kind of metatextual
level of communication, in that the meaning of the juxtaposition lies in

the space between narrative and image, rather than in the explanation or exemplification of one by the other. That meaning is ambivalent: it might be a means of distancing the narrator from the author, providing 'evidence' of his oversights. Or it might be a dry joke along similar lines to that of T. S. Eliot on London Bridge in the 'Unreal City' of *The Waste Land* (1922), who, among the throngs of people, 'had not thought that death had undone so many' (Eliot 1961: 53). Either way, the reader is invited into a kind of coalescence with authorial irony, outside the level of the language and image.

The witness is not only visual: Sebald's writing, in its most fundamental and consistent form, is the performance of an extraordinary feat of listening and memory. It is hard to imagine a method more at odds with that recommended in the Royal Society's motto, *nullius in verbum* (nothing upon another's word), than Sebald's texts. Not only are his texts full of the words of others; nor is it only that he at times relies, with irony, on the guidelines of unreliable sources as if they were reliable (such as an encyclopaedia published in 1911 (Sebald 1998: 9), or an instance in which the traveller is surprised to discover that a hotel does not live up to the description in his guidebook, published 'shortly after the turn of the century' (1998: 42)). One of the most striking features of Sebald's writing is its absorption of reported speech and literary texts into a single, holistic narrative, in which countless voices are subsumed into Sebald's voice (or vice versa), without speech marks designating where one voice begins and another ends. The voice is individual and distinct in the cadences of the tone, and yet compound and diffuse in that the source of the voice is often ramified through many layers. Were we to open a page at random, it would be difficult to know if the narrating 'I' were the narrator himself, or Thomas Browne, or the Vicomte de Chateaubriand, or a gardener the traveller happened to meet. All speak with the same archaic eloquence. The voices of others reach us through layer upon layer of mediation, creating a kind of chorus in the text, but also registering the distance between the word and the experience. In parallel to the narrative-visual creation of open spaces around the text noted above, what this suggests is a consistent rejection of impersonation, of containing the voices of others – it evokes, without containing, the voices of others.

How does this epistemological indeterminacy interact with Sebald's engagement with the traumata of history? If the above seems to suggest a textual abnegation of documentary evidence and proof, what should we make of a stance of radical uncertainty when taken into the most emotive areas of inquiry, of histories that demand to be addressed? Sebald's work, for all the self-conscious and arguably postmodern sense of the relativity of experience, seems guided at all times by a wish not to trespass on the experience itself. The consciousness of the mediatedness of the account, both visually and textually, never strives for telekinetic or appropriative intensity, but rather points outside its own frame of reference towards that which cannot be captured. As Roland Barthes discusses photographs as 'emanations' (2000), so Sebald's forms of witness strive for a kind of receptivity that – again – evokes, rather than contains, the experiences of others.

One of the formative experiences to which Sebald returns again and again in his work goes back to his childhood days in the village of Wertach im Allgäu in the south German Alps, and the 'sense that while I grew up in what was, after all, quite an idyllic environment, at the same time the most horrendous things happened in other parts of Europe' (Bigsby 2001: 144). If one aspect of Sebald's work brings into question the reliability of the witness in terms of that which is present, another is the issue of precisely that which has not been witnessed, but nevertheless registers as being implicated in the traveller's consciousness and conscience. Sebald continues as follows:

> While I was sitting in my pushchair and being wheeled through the flowering meadows by my mother, the Jews of Corfu were being deported on a four-week trek to Poland. It is the simultaneity of a blissful childhood and these horrific events that now strikes me as quite incomprehensible. I know that these things cast a very long shadow over my life. (qtd Bigsby 2001: 144)

What Sebald presents here as the awareness of an 'incomprehensible simultaneity' illustrates the pivotal significance of what we have discussed already as the 'meanwhile problem' (Buzard 1998): the sense of inhabiting a world in which 'elsewheres' increasingly register as a demand on conscience. As noted in Chapter 3, this idea is presented in Voltaire's observation in his 'Poem on the Lisbon Disaster', that while 'Earth Lisbon swallows', the 'light sons of France / Protract the feast, or lead the sprightly dance' (Voltaire 2000: 100). While Sebald's work opposes what he understands as the aesthetics of violence intrinsic in the literary *Schockeffekt* (Mosbach 2008: 74) – we find nothing shrill in his voice, and no dramatic manipulation in his narrative presentation – there is also a compositional, or perhaps decompositional, approach at work that seems to respond to this concern about simultaneity, and that links to a parallel concern about desensitisation through mediation expressed in Susan Sontag's *On Photography*:

> The vast catalogue of misery and injustice throughout the world has given everyone a certain familiarity with atrocity, making the horrible seem more ordinary – making it appear familiar, remote ('it's only a photograph'), inevitable. At the time of the first photographs of the Nazi camps, there was

nothing banal about these images. After thirty years, a saturation point may have been reached. In these last decades, 'concerned' photography has done at least as much to deaden conscience as to arouse it. (Sontag 1977: 21)

In the third chapter of *The Rings of Saturn*, which accounts for the stretch of the walking tour as it moves south from Lowestoft along the coast towards Southwold, we see one way in which Sebald defamiliarises the photograph in contradistinction to these terms. Its emplotment proceeds as follows: the narrator's reflections on the experience of fishermen who sit on the beach lead into a history of the herring (Sebald 1998: 57), before moving on to the recollection of an article 'clipped from the *Eastern Daily Press* several months before, on the death of Major George Wyndham Le Strange, whose great stone manor house in Henstead stood beyond the lake' (1998: 57):

> During the last War, the report read, Le Strange served in the anti-tank regiment that liberated the camp at Bergen Belsen on the 14th of April [. . .] but immediately after VE-Day returned home from Germany to manage his great uncle's estates in Suffolk, a task he had fulfilled in exemplary manner, at least until the mid-Fifties, as I knew from other sources. (1998: 59–62)

The bracketed ellipsis in the passage stands in for an image of a photograph, given a two-page spread, of what we may assume, though we are not directly informed, must be connected to the camp of Bergen Belsen.

Human corpses cover the forest floor in what might, at first glance, have appeared to be a pastoral scene. The image receives no direct commentary, and the mention of Bergen Belsen is in a sub-clause in the account of Le Strange's eccentric relationship with his housekeeper to whom, according to the *Eastern Daily Express* article that the narrator paraphrases (and of which a photograph is also provided), the Major left his entire fortune (1998: 62). It is this passage that is noted by Mark McCulloh when, summarising the controversy that such juxtaposition arouses, asks: 'Is it tasteful to lump such qualitatively different data together?' (McCulloh 2003: 65). What is clear is that the technique – or habit, depending on how programmatic we find this narrative feature – is so intrinsic to Sebald's approach that we cannot view such juxtapositions as anomalies. It is as endemic to his approach to sites of atrocity as the longer, part-fictionalised biographical engagements with human beings who have suffered them. It is part of Sebald's 'post-memorial' practice. What is the effect? And is this an ethically viable aesthetic?

The initial impact of the image as it appears derives precisely from its incommensurability and from its interruption of the narrative: the lack of explication or emplotment registers, irreducibly, this silence:

Figure 4   W. G. Sebald, *The Rings of Saturn* (1998: 60–1). © 2013, The Estate of W. G. Sebald; image courtesy of Eichborn Verlag.

the image is important in part in that it is indeed part of the story of Le Strange: it cannot be worded into his story; the narrative is literally broken. And we can begin to see Sebald's insertion of the photograph as a kind of psychoanalytic enlargement on that 'detail' of Le Strange's story, volunteering it as a cause implicated in his subsequent silent relationship with his housekeeper. As we move beyond the story of Le Strange, the image becomes part of a wider canvas, again echoing through the narrator's own account as well as Le Strange's (we might also note that the image echoes the photograph a few pages earlier of a haul of herring (Sebald 1998: 54)). The effect is similar to that of montage film, such as Resnais' *Night and Fog* (1955). As Andrew Hebard has argued, the scandal surrounding the film may have 'resulted not so much from the images themselves' but from the 'use of archival material juxtaposed with present day footage' and the sense of 'moral contamination' this involved (Hebard 1997: 89). Sebald's prose, like Resnais' film, frequently allows leakage between the horrific and the everyday, between that which has not been witnessed and that which is present in the environment itself, providing no framework for the logical connections between the different forms of data. Whether this is compositional manipulation, or the expression of a mind in motion resisting the censorship of questionable proximities, it represents an insistence on the implicatedness of such unwitnessed, harrowing histories in the rest of human experience. The sense of 'contamination' is especially subversive in that it threatens the reader's ethical security. In the absence of discursive comparison in the text itself, the reader is implicated in – becomes, in a sense, the medium of – seemingly incommensurable experiences, images and events. This redeployment of images and accounts extricates them, defamiliarises them, returns us to a sense of wonder, in that they are not emplotted within explicatory narratives.

The other side of Sebald's work is that it frequently involves an uncanny return, rendering the familiar strange. In *The Psychopathology of Everyday Life*, Freud argues that 'to the category of the wonderful and uncanny we may also add that strange feeling we perceive in certain moments and situations when it seems as if we had already had exactly the same experience, or had previously found ourselves in the same situation. Yet we are never successful in our attempts to recall clearly those former experiences and situations' (Freud 2010: 136). This experience of déjà vu as something miraculous and uncanny casts doubt on the idea that wonder depends on witnessing that which has never been seen before – an ideology of primacy. And it is an experience recurrent in Sebald's work (almost creating a sense of déjà vu in itself). The most remarkable instance takes place when the traveller recounts visiting the poet and translator Michael Hamburger. To the already nuanced idea of witness that déjà vu implies, it adds a sense that we are reading an account that subverts one of the most basic tenets of the traveller's tale in terms of witness: as the record of the survival of the traveller who lived to tell the tale. The narrator recalls the sensation of being guided around the house 'as if I or someone akin to me had long gone about his business there' (Sebald 1998: 184); the feeling 'that Michael was taking me round a house in which I myself had lived a long time ago' (1998: 185). This unnerving experience leads into a wider consideration of the way that while 'chance happenings' occur 'far more often than we suspect, since we all move, one after the other, along the same roads mapped out for us by our origins and our hopes', the narrator's 'rational

mind is nonetheless unable to lay the ghosts of repetition' that haunt him
'with ever greater frequency':

> Scarcely am I in company but it seems as if I had already heard the same
> opinions expressed by the same people somewhere or other, in the same way,
> with the same words, turns of phrase and gestures. The physical sensation
> closest to this feeling of repetition, which sometimes lasts for several minutes
> and can be quite disconcerting, is that of the peculiar numbness brought on
> by a heavy loss of blood, often resulting in a temporary inability to think, to
> speak, or to move one's limbs, as though, without being aware of it, one had
> suffered a stroke. Perhaps there is in this as yet unexplained phenomenon of
> apparent duplication some kind of anticipation of the end, a venture into the
> void, a sort of disengagement, which, like a gramophone repeatedly playing
> the same sequence of notes, has less to do with damage to the machine itself
> than with an irreparable defect in the programme. (1998: 187–8)

The uncanniness of the experience, as well as its being a 'still unexplained' phenomenon, brings into question the role of the witness as
the conveyor of new worlds as such and suggests wonder at precisely
the point where the world is encountered as disconcertingly, uncannily
familiar. Whether regarding the directly present, the distantly implicated,
the strange or the familiar, *Die Ringe des Saturn* thus places the witness
and the reader in the position of a traveller in undiscovered country. In
the sense of repetition, coincidence and fatedness – and in the preoccupation with mortality – it leads, too, into a kind of metaphysic that has
implications for Sebaldian melancholy, to which we now turn.

'As woe and wonder be them amonge!': Sebaldian melancholy

In some ways, Sebald might be seen as the disenchanted traveller par
excellence – a paradigm case of disappointment and disillusionment.
Though the density of Sebald's texts recalls Walter Benjamin's remark
in relation to Proust, that text comes from the Latin *textum*, meaning
web (Benjamin 1999b: 198), we can nevertheless extricate from this
complex weft and weave a collection of disenchantments of aphoristic
economy: 'On every new thing there lies already the shadow of anni-
hilation' (an allusion to Thomas Browne) (Sebald 1998: 24); 'It takes
just one awful second [. . .] and an entire epoch passes' (1998: 31); the
history of artificial light constitutes 'no more than a negligible setback in
the relentless conquest of darkness' (1998: 59); history 'staggers blindly
from one moment to the next' (1998: 256) and 'is but a long account
of calamities' (1998: 295). With hyperbolic edge, but Stoic consistency,

Sebald writes a version of this melancholic resignation into all of his work, with the fatalistic addendum that 'history has a way of repeating itself' (Sebald 2005a: 13) and that 'humankind is unable to learn from its mistakes' (Sebald 1988: 174). Though it is digression that often propels the narrative, Sebald unearths the traces of devastation with monogamous attention, and amasses their accumulation with promiscuous imagination. Skies are often darkening, the clouds drawing in. Throughout his travels, the sights are often 'disappointing' and leave the narrator wondering, as he does in *Vertigo*, if he should have 'stayed at home' with his 'maps and timetables' (Sebald 2002b: 53); even the possibility of purchasing a single satisfactory meal seems beyond his grasp. Wonder in this context may thus seem condemned to that of the ostensibly 'obsolete' definitions of 'Evil or shameful action; evil', 'Destruction, disaster', 'Great distress or grief'; or the apostrophic exclamation in the popular ballad *Northumberland Betrayed by Douglas*, as collected by Francis J. Child: 'as woe and wonder be them amonge!' (1889, *The English and Scottish Popular Ballads*, Bk III, ii, 411; cited *OED*). Yet, it may be argued that while the melancholic tone is undeniable in Sebald's writing, it is a melancholy that is far from resigned. Rather, it is infused with a sense of wonder that always brings into question the resignation it dramatises.

Sebald's melancholy derives in part from the idea we began to explore above in terms of a sense of elsewheres, of the simultaneity, even across time, of events not causally related. He quotes the philosopher Emil Cioran's dictum that living is only possible '*par les deficiences de notre imagination et de notre mémoire* [through the deficiencies in our imagination and our memory]' (Sebald 2005a: 169). As a narrative, *The Rings of Saturn* performs the effort to live in imagination and in memory. Just as Sebald strenuously resisted having his work categorised as 'Holocaust Literature', condemning it as 'a dreadful idea that you can have a sub-genre and make a speciality out of it; it's grotesque' (Jaggi 2001: no pagination), so his sense of melancholy derives, in part, from a resistance to the impulse to sub-categorise or compartmentalise: a sense that no space or time is entirely discrete. We see this dilemma expressed in Sebald's frequent narration of newspaper calendar columns. The day on which the narrator brings *The Rings of Saturn* to completion is 13 April 1995: 'It is Maundy Thursday, the feast day on which Christ's washing of the disciples' feet is remembered, and also the feast day of Saints Agathon, Carpus, Papylus and Hermengild. On this very day three hundred and ninety-seven years ago, Henry IV promulgated the Edict of Nantes' (Sebald 1998: 294–5). But as the list continues, increasingly incommensurable events are linked together: the anniversary of the first performance of Handel's *Messiah* coincides with the day on which the Anti-Semitic League was founded. And, finally, Maundy Thursday, 13 April 1995, was also the day on which the narrator's wife's father died.

Sebald's melancholy is thus, at the level of this historical metaphysic, as much concerned with resistance as with resignation: a subversion of the movement of progress in its objection to forgetting the past as a component of the present, in line with Walter Benjamin's concern that 'every image of the past that is not recognized by the present as one of its own concerns threatens to disappear irretrievably' (Benjamin 1999a: 247). Sebald had expressed the view in his broadly critical doctoral thesis on the work of Alfred Döblin, 'Der Mythos der Zerstörung' ('The Myth of Destruction'), which is to be found, in English, in the Sebald archive at the Deutsches Literararchiv. In terms that suggest one ethical source of his adoption of a melancholy worldview and tone in his work, Sebald writes: 'The resistance offered by melancholy becomes the last bastion of a humanist world-view in the great German novels of this century, in Kafka's fiction and in Mann's *Doktor Faustus*' (though not, he suggests, in Döblin's work) (Sebald, 'The Myth of Destruction': 20). And it is a melancholy that resists forgetting, rather than resigns to accepting. In *Die Beschreibung des Ünglucks* (1985) – that is, '*The Description of* . . .' *Unglück*, which can mean unhappiness, misfortune, disaster, accident – Sebald provides the definitive statement concerning his own understanding of melancholy as an elected stance:

> Melancholy, the contemplation of ongoing misfortune [*Unglück*], has nothing in common with the death wish. It is a form of resistance. And at the level of art especially its function is anything other than purely reactive or reactionary. If melancholy, with a staring gaze, once again calculates that it can only be as it is, then it shows that the mechanism [*Motorik*] of comfortlessness [*Trostlosigkeit*] and that of recognition [*Erkenntnis*] are identical. The description of misfortune contains within itself the possibility of overcoming it. (Sebald 2003: 12; my translation)

If we can see the melancholic view as one of political engagement, however, Eric Santner nevertheless pinpoints an important issue in asking the question, 'why do so many readers find Sebaldian melancholy so *pleasurable*, and how might one imagine the ethical and political dimensions of this pleasure?' (Santner 2006: 62; emphasis in original):

> Is the kind of dark beauty that Sebald so wondrously perfected an invitation toward self-extension into the world in all its brutal and often disastrous complexity, or does it offer the seductions of a kind of quietist complacency in the guise of morally charged sentiment and 'memory work'? (2006: 63)

If Sebald insists on the resistance involved in melancholy, he is also alert to the ethical implications of the consolation the melancholic may take in it. In *Kafka's Other Trial*, Elias Canetti writes that '[i]n the face of life's horror – luckily most people notice it only on occasion, but a few whom inner forces appoint to bear witness are always conscious of it – there is only one comfort: its alignment with the horror experienced by previous witnesses' (Canetti 1974: 4). This ethically unsettling idea – that the horror experienced by others provides the only comfort for those 'whom inner forces appoint to bear witness' (1974: 4) – is a psychological mechanism echoed closely in Sebald's own writing from early on. In his first non-academic publication, *Nach der Natur: Ein Elementargedicht* (1988), translated by Michael Hamburger and published as *After Nature*, the narrator reflects that if life is like a 'Nordic chess tragedy', and an 'arduous enterprise', then 'For comfort there remains nothing but other people's / misfortune [. . .]' (Sebald 2002a: 92–3). The ethical commitment to memory is thus accompanied by the open admission of the comforts of other people's sufferings.

As this suggests, melancholy is not a rational, intellectual position alone; and it too involves framing reality in a specific way, cast in a certain light. The simultaneous assembly and disassembly – the juxtaposition of the incommensurable, the interconnecting of the disparate and diachronic into a medley history that undermines history as a causal narrative – works in two directions. It treads a line between coincidence and fate as two sides of the same coin (in that the one can always be reinterpreted as the other). This tension between freedom and fate, trangression and systematisation, is crucial in the melancholy of *The Rings of Saturn* in terms of the narrator's own sense of fatedness – and resistance to it. *The Rings of Saturn* is characterised by a tension between its digressive wanderings and the rigorous circularity of its narrative composition, between the narrative's liberal disregard for causality in its associative leaps and its gathering sense of intricate patterns across time and space. As the title already intimates, *The Rings of Saturn* is formed in circles, and might be read as recovering the ancient, worldwide form of the 'ring composition' as presented in Mary Douglas' *Thinking in Circles*, for which the 'minimum criterion [. . .] is for the end to join up with the beginning' (Douglas 2007: 1) but which can involve intricate compositional parallelisms and chiasmic symmetries. Douglas' key example is the Book of Numbers which 'has the reputation of a disorderly, unstructured book' but can be read as a 'highly structured ring composition' (2007: 43). The same can be said of *The Rings of Saturn*. At the outset, the narrator tells us that 'several times during the day I felt a desire to assure myself of a reality that I feared had vanished forever by looking out of that hospital window, which, for some strange reason, was draped with black netting' (Sebald 1998: 4). A photograph depicting such a window is inserted into the narrative. This opening scene is echoed in the closing passage in the book, which loops back into the references of the opening chapter, returning again to Thomas Browne, who, Sebald writes,

> remarks in a passage of the *Pseudodoxia Epidemica* that I can no longer find that in the Holland of his time it was customary, in a home where there had been a death, to drape black mourning ribbons over all the mirrors and all canvasses depicting landscapes or people of the fruits of the field, so that the soul, as it left the body, would not be distracted on its final journey, either by a reflection of itself or by a last glimpse of the land now being lost forever. (1998: 296)

The black netting on the hospital window thus becomes, symbolically and retrospectively, a portent of death, and speaks to the recurrent sense in *The Rings of Saturn* that the traveller is already in the country from whose bourn no traveller returns (cf. Beck 2004: 77). Sebald's book is so carefully composed that this must be more than coincidence, and it is perhaps significant that the observation of the black netting across the hospital window does not appear in the first draft of the chapter, and was added after the completion of the full draft (as can be seen by examining the working drafts of *Die Ringge des Saturn in* Folders 7–9 of the Sebald archive). The journey travels south, towards Orford Ness, and – as we saw with relation to Chatwin – to travel south, drawing on Dante, evokes a descent into hell, a journey towards death (Hulme 2002a: 227). The intricacy of the design and its melancholic sense that the end is contained in the beginning is one of the ways in which Sebald's narrative engages with mortality; but the more insistent this compositional fatedness, the deeper the sense of melancholy dramatised becomes, the more autonomous, the more resistant, is the existence of the writing itself.

One of the powerful and recurrent readings of Sebald's writing, nevertheless, suggests that it brings into question an idea of departure, of open encounter with the unknown, insisting instead on the haunting presence of the past as the shaper of the present and future, and – in the most categorical argument in this vein – on 'The Impossibility of Getting Lost' (Zilcosky 2007):

> Whereas traditional literary travellers get lost in order to find their way back home, Sebald undermines this narrative, but not as we might expect: he does not claim that we are all hopelessly lost and thus unable to come home. Rather, he demonstrates how our disorientations never lead to new discoveries, only to a series of uncanny, intertextual returns [. . .] Instead of

providing accounts of nomadism, Sebald tells stories in which subjects can never become sufficiently disoriented, can never really lose their way. Like Freud, Sebald thus views modern travel as primarily uncanny [. . .] producing the sensation that the traveller, no matter how far away he journeys, can never leave his home. (2007: 102–3)

A similar line is taken by Margaret Bruzelius (2007), in reading *The Rings of Saturn* as part of the romance genre in the vein of Walter Scott, suggesting that in Sebald 'adventure transmutes into a self-conscious melancholia: the form imposes itself as an alienated yet inescapable plot' (Bruzelius 2007: 22):

> [T]he consciousness of operating in a highly formalized plot structure is experienced as a luxurious, melancholic imprisonment, for the narrators [Sebald and Joseph Conrad] share the fundamental traits of the adventure hero: they are lucky, they come home safe [. . .] [A]dventure, despite the derring-do, is always about stasis. Conrad and Sebald completely conform to this generic imperative [. . .] despite the continuous emphasis on motion across a rebarbative and ultimately meaningless landscape, adventure only returns us to where we already are. (2007: 186)

Such arguments highlight crucial aspects of Sebald's texts: as we have seen already, the narrative provides ample substantiation of 'melancholic imprisonment'. But they identify the issue Sebald engages with, rather than the life of the writing in its resistance to this resignation. It does beg the question of whether Sebald's text can be read in such direct terms: does the performance of a formalised plot structure necessarily involve, at the level of tone, subscription to its perceived values? Does the unnerving experience of *Unheimlichkeit* fall so neatly on one side of an either/or model of displacement? And does Sebald's dramatisation of the experience of being unable to break the circuits of a melancholic network, formal and thematic, not register resistance to these perceived laws in the existence of the writing? In what follows, I will develop the suggestion made by Deane Blackler that 'Sebald's engagement with the patterns discernible in the coincidences and contiguities of one kind and another suggests that his primary position is one of wonder rather than the melancholy one he ironizes in the lighter caricature of the ubiquitous writerly narrator constructed in his own image' (Blackler 2007: x).

It is with this in mind that we might consider the complaints of contrivance, as in the case of Alan Bennett's remarks in his diaries:

> I persevere with Sebald but the contrivance of it, particularly his un-peopling of the landscape, never fails to irritate [. . .] Maybe East Anglia is like this (or more like it than West Yorkshire, say) but Sebald seems to stage-manage both the landscape and the weather to suit his (seldom cheerful) mood. Kafka has

been invoked in this connection, but Kafka dealt with the world as he found it and didn't dress it up (or down) to suit him. (Bennett 2005: 308)

Of this 'stage-management', Bennett comments, in a remark that is, perhaps, more insightful into Sebald's tone than it claims: 'Once noticed, Sebald's technique seems almost comic' (2005: 380). Will Self, too – though with a shared sense of irony – notes that critics have been 'taken by the improbability of anyone walking – as Sebald's alter ego does – for the 25-odd coastal miles from Lowestoft to Middleton in Suffolk, without meeting a considerable number of *people*' (Self 2009: no pagination).

There can be no doubt that Sebald did indeed 'stage-manage' the landscape, and the weather in particular. The opening sentence of the second chapter of the draft for *Die Ringe des Saturn* is, notably, entirely contradictory of the first sentence of the published version. Instead of a 'grey, overcast day' (Sebald 1998: 29), we have: '*Es war ein heller Tag, als ich im August 1992 mit dem Dieseltriebwagen, der zwischen Norwich & Lowestoft verkehrt, an die Küste hinunterfuhr.* [It was a bright day in August that I travelled down along the coast by the diesel train which ran between Norwich and Lowestoft]' (Sebald, 'Handwritten Drafts', Fol. 3: 5). But digging out the meteorological reports for August 1992 to establish what the weather was really like on that bright overcast day in August 1992 would not contribute to our understanding of the book. Nor is the point to be dealt with by insisting, as we might, that while Sebald may exaggerate, he surely does not entirely fabricate the idea that rural Suffolk is a sparsely populated part of the world. We could ask: has ever a book been more densely populated than *The Rings of Saturn*, by both the living and the dead and – perhaps the most delicate fear and longing in its pages – those somewhere in-between? Every page of *The Rings of Saturn* is dense with the lives of others.

Perhaps most importantly, the ironisation of this position, its humour, should not be underestimated. As Michael Hulse has remarked, '[i]n his writing [Sebald] comes across as a melancholy man, but he's really a very funny man' (Atlas 1999: 292). Asked about the apparent contrast between his 'sombre world view and his equable disposition' (1999: 292) Sebald replied, '"One is born with a certain psychological constitution, and then one discovers that life is partly dispiriting and partly exhilarating in its oddness"' (qtd 1999: 278). The melancholic resignation is consistently ironised and brought into question in Sebald's writing, and the role of self-aware humour – and its etymological link to humility – is crucial in Sebald's nuancing of the temptation to paranoid totalisation. The link between melancholy and humour is a deep one.

As Klibansky, Panovsky and Saxl write in *Saturn and Melancholy*, the '[m]elancholic and humourist both feed on the metaphysical contradiction between finite and infinite, time and eternity, or whatever one may choose to call it. Both share the characteristic of achieving at the same time pleasure and sorrow from the consciousness of this contradiction':

> The melancholic primarily suffers from the contradiction between time and infinity, while at the same time giving a positive value to his own sorrow 'sub specie aeternitatis', since he feels that through his very melancholy he has a share in eternity. The humorist, however, is primarily amused by the same contradiction, while at the same time deprecating his own amusement 'sub specie aeternitatis' since he recognises that he himself is fettered once and for all to the temporal. Hence it can be understood how in modern man 'Humour', with its sense of the limitation of the Self, developed alongside Melancholy which had become a feeling of an enhanced Self. (Klibansky et al. 1964: 234–5)

Sebald's lugubrious hyperbole sounds a lot like that of Joseph Roth in '»Romantik« des Reisens' (an echo and further ironisation of the Conrad essay, 'The Romance of Travel' considered in Part I, Chapter 2):

> The pleasure that one may experience before a journey is always lesser than the annoyance that journey causes in the end. Nothing is so annoying as a huge railway station, that looks like a monastery, before the entrance of which I always consider, for a moment, whether I shouldn't rather take off my shoes than call the luggage carrier [. . .] I must always force myself to inform the counter clerk, shut off from the entire world, of my destination. He has only a single open square, from which to receive money and noise. I always wonder that he wouldn't rather listen with his hands . . . (Roth 2006: 221–2; my translation)

The Sebaldian traveller's own sufferings are either serious and decisive (and in this case only hinted at) or incidental and trivial (and in this case lugubriously exaggerated, to comic effect). Indeed, we see in Sebald's working methods a kind of process of increasing humility. Take the passage that, in Michael Hulse's translation, appears as follows: 'Several times during the day I felt a desire to assure myself of a reality I feared had vanished forever by looking out of that hospital window, which, for some strange reason, was draped with black netting [. . .]' (Sebald 1998: 4). In the working draft of the first chapter of *Die Ringe des Saturn*, Sebald wrote the sentence that eventually appeared as above, as follows: *'Das im Laufe des Tages in mir verschiedentlich sich rührende Bedürfnis, der, wie ich befürchtete, für immer verschwundenen Wirklichkeit durch einen Blick aus diesem Fenster mich zu versichern [. . .]'* (Sebald, 'Handwritten Drafts', Fol. 3: no pagination). In the published version, the sentence has been adapted: '*Der im Laufe des Tages des öfteren schon in mir aufgestiegene Wunsch, der, wie ich befürchtete, für immer entschwundenen Wirklichkeit durch einen Blick aus diesem sonderbarerweise mit einem schwarzen Netz verhängten Krankenhausfenster mich zu versichern*' (Sebald 2011: 13). The significance of the addition of the reference to the black netting – '*mit einem schwarzen Netz*' – has already been noted. But other differences here are also quite telling: '*Bedürfnis*' [need] becomes '*Wunsch*' [wish]; '*ver*schwundenen Wirklichkeit' [disappearing reality] becomes 'ent*schwundenen Wirklichkeit*' – a subtle alteration which suggests that the reality is disappearing from the first-person, rather than transforming or transporting itself into nothing ('*ver*' indicates a transformation; '*ent*' negation). So a 'need' is downplayed – as if, on reflection, this seems immoderate, self-indulgent – to a wish. A reality feared to be disappearing from 'the' world, on reflection, was feared to be disappearing from 'a' world – that of the narrator. Both changes illustrate the workings of Sebald's conscience over his text – a modesty of admission which is also a kind of realism, repressing and qualifying the exaggerations of desires and perceptions into more objective wordings (more objective in that they acknowledge the subjectivity of the feelings themselves).

Nearly all of Sebald's travel narratives describe setting out in the hope of getting over periods that are described as 'difficult', but the specifics of these difficulties hover in the background. The sufferings Sebald the traveller chooses to mention are, on the whole, closer to tribulations than traumas. A sleepless night in a hotel (one closes the hotel window, it's too hot; opens it, and the traffic is too noisy) (Sebald 1998: 82); the apparent impossibility of ever finding a satisfactory meal and thus settling, yet again, for a 'burger combination' as a surprisingly frequent customer at McDonald's (1998: 85); the necessity of quenching one's thirst with cherry coke instead of the requested mineral water, 'drained at a draught like a cup of hemlock' (1998: 176). They are not the ordeals of an Odysseus, and are closer to what Andrew Motion has described as Sebald's 'occasionally Eeyore-ish, lugubrious manner' (Motion 2001: no pagination). To describe the marvellously weighted set-piece in which the narrator, in the most self-ironising parody of *Moby-Dick* imaginable, engages at length in one-to-one combat with a plate of fish and chips, to no avail, as 'involuntary comedy' and a 'stylistic faux pas' (Bond 2006: 39), and to explain it as what 'happens when the melancholic gaze has to be upheld at all costs' (2006: 41), is to repeat a joke without noticing that it was told as such in the first place.

We began this section by considering the way that Sebald's writing has written through it a litany of melancholic fatalisms, and the way this leads into a melancholic sense of the interconnection of different times and places in one another. In extricating such statements from the network of the texts, however, we read on the level of rhetoric, rather than of the tone that emerges, in the way these instances interact with one another compositionally. One of the ways in which the resignation – but not the melancholy itself – is most subtly ironised is in the open side of the intricate interconnections within the text. How close the lines that Sebald writes towards the end of the book sound to those attributed the Dowager Empress Tz'u-hsi: Sebald's narrator writes, ostensibly in bringing his narrative towards resolution: 'Now as I write, and think once more of our history, which is but a long account of calamities [. . .]' (Sebald 1998: 295). This assertion echoes the very words of the empress, who had found in the silkworm the 'ideal subjects, diligent in service, ready to die' (1998: 151): 'Looking back, she said, she realized that history consists of nothing but misfortune and the troubles that afflict us, so that in all our days on earth we never know one single moment that is genuinely free of fear' (1998: 153). In such ways, *The Rings of Saturn* always presents more than can be contained within its argument, opening out into uncertainty and wonder even at the moments in which it appears to make its most categorical assertions.

Unheimliche Heimat: travel and translation

It might already seem unlikely, as is reported in *The Rings of Saturn*, that one of Norwich City Hospital's nurses should remark to another that 'the Maltese, with a death-defying insouciance quite beyond comprehension, drove neither on the left nor on the right, but always on the shady side of the road' (1998: 18). That 'Lizzie', as is reported in *Die Ringe des Saturn*, uttered the words, '*die Malteser mit unbegreiflicher Todesverachtung nicht links fahren und nicht rechts, sondern stets auf der schattigen Seite der Straße*' (Sebald 2011: 29), even less so. Yet, while the German-language text often includes reported speech in the English language – usually marked out from the rest of the text through the use of italics: a distinction not made in the English versions – much of the language is presented in the German language. It is translated, as well as adapted and absorbed, into the narrator's fluent though also idiosyncratic, almost archaic German.

I open this section on the issue of travel and translation by remarking this feature to illustrate that issues of translation are central to Sebald's enterprise, and more overtly thematised than in many traveller's tales, before we even begin to consider the remarkable history of the translations themselves and the international history of their reception. Indeed, Sebald's writing literally comes into being, in part, through acts of translation. The German-language texts, punctuated as they are with English, French and Italian (in descending order of frequency and among other languages), largely involve travel through other, primarily European, linguistic cultures, and are made up in no small part of the reported speech of the people the traveller encounters on his journeys. And Sebald's work always inherently involves – and is, I will suggest, deeply concerned with – translation as part of the experience of travel and language: this is one of the ways in which *Die Ringe des Saturn* and *The Rings of Saturn* involve travelling through '*das unentdeckte Land*' – or 'the undiscovered country'. The translations contribute something essential to the work in itself: its sense of inhabiting what, to borrow the title of one of Sebald's studies of Austrian literature, we may call an *Unheimliche Heimat* (1991) – an unhomely, or uncanny, homeland.

Sebald's deep involvement in the translation of his work into English is widely noted. (Less often observed in Anglophone criticism is that Sebald was also involved in the translation of his work into French.) And Sebald was himself an active and influential agent in terms of translation: he was the first director of the British Centre for Literary Translation at Norwich (Denham and McCulloh 2006: 8). In terms of the reception of his work, Sebald's ascent to being widely regarded as one of the most important writers in world literature was, initially, carried out largely in response to the English translations (an unusual event in English-language book culture in itself), while there was a somewhat more sceptical response in terms of both critical appraisal and sales in Germany (cf. Denham and McCulloh 2006: 1). Mark McCulloh writes in terms of 'Two Languages, Two Audiences: The Tandem Literary Œuvres of W. G. Sebald' (McCulloh 2006). English-language scholarship often prioritises Sebald's reception in English over his production in German as a chart of the evolution of his output (as if the power and value of the texts lay in their effect more than in their causes) (see McCulloh 2003; Patt 2007). And it is quite striking that Sebald has almost as much, if not more presence as a figure in 'English Literature' as he does in 'German Literature' or Germanistik. While Sebald receives substantial commentary in the *Cambridge History of Twentieth-Century English Literature* (Marcus and Nichols 2004: 433–5, 765), he is not mentioned in the *Cambridge History of German Literature* (Watanabe-O'Kelly 1997) at all.[1] Sebald's work thematises the issues this raises from the first. It is this, and the role of and relations between travel and translation in the book itself – or rather, books themselves – that will primarily concern us here.

As Michael Cronin has argued in *Across the Lines*, there has been a relative neglect in studies in travel and travel writing of the 'the role of language in the construction of identity of both the traveller and the other'; and this '[i]ndifference to the question of language [. . .] has led to a serious misrepresentation of both the experience of travel and the construction of narrative accounts of these experiences' (Cronin 2000: 2–3). One of Cronin's points, as we saw in Part I, is that 'the detailed encounter with language difference points to the bankruptcy of the widespread rhetoric of exhaustion on the subject of travel' (2000: 2–3). The neglect is 'all the more telling', Cronin suggests, in that 'one of the most commonplace experiences of the traveller is the sudden humiliation of language loss as things go disastrously wrong and familiar words reveal themselves to be worse than useless' (2000: 2). Sebald's traveller in *The Rings of Saturn* reflects on this experience, in a slightly modified form, when his appearance and English causes the shop assistant in a grocer's shop to 'gape [. . .] with her mouth half open' as if he had 'landed from another planet' (Sebald 1998: 175–6). The sense of extraterritoriality, of an unknown environment, is magnified by such linguistic encounters.

Sebald is, among other things, an interpreter of English culture from the perspective of a foreigner. The journey described is that of a German emigrant resident in Suffolk, England, who goes on a solitary walking tour of the county. The traveller – like the traveller of *The Enigma of Arrival* – is both a long way from his original home and close to his adopted home: that is, the journey he makes is not far, but the point of departure is itself already deferred, the result of a previous journey, an emigration. Unlike Naipaul's traveller, Sebald's traveller stays within the one 'world' of Europe, but he moves further in terms of language: with this traveller, the language he speaks in and thinks in and writes in is not that of those around him (he would expect that the majority of the indigenous population will not be able to understand his language, though the sound of the language may be common knowledge). He is describing his environment in a way many of its inhabitants cannot understand. Where Naipaul's language, as we have seen, travels with different associations in different places, Sebald's things travel but have different names. In the story about a Paul Bereyter, a former school teacher of the narrator's, it is recalled that in French lessons in the May meadows, 'we easily grasped what *un beau jour* meant, and that a chestnut tree might just as well be called *un chataignier en fleurs*' (Sebald 2002c: 38). Sebald is a learner of other languages, including those of specialised vocabularies: the multilingual quality of the prose has a complement in the usage of terminologies drawn from diverse fields: the teller of the first tale in *The Emigrants* knows (or finds out, or remembers on hearing) that the ivy is Virginia creeper, and the trees are lime, elm, and 'holm' oak (Sebald 2002c: 4); that when a bird is shot in flight, what falls to the ground is called 'the report' (2002c: 11).

Sebald's readership, in the first writing, is a German-language one: in the first instance, the book, as 'travel report', thus has the character of a report back to the homeland. And the language more subtly orients itself back to Germany in the German original: '*der deutsche Ozean*' ['the German ocean'] (Sebald 2011: 69) rather than '*die Nordsee*' ['the North Sea'] (Sebald 1998: 53). Conversely, the translation often involves substantial adaptation in what appears to concern the protection of privacy: a photograph is provided of Thomas Abrams' house in the German (Sebald 2011: 287), but not in the English. The comparison foregrounds the way in which Sebald's writing thematises the pronounced sense in travel narratives, that they register an idea of putative readership or projected audience. To travel across the lines of language is to highlight (or disavow) the specificity of the linguistic representation or reproduction of the environment encountered.

The English translation, strangely enough, brings the 'original' text closer to the original 'material'. The German is already a translation (and adaptation); the original comes into being in an act of linguistic translation. The English translation is a translation 'back' – in a sense, it precedes as well as succeeds the German original. What Sebald's narrator remembers – as in the case of the nurses' dialogue above – is a translation. A memory is overlaid by translation as much as by imagination. It emphasises the absence in the text of a direct referentiality. In the German text, English words appear italicised. The gardener the traveller meets in the second chapter, Hazel – who pre-echoes many of the ideas that Sebald would express later in *The Natural History of Destruction* – recalls the '*dog fight*' (1998: 40), italicised in the German, and is reported to have spoken as follows: '*It had seemed like a friendly game*, sagte Hazel, *and yet now they fell, almost instantly*' (1998: 40). It lends the German inclusions of English a kind of talismanic resonance, as if the narrative were possessed momentarily by the voice of another.

One of the most pertinent scenes in which such issues are raised is the encounter, noted earlier, between the traveller and the poet and translator Michael Hamburger. The approach to the meeting involves carefully deployed allusions to the translator's work. As the traveller emerges from Dunwich Heath as night falls, the narrative includes (italicised in the German) the phrase, '*Night, the astonishing, the stranger to all that is human, over the mountain-tops mournful and gleaming draws on*' (1998: 206). This is from Hölderlin's 'Bread and Wine' (1800–1). It appears in the German-language original in English translation, and is a slight adaptation of Michael Hamburger's own translation: 'Night, the astonishing, *there*, the stranger to all that is human, / Over the mountain-tops mournful and gleaming draws on' (Hölderlin 1998: 249). This leads into a biographical portrait of Hamburger's emigration from Germany to England, before the encounter itself. A central moment in the meeting concerns what are attributed to Hamburger as his own words, in German in *Die Ringe des Saturn*, in English in *The Rings of Saturn*:

> Does one follow in Hölderlin's footsteps, simply because one's birthday happened to fall two days after his? Is that why one is tempted to cast reason aside like an old coat, to sign one's poems and letters 'your humble servant Scardinelli' [. . .]? Does one begin to translate elegies at the age of fifteen or sixteen because one has been exiled from one's homeland? Is it possible that later one would settle in this house in Suffolk because a water pump in the garden bears the date 1770, the year of Hölderlin's birth? For when I heard that one of the near islands was Patmos, I greatly desired there to be lodged, and there to approach the dark grotto. And did Hölderlin not dedicate his Patmos hymn to the Landgrave of Homburg, and was not Homburg also the maiden name of Mother? Across what distances in time do the elective affinities and correspondences connect? How is it that one perceives oneself in another human being, or, if not oneself, then one's precursor? The fact that I first passed through British Customs thirty-three years after Michael [. . .] (Sebald 1998: 182)

The passage expresses some of the mainsprings of Sebald's thought; and translation plays a central role. The only part of this passage that appears in English in the German is the sentence beginning with the words, 'For when I heard', which is itself an allusion to Hamburger's translation of Hölderlin. And the narrative here textually performs the idea expressed in the passage. Hamburger's reported identification with Hölderlin transforms, in the course of two sentences, into the narrator's with Hamburger. The sentences, 'Across what distance in time do the elective affinities and correspondences connect?' and, 'How is it that one perceives oneself in another human being?' could be either those of Hamburger or those of Sebald's narrator; in both the German and the English, the 'original' language is untraceable. The 'source' of the narrative voice here is unidentifiable, and mediated through layers of translation. No narratorial marker distinguishes between the voice that is demonstrably Hamburger's in reference to Hölderlin, and that of Sebald's narrator, demonstrably the 'speaker' of the sentence, 'The fact that I passed through British Customs thirty-three years after Michael [. . .]' The sentence midway is acutely apposite: 'How is it that one perceives oneself in another human being, or if not oneself, then one's precursor?' (1998: 182). It reflects – in both the English and the German

– a haunting quality of indeterminacy that is in keeping with the sense of exile described.

Sebald persistently breaks the basic grammar of the German language.[2] Sebald's German has syntactical marks of Englishness in the ordering of subject, object, verb. It is a German with an almost English-language sentence structure, with subject followed by predicate followed by object. One of the first rules learned by the student of German is that the verb often goes at the end of the sentence. The out of place verbs in the following, drawn from the opening pages of *Die Ringe des Saturn*, are highlighted in non-italics:

> *Vielleicht war es darum auf den Tag genau ein Jahr nach dem Beginn meiner Reise, daß ich, in einem Zustand nahezu gänzlicher Unbeweglichkeit,* eingeliefert wurde *in das Spital der Provinzhauptstadt Norwich, wo ich dann, in Gedanken zumindest,* begonnen habe *mit der Niederschrift der nachstehenden Seiten.* (Sebald 2011: 11–12)

Michael Hulse's translation into English in *The Rings of Saturn* is in the elegant English that follows:

> Perhaps it was because of this that, a year to the day after I began my tour, I was taken into hospital in Norwich in a state of almost total immobility. It was then that I began in my thoughts to write these pages. (Sebald 1998: 3–4)

Yet – without in any way suggesting this would have been a preferable translation – the most literal translation of the sentence in terms of grammar might without too much exaggeration have been:

> Perhaps it was because of this that, a year to the day after I began my tour, I, in a state of almost total immobility, into hospital in Norwich was taken, where I, in my thoughts at least, with the writing of these pages began.

It is possible that Sebald's persistent anti-grammar may derive from living in England for most of his adult life, given that the sentence structure is closely aligned to standard English. To this degree, the syntax may have arisen out of circumstance. But we are not dealing with a simple case of 'D-English' in reverse (*engleutsch?*). However it arose, there can be no doubt that a writer who so extensively and thoroughly worked on draft after draft, sentence by sentence, chose to retain this peculiarity in his finished prose. The effects are of special relevance to us here. The merger of German and English structures, the voice's advertent and diverting linguistic emigration, is itself significant as a mark of the estrangement of the traveller. Equally important is the effect on the reader: disturbances in the grammar jar and jolt; prevent slips in vigilance. The sentence structure makes it more likely that the reader will have to go back and read the sentence again. It makes Sebald's writing recognisable. It makes the language strange. It makes it sound archaic and acutely formulated. It sounds like it comes from the past. In short, it condenses in the very structure of the language many of the thematic preoccupations that characterise Sebald's work generally. In both the German and the English, the language itself is manipulated in such a way as to register the disorientation of the narrator, and disorient the reader: the mesmeric elegance of the English is effective in the same way the expatriated German is, as an unmooring, almost anachronistic effect.

Mark McCulloh has observed that 'a certain playfulness, based in allusions and linguistic associations, is sometimes vacated in the English versions in favour of pensive earnestness, while on the other hand the drier, more matter-of-fact descriptions in the German original often take on a more luminous, poetic character in the translations' (McCulloh 2006: 13). The German text often includes far more specific and detailed measurements and dates. The measurements for Rembrandt's *Anatomy Lesson* are given in more precise detail in the German – '*eineinhalb*' (one-and-a-half) in the German, 'large' in the English (Sebald 2011: 23; 1998: 13). Measurements are Anglicised ('*zwanzig Meter*' becomes 'twenty yards' ([1995] 2011: 87; [1995] 1998: 68). The name of Frederick Farrar is consistently given in full in the German, only the second name in the English (2011: 64; 1998: 47). There may be in this a kind of equivalence at work, in that both effects are unsettling.

Sebald's deep involvement in the English and the French translations, along with the poetic dedication of his translators (thus far, into English, Michael Hamburger, Michael Hulse, Anthea Bell, Iain Gailbraith and Jo Catling), make the prospect of later translations unlikely. And we may speak, I think, of 'versions', not only because of this collabora-tive involvement, but because Sebald's writing is concerned with its own translatability or untranslatability from the first. Its passage into other languages is one of its inherent features as a voyage of recovery and renewal, and part of an epistemology in which the referent, or the subject, is largely evoked through the silences in the texts. It has some-thing of Mallarmé's sense of the relations between language and reality in the passage cited by Walter Benjamin in 'The Task of the Translator':

> The imperfection of languages consists in their plurality, the supreme one is lacking: thinking is writing without accessories or even whispering, the immortal word still remains silent; the diversity of idioms on earth prevents everybody from uttering the words which otherwise, at one single stroke, would materialize as truth. (qtd Benjamin 1999b: 78)

Perhaps the most prominent change made between the German and the English, besides the omission of *'eine englische Wallfahrt'*, concerns this sense of the silence that is evoked, but not captured in language. Within the texts, too, there is this difference. Walsingham is designated as a destination for pilgrimages (reference is to the '*Wallfahrtsort*' of 'Walsingham' in the German (Sebald 2011: 37), but only 'Walsingham' in the English (Sebald 1998: 24). Is it that within the linguistic community of English, the designation is implied already by an expectation of cultural memory of the significance of the place? Or is it, rather, part of the thematisation of translation as part of the process of emigration? In the closing lines of the books, the '*bald auf immer verlorene Heimat*' (2011: 350) – the *Heimat*, both home and land, soon to be lost forever – is lost again to become 'the land now being lost forever' (1998: 296). The questions of travel and translation, including the ways in which translation itself thematises loss, thus becomes one of the most fundamental ways in which Sebald's work addresses its own themes.

On the lives of silkworms: Sebald's living forms

At the end of the first chapter of *The Rings of Saturn*, the narrative asks an open question which, though never answered directly, defines the rest of the narrative as, at one level, an oblique answer to it. It concerns Thomas Browne's reflections on the urn of Patroclus:

> since the heaviest stone that melancholy can throw at a man is to tell him he is at the end of his nature, Browne scrutinizes that which escaped annihilation for any sign of the mysterious capacity for transmigration he has so often observed in caterpillars and moths. That purple piece of silk he refers to, then, in the urn of Patroclus – what does it mean? (Sebald 1998: 26)

While the question is left to linger, open, across the subsequent text, the thread of silk is densely woven into its fibre, creating a web of associations and echoes rather as Sebald's calendar columns connect the disparate and diachronic around the coincidence of the date. There are the 'birds of paradise and the golden pheasants on the silken tapestries' at Somerleyton Hall (1998: 33); the North Sea fishermen's herring nets of 'coarse Persian silk' (1998: 56); the resemblance of Swinburne to the 'ashy grey silkworm, *Bombyx Mori*' (1998: 165); the 'silken rope' by which one of the estate managers of Earl Ferrers is publicly hanged (1998: 262) – to note only a few. The motif of silk arises most overtly as the focus of the narrative at the outset, in the sixth chapter (that is, one of the two central chapters among ten), and in the last chapter.

This organisation is one of the features that links Sebald's narrative to the 'ring composition' structure noted above (in which, in the classical ring composition, the 'whole burden of its message' is 'condensed into the mid-turn' (Douglas 2007: 258)). Both the central and the final chapter concern the question of silk cultivation: under the dominion of the Dowager Empress Tz'u-hsi at the heart of the Chinese Empire in the nineteenth century in the central chapter; and, in the final chapter, as a drawing together of the many threads of the preceding narrative in an encompassing, broad history of sericulture.

The method by which silk is threaded through the narrative, and the methods by which it is cultivated, are notably at odds. And it would not be entirely fanciful to suggest of *The Rings of Saturn* that one way of reading the book is to see the 'whole burden of its message' (Douglas 2007: 258) lying in the tension between them. It is a tension between an ideology of utility, of life utilised as a means to an end, and one of openness to life in and of itself. The dowager empress is presented as a kind of imperial inversion of the melancholic: 'The more ostentatious the demonstrations of her authority became [. . .] the more the fear of losing the infinite power she had so insidiously acquired grew within her' (Sebald 1998: 150) – through to her last words (thus reported), as a pre-echo of the narrator's closing passage, that 'history consists of nothing but misfortune and the troubles that afflict us' (1998: 153). The only living creature to 'arouse strong affection in her' is the silkworm:

> These pale, almost transparent creatures, which would presently give their lives for the fine thread they were spinning, she saw as her true loyal followers. To her they seemed the ideal subjects, diligent in service, ready to die, capable of multiplying vastly within a short span of time, and fixed on their one sole preordained aim, wholly unlike human beings, on whom there was basically no relying, neither on the nameless masses in the empire nor on those who constituted the inmost circle about her and who, she suspected, might go over at any time to the side of the second child Emperor she had installed. (1998: 152)

The cultivation of the silkworm and the manufacture of silk becomes, in the final chapter, a kind of emblematic record of human society. Sericulture connects the Chinese Empire of 2700 BCE, in which Huang Ti instructed that silk manufacture provide employment for and 'increase the happiness' of the people (1998: 276) to the internecine political wrangling of the Duc de Sully and Olivier de Serres in seventeenth-century France over the benefits of silk cultivation in agricultural France (1998: 277–9); it connects the eighteenth-century Norwich manufactories (1998: 286) to the revival of sericulture in Germany under the fascists (1998: 291–4) to the Amritsar massacre by the British in India, in 1919 (1998: 295). All of the stories combine power relations and suffering with the desire for beauty or progress, and even the tradition of mourning, in wearing 'heavy black silk taffeta' (1998: 296) becomes implicated in a more complex history.

Sebald, who has elucidated so many aspects of Kafka's writing, would likely have agreed that '[n]othing alive can be calculated' (Kafka 2002: 116). The incalculable complexity of this history, and Sebald's investment of his narrative with so many instances that open out into yet more potential interrelations and implications, is less a system of relations than a recognition of the irreducibly complex, which never loses sight of the living experience of its 'subjects' as something beyond its final understanding. That last image, then, of the silk mourning ribbons being placed over the mirrors and canvases 'so that the soul, as it left the body, would not be distracted on its final journey, either by a reflection of itself or by a last glimpse of the land now being lost forever' (Sebald 1998: 296) is at once a portent of death, a glimpse of the transmigration of souls, and a thread leading out into a network of complexity that defies the closure of its own symbolism. It links back to the black netting draped over the hospital window in the book's opening scene (1998: 4), suggesting, structurally and subtly, that we are reading the account of one in limbo between life and death, distracted on his final journey. It recalls that the silkworm is the creature that Thomas Browne had studied as evidence of the transmigration of living things. But the silk, covering the distractions of a reflection of the self or the land being lost forever, itself becomes less a note of conclusion, than one of wonder, a distraction that leads towards the unimaginably complex network of relations between living forms.

Coda: 'Der Sebald Weg'

'Der Sebald Weg' is the name of a walk that has been established by the village council of Wertach im Allgäu, Sebald's birthplace, high in the Bavarian Alps. It follows the path Sebald describes in the 'Il ritorno in patria' section of Vertigo (2002b: 171–263), leading from Oberjoch via Unterjoch to the house in which he was born, in the village of 'W.' – the cipher that alerts us to the fictionalising process involved in the presentation of Wertach, and an echo of Georges Perec's W, or The Memory of Childhood, as well as Kafka's hieroglyph of identity in 'K.'

What is most remarkable about the way in which Sebald's traces have been followed, however, is not only the way Sebald's work has been absorbed into the phenomenon of 'literary tourism' (Watson 2006). It is rather the way that Sebald's work has generated an extraordinary range of literary and artistic homage. In 'following' Sebald, many not only track the ways he took, but attempt to adopt his way of taking them: his way of walking, as well as his walks, so to speak. The Sebaldian venture has involved artists in other media as well as literature, most notably in a multi-media exhibition, 'Waterlog' (with an accompanying catalogue now published (see Bode et al. 2007), and a large-scale project orchestrated by the Institute of Cultural Inquiry in Los Angeles, *Searching for Sebald: Photography after W. G. Sebald* (Patt 2007). Robert MacFarlane writes of his engagement in an 'unconventional biography' of Sebald produced by 'footstepping' the author's journeys as recounted in his work (MacFarlane 2007). Will Self, too, made a three-and-a-half day walk of the East Yorkshire coast in homage to Sebald's *The Rings of Saturn* in response to an 'ineluctable burgeoning affinity' (Self 2009: no pagination). Most recently, there has been a film, *Patience (After Sebald)*, directed by Grant Gee. The regenerative impact of Sebald's work, the way its rings keep entering into ever-increasing cycles, the way its sense of the porous borders between selves, living and dead, present and absent carries over into the reader (or viewer), is a mark of the power of Sebald's achievement as a writer whose work can infiltrate one's field of vision. And much of the work 'after' Sebald has been of independent value, as well as full of insight. At times, however, the sense of affinity may have transmuted into the kind of emotional trespass that Sebald was so wary of in his work. When encountering the numerous critics who refer to Sebald using the name by which he was known to friends – Max Sebald – it is tempting to recall Walter Benjamin's letter on Max Brod's 1938 book, *Franz Kafka: Eine Biographie* (Benjamin 1999b: 136–43). Benjamin reproaches Brod for a 'pietistic stance of ostentatious intimacy', in which there is a 'fundamental contradiction' between Brod's thesis (that Kafka was on the 'road to holiness') and the 'attitude' (one of 'supreme bonhomie' (1999b: 136)). But the reproducibility of Sebald's 'method' is of interest in itself.

Many of the features of Sebald's writing exist as a kind of process that assumes its own entry into a process of reformulation and recycling. We might see in this reproducibility a spatial denial of borders, and a temporal deferral of death; a procedure of potentially endless renewal in which one thing is always part of another, in which each thing, so defined, is always endlessly ramified in its associations, known or unknown. In a sense, Sebald's work invites our followings: an attentiveness to the traces of the past; a sense of the implication of the here-and-now in the there-and-then. Yet *The Rings of Saturn*, even as it is composed in such a way as to be a model of circularity, always opens out into a sense of wonder that unsettles its own logic. In its form, in its texture, it brings things together but also lifts them out of the trammellings of habit, maintaining a stance of wonder as part of woe. His writing estranges the world and our understanding of it, and in so doing invites us to attend to it all the more closely. Perhaps the poet Hans Magnus Enzensberger – Sebald's publisher at Die Andere Bibliothek at the time of *Die Ringe des Saturn* – supplies the most fitting point on which to close, in a poem which prefaces *Unrecounted*. 'A Parting from Max Sebald' acknowledges the distance, as well as the affinity, from which Sebald's voice reaches us:

> He who was close to us
> from far off seemed to have come
> into our uncanny homeland. (Enzensberger 2004: no pagination)

Notes

1. It should be noted that the last essay of the *Cambridge History to German Literature* deals with 'German Writing in the West (1945 to 1990)' (Watanabe-O'Kelly 1997: 440–506), in which period only two of Sebald's books had been published (*Nach der Natur*, in 1988, and *Schwindel. Gefühle*, in 1990).
2. My thanks to Michael Basseler and to Anna Rettberg for bringing this feature of Sebald's German to my attention.

Afterword: The 'unlimited vicissitudes of travelling'

> It is in classifications that life flashes through so tantalisingly, in the registers that attempt to catalogue it and in so doing expose its irreducible residuum of mystery and enchantment. In the same way the project [. . .], set out like Wittgenstein's *Tractatus* (I.I, I.2, 2.II, 2.I2 etc.), affords us in the truly minimal gaps between one number and the next a glimpse of the unlimited vicissitudes of travelling.
>
> Claudio Magris, *Danube* (2001: 17)

This study began with a consideration of dimensions of the literary and cultural horizon of expectations that are often brought to bear when encountering travels in contemporary literature; that is, what we may bring with us upon 'arrival'. Before closing, it may be appropriate to offer a consideration of what we take with us when we 'leave'. The question is not so much, as is often the case in studies in travel writing, 'where next?' This study has attempted to question a model of reading travels as exclusively or primarily documents of geographical discovery, rendered precarious by the increasingly full and competing versions of the world. My area of concern here has more to do with the question of 'how next?' The texts that have been gathered together in 'an attempt to catalogue' the form of traveller's tale of wonder in contemporary literature has been conducted from the first with the hope that it would expose the 'irreducible residuum of mystery and enchantment' that the texts considered evoke. What, then, do we take from them, having brought these texts together in terms of the literary and cultural history of travels? And how do the literary and cultural forms we have considered open out into literary and cultural history once more? What Magris (a writer whose travel account, *Danube*, bears notable similarities to the voyages we have considered here) describes as the 'unlimited vicissitudes of travelling' – that is, the inexhaustible variety of any journey, as well as that of the journeys that might be made – has implications for approaches to literary and cultural history, as well as for travel in itself.

The readings of travellers' tales of wonder in contemporary literature have brought out a range of shared concerns, thematic and formal. Chatwin, Naipaul and Sebald each engage with questions of form, both recovering and renewing old forms of writing, and crossing and redefining the boundaries of conventional genres in the present. Each brings into question an ideology of primacy, focusing in their travels on the traces of the past, the role of imagination in experience, and hidden or suppressed histories and connections – thus challenging a 'rhetoric of exhaustion' (Cronin 2000: 2) both by registering the role of perspective, imagination and desire in any traveller's account, and by a deep engagement with the changingness of the world and our multiple encounters with it. Their adaptation of narrative itself – whether in Chatwin's dazzling interconnections, the radiation of words and episodes across Naipaul's texts, or the narration of the calendar column in Sebald's writing – suggests a literary-historical adaptation of form to the contexts of late modernity, and one in which the power of genre to shape the encounter is implicitly or explicitly interrogated. Bringing together writers of internationally diverse backgrounds – in contrast to a tendency to classify travels according to either origin or destination – has been an effort to stress that the travels of the writers considered suggest, or require, a more comparative perspective in literary history if we are fully to account for their contributions in literary terms. And in reading their work closely for the literary techniques and voice, this has been an attempt to contribute to an approach in which contemporary travels may be read for the perspectives they offer, rather than primarily for the symptoms they may display. A literary history can be delineated. But the value of the works, taken in sum, derives more from the liberating effect of the writing on issues of form than from any emergent orthodoxy. And it is the sense of wonder in each writer's work that has the widest implications.

Their journeys can be followed; their narrative forms can be adopted. But it is in the sense of wonder that is so pivotal to their aesthetics and ethics that the works considered here have their most enduring effect in both literary and cultural history. Their journeys do not require us to travel to Patagonia, or to Wiltshire, or to Suffolk – or anywhere else. But this is not because a 'travel book, at its purest, is addressed to those who do not plan to follow the traveler at all, but who require the exotic or comic anomalies, wonders, and scandals [. . .] which their own place or time cannot entirely supply' (Fussell 1980: 203). Nor is it because their accounts deplete what may be encountered with wonder, rendering another area one degree closer to comprehensive exhaustion. The experiences of the world are part of it; a source, rather than a scourge, of wonder. Travellers' tales of wonder compel us to acknowledge that the world and our experiences in it are far from comprehensively known. Their gift is to invite us to a sense that, if we wish to encounter a world in which wonder is possible or necessary – a wonder that mixes enchantment and engagement, elegy and celebration – we are already there.

Bibliography

Adams, Percy G. (1983), *Travel Literature and the Evolution of the Novel*, Lexington: The University Press of Kentucky.

Amann, Jürg (1985), *Patagonien: Prosa*, Munich and Zurich: Piper.

Andrews, Robert, Jules Brown, Phil Lee and Rob Humphreys (2009), *The Rough Guide to England*, 8th edn, London and New York: Rough Guides.

Aragon, Louis [1926] (1994), *Paris Peasant*, trans. Simon Watson Taylor, Boston, MA: Exact Change.

Atlas, James (1994), 'An erudite author in a genre all his own', *The New York Times*, 14 December, available at <http://www.nytimes.com/1994/12/14/books/an-erudite-author-in-a-genre-all-his-own.html?pagewanted=all&src=pm> (last accessed 15 July 2012).

——(1999), 'W. G. Sebald: A Profile', *Paris Review*, 151 (Summer): 278–95.

Auden, W. H. and Louis MacNeice [1937] (1985), *Letters from Iceland*, London and Boston: Faber and Faber.

Bacon, Francis (1857–74), *The Works of Francis Bacon*, ed. J. Spedding, Robert Leslie Ellis and Douglas Denon Heath, 14 vols, London: Longman, Green, Longman and Roberts.

Bal, Mieke (2002), *Travelling Concepts in the Humanities: A Rough Guide*, Toronto: University of Toronto Press.

Balzac, Honoré de [1831] (1977), *The Wild Ass's Skin*, trans. Herbert J. Hunt, London: Penguin.

Banville, John (2001), 'The Rubble Artist', *The New Republic Online*, 6 December, available at <http://www.powells.com/review/2001_12_06> (last accessed 16 July 2012).

Barkham, John (1978), 'Youthful Briton Finds Adventure in Harsh Land', *Youngstown, Ohio Indicator*, 16 July; review also published as 'The Uttermost End of the Earth', *The Philadelphia Inquirer*, 20 August. MS. Eng. C. 7846.

Barron, Neil (ed.) (2004), *Anatomy of Wonder: A Critical Guide to Science Fiction*, London: Libraries Unlimited.

Barth, John [1967] (1984), 'The Literature of Exhaustion', in *The Friday Book: Essays and Other Nonfiction*, New York: Perigee Books, pp. 62–76.

——(1984), *The Friday Book and Other Essays*, New York: Putnam.

Barthes, Roland [1970] (1983), *Empire of Signs*, trans. Richard Howard, New York: Hill and Wang.

——[1980] (2000), *Camera Lucida*, London: Vintage.

Bassnett, Susan (1993), *Comparative Literature: A Critical Introduction*, Oxford and Cambridge, MA: Blackwell.

Baudelaire, Charles [1859] (2006), 'Le Voyage', in *The Complete Verse*, trans. Francis Scarfe, London: Anvil Press, pp. 241–7.

Baudrillard, Jean (1983), *Simulations*, trans. Phil Bleitchman, Paul Foss and Paul Patton, Los Angeles, CA: Semiotext[e].

Bauman, Zygmunt (1991), *Modernity and Ambivalence*, Ithaca: New York University Press.

——[1989] (2000), *Modernity and the Holocaust*, Cambridge: Polity.

Beck, John (2004), 'Reading Room: Erosion and Sedimentation in Sebald's Suffolk', in J. J. Long and A. Whitehead (eds), *W. G. Sebald: A Critical Companion*, Edinburgh: Edinburgh University Press, pp. 75–88.

Bedford, Sybille (1978), 'On the Go', *London Review of Books*, 9 Nov.: 45–6.

——[1960] (1990), *A Visit to Don Otavio: A Traveller's Tale from Mexico*, London: Folio Society.

Beer, Gillian (1987), 'Problems of Description in the Language of Discovery', in George Levine (ed.), *One Culture: Essays in Science and Literature*, Wisconsin and London: University of Wisconsin Press, pp. 35–58.

Behdad, Ali (1994), *Belated Travelers: Orientalism in the Age of Colonial Dissolution*, Durham, NC and London: Duke University Press.

Benjamin, Walter [1955] (1977), *Illuminationen*, Frankfurt: Suhrkamp.

——[1950] (1999a), 'Theses on the Philosophy of History', in Hannah Arendt (ed.), *Illuminations*, trans. Harry Zorn, London: Pimlico, pp. 245–55.

——[1955] (1999b), *Illuminations*, ed. Hannah Arendt, trans. Harry Zorn, London: Pimlico.

Bennett, Alan (2005), *Untold Stories*, London: Faber and Faber.

Bigsby, Christopher (2001), 'In Conversation with W. G. Sebald', in *Writers in Conversation with Christopher Bigsby*, Norwich: University of East Anglia, pp. 139–65.

Bishop, T. G. (1996), *Shakespeare and the Theatre of Wonder*, Cambridge: Cambridge University Press.

Blackler, Deane (2007), *Reading W. G. Sebald: Adventure and Disobedience*, New York: Camden.

Bloom, Harold [1973] (1997), *The Anxiety of Influence: A Theory of Poetry*, New York: Oxford University Press.

Bode, Stephen, Jeremy Millar and Nina Ernst (eds) (2007), *Waterlog: Journeys Around an Exhibition*, London: Film and Video Umbrella.

Bond, Greg [2004] (2006), 'On the Misery of Nature and the Nature of Misery: W. G. Sebald's Landscapes', in J. J. Long and Anne Whitehead (eds), *W. G. Sebald: A Critical Companion*, Edinburgh: Edinburgh University Press, pp. 31–44.

Boorstin, Daniel J. [1961] (1985), *The Image: A Guide to Pseudo-Events in America*, New York: Atheneum.

Borges, Jorge Luis and Adolfo Bioy Cesares [1967] (1971), *Extraordinary Tales*, ed. and trans. A. Kerrigan, London: Souvenir.

——(1982), 'The Gaucho and the City', *The New Republic*, May. [G. l 'Research': MSS. Eng. c. 7836].

Borm, Jan [2004] (2007a), 'Defining Travel: On the Travel Book, Travel Writing and Terminology', in Glenn Hooper and Tim Youngs (eds), *Perspectives on Travel Writing*, Aldershot and Burlington, VT: Ashgate, pp. 13–26.

—— (2007b), '"What Am I Doing Here": Contemporary British Travel Writing: From Revival to Renewal', *Literatūra* 49: 5, 9–16.

Bowker, Geoffrey C. and Susan Leigh Star (1999), *Sorting Things Out: Classification and its Consequences*, Cambridge, MA and London: Massachusetts Institute of Technology.

Boym, Svetlana (2001), *The Future of Nostalgia*, New York: Basic Books.

Brecht, Bertolt [1939] (1973), 'An die Nachgeborenen', in *Svendborger Gedichte*, Frankfurt: Suhrkamp, pp. 98–101.

Bridges, Lucas (1948), *Uttermost Part of the Earth*, London: Hodder and Stoughton.

Brisson, Ulrike (2005), 'Teaching Travel Writing: A Voyage of Discovery', in E. Groom (ed.), *Methods for Teaching Travel Literature and Writing: Exploring the World and Self*, New York: Peter Lang, pp. 13–30.

Brooks, Peter (1984), *Reading for the Plot: Design and Intention in Narrative*, Oxford: Clarendon.

Bruner, Jerome (1991), 'The Narrative Construction of Reality', *Critical Inquiry*, 18: 1–21.

Bruzelius, Margaret (2007), *Romancing the Novel: Adventure from Scott to Sebald*, Lewisburg, PA: Bucknell University Press.

Buford, Bill (ed.) (1984), *Granta – Travel Writing*, Issue 10, London: Penguin.

Buzard, James [1993] (1998), *The Beaten Track: European Tourism, Literature and the Ways to 'Culture' 1800–1918*, Oxford: Clarendon Press.

Byron, Robert [1937] (2007), *The Road to Oxiana*, Oxford: Oxford University Press.

Calvino, Italo [1988] (1996), *Six Memos for the Next Millennium*, trans. Patrick Creagh, London: Vintage.

Campbell, Mary Baine (1988), *The Witness and the Other World: Exotic European Travel Writing 400–1600*, New York: Cornell.

—— (2002), 'Travel Writing and its Theory', in P. Hulme and T. Youngs eds, *The Cambridge Companion to Travel Writing*, Cambridge: Cambridge University Press, pp. 261–78.

Canetti, Elias [1960] (1962), *Crowds and Power*, trans. Carol Stewart, London: Victor Gollancz Ltd.

—— (1974), *Kafka's Other Trial: The Letters to Felice*, trans. Christopher Middleton, New York: Schocken Books.

Carroll, David [1990] (1997), 'Foreword: The Memory of Devastation and the Responsibilities of Thought: "And let's not talk about that"', in F. Lyotard, *Heidegger and "the jews"*, trans. Robert Michel and Mark Roberts, Minneapolis: University of Minnesota Press, pp. vii–xx.

Casanova, Pascale [1999] (2004), *The World Republic of Letters*, trans. M. B. DeBevoise, Cambridge, MA and London: Harvard University Press.

Catling, Jo [2002] (2010), 'Silent Catastrophe: In Memoriam W. G. (Max) Sebald 1944–2001', available at <http://www.new-books-in-german.com/featur27.htm> (last accessed 15 July 2012).

Cendrars, Blaise [1913] (2001), *Prose of the Trans-Siberian & of the Little Jeanne de France*, trans. Tony Baker, Sheffield: West House Books.

Chatwin Archive. Oxford, Bodleian Library. Catalogue of Papers of (Charles)

Bruce Chatwin, 1963–1989. Oxford, Bodleian Library, Department of Special Collections and Western Manuscripts. Catalogued by Nicholas Shakespeare and Matthew Neely, 2011. Table of contents available at <www.bodl ey.ox.ac.uk/dept/scwmss/wmss/online/modern/chatwin/chatwin.html/> (last accessed 31 July 2012).

——(B 'On the Silk Road' ('Papers concerning Afghanistan, 1963–4, 1969, n.d.') [MSS. Eng. c. 7834].

——(G.1 'Research' ('Papers concerning unpublished work "The Nomadic Alternative", mainly c. 1968–73': 'Research Material and Notes') [MSS. Eng. c. 7836].

——(G.1 'Nomadic Alternative' ('Unpublished draft of "The Nomadic Alternative", 1972') [MS. Eng. 7838].

——(I.1 'O Patagonia' ('Proposal, written at the request of literary agent Gillon Aitken, for *In Patagonia*, October 1974') [MS. Eng. d. 3975 (Fol. 1)].

——(I.3 'Patagonia Notebook 1' ('Notebook [c. Feb. 1975]) [MS. Eng. e. 3733].

——(I.4 'Milward's Memoirs' ('Photocopy of typescript version of Milward's journal' [M.S. Eng. c. 7482].

——I.4 'Letter to Milward' ('Photocopy of letter to Milward, from unidentified correspondent, appraising his work') [MS. Eng. c. 7842].

——(I.6 'First draft' ('1st draft of *In Patagonia*, n.d.') [MS. Eng. d. 3976].

——(I.8 'Reviews' ('Reviews, Oct. 1977–Sept. 1979, n.d.') [MS. Eng. c. 7846].

Chatwin, Bruce (1977), *In Patagonia*, London: Jonathan Cape.

——[1982] (1983), *On the Black Hill*, London: Picador.

——[1988] (1989), *Utz*, London: Penguin Books.

——[1993], *Far Journeys: Photographs and Notebooks*, ed. David King and Francis Wyndham, New York and London: Penguin.

——[1989] (1996), *What Am I Doing Here*, London: Penguin Books.

——[1996] (1997), *Anatomy of Restlessness: Selected Writings, 1969–1989*, ed. Jan Borm and Matthew Graves, London: Penguin.

——[1980] (1998), *The Viceroy of Ouidah*, London: Vintage Classics.

——[1998] (1999), *Winding Paths: Photographs by Bruce Chatwin*, London: Jonathan Cape.

——[1987] (2005), *The Songlines*, London: Vintage.

——(2010), *Under the Sun: The Letters of Bruce Chatwin*, ed. Elizabeth Chatwin and Nicholas Shakespeare, London: Jonathan Cape.

Chatwin, Bruce and Paul Theroux [1985] (1992), *Patagonia Revisited*, London: Jonathan Cape.

Clapp, Susannah (1989), 'What am I doing here', *The Guardian*, 19 January, p. 37.

——(1997), *With Chatwin: Portrait of a Writer*, London: Jonathan Cape.

Clark, Steve (ed.) (1999), *Travel Writing and Empire: Postcolonial Theory in Transit*, London: Zed Books.

Clifford, James (1986), *The Predicament of Culture: Twentieth-Century Ethnography, Literature and Art*, Cambridge, MA: Harvard University Press.

——(1989), 'Notes on Theory and Travel', *Insriptions*, 5, available at <http://www2.ucsc.edu/culturalstudies/PUBS/Inscriptions/vol_5/clifford.html>(last accessed 15 July 2012).

——(1997), *Routes: Travel and Translation in the Late Twentieth Century*, Cambridge, MA: Harvard University Press.

Cocker, Mark (1992), *Loneliness and Time: The Story of British Travel Writing*, New York: Pantheon Books.

Conrad, Joseph (1926), 'Geography and Some Explorers', in R. Curle (ed.), *Last Essays*, London: J. M. Dent and Sons, pp. 1–31.

——[1899/1901] (1998), *Heart of Darkness*, ed. Robert Kimbrough, New York and London: Norton and Company.

——[1916] (2003), *The Shadow-Line*, Oxford: Oxford University Press.

Cooper, Helen (ed.) (2008), *Sir Gawain and the Green Knight*, trans. Keith Harrison, Oxford: Oxford University Press.

Cronin, Michael (2000), *Across the Lines: Travel, Language, Translation*, Cork: Cork University Press.

Cunha, Euclides da (1944), *Rebellion in the Backlands*, trans. Samuel Putnam, Chicago and London: University of Chicago Press.

Daston, Lorraine and Katharine Park (1998), *Wonders and the Order of Nature: 1150–1750*, New York: Zone Books.

Davidson, Robyn [1980] (1989), *Tracks*, London: Paladin.

——(ed.) (2001), *The Picador Book of Journeys*, London: Picador.

Delbanco, Nicholas (2005), *Anywhere Out of the World: Essays on Travel, Writing, Death*, New York: Columbia University Press.

Deleuze, Gilles and Félix Guattari [1980] (1987), *A Thousand Plateaus: Capitalism and Schizophrenia*, trans. Brian Massumi, London and New York: Continuum.

Denham, Scott and Mark McCulloh (eds) (2006), *W. G. Sebald: History – Memory – Trauma*, Berlin and New York: De Gruyter.

Derrida, Jacques [1967] (1976), *Of Grammatology*, trans. Gayatri Chakravorty Spivak, Baltimore and London: Johns Hopkins University Press.

——[1980] (1987), *The Post Card: From Socrates to Freud and Beyond*, Chicago: University of Chicago Press.

Diski, Jenny [2002] (2004), *Stranger on a Train: Daydreaming and Smoking around America with Interruptions*, London: Virago.

Dodd, Philip (ed.) (1982), *The Art of Travel: Essays on Travel Writing*, London and Totowa, NJ: Frank Cass.

Douglas, Mary (2007), *Thinking in Circles: An Essay on Ring Composition*, New Haven, CT and London: Yale University Press.

Driver, Felix (2001), *Geography Militant: Cultures of Exploration and Empire*, Oxford: Blackwell.

Dupont, Florence (1999), *The Invention of Literature: From Greek Intoxication to the Latin Book*, Baltimore: Johns Hopkins University Press.

Dyer, Geoff (2006), 'Introduction', in R. West [1942] (2006), *Black Lamb and Grey Falcon: A Journey through Yugoslavia*, Edinburgh, New York and Melbourne: Canongate, pp. xiii–xxiii.

Eliot, T. S. [1917] (1961), *Selected Poems*, London: Faber and Faber.

Elsner, John and Roger Cardinal (eds) (1994), *The Cultures of Collecting*, London: Reaktion Books.

Elsner, Jaś and Joan-Pau Rubiés (eds) (1999), *Voyages and Visions: Towards a Cultural History of Travel*, London: Reaktion Books.

Engdahl, Horace (2001), 'The Nobel Prize in Literature 2001: V. S. Naipaul',

Swedish Academy, Press Release, 11 October, available at <http://nobel-prize.org/nobel_prizes/literature/laureates/2001/press.html> (last accessed 1 January 2010).

——(2002), 'Philomena's Tongue: Introductory Remarks on Witness Literature', in *Witness Literature. Proceedings of the Nobel Centennial Symposium*, ed. H. Engdahl, World Scientific Publishing Company, pp. 1–14.

——(2008), 'Canonization and World Literature: The Nobel Experience', in Karen-Margrethe Simonsen and Jakob Stougaard-Nielsen (eds), *World Literature, World Culture*, Aarhus: Aarhus University Press, pp. 195–214.

Enzensberger, Hans Magnus [2003] (2004), 'A Parting from Max Sebald', in W. G. Sebald and Jan Peter Trip, *Unrecounted*, trans. Michael Hamburger, London: Hamish Hamilton, p. 10.

Equiano, Olaudah [1789] (2003), *An Interesting Narrative and Other Writings*, London: Penguin.

Ette, Ottmar [2001] (2003), *Literature on the Move: Space and Dynamics of Bordercrossing Writings in Europe and America*, trans. Katharina Vester, Amsterdam and New York: Rodopi Verlag.

Evans, R. J. W. and Alexander Marr (eds) (2006), *Curiosity and Wonder from the Renaissance to the Enlightenment*, Aldershot and Burlington, VT: Ashgate.

Fabian, Johannes [1983] (2002), *Time and the Other: How Anthropology Makes Its Object*, New York: Columbia University Press.

Fanon, Frantz [1963] (2004), *The Wretched of the Earth*, trans. Richard Philcox, New York: Grove Press.

Felman, Shoshana and Dori Laub (1992), *Testimony: Crises of Witnessing in Literature, Psychoanalysis, and History*, New York and London: Routledge.

Fernández-Armesto, Felipe (2006), *Pathfinders: A Global History of Exploration*, Oxford: Oxford University Press.

Fischer, Gerhard (ed.) (2010), *W. G. Sebald: Schreiben ex patria / Expatriate Writing*. Amsterdam: Rodopi.

Fisher, Philip (1999), *Wonder, the Rainbow, and the Aesthetics of Rare Experiences*, Cambridge, MA: Harvard University Press.

Forsdick, Charles (2005), *Travel in Twentieth-Century French and Francophone Cultures: The Persistence of Diversity*, Oxford: Oxford University Press.

Foucault, Michel [1966] (1989), *The Order of Things: An Archaeology of the Human Sciences*, trans. A. M. Sheridan Smith, London: Routledge.

——[1969] (2008), *The Archaeology of Knowledge*, London: Routledge.

French, Patrick (2008), *The World Is What It Is: The Authorised Biography of VS Naipaul*, London: Picador.

Freud, Sigmund [1914] (2003), *Beyond the Pleasure Principle and Other Writings*, ed. Adam Philips, trans. John Reddick, London and New York: Penguin.

——[1899] (2008), *The Interpretation of Dreams*, trans. Joyce Crick, Oxford: Oxford University Press.

——[1901] (2010), *Psychopathology and Everyday Life*, trans. A. A. Brill, Seattle: Pacific Publishing Studio.

—Fritzsche, Peter (2004), *Stranded in the Present: Modern Time and the Melancholy of History*, London and Cambridge, MA: Harvard University Press.

Fussell, Paul (1980), *Abroad: British Literary Traveling Between the Wars*, New York: Oxford University Press.

——(ed.) (1987), *The Norton Book of Travel*, New York: Norton.

Garland, Henry and Mary Garland (ed.) (1997), *The Oxford Companion to German Literature*, 3rd edn, Oxford: Oxford University Press.

Garro, H. (1918), *Tout lou Mond*, extract anthologised in J. L. Borges and A. B. Casares [1967] (1971), *Extraordinary Tales*, London: Souvenir.

Geertz, Clifford (1980), 'Blurred Genres: The Reconfiguration of Social Thought', *American Scholar*, 49.1: 65–79.

——(1983), *Local Knowledge: Further Essays in Interpretive Anthropology*, New York: Basic Books.

George, Andrew (trans.) (1999), *The Epic of Gilgamesh*, London: Penguin.

Ghosh, Amitav [1992] (1994), *In an Antique Land*, New York: Vintage.

Gide, André [1902] (2001), *The Immoralist*, trans. David Watson, London: Penguin.

Gilbert, Helen and Johnston, Anna (eds) (2002), *In Transit: Travel, Text, Empire*, New York: Peter Lang.

Gilroy, Amanda (ed.) (2000), *Romantic Geographies: Discourses of Travel, 1775–1844*, Manchester: Manchester University Press.

Gingras, George E. (ed. and trans.) (1970), *Egeria: Diary of a Pilgrimage*, New York: Newman Press.

Goodman, Nelson [1978] (1992), *Ways of Worldmaking*, Indianapolis, IN: Hackett.

Görner, Rüdiger (ed.) (2003), *The Anatomist of Melancholy – Essays in Memory of W. G. Sebald*, München: IUDICIUM Verlag GmbH.

Gourevitch, Philip [1998] (2000), *We Wish to Inform You that Tomorrow We Will Be Killed with Our Families: Stories from Rwanda*, London: Picador.

Graham, Gordon (2007), *The Re-Enchantment of the World: Art versus Religion*, Oxford: Oxford University Press.

Graves, Matthew (2003), ' "Nowhere Left to Go?" The Death and Renaissance of the Travel Book', *World Literature Today*, 77.3/4 (October–December): 52–6.

Greenblatt, Stephen (1991), *Marvelous Possessions: The Wonder of the New World*, Chicago: University of Chicago Press.

Greil, Marcus (1978), 'The Pleasures of Patagonia', *Rolling Stone*, 10 August. MS. Eng. C. 7846.

Gussow, Mel (1987), 'The enigma of V. S. Naipaul's search for himself in writing', *The New York Times*, 25 April: no pagination.

Hamburger, Michael (2004), 'Translator's Note', in W. G. Sebald and J. P. Tripp, *Unrecounted*, trans. M. Hamburger, London: Hamish Hamilton, pp. 1–9.

Hamner, Robert D. (ed.) (1977), *Critical Perspectives on V. S. Naipaul*, Washington, DC: Three Continents Press.

Harrison, Robert Pogue (2003), *The Dominion of the Dead*, Chicago and London: University of Chicago Press.

——(2009), 'Homeless Gardens', in J. Landy and M. Saler (eds), *The Re-enchantment of the World: Secular Magic in a Rational Age*, Stanford: Stanford University Press, pp. 72–80.

Hawks, Tony (1998), *Round Ireland with a Fridge*, London: Ebury.

Hayward, Helen (2002), *The Enigma of V. S. Naipaul*, Basingstoke and New York: Macmillan.

——[2002] (2006), *The Enigma of V. S. Naipaul*, Houndmills and New York: Palgrave Macmillan.

Hebard, Andrew (1997), 'Disruptive Pasts: Towards a Radical Politics of Remembrance in Alain Resnais' *Night and Fog*', *New German Critique* (Fall): 87–113.

Hemingway, Ernest (1925), *In Our Time*, New York: Boni and Liveright.

Hernstein Smith, Barbara (1968), *Poetic Closure: A Study of How Poems End*, Chicago: University of Chicago Press.

Herodotus [1996] (2003), *The Histories*, ed. J. Marincola, trans. A. de Sélincourt, London: Penguin.

Hirsch, Marianne (1997), *Family Frames: Photography, Narrative and Postmemory*, Cambridge, MA: Harvard University Press.

Hofer, Johannes [1688] (1934), 'Medical Dissertation on Nostalgia', trans. Carolyn Kiser Anspach, *Bulletin of the Institute of the History of Medicine*, 2.6: 376–91.

Höfele, Andreas and Werner von Koppenfels (eds) (2005), *Renaissance Go-Betweens: Cultural Exchange in Early Modern Europe*, Berlin: Walter de Gruyter.

Hoggart, Richard [1957] (2004), *The Uses of Literacy*, New Brunswick, NJ: Transaction Publishers.

——[1961] (2005), 'The Defence Witnesses: Richard Hoggart', in C. H. Rolph (ed.), *Lady Chatterley's Trial*, London: Penguin, pp. 21–9.

Hölderlin, Friedrich (1998), *Selected Poems and Fragments*, trans. Michael Hamburger, London: Penguin.

Holland, Patrick and Graham Huggan [1998] (2000), *Tourists with Typewriters: Critical Reflections on Contemporary Travel Writing*, Ann Arbor: University of Michigan Press.

——(2004), 'Varieties of Nostalgia in Contemporary Travel Writing', in G. Hooper and T. Youngs (eds), *Perspectives on Travel Writing*, Aldershot and Burlington, VT: Ashgate, pp. 139–51.

Holloway, David (1977), 'Footloose in Patagonia', newspaper review, original source unclear. Consulted in the Chatwin Archive, shelfmark MS. Eng. c. 7846.

Holmes, Richard [1985] (2005), *Footsteps: Adventures of a Romantic Biographer*, London, New York, Toronto and Sydney: Harper.

——(2008), *The Age of Wonder: How the Romantic Generation Discovered the Beauty and Terror of Science*, London: Harper Press.

Hooper, Glenn and Tim Youngs, (eds) [2004] (2007), *Perspectives on Travel Writing*, Burlington, VT and Aldershot: Ashgate.

Horstkotte, Silke (2005), 'The Double Dynamics of Focalization in W. G. Sebald's *The Rings of Saturn*', in J. C. Meister (ed.), *Narratology beyond Literary Criticism: Mediality, Disciplinarity*, Berlin and New York: de Gruyter, pp. 25–44.

Hudson, W. H. [1893] (2006), *Idle Days in Patagonia*, New York: E. P. Dutton and Co.

Hughes, Peter (1997), 'Review: Tropics of Candor: V. S. Naipaul', *Contemporary Literature*, 38.1 (Spring): 205–12.

Hulme, Peter (2002a), 'Patagonian Cases: Travel Writing, Fiction, History', in Jan Borm (ed.), *Seuils & traverses: enjeux de l'écriture du voyage*, vol. II, Brest: Centre de Recherche Bretonne et Celtique, pp. 223–38.

——(2002b), 'Travelling to Write (1940–2000), in Peter Hulme and Tim Youngs (eds), *The Cambridge Companion to Travel Writing*, Cambridge: Cambridge University Press, pp. 87–101.

Hulme, Peter and Tim Youngs (eds) (2002), *The Cambridge Companion to Travel Writing*, Cambridge: Cambridge University Press.

Humboldt, Alexander von [1807] (1995), *Personal Narrative of a Journey to the Equinoctial Regions of the New Continent*, trans. Jason Wilson, London: Penguin.

Hussein, Aamer [1994] (1997), 'Delivering the Truth: An Interview with V. S. Naipaul', in F. Fussawalla (ed.), *Conversations with V. S. Naipaul*, Jackson: University Press of Mississippi, pp. 154–61.

Hutton, Adrian Gimenez [1998] (1999), *La Patagonia de Chatwin*, Buenos Aires: Editorial Sudamericana.

Isherwood, Christopher [1939] (1998), *Goodbye to Berlin*, London: Vintage.

Jack, Ian (ed.) (2006), *Granta 94 – On the Road Again – Where Travel Writing Went Next*, London: Granta.

Jacobs, Joseph, and John D. Batten [1913] (2008), *The Book of Wonder Voyages*, London: Adams Press.

Jaggi, Maya (2001), '*The Guardian* profile: W. G. Sebald. Recovered memories', *The Guardian*, 22 September, available at <http://www.guardian.co.uk/saturday_review/story/0,3605,555861,00.html> (last accessed 15 July 2012).

Jameson, Fredric [1981] (1983), *The Political Unconscious: Narrative as a Socially Symbolic Act*, London: Methuen.

Janouch, Gustav [1968] (1971), *Gespräche mit Kafka: Aufzeichnungen und Erinnerungen*, Frankfurt am Main: Fischer Verlag.

Jauss, Hans Robert [1972] (1982), *Toward an Aesthetic of Reception*, trans. Timothy Bahti, Brighton: The Harvester Press.

Jussawalla, Feroza (ed.) (1997), *Conversations with V. S. Naipaul*, Jackson: University Press of Mississippi.

Kafka, Franz [1953] (2002), 'Letter to His Father', in Helmut Kiesel (ed.), *The Metamorphosis and Other Writings*, trans. Ernst Kaiser and Eithne Wilkins, New York and London: Continuum, pp. 175–229.

Kapuściński, Ryszard [1976] (2001a), *Another Day of Life*, trans. William R. Brand and Katarzyna Mroczkowska-Brand, updated material trans. Klara Glowczewska, New York: Vintage.

——[1998] (2001b), *Shadow of the Sun: My African Life*, trans. Klara Glowczewska, London: Penguin.

——(2008), *The Other*, trans. Antonia Lloyd-Jones, London and New York: Verso.

Karkov, Catherine E. (1998), 'Anglo-Saxon Art', in Paul Szarmach, M. Teresa Tavormina and Joel T. Rosenthal (eds), *Medieval England: An Encyclopaedia*, New York: Garland Publications, pp. 111–25.

Kermode, Frank (1987), 'In the garden of the oppressor', *The New York Times*, 22 March, available at <http://www.nytimes.com/1987/03/22/books/in-the-garden-of-the-oppressor.html?pagewanted=1> (last accessed 15 July 2012).

——[1966] (1999), *The Sense of an Ending: Studies in the Theory of Fiction*, Oxford: Oxford University Press.

—Kern, Stephen (1983), *The Culture of Time and Space 1880–1918*, Cambridge, MA: Harvard University Press.

King, Bruce [1993] (2003), *V. S. Naipaul*, Houndsmills: Palgrave Macmillan.

Klibansky, Raymond, Erwin Panofsky and Fritz Saxl (1964), *Saturn and Melancholy: Studies in the History of Natural Philosophy, Religion and Art*, London: Thomas Nelson and Sons.

Knight, Damon (1967), *In Search of Wonder: Essays on Science Fiction*, Chicago: Advent Publishers, Inc.

Korte, Barbara (1996), *Der englische Reisebericht. Von der Pilgerfahrt bis zur Postmoderne*, Darmstadt: Wissenschaftliche Buchgesellschaft.

Koshar, Rudy (2000), *German Travel Cultures*, Oxford and New York: Berg.

Kristeva, Julia (1991), *Strangers to Ourselves*, trans. Leon Roudiez, Hemel Hempstead: Harvester Wheatsheaf.

Kundera, Milan [1992] (1996), *Testaments Betrayed: An Essay in Nine Parts*, trans. Linda Asher, London: Harper Perennial.

LaCapra, Dominick (1994), *Representing the Holocaust: History, Theory, Trauma*, Ithaca, NY: Cornell University Press.

Landy, Joshua and Michael Saler (eds) (2009), *The Re-enchantment of the World: Secular Magic in a Rational Age*, Stanford: Stanford University Press.

Lanzmann, Claude (2009), *Le lièvre de Patagonie: mémoires*, Paris: Gallimard.

Lawrence, D. H. [1921] (2007), *Sea and Sardinia*, in Simonetta de Filippis, Paul Eggert and Mara Kalnins (eds), *D. H. Lawrence and Italy*, London: Penguin, pp. 137–326.

Leask, Nigel (2002), *Curiosity and the Aesthetics of Travel Writing, 1770–1840*, Oxford: Oxford University Press.

le Clézio, J. M. G [1969] (2008), *The Book of Flights: An Adventure Story*, trans. Simon Watson Taylor, London: Vintage Books.

——[1988] (2009), *The Mexican Dream, Or, The Interrupted Thought of Amerindian Civilizations*, trans. Teresa Lavender Fagan, Chicago and London: University of Chicago Press.

Lejeune, Philippe (1975), *Le Pacte autobiographique*, Paris: Seuil.

Levi, Primo [1986] (1988), *The Drowned and the Saved*, trans. Raymond Rosenthal, New York: Simon and Schuster.

——[1958] (2004), *If This Is A Man / The Truce*, trans. Stuart Woolf, London: Abacus.

Levine, George (ed.), *One Culture: Essays in Science and Literature*, Wisconsin and London: University of Wisconsin Press.

Lévi-Strauss, Claude [1955] (1976), *Tristes tropiques*, trans. John and Doreen Weightman, Harmondsworth: Penguin.

Lincoln, Margarete, 'Tales of Wonder, 1650–1750', *Journal for Eighteenth-Century Studies*, 27.2: 219–32.

Lisle, Debbie (2006), *The Global Politics of Contemporary Travel Writing*, Cambridge: Cambridge University Press.

Long, J. J. (2007), *W. G. Sebald: Image, Archive, Modernity*, Edinburgh: Edinburgh University Press.

Long, J. J. and Ann Whitehead (eds) (2004), *W. G. Sebald: A Critical Companion*, Edinburgh: Edinburgh University Press.

Lucian (2007), *A True Story*, trans. A. M. Harmon, Charlestown, SC: Forgotten Books.

Lyotard, Jean-François [1990] (1997), *Heidegger and 'the jews'*, trans. Robert Michel and Mark Roberts, Minneapolis: University of Minnesota Press.

McCannell, Dean (1999), *The Tourist: A New Theory of the Leisure Class*, Berkeley: University of California Press.

McCulloh, Mark (2003), *Understanding W. G. Sebald*, Columbia: University of South Carolina Press.

——(2006), 'Two Languages, Two Audiences: The Tandem Literary Oeuvres of W. G. Sebald', in Scott Denham and Mark McCulloh (eds), *W. G. Sebald: History, Memory, Trauma*, Berlin and New York: De Gruyter, pp. 7–20.

MacFarlane, Robert (2007), 'Afterglow, or Sebald the Walker', in S. Bode, J. Millar and N. Ernst (eds), *Waterlog: Journeys around an Exhibition*, London: Film and Video Umbrella, pp. 78–83.

McLuhan, Marshall [1962] (1988), *The Gutenberg Galaxy: The Making of Typographic Man*, Toronto: University of Toronto Press.

Magris, Claudio [1989] (2001), *Danube*, trans. Patrick Creagh, London: Harvill.

Malabou, Catherine and Jacques Derrida [1999] (2004), *Counterpaths: Traveling with Jacques Derrida*, trans. David Wills, Stanford: Stanford University Press.

'Mandeville, John' [1356–66] (2005), *The Travels of John Mandeville*, trans. C. W. R. D. Moseley, London: Penguin.

Marcus, George E. and Michael M. J. Fischer [1986] (1999), *Anthropology as Cultural Critique: An Experimental Moment in the Human Sciences*, Chicago: University of Chicago Press.

Marcus, Laura and Peter Nichols (eds) (2004), *The Cambridge History of Twentieth-Century English Literature*, Cambridge: Cambridge University Press.

Marincola, John [1996] (2003), 'Introduction' in Herodotus, *The Histories*, ed. J. Marincola, trans. Aubrey de Sélincourt, London: Penguin, pp. ix–xiv.

Martels, Zweder von (1994), *Travel Fact and Travel Fiction: Studies on Fiction, Literary Tradition, Scholarly Discovery and Observation in Travel Writing*, Leiden, NY and Cologne: E. J. Brill.

Mascaró, Juan (trans.) (2003), *The Bhagavad Gita*, London: Penguin.

Mason, Peter (1998), *Infelicities: Representations of the Exotic*, Baltimore: Johns Hopkins Press.

Mathews, Timothy (2007), 'Reading W. G. Sebald with Alberto Giacometti', in H. Buesco and J. F. Duarte (eds), *Stories and Portraits of the Self*, Amsterdam and New York: Rodopi, pp. 237–53.

Matthiessen, Peter [1978] (1996), *The Snow Leopard*, New York: Penguin.

Matvejević, Predrag [1987] (1999), *Mediterranean: A Cultural Landscape*, trans. Michael Henry Heim, Berkeley, Los Angeles and London: University of California Press.

Meanor, Patrick (1997), *Bruce Chatwin*, London and New York: Twayne.

Medwick, Cathleen [1981] (1997), 'Life, Literature, and Politics: An Interview with V. S. Naipaul', in F. Jussawalla (ed.), *Conversations with V. S. Naipaul*, Jackson: University of Mississippi Press, pp. 57–63.

Melikoğlu, Koray (ed.) (2006), *Life Writing: Autobiography, Biography, and Travel Writing in Contemporary Literature*, Stuttgart: Ibidem Verlag.

Melville, Herman [1851] (2002), *Moby-Dick*, ed. H. Parker and H. Hayford, New York: Norton.

Michener, Charles [1981] (1997), 'The Dark Visions of V. S. Naipaul', in *Conversations with V. S. Naipaul*, ed. F. Jussawalla, Jackson: University of Mississippi Press, pp. 63–74.

Millar, Jeremy (2007), 'Who Is This Who Is Coming?', in S. Bode, J. Millar and N. Ernst (eds), *Waterlog: Journeys around an Exhibition*, London: Film and Video Umbrella, pp. 112–13.

Mills, Sara [1991] (2003), *Discourses of Difference: An Analysis of Women's Travel Writing and Colonialism*, London: Routledge.

Milton, John [1667] (1989), *Paradise Lost*, ed. Christopher Ricks, London: Penguin.

Mishra, Pankaj (2003), 'Introduction', in V. S. Naipaul, *Literary Occasions: Essays*, New York: Alfred A. Knopf, pp. vii–xvi.

Montaigne, Michel de [1580] (1958), *Essays*, trans. J. M. Cohen, London: Penguin.

Morgan, Ted (1978), 'Home of the unicorn', *The New York Times Book Review*, 16 July, p. 7. MS. Eng. c. 7846.

Mosbach, Bettina (2008), *Figurationen der Katastrophe: Ästhetische Verfahren in W, G, Sebalds* Die Ringe des Saturn *und* Austerlitz, Bielefeld: Aisthesis.

Moss, Chris (2008), *Patagonia: A Cultural History*, Oxford: Signal Books.

Motion, Andrew (2001), 'Author W. G. Sebald killed in road accident', *The Independent on Sunday*, 16 December, available at <http://www.independent.co.uk/news/uk/home-news/author-wg-sebald-killed-in-road-accident-620349.html> (last accessed 15 July 2012).

——(2007), 'Mapping nature's heartlands', *The Guardian*, 25 August, available at <http://www.guardian.co.uk/books/2007/aug/25/featuresreviews.guardianreview4> (last accessed 15 July 2012).

Muckherjee, Bharati and Robert Boyers [1981] (1997), 'A Conversation with V. S. Naipaul', in *Conversations with V. S. Naipaul*, ed. F. Jussawalla, Jackson: University of Mississippi Press, pp. 75–92.

Munro, Alice (2006), *The View from Castle Rock*, London: Chatto and Windus.

Murray, Nicholas (1993), *Bruce Chatwin*, Bridgend: Seren.

Musgrove, Brian (1999), 'Travel and Unsettlement: Freud on Vacation', in S. Clark (ed.), *Travel Writing and Empire: Postcolonial Theory in Transit*, London: Zed Books, pp. 31–44.

Naipaul, V. S. (1972), *The Overcrowded Barracoon and Other Articles*, London: André Deutsch.

——(1975), *Guerrillas*, London: André Deutsch.

——[1958] (1976a), *The Suffrage of Elvira*, London: Penguin.

——[1959] (1976b), *Miguel Street*, London: André Deutsch.

——(1977), *India: A Wounded Civilization*, London: André Deutsch

——[1957] (1978), *The Mystic Masseur*, London: André Deutsch.

——(1984), *Finding the Centre: Two Narratives*, London: André Deutsch.

—— [1964] (1985), *An Area of Darkness*, London: André Deutsch.
—— [1990] (1991), *India: A Million Mutinies Now*, London: Vintage.
—— (1994), *A Way in the World: A Sequence*, London: William Heinemann.
—— [1998] (1999), *Winding Paths: Photographs by Bruce Chatwin*, London: Jonathan Cape.
—— [1962] (2001a), *The Middle Passage: A Caribbean Journey*, London: Picador.
—— [1971] (2001b), *In a Free State*, London: Picador.
—— [1981] (2001c), *Among the Believers: An Islamic Journey*, London: Picador.
—— [1987] (2002), *The Enigma of Arrival: A Novel in Five Sections*, London: Picador.
—— [1961] (2003a), *A House for Mr Biswas*, London: Picador.
—— [1969] (2003b), *The Loss of El Dorado: A Colonial History*, London: Vintage.
—— (2003c), *Literary Occasions: Essays*, New York: Alfred A. Knopf.
—— (2007), *A Writer's People: Ways of Looking and Feeling*, London: Picador.
Nicolson, Malcolm (1995), 'Historical Introduction', in A. von Humboldt, *Personal Narrative of a Journey to the Equinoctial Regions of the New Continent*, trans. Jason Wilson, London: Penguin, pp. ix–xxxiv.
Nietzsche, Friedrich [1879] (1964), *Human, All-Too-Human: A Book for Free Spirits*, trans. Helen Zimmern, New York: Russell and Russell Inc.
Nixon, Rob (1992), *London Calling: V. S. Naipaul, Postcolonial Mandarin*, New York and Oxford: Oxford University Press.
Nooteboom, Cees [1992] (1998), *Roads to Santiago: Detours and Riddles in the Lands and History of Spain*, trans. Ina Rilke, London: Harcourt.
—— [2006] (2007), *Nomad's Hotel: Travels in Time and Space*, trans. Ina Rilke, London: Vintage.
Nünning, Ansgar (2008), 'Zur mehrfachen Präfiguration / Prämediation der Wirklichkeitsdarstellung im Reisebericht: Grundzüge einer narratologis-chen Theorie, Typologie und Poetik der Reiseliteratur', in M. Gymnich, A. Nünning, V. Nünning and E. Wåghäll Nivre (eds), *Points of Arrival: Travels in Time, Space and Self / Zielpunkte: Unterwegs in Zeit, Raum und Selbst*, Tübingen: Francke Verlag, pp. 11–32.
Nünning, Vera and Ansgar Nünning (1996), *Intercultural Studies: Fictions of Empire*, Heidelberg: Universitätsverlag C. Winter.
Orwell, George [1938] (2000), *Homage to Catalonia*, London: Penguin.
Ousby, Ian (1990), *The Englishman's England: Travel, Taste, and the Rise of Tourism*, Cambridge: Cambridge University Press.
Pamuk, Orhan [2005] (2006), *Istanbul: Memories of a City*, trans. Maureen Freely, London: Faber and Faber.
Parry, Ann (1997), 'Idioms for the Unrepresentable: Post-War Fiction and the Shoah', *Journal of European Studies*, 27.4: 417–32.
Patt, Lise (ed.) (2007), *Searching for Sebald: Photography After W. G. Sebald*, Los Angeles: The Institute for Cultural Inquiry.
Perec, Georges [1975] (2003), *W, or The Memory of Childhood*, trans. David Bellos, Boston, MA: David R. Godine.
Pendry, Helen (2004), *A Brand New Sense of Wonder? Novels of Childhood in the Era of Transnational Capitalism*, Salford: University of Salford Press.

Pfister, Manfred (1993), 'Intertextuelles Reisen, oder: Der Reisebericht als Intertext', in H. Foltinek. W. Reihle, W. Zacharasiewicz (eds), *Tales and their 'telling difference': Zur Theorie und Geschichte der Narrativik – Festschrift für Franz K. Stanzel*, Heidelberg: Universitätsverlag C. Winter, pp. 109–32.

——(1996), 'Bruce Chatwin and the Postmodernization of the Travelogue', *Literature, Interpretation, Theory*, 7: 253–67.

——(2006), 'Travellers and Traces: The Quest for One's Self in Eighteenth- to Twentieth-Century Travel Writing', in Koray Melikoğlu (ed.), *Life Writing: Autobiography, Biography, and Travel Writing*, Stuttgart: Ibidem, pp. 1–13.

Philips, Adam (2004), 'Close Ups', *History Workshop Journal*, 57: 142–9.

Phillips, John (1999), 'Lagging Behind: Bhabha, Postcolonial Theory and the Future', in Steve Clark (ed.), *Travel Writing and Empire: Postcolonial Theory in Transit*, London: Zed Books, pp. 63–80.

Piedra, José (1989), 'Review: The Game of Critical Arrival', *Diacritics*, 19.1 (Spring): 34–61.

Pilkington, John (1991), *An Englishman in Patagonia*, London: Century.

Platt, Peter G. (1997), *Reason Diminished: Shakespeare and the Marvelous*, Lincoln: University of Nebraska Press.

——(ed.) (1999), *Wonders, Marvels, and Monsters in Early Modern Culture*, London and Newark: University of Delaware Press.

Polo, Marco *Il milione* (1928), ed. L. F. Benedetto, Florence: Comitato Geografico Nazionale Italiano Pubbl.

——[1938] (1976), *The Description of the World*, trans. A. C. Moule and Paul Pelliot, New York: AMS Press and London: Routledge.

Pomian, K. (1990), *Collectors and Curiosities: Paris and Venice, 1500–1800*, Cambridge: Cambridge University Press.

Popper, Karl (1969), *Conjectures and Refutations: The Growth of Scientific Knowledge*, London: Routledge.

Pordzik, Ralph (2005), *The Wonder of Travel: Fiction, Tourism, and the Social Construction of the Nostalgic*, Heidelberg: Universitätsverlag Winter GmbH.

Porter, Dennis (1991), *Haunted Journeys: Desire and Transgression in European Travel Writing*, Princeton: Princeton University Press.

Prager, Brad (2010), 'Convergence Insufficiency: On Seeing Passages between W. G. Sebald and the "Travel Writer" Bruce Chatwin', in M. Zisselsberger (ed.), *The Undiscover'd Country: W. G. Sebald and the Poetics of Travel*, New York: Camden House, pp. 189–212.

Pratt, Mary-Louise (1992), *Imperial Eyes: Travel Writing and Transculturation*, London and New York: Routledge.

Proust, Marcel (1997), 'Contre Sainte–Beuve', in *Marcel Proust on Art and Literature 1896–1919*, New York: Carroll and Graf, pp. 17–276.

——[1913–27] (2000), *In Search of Lost Time. In Six Volumes*, trans. C. K. Scott Moncrieff, Terence Kilmartin and Andreas Mayor; rev. D. J. Enright, London: Vintage.

Pye, Michael (2003), 'On the natural history of destruction: don't mention the war', *The Scotsman*, 15 February, p. 15.

Raban, Jonathan [1986] (1987a), *Coasting*, London: Picador.

——(1987b), *For Love & Money: Writing, Reading, Travelling 1969–1987*, London: Collins.

——[1999] (2000), *Passage to Juneau: A Sea and its Meanings*, New York: Vintage Departures.

Ralegh, Walter [1596] (1970), *The Discoverie of the Large, Rich, and Bewtiful Empire of Guiana, with a Relation of the Great and Golden City of Manoa (which the Spaniards call El Dorado)*, ed. Robert H. Schomberg, for the Hayklut Society, 1848; reprint, New York: Lenox Hill.

Rashid, Ahmed [1995] (1997), 'The Last Lion', in Feroza Jussawalla (ed.), *Conversations with V. S. Naipaul*, Jackson: University Press of Mississippi, pp. 166–9.

Reed-Danahay, Deborah (ed.) (1997), *Auto/ethnography: Rewriting the Self and the Social*, Oxford: Berg.

Reid, Alastair (1978), 'The Giant Sloth Skin and Other Wonders', *The New Yorker*, 9 October, pp. 186–90. MS. Eng. c. 7846.

Rennie, Neil [1995] (1998), *Far-fetched Facts: The Literature of Travel and the Idea of the South Seas*, Oxford: Clarendon Press.

Ricoeur, Paul [1983] (1984), *Time and Narrative*, vol. 1, trans. K. McLaughlin and D. Pellauer, Chicago: University of Chicago Press.

Roberson, Susan L. (ed.) (2001), *Defining Travel: Diverse Visions*, Jackson: University Press of Mississippi.

Robinson, Tim (1986), *Stones of Aran: Pilgrimage*, New York: New York Review of Books.

Rose, Gillian (1993), *Feminism and Geography: The Limits of Geographical Knowledge*, Minneapolis: University of Minnesota Press.

Roth, Joseph (2006), '»Romantik« des Reisens', in *Sehnsucht nach Paris, Heimweh nach Prag: Ein Leben in Selbstzeugnissen*, Cologne: Kiepenheuer and Witsch, pp. 221–6.

Rowe-Evans, Adrian [1971] (1997), 'A *Transition* Interview', in *Conversations with V. S. Naipaul*, ed. F. Jussawalla, Jackson: University of Mississippi Press, pp. 24–36.

Rushdie, Salman (1987), 'A sad pastoral: *The Enigma of Arrival* by V. S. Naipaul', *The Guardian*, 13 March, available at <http://www.guardian.co.uk/books/1987/mar/13/fiction.vsnaipaul> (last accessed 15 July 2012).

——(1991), *Imaginary Homelands*, London: Granta.

——(2002), 'In Defence of the Novel, Yet Again', in *Step Across this Line: Collected Non-Fiction, 1992–2002*, London: Jonathan Cape, pp. 54–63.

Russell, Alison (2000), *Crossing Boundaries: Postmodern Travel Writing*, London: Palgrave.

Said, Edward (1978), *Orientalism: Western Conceptions of the Orient*, New York: Pantheon Books.

——(1986), 'Intellectuals in the Post-Colonial World', *Salmagundi* (Spring–Summer): 44–64.

——(1994), *Cultural Imperialism*, New York: Vintage Books.

Santner, Eric L. (2006), *On Creaturely Life: Rilke, Benjamin, Sebald*, Chicago and London: University of Chicago Press.

Schama, Simon [1995] (2004), *Landscape and Memory*, London: Harper Collins.

Schiff, Stephen [1994] (1997), 'The Ultimate Exile', in *Conversations with V. S. Naipaul*, ed. F. Jussawalla, Jackson: University of Mississippi Press, pp. 135–53.

Schmitz, Kenneth, L. (2005), *The Recovery of Wonder: The New Freedom and the Asceticism of Power*, Chesham: McGill-Queen's University Press.

Schulz-Forberg, Hagen (ed.) (2005), *Unravelling Civilisation: European Travel and Travel Writing*, Brussels, Bern, Berlin, Frankfurt am Main, New York, Oxford, Wien: Peter Lang.

Schwartz, Lynne Sharon (ed.) (2007), *The Emergence of Memory: Conversations with W. G. Sebald*, New York: Seven Stories Press.

Sebald *Nachlaß* [Estate]. Deutsches Literaturarchiv Marbach, Germany.

——('Handwritten Drafts' (*'Die Ringe des Saturn: Handschrift'*) [*Handschriftensammlung*: A: Sebald (Mappe 3; 7–9)].

——('The Myth of Destruction' ('Der Mythos der Zerstörung') [Handschriftensammlung: A: Sebald (Mappe 3)].

Sebald, W. G. (ed.) (1988), *A Radical Stage: Theatre in Germany in the 1970s and 1980s*, Oxford: Berg.

——[1995] (1998), *The Rings of Saturn*, trans. Michael Hulse, London: Harvill.

——(2001) *Austerlitz*, trans. Anthea Bell, London: Penguin.

——[1988] (2002a), *After Nature*, trans. Michael Hamburger, New York and Toronto: Random House.

——[1990] (2002b), *Vertigo*, trans. Michael Hulse, London: Vintage.

——[1992] (2002c), *The Emigrants*, trans. Michael Hulse, London: Vintage.

——[1998] (2002d), *Logis in einem Landhaus*, Frankfurt: Fischer Tagenbuch Verlag.

——[1985] (2003a), *Die Beschreibung des Unglücks: Zur östereichischen Literatur von Stifter bis Handke*, Frankfurt: Fischer Taschenbuch Verlag.

——[1999] (2003b), *On the Natural History of Destruction: With Essays on Alfred Andersch, Jean Améry and Peter Weiss*, trans. Anthea Bell, London: Penguin.

——[1991] (2004), *Unheimliche Heimat: Essays zur österreichischen Literatur*, Frankfurt: Fischer Taschenbuch Verlag.

——(2005), *Campo Santo*, trans. Anthea Bell, London: Hamish Hamilton.

——(2008), *Über das Land und das Wasser: Ausgewählte Gedichte 1964–2001*, ed. Sven Meyer, Munich: Carl Hanser Verlag.

——[1995] (2011), *Die Ringe des Saturn: eine* englische *Wallfahrt*, Frankfurt am Main: Fischer Taschenbuch Verlag.

Sebald, W. G. (poems) and Tess Jaray (artwork) (2001), *For Years Now*, London: Short Books.

Sebald, W. G. (poems) and Jan Peter Tripp (artwork) (2004), *Unrecounted*, trans. Michael Hamburger, London: Hamish Hamilton.

Self, Will (2009), 'Incidents along the road', *The Guardian*, 7 February, available at <http:www.guardian.co.uk/books/2009/feb/07/wg-sebald-austerlitz-will-self-fiction> (last accessed 20 Sept. 2012).

Sell, Jonathan P. A. (2006), *Rhetoric and Wonder in English Travel Writing, 1560–1613*, Aldershot: Ashgate.

Shakespeare, Nicholas (1999), *Bruce Chatwin*, London: Harvill.

——(2003), '*In Patagonia*: An Introduction', in B. Chatwin, *In Patagonia*, London: Penguin, pp. vii–xxiv.

——(2007), 'The ability to see and not to see', *Daily Telegraph*, 1 September, available at <http://www.telegraph.co.uk/culture/books/3667614/The-ability-to-see-and-not-to-see.html> (last accessed 17 September 2012).

Shankar, S. (2001), *Textual Traffic: Colonialism, Modernity, and the Economy of the Text*, Albany: SUNY Press.

Shehadeh, Raja (2007), *Palestinian Walks: Notes on a Vanishing Landscape*, London: Profile Books.

Shelton, Anthony Alan (1994), 'Cabinets of Transgression: Renaissance Collections and the Incorporation of the New World', in J. Elsner and Cardinal (eds), *The Cultures of Collecting*, London: Reaktion Books, pp. 177–203.

Simpson, George Gaylord [1934] (1982), *Attending Marvels: A Patagonian Journal*, Alexandria, VA: Time-Life Books.

Sinclair, Iain (2005), *Edge of the Orison: In the Traces of John Clare's 'Journey out of Essex'*, London: Hamish Hamilton.

Sontag, Susan (1977), *On Photography*, London: Penguin.

——[1972] (1980), *Under the Sign of Saturn*, New York: Farrar, Straus and Giroux.

——(1984), 'Model Destinations', *Times Literary Supplement*, 22 June, pp. 699–70.

——(2000), 'A mind in mourning', *Times Literary Supplement*, 25 February, p. 3.

——[2003] (2004), *Regarding the Pain of Others*, London: Penguin.

——(2007), *At the Same Time: Essays and Speeches*, London: Hamish Hamilton.

Spitzweg, Carl (1976), 'Der arme Poet. Gemälde, 1837', in *Carl Spitzweg*, Ramerding: Berghaus Verlag, p. 37.

Spratt, Thomas [1667] (1722), *The History of the Royal Society of London, for the Improving of Natural Knowledge*, London: Knapton.

Stefanovska, Malina (2009), 'Exemplary or Singular? The Anecdote in Historical Narrative', *SubStance: A Review of Theory and Literary Criticism, 'The Anecdote'*, 38.1: 16–30.

Steiner, George (1971), *In Bluebeard's Castle: Some Notes Towards the Redefinition of Culture*, New Haven, CT: Yale University Press.

Sterne, Laurence [1768] (2005), *A Sentimental Journey through France and Italy by Mr. Yorick*, London: Penguin.

Sugnet, Charles (1991), 'Vile Bodies, Vile Places: Traveling with Granta', *Transition*, 51: 70–85.

Sepúlveda, Luis [1995] (1989), *Full Circle: A South American Journey*, trans. Cris Andrews, Melbourne: Lonely Planet.

Swales, Martin (2004), 'Theoretical Reflections on the work of W. G. Sebald', in J. J. Long and A. Whitehead (eds), *W. G. Sebald: A Critical Companion*, Edinburgh: Edinburgh University Press, pp. 23–7.

Tappan, Eva March (ed.) (1914), 'The Shipwrecked Sailor', trans. W. K. Flinders, in *The World's Story: A History of the World in Story, Song and Are*, Boston: Houghton Mifflin, pp. 41–6.

Taylor, David (1999), 'Bruce Chatwin: Connoisseur of Exile, Exile as Connoisseur', in S. Clark (ed.), *Travel Writing and Empire: Postcolonial Theory in Transit*, London: Zed Books, pp. 195–211.

Theroux, Paul (1972), *V. S. Naipaul: An Introduction to His Work*, London: André Deutsch.

——(1977), 'Down in old Pat.', *The Times*, 13 October. MS. Eng. c. 7846.

——[1998] (2000), *Sir Vidia's Shadow: A Friendship across Five Continents*, New York: First Mariner Books.

——[1979] (2008a), *The Old Patagonian Express. By Train through the Americas*, London: Penguin.

——(2008b), *Ghost Train to the Eastern Star: On the Tracks of 'The Great Railway Bazaar'*, London: Penguin.

Thieme, John (1982), 'Authorial Voice in V. S. Naipaul's *The Middle Passage*', in P. Dodd (ed.), *The Art of Travel: Essays on Travel Writing*, London and Totowa, NJ: Frank Cass, pp. 139–50.

——(1987), 'Review: Thinly-Veiled Autobiography', *Third World Quarterly*, 9.4 (October): 1376–8.

Thorpe, Michael (1976), *V. S. Naipaul*, published for the British Council, Harlow: Longman Group.

Thubron, Colin [1999] (2000), *In Siberia*, London: Penguin.

Tiffin, Helen (1988), 'Rites of Resistance: Counter-Discourse and West Indian Biography', *Journal of West Indian Literature*, 3: 28–46.

Todorov, Tzvetan [1991] (1995), 'The Journey and its Narratives', in *The Morals of History*, trans. Alyson Waters, pp. 60–70.

——[1982] (1999), *The Conquest of America: The Question of the Other*, trans. Richard Howard, Norman: University of Oklahoma Press.

Ure, John (2003), *Searching for Nomads: An English Obsession from Hester Stanhope to Bruce Chatwin*, London: Constable.

Veit, Walter F. (2000), 'Voyages of Discovery and the Critique of European Civilization', in M. A. Seixo and M. Alzira (eds), *Travel Writing and Cultural Memory – Écriture du voyage et mémoire culturelle*, Amsterdam and Atlanta: Rodopi, pp. 57–82.

Voltaire [1759] (2000), *Candide and Related Texts*, trans. David Wootton, Indianapolis: Hackett Publishing Company.

Walcott, Derek (1998), 'The Garden Path: V. S. Naipaul', in *What the Twilight Says: Essays*, New York: Farrar, Straus and Giroux, pp. 121–33.

Washburn, Gordon Bailey (1970), 'Foreword', in Emma C. Bunker, C. Bruce Chatwin and Ann R. Farkas (eds), *'Animal Style' Art from East to West*, New York: An Asia House Gallery Publication by the Asia Society, p. 7.

Watanabe-O'Kelly, Helen (ed.) (1997), *The Cambridge History of German Literature*, Cambridge: Cambridge University Press.

Watson, Jay (1993), 'The Rhetoric of Exhaustion and the Exhaustion of Rhetoric: Erskine Caldwell in the Thirties', *The Mississippi Quarterly*, 46: 215–29.

Watson, Nicola (2006), *The Literary Tourist: Readers and Places in Romantic and Victorian Britain*, London: Palgrave.

Waugh, Evelyn [1946] (2011), *When the Going Was Good*, London: Penguin.

Weber, Max [1917] (1946), *Max Weber: Essays in Sociology*, ed. and trans. H. H. Gerth and C. Wright Mills, Oxford: Oxford University Press.

Weiss, Timothy F. (1992), *On the Margins: The Art of Exile in V. S. Naipaul*, Amherst: University of Massachusetts Press.

Welsch, Wolfgang (2002), 'On Reason and Transition: On the Concepts of Transversal Reason', available at http://www2.uni-jena.de/welsch/Papers/reasTrans.html (last accessed 14 Sept. 2012).

Wesseling, Elisabeth (1991), *Writing History as a Prophet: Postmodernist*

Innovations of the Historical Novel, Amsterdam and Philadelphia: John Benjamins.

West, Rebecca [1942] (2006), *Black Lamb & Grey Falcon: A Journey through Yugoslavia*, Edinburgh, New York and Melbourne: Canongate.

White, Edmund (2004), 'Bruce Chatwin', in E. White, *Arts and Letters*, San Francisco: Cleis, pp. 123–7.

White, Hayden (1987), *The Content of the Form: Narrative Discourse and Historical Representation*, Baltimore and London: Johns Hopkins University Press.

White, Jonathan (ed.) (1993), *Recasting the World: Writing after Colonialism*, Baltimore and London: Johns Hopkins University Press.

Whitfield, Peter (2011), *Travel: A Literary History*, Oxford: Bodleian Library.

Williams, Arthur (2000), 'W. G. Sebald: A Holistic Approach to Borders, Texts and Perspectives', in Arthur Williams, Stuart Parkes and Julian Preece (eds), *German Language Literature Today: International and Popular?*, Bern: Peter Lang, p. 106.

Winokur, Scott [1991] (1997), 'The Unsparing Vision of V. S. Naipaul', in F. Jussawala (ed.), *Conversations with V. S. Naipaul*, Jackson: University Press of Mississippi, pp. 114–29.

Wood, James (1999), 'Sebald's Uncertainty', in *The Broken Estate – Essays on Literature and Belief*, New York: Random House, pp. 232–41.

——(2008), 'Wounder and Wounded: V. S. Naipaul's Empire', *The New Yorker*, 1 December, available at <http://www.newyorker.com/arts/critics/books/2008/12/01/081201crbo_books_wood> (last accessed 15 July 2012).

Woolf, Virginia (2008), *Selected Essays*, ed. David Bradshaw, Oxford: Oxford University Press.

World Tourism Organization UNTWO website, 'Why Tourism?', available at <http://www.untwo.org/aboutwto/why/en/why.php?op=1> (last accessed 16 July 2012).

Youngs, Tim (1997), 'Punctuating Travel: Paul Theroux and Bruce Chatwin', *Literature and History*, 6: 2, 73–88.

——(2004a), 'The Importance of Travel Writing', *The European English Messenger*, 12. 2: 55–62.

——(2004b) 'Where Are We Going? Cross-border Approaches to Travel Writing', in G. Hooper and T. Youngs (eds), *Perspectives on Travel Writing*, Aldershot: Ashgate, pp. 167–80.

Zilcosky, John (2007), 'Sebald's Uncanny Travels: The Impossibility of Getting Lost', in J. J. Long and A. Whitehead (eds), *W. G. Sebald: A Critical Companion*, Edinburgh: Edinburgh University Press, pp. 102–22.

——(ed.) (2008), *Writing Travel: The Poetics and Politics of the Modern Journey*, Toronto and London: University of Toronto Press.

Zisselsberger, Markus (ed.) (2010), *The Undiscover'd Country: W. G. Sebald and the Poetics of Travel*, London: Camden House.

Index